CHASING DEVOTION

LONDON CLARKE

Vinci Books

vinci-books.com

Published by Vinci Books Ltd in 2026

1

The publisher and the author have made every effort to obtain permissions for any third party material used in this book and to comply with copyright law. Any queries in this respect should be brought to the attention of the publisher and any omissions will be corrected in future editions.

A CIP catalogue record for this book is available from the British Library.

Paperback ISBN: 9781036738143

The EU GPSR authorised representative is Logos Europe, 9 rue Nicolas Poussion, 17000 La Rochelle, France contact@logoseurope.eu

Songs featured on the band Cutter's 1999 album, Den of
Vipers
The Snare
Bring It All Back
The Eye of Scorn
The Weight of Sound
The Flight
Inside My Mind
Sound of Salvation
Dead of Morning
Cold Morning, Bright Lies
Chains of Time
The One Who Ran
All for You
When the Lights Go Out
Songs for Ghosts

Songs featured on the follow-up album, Millennial
Breakdown
Glass and Fire
Emotional Hangover
Songs for Ghosts Part II
In the Afterglow
The Detour
The Real Thing
Stark Daylight
The Shift
Peace and Love
The Abyss
My Escape
Live Wire
Y2K

*For Scott Stapp, and for the bands Creed and Alter Bridge—
Your music has always conveyed messages of devotion, fall, and
redemption. Thank you for the songs that carried this story (and this
series) into being.*

Chapter One

NOW

The red light above the mic glows like a warning flare. *Recording*.

"Welcome back to The Exit Door. I'm Brynn Cole, and in case you're new here, this is where we talk about getting out. Of groups. Of mindsets. Of lives we no longer want to live in."

My voice is calm, practiced. In the five years I've hosted this podcast, I've learned to keep it neutral and non-emotional, especially during live shows.

"We're talking to Alyssa Chambers—former member of a high-control group, now a student at the College of Charleston and a volunteer with The Exit Project. Alyssa, thanks for being here."

Alyssa sits across from me, headphones covering her ears. She leans toward the microphone. "Thanks for having me."

We're sitting in the studio at The Exit Project's office, a converted mill building with creaky floors and bad insulation. My business partner and I have been modernizing little by little, starting with the soundproofing in the studio. Hopefully, within the next six months, we can renovate the office spaces.

When I co-founded this nonprofit two years ago, I didn't picture myself doing podcasts, but it was the next logical step after my memoir about my preteen years in a cult became a minor bestseller.

I lean toward the mic. "Tonight's topic is the afterlife— I'm not talking about heaven, but the life you live *after* you leave a high-control group—the one where you wake up one day and realize you don't know who you are anymore." I shift my eyes to my guest. "And Alyssa, you know as well as I do that sometimes after leaving, freedom can be heavier than captivity."

She nods. "That's so true."

I glance through the glass panel where Paul, my co-founder, audio engineer, and executive producer, sits at the small control desk, giving me a thumbs-up. His gray-streaked brown hair looks almost gold under the amber studio lights.

I turn back to the mic. "Alyssa, you've talked about what it was like to leave the community you were involved with. Many of our listeners struggle with what comes *after.* The world doesn't exactly hand you a manual."

A soft laugh. "Honey, you are not wrong about that. It's *hard.* I didn't even know how to rent an apartment or open a bank account. I'd never had a phone, never used email. I was twenty-three, and the first night I slept alone, I thought the silence was going to kill me."

Alyssa's "life after" has been harder than mine. The community she was born into was restrictive, with little to no contact with the outside world. My group had plenty of the outside world's influences—movies, music, makeup, and money. All filtered through the lens of one woman's vision of Utopia.

Alyssa is thirty-five, but she looks ten years older, closer to my age. She escaped more than a decade ago, but her dark eyes still carry the haunted rooms and cobweb-crusted corners of life lived within a group that abused her mind, body, and soul. Her hair is thinning at the part. The stress has followed her like a demon. But when she speaks, there's that soft, lilting strength I've always associated with Southern women—the kind who smile sweetly while bracing for impact.

"When I first left," she says, "I stayed in shelters, hostels. I worked at fast-food places." Her voice falters as she's probably deciding how much truth to give away. "But what I found was that the dangers that had been inside the group were still waiting for me outside as well. I quickly discovered what bars were good for—that whiskey was really good for numbing pain."

I glance over at my travel mug—coffee laced with Kahlúa—my dirty little secret. My mouth waters to take a swig. I lean back in my swivel chair, which squeaks every time I move.

"In one of the bars, I met this man who—" She stops, draws a shaky breath. "He said he wanted to help. Said he'd been through something similar. Told me he'd gotten himself out of a cult too." She swallows. "I didn't know any better back then. Thought that meant he was safe. Ended up staying with him a while. And before I knew it … it felt real familiar." A faint, humorless smile. "Had to ask before I left the house. Had to explain if I wanted to spend five dollars. Lord help me, I had to justify eating ice cream. So, I started saving change. Kept it in a little jar behind the cleaning supplies. Bought those tiny bottles of whiskey with it." She lets out a soft breath. "He found out eventually. They always do. So I left. Again." A dark laugh. "That's the only decent thing whiskey ever did for me. I wanted it worse than I wanted to stay." She glances toward the glass panel. "Not long after that, I met Paul. He told me about The Exit Project. That's when I finally got some real help." Alyssa unbuttons the cuff of her flannel shirt. "You think once you're out, the worst part's behind you. But there are folks out here who can smell it on you—the fear, the need to belong. They find you. Sometimes you trade one cult for another."

"I know," I say. And I really do know.

From the control room, Paul signals to me with a hang-ten hand gesture that calls are coming through the phone line. His voice filters through my headset. "Patching a call from Pawley's Island, South Carolina."

Something tightens low in my chest—an old, reflexive response to a mental image of salt air, marsh water, the sound of waves through open windows.

"It looks like we have a caller on the line," I say. "Ivy, calling from South Carolina."

Then, through the headset, a hesitant voice cuts in. "Hello?"

"Hello, Ivy. Welcome to The Exit Door. Do you have a question for Alyssa?"

"Hi, Brynn. Wow. It's so great to finally talk to you. I've been listening to you for, like, years and always wanted to call in."

"We're so glad you did. How are things in Pawley's Island? We're kind of neighbors. Our show broadcasts from Charleston, so we've got a same-state connection."

"Yes." She laughs a little. "We have another connection too."

"We do?"

"Yeah, you know a friend of mine."

"Really? Who's your friend?"

A pause, and then, "Sullivan Stonecutter."

The name hits like a bomb. For a second, I'm sure I've misheard her. I focus on a wall poster outlining how to recognize a high-control group. Then I shift my gaze to Alyssa to refocus on the present moment.

"Hello?" Ivy's voice again. She sounds young.

"Yes. Yes, I'm here."

I glance toward the control booth. Paul's eyes meet mine.

I clear my throat, which turns into a laugh. "Oh, right. How do you know Sullivan?"

She laughs too, a nervous sound. "It's a long story. We're, like, friends."

Girlfriend, more likely.

"He talks about you—a lot actually."

"About me?"

"Yes. Like, all the time." A fragile, bottomless pause.

I've not seen or heard from Sullivan in more than twenty years. The only contact I've had with him was through his attorney a few years ago, when I needed him to sign off on using his name in my book. Otherwise, I only know what the rest of the world knows. Rock star. Former lead singer of Cutter. Now a solo artist who mostly plays clubs.

I grab my coffee, take a sip, allow the sweet burn to slide over my tongue, down my throat. "Ivy, do you have a question for Alyssa?"

"Um, my question is for you, actually."

I dig my fingernails into the vinyl on the arms of the chair. Bracing myself for ... something. "OK."

Her words tumble out in quick succession. "How do you help someone who left a high-control group a long time ago but still isn't really free?"

I press gently, the way I've done with hundreds of callers. "What do you mean when you say they're not really free?"

"I mean like, their ability to trust, to love is impaired by what happened before," she says. "Like, they say they want a real relationship, but every time it gets close to that, they pull away."

"Is he—this person—this is someone you've known for a long time?" Cringe. I said *he*.

"Several years, yeah." She rushes on. "It's not that they're going back to the cult or anything, just that they seem tied to the past, unable to get beyond it."

Alyssa seems to sense the change in the air and mercifully jumps in. "Ivy, honey, this is Alyssa. I completely understand what you're saying. And that can happen. No matter how long it's been since we left, the past still gets under our skin, makes repeat visits. Lordy, sometimes even decades later."

I find my tongue again. "It's why it's so important for those of us who have come out of these groups to stay in therapy, in community. We need people to talk to, who will ask us how we're doing—make sure we're OK." I take another sip of my spiked coffee. "Does he—this person—this friend of yours have a support community?"

"I—I think so. I mean, he has me." She goes along with my pronoun. "Anyway, I think something in him is still trapped. There's something he's never worked through. Something he left behind."

Alyssa and I tag-team our advice. Counselors. Books. Resources. The Exit Project's website.

Finally, Paul whirls his hand in the air. *Wrap it up.*

"Ivy, maybe we can talk off air sometime," I say. "Why don't you send me an email?"

"OK," she says. "From your website, or——"

Paul has already disconnected Ivy and pulled up another caller. *Natalie from Memphis.*

And now I'm on to talking about a different cult but the same sort of fallout.

Somehow, I make it through the rest of the podcast. Somehow, I manage to end the episode with my usual, "That's all for tonight's episode of The Exit Door. For anyone who's still finding their way out—keep walking. Sometimes freedom isn't a clear path. Sometimes it's a long road back to yourself."

The red light goes dark. Broadcast over.

I muster small talk with Alyssa, thank-yous for coming on the broadcast, and promises to meet up the following week for coffee.

When the door shuts behind her, I sink back in my chair. My headset slides into my lap.

A few seconds later, the hinges squeal on the control-room door as Paul pushes it open.

"You OK?"

"I'm fine," I say automatically, rubbing the spot between my eyebrows. "That was just … an unexpected call."

He steps closer, resting one hand on the edge of the desk. "I saw your face when she said his name."

I let out a humorless laugh. "Yeah. Not my best poker-face moment."

He hesitates, and his dark eyes brim with concern. "You want me to cut that segment before we upload to the website? Or bleep his name? We can anonymize it. Or we can lose the call altogether, no problem."

I shake my head. "It took me by surprise—"

"You might get some questions about it."

I gaze at the photo of Paul and me sitting beside my computer screen. Both of us are smiling. The banner behind us reads *The Exit Project: Helping Survivors of Cults and High-Control Groups*. "Leave it. That's the point of the show, right? Real stories. Real consequences."

He folds his arms over his chest. "Real triggers, too."

I huff out a breath. "Thanks, Dr. Paul. I'm OK." I reach for my mug.

Paul puts a hand on my shoulder. "You got more than coffee in that mug?"

I meet his gaze. "A little cream, a little sugar."

"A little liquor?"

I shrug. "Eh. It's so watered down it's more like a hard Yoo-hoo."

He drops his head. "Brynn."

"No lectures, OK?"

He nods. "OK. We still on for dinner and the comedy club tomorrow?"

I'd almost forgotten. "Right."

"Unless you want to reschedule."

"No. I want to go." I smile. "As long as we call it a business meeting. I don't want anyone else on staff to know we're … fraternizing for fun."

He gives me a mock salute. "Business meeting, it is."

The truth is, I like Paul. He's amazing at what he does—the best interventionist I've ever met. He has this uncanny ability to walk into someone's pain without flinching, to pull them out of the wreckage without making them feel damaged. More than once, I've been present while he talked someone down from the ledge. On top of that, Paul is smart, multi-skilled as an audio engineer and producer, not to mention that he's quietly attractive and unencumbered by ex-wives or children.

All those attributes and virtues are exactly why I'll probably screw up this relationship before anything even starts. We're friends. That's good enough. Or it has been up until now.

Paul walks me to my car, and we stand for a minute or two while we talk. I know he wants this to be more—it's stamped right behind his eyes that are so often hidden by an errant, gray-streaked lock of hair that slides across his forehead.

He waits until I'm in the driver's seat and then shuts the door. As I pull out of the lot, the streetlights smear gold across the wet pavement. I should be planning how to frame the next podcast episode, but all I can think about is that voice on the phone.

He talks about you all the time.

Sullivan's name still has a kick to it. I thought I'd become immune to it. Twenty-five years should be enough time to bury the hurt and regrets.

He was my compass once. My proof of life beyond the gates, beyond the silence and fear. The first person who looked at me and saw something more than a scared little girl. I've never loved anyone like that since. I've never believed I could.

Sometimes I wonder if that kind of love only happens once, when you're too young or too naïve to understand what it really means—what it can do to your head, your heart.

Paul is kind. He's also safe. Predictable. He doesn't make my pulse race or my stomach drop, and that should be a relief. Instead, it seems like another loss—one I can't quite name.

I park outside my building, turn off the engine, and sit there listening to the rain on the car's roof and the slow tick of the cooling engine.

Sullivan is still out there—somewhere.

And all those old feelings I buried long ago have just clawed their way out of the grave.

Chapter Two

BIG BEND, FLORIDA, 1990

"The Snare"

People like to say you can't fall into a cage—you walk in. But my mother and I didn't walk in. We drifted like exhausted swimmers dragging ourselves toward any shore that looked brighter than the one behind us.

For us, that brighter shore was a recruiting seminar at the Charleston Harbor Marriott, offering a free sunset cruise just for attending. My mother signed us up because it was free, we hadn't eaten a real meal in two days, and the flyer promised "opportunity" in warm gold lettering that made everything else in our lives look gray by comparison.

That night, my mother put on mascara for the first time in months. I wore my one good dress. We stood on the deck of a yacht, a word I didn't even know how to pronounce before that night. I sipped Sprite from a plastic cup while Mama drank white wine and listened to a woman in a linen jumpsuit talk about Crystal Cliffs—its community, its purpose, its promise.

The woman's name was Astra Cynthia, and she spoke in a way that suggested her every word was a gift, a mission, a lifeline.

"What if you could start over?" she asked the group of mostly women, with a few men standing in the back. "What if you could have built-in support? Housing? Safety? A future? Community? What if you never had to struggle on your own again?"

The word that hooked my mother wasn't "housing" or "safety." It was "community."

We'd been living alone for too long, just the two of us, in a double-wide outside of Myrtle Beach, where everything we had was borrowed, including the double-wide.

Standing on a yacht with twenty-five other people all salivating to break out of their gravel-road grind, I knew that everything was about to change.

Mama kept confirming it. "Tonight could elevate our lives, Brynn. This could be the break we've been waiting for."

At eleven years old, I wasn't sure what "a break" looked like. A break from eating oatmeal or rice for dinner. A break from sharing a bed with Mama when it rained because the ceiling leaked where I slept. A break from having to stay with Mama's friends whenever it stormed because the double-wide might blow away.

People imagine cult-recruiting seminars as dark, intense, and obvious—windowless rooms and brainwashing chants. The truth was more like the slippery fish I remember my Uncle Malachai catching out of his skiff when we lived on that mosquito-laden lake near Beaufort, South Carolina. It seemed like I had it, until the fish slipped right out of my hands and into the water.

On the yacht with Astra Cynthia, change tasted like free

appetizers and sunsets and sea air. This was what real life *could* be. We could be rich. We could cruise on yachts forever.

For the first time in years, Mama looked happy. Her wavy brown hair snaked over her pink sweater. The sunset wove gold through the strands and coaxed the smile that made her eyes sparkle. Mama believed everything she heard that night. She was sure we could sail away from the muck and mire that had moored us after Daddy died.

As Astra Cynthia moved through the assembled would-be members, I fixated on the hole in the pocket of Mama's worn pink cardigan. Would Astra Cynthia see it? Would that disqualify us from this life that Mama coveted?

Astra Cynthia was tall, with sun-burnished skin, honey-colored hair knotted in a loose braid, her linen jumpsuit fluttering in the breeze. She looked like she'd stepped out of a lifestyle magazine instead of a recruitment machine.

When she spoke, people leaned in. She radiated something most of us hadn't felt in a long time—or ever. Certainty and confidence. She talked about the Crystal Cliffs community the way other people talk about miracles.

The Collective, we would find out, was the community's supercenter, a self-contained world where food, clothing, household goods, and anything anyone could ever want was provided, including employment.

"We have openings for every position right now," she told us. "Everything from stock crew to cashiers to buyers and distributors and marketers and designers. Whatever your talent, there is a place for you."

I imagined the Land of Oz—golden streets and flying monkeys, magically transporting anything anyone could ever need. Maybe there were mansions like the ones my mother watched in her evening shows, homes where the rich and famous lived in luxury.

Astra Cynthia paced the length of the deck where the audience congregated, stopping right in front of Mama. "You'll never have to wonder if you matter. You'll be supported from day one." She beamed and held her arms open. "Housing. Food. Jobs. Community. So, this is where you have to ask yourself, 'Why *wouldn't* I join?'"

My mother's eyes fluttered closed for a second, no doubt envisioning the dream Astra Cynthia described.

Astra Cynthia bent her arms into a Shiva-esque pose. "If there's something you need, just say it. All we ask is that you work hard, uphold Crystal Cliff's principles, and always offer light and love and a positive attitude to further the mission."

If Mama's new job would let us have the kind of food I'd had that night, I was all for it. Silver trays lined the deck railings, with heaping piles of shrimp cocktail on crushed ice, glistening fruit cups layered like jewels, chicken skewers dripping with honey glaze, tiny caprese bites with perfect basil leaves impaled on a stick. Mama ate the shrimp as if she might never see another crustacean.

It was the bread that did it for me. There could never be enough bread in the world. Warm rolls in baskets lined with white cloth, steam curling up. You could smell it from six feet away. It was like the days when Mama used to make muffins in the morning, before she had to choose between flour and rent.

That was the moment Astra Cynthia closed the deal.

She rested a hip against the railing and looked down at me. "Your mama's been through a lot." Her voice was almost a whisper, as if confiding, as if I didn't know. "You're doing your best. You deserve support too."

It was a frighteningly precise statement, considering she hadn't asked me a single question. Years later, I would remember that moment and understand that Astra Cynthia wasn't guessing our background. She was reading every frayed thread of my mother's cardigan. The lines of exhaustion in her face. Our cheap haircuts and thrifted purses. Our polite smiles.

She shifted her eyes to Mama's. "Where are y'all living now, Brandy?"

"We're … between places right now." Mama's smile slipped. "We lost the place we were living in."

It was the first time I'd heard this. I'd thought the leak in the ceiling had been the last straw before we gave the place up.

Astra Cynthia nodded, her green eyes sparkling, a curl of her hair hanging to her elbow.

I wanted to touch it. I knew it would be like silk.

"You and Brynn are exactly who we help," she said.

She slipped a stapled packet into my mother's hands. "Take this home. Read it. No pressure. No commitment. If you join us, it's because it feels right in your spirit."

Her hand came down on my mother's shoulder, light and reassuring.

Mama had spent the past four years being judged by landlords, denied by employers, and ignored by anyone who had the power to help. Astra Cynthia listened. She praised. She spoke to Mama as a fellow woman who needed a hand.

By the time the boat docked, Mama walked off in a daze, grinning like she'd been holding a 300-pound weight over her head and had finally thrown it overboard.

Back at our motel that night, I turned on the television. Familiar yellow faces and crown-like hair appeared on the screen. Bart and Homer.

"Yay, *The Simpsons* is on." I climbed onto the queen-sized bed and sat cross-legged, bouncing up and down. It was one of my favorite shows, and I hadn't been able to watch it since our cable was cut off several months earlier. This night seemed too good to be true—a full belly and *The Simpsons*.

Mama perched on the edge, feet still in her shoes, holding the papers Astra Cynthia had given her. Her hands shook a little as she read through them.

"You're really happy about this, aren't you?"

I nodded, my eyes glued to Marge's blue hair.

"They'll help me get certified in business management. It's like a miracle."

I nodded again as the brown greyhound the family had named Santa's Little Helper bounded onto the screen. "If we move there, can we get a dog?"

She laughed a little. "I don't know. Maybe. We'll have to see."

Mama filled out the forms. By morning, she'd signed the contract. By the end of the week, she had a new job, and we were living in Crystal Cliffs. We were part of a community.

Even though, as in our life before, nothing really belonged to us. Not our nice, clean new house, and nothing inside it. We were still living a borrowed life.

But Mama was smiling again. And that was enough for me.

Mama was hired as a cashier at The Collective with assurances from Astra Cynthia that she would quickly work her way up to manager.

We had a roof over our head—a two-bedroom, two-bathroom house with new appliances in the kitchen.

"It's like we've hit the lottery," Mama said.

She was assigned a mentor at work, Honey Barrett. Honey was five feet eleven, and although her name suggested a certain delicacy, she was about as graceful as a drunk bear. As proven by the first time she set foot in our entryway, collided with a decorative column, tripped on the rug, and ran headlong into a hall table.

Even so, Honey was kind and took us under her large, capable arm, showing us what life in the community could be like if we made every effort to assimilate and took the opportunities that came down the assembly line.

One day, after Mama came home from The Collective, the two women joined me on the front porch, where I was drinking ginger ale and finishing my homework. Mama took off her shoes and rubbed her feet while Honey fed us information about every person who lived on our street.

"You've got great neighbors." Honey pointed a long finger toward the house next door. "Have you met the Stonecutters yet?"

Mom shrugged. "I've seen a woman coming and going, but I haven't met her."

"Kristen's a veteran worker at The Collective," Honey said. "Works in the warehouse. She's been in Crystal Cliffs for two years now and is a member in excellent standing."

Mama winced as she rubbed her red toes. "She lives there alone?"

Honey smiled. "She's divorced, with a son—Sullivan."

Honey's eyes traveled toward me. "He's about your age, Brynn. Maybe a little older."

I moved to the porch steps with my ginger ale and watched the afternoon sun bake the gravel path until it shimmered.

Next door, the screen creaked open, and a boy came out.

Tall. Broad-shouldered. Sandy-blond hair falling into his eyes. He wore one of the standard Collective T-shirts, bright blue with white lettering, but his was faded at the sleeves as if it had been washed too many times. He held a clipboard to his chest.

His gaze landed on me. Not with curiosity or even annoyance. More like observation. A flashlight beam sweeping across a room, catching all my dust and secrets— as if I had any to hide.

"I guess you're the new neighbors." His voice startled me. It was lower than most of the boys I knew.

"Yeah," I managed, my fingers nervously peeling at the label on my ginger ale.

His voice must have startled Mama too, because she broke off her conversation with Honey.

The boy sauntered over to our porch and stood in front of me. "I'm Sullivan."

My mom came to the edge of the porch. "Hey there. I'm Brandy, and this is my daughter, Brynn."

I stood, meeting his gaze. Ice-blue eyes.

Next door, the screen opened again. A woman with blond hair piled in a messy bun emerged. She wore a tank top showing off a bright tattoo of stars and vines trailing up her arms, and she carried a laundry basket on her hip.

"There you are," she called out to her son. "We have sheets to wash." Then her gaze moved from Sullivan to the gathering on my porch. "Oh! Hello." She waved with her free arm. "Hi, Honey."

"Hi, Kristen." Honey stood. "These are your new neighbors, Brandy and her daughter, Brynn."

Kristen set down the laundry basket. "Glad to finally have someone move into that house. It's been empty too long." She motioned toward her son. "I guess you've met Sullivan." Kristen beamed at me, then glanced toward Mama. "You working at The Collective?"

Mama nodded, her face glowing. "Just started yesterday. Cashier."

"I work in the warehouse. I drive the lift, help label boxes." Kristen flipped her long blond hair over her shoulder. Its length and color were reminiscent of Astra Cynthia's. "Let me or Sullivan know if you need anything. It's always good to have someone show you the ropes." She lowered her voice conspiratorially. "Lots of rules here. Lots of eyes. You'll figure out which ones matter."

Mama smiled. "Stop by anytime."

I cringed a little at the awkwardness in Mama's words, the desperation to connect with someone, to make a friend.

Hopefully, Kristen wouldn't think we were weird.

"Thanks," Kristen said, "but don't invite me if you don't mean it. I'm notorious for dropping by." She swung the basket up against her hip and stepped off the porch.

Sullivan followed her, but not before glancing back at me once more.

As the mother and son pair disappeared around the side of the house, I looked toward the path they'd taken, thought of Sullivan's quiet, clear eyes.

It seemed like the beginning of something. I just didn't know what yet.

Chapter Three

NOW

I replay the caller's words the way you agitate a loose tooth when you're a kid—tongue pressing against it again and again, knowing it'll hurt but unable to stop.

He still talks about you.

She didn't say "he *used to.*" She used present tense. Ongoing. What am I supposed to make of that? Maybe she only said it because she was calling my show. People say things they think you want to hear when they want something from you.

I wander into my home office. I don't turn on the lights —the bluish glow from my screen is enough.

The thing is, ever since I left Crystal Cliffs all those years ago, I've built a life with plenty of escape routes. My whole world is about teaching people how to leave their prison without looking back. The past loosens its grip if you keep walking forward. I say it with conviction. With practice.

Tonight, though, I wonder—am *I* really finished with the past?

The moment the caller said his name, everything I

thought was finished rose up, fully formed. The ache. The pull. The part of me that remembers Sullivan Stonecutter all too well.

I sit at my desk. Wake the desktop. Check my email.

A few messages from the office. A donation receipt. A calendar reminder I forgot to dismiss. Then, I see his name. Right there. In my inbox.

From: Sullivan Stonecutter
Subject: It's been a while

My pulse spikes so hard it makes me lightheaded.

For a second, I don't click it. I stare, like the words might rearrange themselves into something less impossible if I give them time.

They don't.

My finger weighs heavily on the mouse. Then I click the email and open it.

Brynn,

Even as I write this, I'm not sure if I should be contacting you or if you even want to hear from me. I've been thinking about reaching out for a while.

My friend Ivy called me tonight. She told me she'd called your show and that you gave her a green light to email you, so I figured—maybe that was a door cracked open, even if it wasn't meant for me.

So here I am, knocking.

I live in Nashville most of the time now. Have for a while.

Put down some roots a few years ago, and I've tried to make this my home. I lead a pretty quiet life. I still tour though, still singing, writing songs.

I think about you more than I probably should. I regret a lot of things—especially what happened between us. I've had time to think about all that. Too much time, maybe.

I don't expect anything. I just want you to know I'm out here, and that I hope you're well.

If you feel like it, drop me a line. I'd really like to know how you are.

—Sullivan

My equilibrium tilts like I'm sliding off a platform, desperately grasping for something to hold on to.

First, the caller—his friend—Ivy.

Now this.

I push back from the desk, and the chair wheels scrape against the floor. My heart is pounding like I've been running, like I've been chased. I press my palms flat against the desk.

Nashville.

He's built a life somewhere, built relationships with other people. He's moved on—well, of course he has.

Still…

I think about you more than I probably should.

The sentence replays, insistent in my head.

I reread the email twice. Three times. Then I sink back into the chair and stare at the screen, the cursor blinking at the bottom of the message, waiting. It assumes a reply is inevitable.

Is it?

Some reckless part of me says it is, and it is already reaching toward him.

But if I open that door, will it set me free? Or undo everything I've built since I walked away?

From: Brynn Cole
Subject: Re: It's been a while
Sullivan,
Wow. I wasn't expecting to hear from you. You're right. It has been a
while. I'm glad to hear you're well.
I did tell your friend she could email me. I was a little taken aback by
her call, I'm not going to lie. But I'm glad she reached out. I'm glad
you did too. Your message meant more to me than I can explain in a
few sentences.
I live in Charleston now. As you may know, I run a nonprofit called
The Exit Project, and I host a podcast.
It's strange, the paths life takes us down.
I hope Nashville's been kind to you.
—Brynn

Changing your hair is never a good idea when you're in the middle of a crisis.

After having been a brunette for my whole life, I chose today of all days to experiment with a coppery red.

The processing time took longer than I planned, and now I'm late for an early dinner with Paul.

I take an Uber to the restaurant, then bust through the door, still trying to close my umbrella as I approach the hostess stand.

"I'm meeting someone," I tell the young hostess. "I'm late. Reservation is under Paul—"

Behind her, a hand sweeps through the air.

I start walking. "Never mind. I see him."

The restaurant is dim and warm, all amber light and low conversation. It's raining again, and tears streak the windows, silver threads along the glass. I fall into the chair across from Paul, breathing out a string of apologies.

My hand immediately flies to my hair. "I, uh, had a hair appointment."

He shoots me a small smile. "Red."

I wince, pull a lock of it away from my head, and eye the strands. "Is it terrible?"

Fine lines trail out from his eyes as his smile widens. "It looks great, Brynn."

Paul looks different. Normally, he has the makings of a graying beard, but tonight it's more like a shadow, his hair still damp from the rain.

He squares the menu in front of him. "I was beginning to think you were going to cancel."

"I almost did." I twist my napkin in my lap, managing a reassuring smile as I quickly add, "After I saw my hair in the mirror, I was pretty sure I made a mistake."

His gaze intensifies. "Red suits you."

I quickly change the subject. "Work's been insane."

"I know," he quips. "We work at the same place, remember?"

I take a sip of water, grateful for the excuse to look away. "I'm trying to line up some interviews for the next podcast."

"Did you find someone for next week?"

"Yeah. Her name's Shawna. She came out of a high-control group called Clear View, run by Bodhi Caspian. Remember him?"

Paul nods. "Yeah. He's in jail now. I read a bunch of stuff last year about Clear View—I think they later changed their name to Elevate or something."

I scan the menu. "Yep, that's them."

Paul tells me about a client he's working with—someone trying to get their daughter out of a sex cult.

I bob my head, passively listening, but my thoughts turn back to Sullivan and whether I should mention the email to Paul. He knows my story. But how much does he really want to hear?

He leans back. "You seem a little distracted."

I jerk my head up. "Sorry."

"Anything you want to tell me?"

"It's … complicated."

He groans. "I hate that phrase." He opens his menu and scans it silently for several minutes. Finally, he sets it down. "Have you been thinking about him since the call last night?"

The question shouldn't surprise me, but it does. "Who?"

He gives a small, crooked grin. "Come on, Brynn. You know who."

I glance down, tracing the rim of my glass with a finger. Damn, I could use that drink right now. "I got an email from him," I blurt.

Paul doesn't react right away. No sharp intake of breath or tightening of his jaw. Just a slow, thoughtful blink, like he's mulling over the information.

Our server stops at our table and introduces himself as Brett. Brett has cherubic cheeks and thinning, curly black hair, and when he holds out a drink menu, I practically tear it from his hand.

"I'll give you a minute to look and—"

"I'll have an old-fashioned," I say.

He smiles, revealing braces. "Oh, well, you obviously know what you want."

"Yes, I do," I state without hesitation.

He turns to Paul. "And you, sir?"

"Um, I'll have an iced tea."

I bring my hands down on the table. "You're going to make me drink alone?"

His eyes widen. "I'm the designated driver to the club, remember?"

"So? The club is like three blocks away."

"I'll be right back with those," Brett says, then rushes off.

I fling my hair off my shoulders, glance at Paul, then away again.

"OK," he says. "Do you want to tell me what Sullivan said?"

Relief and dread tangle in my chest. "He said the caller —her name is Ivy—told him we'd talked. He thought he'd reach out." I hesitate and then roll out the truth. "He lives in Nashville now. He said he thinks about me. That he regrets what happened between us."

Paul nods once, absorbing it. He reaches for his water, takes a sip.

I blow the hair out of my eyes.

"And how do you feel about that?" he asks.

"It was like being knocked sideways, to be honest."

His mouth curves at the edges. "Well, look, Brynn, you and Sullivan came from the same group, the same … lie. Shared trauma can connect people for a lifetime." He pauses. "Are you going to reply to his email?"

I suck my lower lip. Move my gaze toward the bar. "I replied this morning."

That earns me another pause. This one longer.

"Thank you for telling me," he says.

A strange warmth spreads through me at his understanding. Paul and I have been friends for a long time, but with this new, developing semi-romantic vibe between us, I'm treading carefully.

"I didn't say much," I rush on. "Just an acknowledgement, really."

Paul studies me. "You don't owe me an explanation for replying."

"I know, but I didn't want you to think I was hiding anything."

The server passes again and drops off a basket of bread.

Paul grabs a roll and drops it on his plate. "Can I be honest?"

"You usually are."

"I don't think this is about whether you should talk to him," he says. "I think it's about whether you're ready for what talking to him might stir up."

My throat tightens.

"I think you're strong enough to handle it," he says. "I just don't want you to tear yourself up about it."

The server brings our drinks. I wrap my hand around the sweating glass, poke the drink straw into my mouth, and wait for the burn. Then I sit back. "You're OK with me talking to him? I mean, I know this is only our second 'date.'" I throw up my fingers to make air quotes. "But here I am telling you about Sullivan and me getting back in touch. Where does that leave you?"

"It leaves me right here. Eating dinner with you." He offers a rueful smile. "But I won't pretend I don't care about you, Brynn."

"Paul…"

"And I think this guy still matters to you."

This was becoming too uncomfortable. "Let's not talk about Sullivan tonight."

"Sounds good to me." Paul lifts his iced tea. "Also, for the record—if this *is* a crisis change of hairstyle, it's one of the better ones I've seen."

I laugh and the tension breaks enough to breathe again.

As the conversation drifts back toward menus and work and weather, and late afternoon turns to evening and a second old-fashioned, I find myself recalling images of Sullivan on stage, head tipped back, guitar strap cutting across his shoulder, eyes closed.

Paul insists on paying for dinner, even though we split everything at work, and he knows I hate it when people buy me things.

"It's your birthday week." He waves me off as the server carries away his credit card. "Let's celebrate."

I roll my eyes. "Eh. It's not a milestone birthday or anything. Forty-five is nothing to celebrate."

"Let me feel like a good friend."

"You *are* a good friend," I say.

He raises an eyebrow, but I recognize the disappointed lines around his mouth. "Then don't fight me on the check."

———

At the comedy club, I order a glass of red wine, and this time, Paul joins me and orders one as well. The club is small and crowded, dark except for the glow of string lights looped around the ceiling rafters.

The comedian is funny, but not as funny as others I've seen over the years. Sullivan and I used to love comedy clubs tucked into basements or behind bars. Bad lights, cheap drinks. It was kind of our thing. I've never told Paul that. He only knows that I like stand-up comedy. Right now, though, I wish we'd gone somewhere else. A movie. The symphony. Anywhere that doesn't feel like borrowed history.

He laughs beside me, an easy, genuine sound, tipping his glass back for a sip of wine.

The comedian onstage paces back and forth, moving onto the next joke about his ex-wife and a Roomba, and everyone around us is losing their minds with laughter.

I smile when the room laughs, even chuckle once or twice in the right places, but my attention drifts—backward, sideways, into memory.

I swirl the wine in the glass, watching it climb the sides. The alcohol is the only thing keeping me from crying right now, and it will probably be the catalyst for my tears later.

Paul nudges me gently with his elbow. "You OK?"

"Yeah," I say. "Just tired."

When the show ends, Paul drives me back to my house. He talks a little about the show, asks if I liked it. I say I did.

He walks me to the door, hands in his pockets, jangling keys.

"You want to come in?" The question flows easily from my lips.

His expression is foreign to me as he follows me into the dark living room—wrinkled forehead, mouth in a line.

I flip on every light I come across, toss my coat over the back of a chair.

Paul has entered my house dozens of times, but never after a "date." It feels strange to me, and it must to him as well. He hovers near the entrance, as if he expects me to send him away.

"You want a drink?"

He shrugs a shoulder. "OK."

I don't know what I plan to do with him, but it won't be anything too exciting. No, it's a very polite, restrained hour during which we sit on the sofa together. Have another drink. More conversation about work, the comedian.

After a while, he stretches his arms. "It's getting late."

My head is a little swimmy, my vision a little bleary. I'm buzzed. The words teeter on the end of my tongue, asking him to stay. I immediately clamp my lips. *Do not ask him to stay. You will so regret that tomorrow.*

It doesn't matter anyway because Paul is focused on my coffee table book.

"*Making Memories in Boxes.*" He opens the cover, flips through several pages of photographed dioramas. "Wow. Cool. What are these?"

I scoot to the edge of the couch. "Sort of my little hobby."

"What—you make these?"

I nod. "I've made them for years. It's kind of therapeutic for me."

He smooths his hand over a page of one of my favorite representations of memory boxes. Little miniatures in each one—like dollhouse scenes.

"What's this all about?" he asks.

It's too hard to explain in words. I stand and hold out my hand. "Come on. I'll show you."

We walk down the hall to the spare room, where my memory boxes live. I open the door and flip on the light.

Paul enters the room slowly, like he's walking into a museum and taking it all in. "Wow. You've made a lot of these."

"Yeah."

Floor-to-ceiling shelves, all handmade cedar and pine, each box carved or painted or burned with something that matters—or hurts—enough to keep.

Some of them are pretty. The ones that aren't, aren't meant to be.

Paul sweeps his gaze across the room. "What are these exactly?"

"They're memories."

He moves toward one that perfectly represents Mama's bedroom in Crystal Cliffs. Right down to the gold mirror that used to sit on her chest of drawers. A room I haven't seen in more than twenty-five years.

"I sometimes wonder if Mama's room still looks the same, wherever she's living now."

"You ever talk to her?"

"Not in several years. Not since she left Crystal Cliffs, and I haven't seen her since I left." I run a finger over the carved figurine of Mama. She looks the way I want to remember her—in trailer park clothes and unstyled hair. All pre-Crystal Cliffs. "Anyway, these are all artifacts of my life. The things I want to remember. At least most of them."

He moves from shelf to shelf, holding his hands behind his back, like he's afraid of breaking something.

"It's fine," I say. "You can touch them."

He picks up one of the boxes from the middle shelf, shaped like an RV with an open side. His fingers trace the carved outline of the name on the roof: *Teddy.* Inside, miniature CDs are spread out on the floor. Beer bottles. Two figurines sit on the couch—a man with curly brown hair and a woman with silver eyes.

Paul lights up. "These are incredible, Brynn."

I shrug, suddenly shy. "It's something I do to sort through the past and organize feelings."

"Healthier than most coping mechanisms," he says. "Healthier than the whiskey and wrecked Jeep that shook me out of my funk years ago."

"That was me too." *Still is sometimes.* "Minus the Jeep."

He sets the Teddy box back on the shelf and reaches for one with the back facing out. Whitewashed wood. Small, delicate vines burned into the sides.

My stomach drops. "Not that one," I say too quickly.

He freezes, box already in his hand. He starts to put it back. "Sorry. I didn't mean to—"

"Never mind. It's fine." I'm not sure why I had such a knee-jerk reaction. It's a box I hardly ever look at, and I certainly never touch it. Of all the ones I should've thrown away, it's the one that has survived every purge. Every cleansing ritual. Every attempt to heal and forget and move on.

Paul looks down at it, curiosity blooming. "This is beautiful. The vines on the back. Whose is—"

He turns it around, and after that, it's easy to see who it was made for. A tie-dyed backdrop with a peace sign. It's a replica of the Woodstock '99 stage, complete with tiny band members. The figure at the microphone is disturbingly similar to the one I watched on that stage when I was twenty.

Paul's eyes flick to mine. "Sullivan?"

I choke out the words. "I threw out most of the boxes I made for him. But not that one."

Paul holds the diorama gently, as if it were a religious artifact. The light glints across the stage, made painstakingly of wood, wire, and paint. I don't tell him that underneath there's a switch that will make the scene light up with blue LED lights.

"I never could bring myself to get rid of that one," I say. "So much work went into it."

"Why would you? It's part of your memories." He runs a finger over the blond figurine. "You've never let him go."

Gut punch.
But he's right. I haven't.
Not completely.
Who am I kidding? Not at all.

Chapter Four

BIG BEND, FLORIDA, 1991

"Bring It All Back"

By the time I was twelve, Crystal Cliffs almost felt like home.

I could walk to the beach from our house. The view from the edge of the fence that separated our community from the ocean could fool you into thinking you'd stumbled into a postcard-worthy setting.

And it was safe. Astra Cynthia said so every time she gave a welcome tour to potential new members.

My mom said it was safe too.

"It's been a year since I felt like I needed to have my shotgun at the ready," she told me. "No men prowlin' around the windows or tappin' at the door."

I'd never known there were men at our windows, but I remembered Mama warning me against ever opening the door unless she or her brother—my Uncle Malachai—was on the other side of it.

Mama seemed happy in Crystal Cliffs. She smiled a lot

more than she used to, and she had friends now. Sullivan's mom, Kristen, quickly became Mama's best friend.

Kristen was the most beautiful woman I'd ever seen among women my mom's age. She had golden hair and eyes like diamonds. Sullivan's eyes were like hers—clear as glass.

Every morning before school, I dressed in my uniform, braided my hair the way all the girls were supposed to, threw my backpack over my shoulder, and made my way toward the community school along the sidewalk, past the large, glowing clock on its stone tower, shining over the neighborhood. Our subdivision was built around the structure, reminding us that time was the most important part of our lives. Astra Cynthia said making the most of every moment and not wasting a second was what made productive human beings.

Every afternoon after homework, the community children were expected to volunteer at The Collective, each of us assigned to a specific role. I usually helped mop the café's floors, sort clothes to hang on the racks, or stock cans in the grocery section. Mama still worked full-time at the register, even though Honey Barrett promised her that by year five she'd be managing the home goods department.

Kristen Stonecutter had moved positions, shifting from forklifts and labels to running the front registers with a flair no uniform could suppress. If a bored teenager or a tired mother came through her line, Kristen knew exactly how to make them laugh by saying something witty and then tossing her palomino ponytail.

I'd started wearing my hair like Kristen's, except mine was dark brown and wasn't quite long enough to hang to the middle of my back like hers.

Mama and Kristine had coffee together before shifts,

discussed community meetings, swapped recipes, and whispered things—most of which they never let me hear.

Mama's friendship with Kristen also meant I saw Sullivan a lot.

And that was not a bad thing.

In the year I'd known him, Sullivan had turned fifteen and had shot up fast, all limbs and angles, but his face had settled into clearly defined cheekbones sloping down to hollows, sun-browned skin, sandy-blond hair that never stayed where he combed it. And those eyes—shockingly blue.

I often glimpsed Sullivan while volunteering after school, but only in passing. Sometimes he was hauling boxes for the store or helping the groundskeepers.

Girls in the community school whispered about him behind their textbooks. They wrote his name in the margins of their worksheets. Some made excuses to pass by our houses, giggling and hopeful. Sullivan didn't seem to notice any of it. Or maybe he did and pretended not to care.

One night, when I came home from The Collective, Kristen and Mama were sitting at our kitchen table, drinking something red from dark blue plastic cups. I greeted Kristen, then slipped into the den, with the television on low, my history textbook in my lap. I stared at the words on the page, but my focus was on deciphering what they were talking about. Every so often, one of them would say something a little too loud.

"Shhh," Kristen shushed.

"No one can hear us."

"You'd be surprised," Kristen said. "Say that too loud, and we'll both end up in the Think Tank."

That was the second time I'd heard that term—the Think Tank—and both times it was described as a place no one wanted to go. From what I gathered, it was a facility somewhere in the neighborhood, where people who weren't on board with the community's mission were sent.

"I'm just saying that sometimes I wonder about the way they handle discipline in the community," Mama said. "All that screaming—those stabilizing sessions? They're so … violent. Don't you wonder about whether that's right?"

"I can't afford to wonder," Kristen said. "Sullivan's on a trajectory for staff training, so we've got to toe the line."

"I'm not surprised they've singled him out," Mama answered. "He's the model of excellence."

"He is—I'll say that even if he's mine," Kristen agreed. "Astra Cynthia has been watching him. She's eyeing him for management—or maybe even administration."

Mama lowered her voice another decibel. "You think she's eyeing him for professional potential or for *other* reasons."

Kristen snorted. "Well, I hope it's not for *that*."

"Don't get me wrong. I love Astra Cynthia, but I've heard some stories about her preference for younger men."

"Sullivan would be a little *too* young for her," Kristen said. "At least I hope he would."

A long pause. Then Mama's voice again. "Does he *want* to go into management? Or would he rather be part of distribution or something?"

Kristen made a sound in the back of her throat. "Whatever he does, he's going to need a lot of prodding. I don't know what the hell that kid is thinking. Says he wants to leave Crystal Cliffs, go to California, and be a rock star."

Mama groaned. "Oh no."

"Yeah. I told him no way. He has too much potential. He needs to stay right here in Crystal Cliffs, find a good wife, work for The Collective, and he can play his guitar at the Crystal Club if he wants to." She made that sound in the back of her throat again. "He's going to be a challenge, though. He's hitting that age where he's not easy. Fights me on everything."

"Don't let anyone know about him thinking that way," Mama said. "I'd hate to see *him* in a stabilizing session." More liquid glugged into plastic cups. "Maybe he'll find a cute girlfriend here, and that will change his mind about the rock star stuff."

"Yeah," Kristen yawned loudly. "I think I'm going to have to marry him off early to keep him from going into the Gray."

The Gray—a term for the world beyond Crystal Cliffs, a world filled with Gray Ones, people that lived by their own rules.

"Hey," she continued. "Maybe we can arrange a marriage between Sullivan and Brynn once she's old enough. That would be perfect."

The two women cackled.

I sat up and turned down the television another notch. They weren't serious, of course. They couldn't be. Even so, that didn't squelch the image coursing through my almost-thirteen-year-old brain of Sullivan and me standing at an altar.

"We'd be sisters-in-law," Mama screeched. "Well, sort of."

The sound of their laughter was punctuated by the *thunk* of their hands slapping the table.

"Brandy," Kristen wheezed. "I love you so much."

"Me too, girl. If you or Sullivan ever need anything, I'm here for you both. I'll do anything I can."

Their words were starting to roll into each other's as they laughed so hard they broke into coughing fits. Mama didn't even sound like herself. What was wrong with them?

"I think we need some food," Kristen said. "I'm drunk as a skunk."

Now it made sense—the red in the glasses wasn't Cherry Coke. It was wine. It was the first time my mom had been drunk since we left the double-wide a year before.

The last time Mama drank, she'd spent the night crying in her bedroom. Then she'd called Francis Alewood from down the lane to come over. He didn't leave until morning. I hoped that wouldn't happen this time. There weren't that many men in Crystal Cliffs. Other than a few husbands and boyfriends, male community members were mostly like Sullivan—kids and teenagers.

One day, Sullivan wouldn't be a teenager anymore. One day, I wouldn't either.

***

I was sitting on the porch steps of our house after school, carving little spirals into a strip of soft wood with a small pocketknife. If all went well, the figurine would start to look like Kristen, and I'd give it to her as a gift. The shoulders were pretty level. The neck was a little long, and I'd left plenty of extra wood exposed to work on the waves of the hair. I'd do that last. I started to work on the face. Getting the nose right was harder than I thought.

The sun was low, honey-colored. A few younger kids darted past, chasing each other with Sock'em Boppers—big inflatable blue and green devices to pummel each other.

A few minutes later, Sullivan loped by, backpack slung over his shoulder, clipboard in hand—always the clipboard.

"No Crayons today?" he called out.

I looked up, startled. "No. Why?"

Crayons? When had he ever seen me with Crayons?

He grinned, his teeth practically shining in the late-day sun. "I'm kidding you."

"Oh." I blinked up at him.

"The other day I came by, and you were out here drawing or something—with colored pencils, I guess."

I forced a smile. "Oh, yeah. I was."

"You're kind of artsy, huh?"

I shrugged. "Yeah. I guess."

Then, it was like my brain shut down its conversation center. He stood there, seemingly waiting for me to say something else.

Finally, he nodded toward the wood shavings around my feet. "You carving?"

I looked down at the figurine in my hand. I'd accidentally nicked the wood when Sullivan had shown up, and there was a hollow in the middle of the face where the nose should have been.

He approached the steps and leaned against the railing. "Can I see?"

I didn't want to show him. My fingers tightened around the wood as he peered down at the sculpture.

"Oh, cool. It's like a woman."

It wasn't *like* a woman—it was Kristen.

He lowered his backpack and his clipboard onto the step and sat next to me. "I thought I saw you at The Collective today. Were you volunteering in the café?"

"I was cleaning the coffee carafes."

He made a sympathetic noise. "Oh, yeah. I used to do that too when I first started working there." He leaned toward me, bumped my shoulder with his. "Pretty soon you'll be working in the stock room like me, checking supplies."

I glanced over at his clipboard. "Is that why you're always carrying that around?"

"Unfortunately."

I made eye contact with him, then looked away. In the late afternoon sun, his eyes were as clear as water. "Do you like doing that? Working in the stock room?"

He shrugged a shoulder. "It's … I mean, not really. At least I get paid a little." He dragged his backpack closer and unzipped it. "You like music?"

"Yeah." I didn't know much about music. Mama listened to country, and there was a girl in my class named Maeve who let me use her Walkman between classes to listen to rock bands. "I was listening to Black Crowes today."

"They're pretty good. Do you like Soundgarden?"

I didn't know if I did or not, but I nodded anyway. "Sure."

He pulled out a jewel case from his backpack. "Just got their newest album. Chris Cornell, I mean, *come on*! His voice is like … damn!" He passed me the CD. "Here. Take it. Get it back to me sometime this week once you've listened."

I balanced the plastic case on the tips of my fingers, as if it were made of glass and might break if I closed my hand around it. "Really? Are you sure?"

"Yeah." He slid his clipboard into his backpack and stood. "I'd really like to know what you think of it."

Sullivan wanted to know what I thought of something. Did we even have a CD player in the house? I would find one. Wait, Maeve would let me use hers. Maybe we could listen to it at her place. At least I knew her Walkman played CDs. "Thanks. I'll listen as soon as I can."

"Great." He braced a hand on my shoulder as he stood, although he didn't press down too hard. "Well, I'd better get home. Mom's got dinner waiting. My mom and your mom picked up a coverage shift for inventory night, so they'll be gone awhile."

He didn't say what we both knew: later shifts meant fewer eyes. Fewer rules.

A rare freedom. Although sometimes it seemed like people in Crystal Cliffs hated having too much free time or free rein.

Sullivan picked up a stray piece of wood from the ground. "Come over and watch some TV if you want."

I froze. Had he really invited me to his house, with no one else home? I wondered if he knew I wasn't even thirteen yet.

"Um, OK. Maybe."

"I mean, only if you want to." He grinned. "We could watch *90210*."

I jerked my head up. "That's like, my favorite show."

He straightened. "I know."

"How did you know?"

"I can tell." He tapped his temple. "I have instincts."

I laughed. "No, you don't."

"Maybe not, but I have popcorn. Buttered. From The Collective."

"I love popcorn," I said.

"I know."

Sullivan's house was like ours. Two bedrooms, two bathrooms. A brightly decorated living room with a border of stenciled flowers that ran along the top of the walls. Sullivan sat on one end of the couch, and I sat on the other. We watched *Beverly Hills 90210*.

It was the episode where Kelly told her friends that she'd been attacked at a Yale fraternity party. I thought I might die of embarrassment. Even the mention of anything sexual in the presence of someone like Sullivan was unbearable.

I stuffed popcorn into my mouth until my cheeks were puffed out like a hamster.

"What a douche," Sullivan said. "That frat guy, I mean."

I made a noise of agreement, filtered through a mouthful of popcorn.

"You know, Astra Cynthia says that guys who rape women should lose their balls." He threw a piece of popcorn in the air, caught it in his mouth, and chewed loudly. "It sounds extreme, but I think I agree with her."

I glanced over at him. His face had hardened, eyes focused on the TV.

"If anyone did anything to my mom," he said, "I think I'd cut their balls off myself."

I swallowed the popcorn. "Where's your dad?"

"Overseas somewhere. Fighting in Iraq, I think. At least, that's what Mom says."

"You ever talk to him?"

He shook his head. "No. I've never even met him. Mom got together with him when she was dancing at a club. I was born nine months later." His mouth quirked into a smile, which he quickly shrugged away. "He sends a check sometimes." He swung his head toward me. "What about you?"

"My dad died like four years ago—in a car accident."

Sullivan's forehead creased. "I'm sorry to hear that."

It seemed like he really meant it.

———

Over the next year, Sullivan and I spent time at each other's houses whenever our moms got together for dinner. Mostly, we figured Mama and Kristen used it as a chance to open a bottle of wine and get a little drunk on a Friday or Saturday night.

The more they drank, the louder they got. Sometimes, when we were watching TV in the den, we heard parts of their conversations that made me want to crawl under the couch. Especially whenever Kristen joked about Sullivan and me getting married, which she did more often these days.

"We ought to arrange it now," Kristen said one night. "Save them the trouble later."

I cringed and whipped my head toward Sullivan, who rolled his eyes.

My mother snorted. "Kris, come on."

"What? It'd be perfect. They like each other, like spending time together. Might as well make it official."

Sullivan stiffened beside me.

I clawed at my jeans, scratching an imaginary itch. Heat flared in my cheeks. "It's a joke."

"Sure it is," Sullivan said with a sarcastic edge.

Lately, the "arranged marriage" joke had become a point of contention between Sullivan and Kristen.

I imagined how I must look to him—scrawny, flat-chested. "I'm sorry they keep saying that."

He gave me a sidelong glance, squinting a little. "How do you feel about them saying that?"

"I—I don't know. It's weird." Not romantic. Not flattering. But it was true. It *was* weird that our mothers kept joking about it. "I'm only thirteen. You're only sixteen. It's stupid."

His cheeks lifted in a small, close-lipped smile. "Don't take this the wrong way, Brynn, but I think it's just my mom trying to figure out how to keep me here."

I wasn't offended, and I knew he was right.

His gaze darted past me to the doorway that led to the kitchen, where our mothers' laughter crackled.

"You know this isn't how most people live." Sullivan motioned toward our bay window.

Nearly everyone had an extra-sized window in their house so that they could see the clock tower.

"Not everyone brushes their teeth to a timer." He sighed. "Not everyone works at the same place, lives in the same community. A lot of kids don't go through the torture of boarding school. Wait until you have to go next year."

I remembered what it was like living out in the Gray. It hadn't been all bad. But I'd been looking forward to going to boarding school, making new friends, and living with lots of other girls my age.

"Astra Cynthia says people live here because they chose a different kind of life," I said.

Sullivan cocked an eyebrow. "I didn't choose this. Did you?"

"No."

He pointed toward the front door. "Down that road are other places—Tallahassee. Head north, and there's Atlanta. You ever been to Atlanta?"

I shook my head.

"Well, I have. It's a whole other world. You can eat in different restaurants. There's a mall with tons of stores, not just one supercenter. You can go to a club and listen to bands." He lowered his voice. "Beau and I snuck into a club last week." His eyes lifted, reliving it. "It was amazing, Brynn. That's what I want. To play music."

Just like Kristen said. Music was Sullivan's dream.

"Yeah," he ran a hand through the top of his hair, and it flopped back into place perfectly. "So, I don't think I'm going to be here for long."

"What do you mean?"

"I'm thinking about making a break for it."

My breath snagged. "Leave Crystal Cliffs?"

Sullivan nodded. "Yeah. I can't live like this the rest of my life. Not after what happened to Jason."

"Jason?"

"Jason Hillsdale." His eyes met mine. "They carted him away about a month ago. I was there, Brynn. I saw it. He was taken by one of the white vans you see parked behind the community building."

His words weren't making any sense to me. "What do you mean they 'took' him? I heard he was mountain climbing in Utah."

Sullivan quirked his mouth. "Yeah. That's where they *say* he is. I was walking back from school when I saw the van pull into the Hillsdales' driveway. A couple of men rushed out, a gurney between them—white sheet strapped down like seatbelts. Someone was under that sheet. Screaming." He shook his head. "I wasn't supposed to see that."

"What do you think happened to him?" I whispered.

Sullivan huffed out a dark sound. "I think he's dead."

The word scratched at my insides. "Dead?"

He snapped his gaze to mine. "I think they killed him. Don't kid yourself. Jason isn't the first."

My mouth fell open. "Why would they kill him?"

"He was talking to reporters, people out in the Gray. Telling them stuff. True stuff. About Astra Cynthia. About Chuck Crow, letting people know that he's her partner in crime. He's as bad as she is, if not worse. They're not good people, Brynn. They made an example of Jason."

"Everything OK in there?" Mama's voice cut through my silent mind machinations of what Jason might have been telling the world that would have gotten him killed.

"Everything's fine," Sullivan yelled back.

A giggle from Kristen. "Not doing anything in there that you shouldn't, are you?"

I chimed in. "We're watching TV."

"OK," Kristen sing-songed.

I dropped my voice to a whisper. "I can't believe that Astra Cynthia would do that. Or Chuck Crow."

Sullivan turned his eyes back to the TV. "Believe what you like. Just watch your step, Brynn. Keep your head down. Keep carving your little people and stay out of trouble."

His words jarred my memory. The wooden figure. The one I'd tried to make look like Kristen hadn't turned out so well, but I'd tried again—and this one was perfect. I hadn't been planning to show it to him yet, but all this talk about him leaving made me want to.

I went across the room, pulled open the cabinet that held my wood and tools, and plucked out my project. The figurine was only about three inches long. I had painted it earlier in the day, and some of the paint on the bottom was still a little sticky.

"Here," I said. "Hold out your hand."

He did, and I carefully laid the figure in his palm.

His eyes flared. "Damn. That's me!"

I beamed, pride coursing through me. "Yep."

"Wow. It looks like me." He looked up. "Can I have it?"

"Yes. It's yours. I made it for you."

His face softened. "Wow. Thanks, Brynn. That's really, really cool." He inspected the figurine again, letting it roll back and forth in his hand.

I'd never felt such a rush of elation. "I'm glad you like it."

"I love it," he said. "I'll keep it forever."

I resumed my place beside him. "Sullivan?"

"Yeah."

"Aren't you scared? That they might kill you too if you try to leave?"

"Yes," he said. "But I'd rather die than stay here." His eyes bored into mine. "And if you tell anyone I said that, I'll deny it."

"I won't tell," I said.

"Not even your mom."

"I swear."

The smoke and fire in his eyes said he was leaving, and nothing would stop him, but I wanted to believe that something—and a childish fantasy prompted me to think maybe it could be me—would anchor him.

Still, after our conversation about Jason, I started looking at my community through a different lens—one that made me think about leaving too.

Chapter Five

NOW

Rain needles my apartment windows, tracing pale veins down the glass. In the city below, cars splash through puddles, an occasional horn bounces off brick.

I should do some work. My lunch date with Paul ran longer than I expected. Official date number three. It's going to be hard to keep calling these "founders' meetings" if we keep kissing at the end of them like we did today.

I sit down at my computer and jiggle the mouse. An outline for next week's podcast opens on my laptop, half a paragraph staring at me expectantly.

Soon. First, I need to fix a drink.

In the kitchen, I light the citrus-and-cedar candle on the counter. I grab my glass from the sink, plonk some ice into it, and pour whiskey over it. I already had two at lunch with Paul. Guilt from having three whiskeys in one day makes me turn on the tap, hold the glass under it for a second, and dilute the drink to amber water. I swish it, take a sip. The burn barely registers anymore.

Paul's voice from lunch replays in my head: *I really enjoy being with you.* He means it. The feeling is mutual. If only I weren't afraid to build something that would have to live in the shadow of a man I once followed across state lines.

I've been checking my email obsessively since I replied to his message. Several days have passed, and he hasn't replied.

Maybe that's for the best.

I return to my desk, pull my chair closer to the screen, and move the mouse to a search bar.

I type in the name: *Sullivan Stonecutter.*

The screen fills instantly—grainy photos, fan pages frozen in time, headlines from two decades ago:

"Cutter's Lead Singer Walks Offstage Mid-Tour."

"Rumors of Another Band Breakup."

"Where Is Sullivan Stonecutter Now?"

I scroll past them all until I find one that catches my eye: *"The Last Song—Frontman Pipes Up About Past, Present and Future."*

The article is about fifteen years old. In the photo, he would have been around thirty-three. His face is chiseled, his hair nearly to his shoulders. The same eyes, though. Piercing. Haunted.

I click the link. The page loads slowly, pixels stuttering. The interview is short, an excerpt from a long-defunct magazine. I read the pull quote at the top:

"Some people spend their lives trying to forget where they came from. Others can't. I think I'm the second kind."

My throat tightens. Shared trauma. That's what Paul called our connection. Maybe that was why it didn't work out for us. The damage ran too deep—down into our core. The mire of our early lives was like quicksand, holding us down, burying us alive.

I return to my email. This is the last time I'll check today.

There are no messages from Sullivan, but another subject line shoots out like a flare.

Subject: *I'm the girl who called the other day—Ivy Delane*

My pulse jumps. Shit. Sullivan's girlfriend.

From: *ivy.delane@firemail.com*

For a moment, I stare at it, the cursor hovering over the unopened message. Then I click.

Hi Brynn,

I'm sorry for calling out of the blue the other day. I should have reached out like this instead. I hope it's OK if I contact you on your work email—it's listed on your nonprofit's site.

I know naming a mutual acquaintance like that probably wasn't the ideal thing to do live, and I'm sorry if it put you in an uncomfortable position. I didn't know how to ask the question without mentioning his name first.

I hope this isn't strange or presumptuous. I've been thinking about it a lot—about you, actually—and I wanted to reach out directly rather than let things feel awkward or unfinished.

I'll be in Charleston for a few days next week to visit my sister. I was hoping—if you're open to it—that we might meet for coffee or lunch. Nothing formal. Just a chance to say hello in person.

Like I said before, Sullivan has spoken about you often, always with so much respect. It would mean a lot to me to finally meet you in person. I'd love it if you would sign a copy of your book for me.

I admire the work you're doing with The Exit Project. It takes courage

to turn experience into something that helps other people find their foot-
ing. I imagine it hasn't always been easy.
Please don't feel any pressure. I understand completely if your schedule
is full or if this isn't something you'd be comfortable with.
Thanks for considering it.
Ivy

The words swim.

No pressure.

It would mean a lot to me.

I almost smile.

This isn't about coffee or Charleston or admiration for my work—though I'm sure that part is genuine enough.

Ivy is smart. She's stepping forward, placing herself between Sullivan and whatever unfinished thing might still exist between us. Letting me see her, know her, humanize her—before I have the chance to become something abstract or dangerous in her imagination.

There's a confidence in it I can't help but respect. And maybe—if I'm being honest—I'm curious too.

She's a connection to Sullivan, and I haven't seen him in so long. She's also a mirror. A way of seeing myself from the outside. Of understanding what part of him is still reaching out to me—and what part has moved on.

I close the email and sit for a moment. Stevie Nicks' raspy voice wails on my Spotify playlist. "Edge of Seventeen." One of Sullivan's favorite songs. We'd danced to it once at a community center gathering, back when we were kids.

The old instinct whispers that I should protect myself. Keep a distance. Say I'm too busy.

Except that instinct is rooted in fear, and I've built my

adult life around walking through doors instead of pretending they aren't there.

If she read my memoir, then she read the words that meant as much to me then as they do now: *Sullivan Stonecutter was the love of my life. He was also one of my greatest agonies.*

I click and open a new email message.

Subject: *RE: Meeting in Charleston*
Hi Ivy,
Thank you for reaching out and for such a thoughtful note. I didn't find it strange or presumptuous at all.
I'd be open to meeting. Coffee or lunch sounds fine. It would be nice to meet a friend of Sullivan's.
Thank you for your kind words about The Exit Project. The work is meaningful to me, even on the hard days.
Let me know your schedule while you're in town, and we'll find something that works.
Safe travels,
Brynn

I hit Send.

For a second, I feel nothing. Then comes the sensation low in my chest, like I've stepped off a curb I didn't see coming.

My fingers curl against the edge of the desk as I glimpse my reflection in the monitor—coppery hair catching the light, unfamiliar and suddenly too bright. A woman I barely recognize looks back at me, mid-transformation, and so much older than I anticipate.

Beneath the planes of my face, coiled tight, is something that scares me far more.

Hope.

Not the reckless, romantic kind I once believed in. This

one doesn't promise anything. It just whispers that whatever's coming won't be faced blindly.

Ivy is probably exhaling, satisfied that she's done the sensible thing.

Here I am—standing in the middle of it all—aware and suddenly very, very awake. There's no undoing it now.

The door is open. I'm obviously going to walk through it.

Chapter Six

BIG BEND, FLORIDA, 1994

"The Eye of Scorn"

I was entering my second year of boarding school in Crystal Cliffs. Mom worked extra shifts at the supercenter to pay for my tuition, and I volunteered every weekend at The Collective's market just outside the community—a weekly occurrence that was part sales and part recruiting.

I still saw Sullivan from time to time, but he never came to our house with Kristen anymore. Mostly, we waved if we saw each other passing in the street, or sometimes I'd see him at The Collective, where he was interning as a manager. It must have felt like prison to him, being groomed for a life he didn't want.

Still, he played guitar and sang in the band at our Friday night gatherings at the community center, and he smiled enough to make me wonder if he'd forgotten all about trying to leave. Maybe he'd finally found some peace in the growing community.

Astra Cynthia's self-improvement book was selling in

reader circles like no one ever expected. People claimed her philosophies had influenced them to start their own businesses, coached them in losing weight and keeping it off, and even taught them how best to rear children. When she'd been featured on a popular talk show, the host had called her "a Renaissance woman and a guru in how to live a stable, contented life."

After Astra Cynthia was featured on the talk show, the community had grown by several thousand members. Television producers approached her about doing her own talk show to share her many nuggets of wisdom. The Collective was exporting goods. The selection process to join the community was tightened, and more stringent requirements were put in place. Housing was no longer free to members.

And there were a lot more rules for everyone.

I'd lived long enough in the community that I thought I knew all the rules. Including the parameters around all the exercises and "games" we participated in at school.

Most of the exercises were designed to reveal our strengths and weaknesses. There were falling games in which our classmates were meant to catch us, and climbing games in which students spotted one another. The Eye Game had a completely different purpose. A contest of staring—unblinking, silent endurance—this exercise was about loyalties. The Eye Game was how they stripped you of your shadows, made you prove you had nothing to hide.

A man we knew as "Uncle Dunn" officiated the game. A man with an air of administrative severity, he'd spent his entire life cataloging other people's obedience. His steel-rimmed spectacles framed a face that never revealed more than mild impatience. His clothes were immaculate—pressed slacks, starched shirt, sleeves rolled to the same precise midpoint every day. Even his wristwatch seemed to tick more sharply than anyone else's.

He recorded everything—reactions, hesitations, tears. A walking ledger of microscopic observation, he prowled the room in measured steps, noting everything.

It was late November, and strangely cold for Big Bend. The air carried an unnatural chill that settled over the peninsula like a spell. The marshes, usually soft with the buzz of insects and the slow lap of water, had gone still. In the early mornings, frost clung to the reeds, and even the gulls sounded different, their cries thinner in the cold air.

That afternoon, a few of us had gone out in one of the jon boats that sat tethered behind the girls' dorm. We weren't supposed to—boats were reserved for "community excursions"—but Maeve Robbins had dared us, and the water was low enough that the mudflats gleamed like dull glass. We'd pushed off, gliding through the narrow cuts between the spartina. For a few minutes, it felt like freedom —the brackish air stinging our cheeks, the sky the color of tin. By the time we dragged the boat back to the dock, our hands were numb, and the world already felt like it was closing in again.

That night, the summons came.

It had been almost two months since the last Eye Game. We thought for sure we'd been caught in the jon boat, and that's why it was happening again. Some of the younger girls told us there were rumors among the boarding school staff that someone was stealing food from storage.

When Uncle Dunn called sixteen of us from the upper dorm to the recreation room, we already knew what was coming. The boys had their own building across the quad, and we never mixed after dark. This was just us—the older girls—fifteen to seventeen. They suspected one of us. It had taken place on our side of the dorm.

We were marched to the room with windows blacked out with paper, and a single lamp burned against the far wall, its yellow beam pooling on the floor like a stage light. The usual buzz of the fluorescents was gone. Expectant silence pressed in.

Melissa Bench stood beside the lamp, hands folded at her waist, the same smirk she always wore, eyes too big for her face peering over us. She was a senior girl. Many of the seniors were recruited to take on leadership roles. Tonight, Melissa had been put in charge.

"Tonight's lesson is about truth," she said. "You can't hide from it. You can't hide behind anything." She lifted a finger to her collar and yanked it. "Even your coverings."

A chill rolled through the room.

"Our coverings?" The word snagged in my throat. She couldn't mean our clothes.

I glanced down at my white shirt, the smear of mud on one knee of my navy pants.

Maeve whipped a hand through wavy brown hair before shooting it into the air. "Excuse me—our coverings?" Her gray eyes narrowed. "What exactly are you asking us to do?"

Uncle Dunn stood in the corner, arms crossed, blue eyes like searchlights.

"Remove your outer layers," Melissa said lightly, as if asking us to take off our shoes. "Anything you could use to conceal your fear."

No one moved.

"You're staying in here?" Maeve asked Uncle Dunn.

He nodded.

"Are you even going to turn around?"

Uncle Dunn lifted his chin. He spoke in clipped syllables, each instruction delivered like an entry in a ritualized report. "Are you showing trust, Maeve—or fear?"

Melissa's gaze cut through her. "Yes, Maeve. Uncle Dunn is an elder. I know you're not accusing him of wasteful thoughts."

Wasteful thoughts. Astra Cynthia's word for a headspace that focused on physical attraction, one that might even lead someone to act upon the desires.

Maeve and I traded a helpless glance. What choice did we have? Buttons clicked, zippers rasped. One by one, we folded sweaters and jackets over chairs until we stood in our underwear.

Shadows climbed the walls, bending our bodies into warped silhouettes.

Melissa paired us off. "The rules are the same," she said. "Eyes forward. No blinking. No turning away. Seek out the truth in each other's gaze. One of you knows something."

Our breaths huffed in and out—small, tight, uneven— like we were lining up for a race.

"You will have one minute," Melissa said.

Uncle Dunn lifted a silver stopwatch, its face flashing in the lamplight.

Click.

Maeve stood across from me, chin lifted, eyes locked. At first, I thought I could handle it—just a stare, only a few seconds. But the longer it went on, the heavier it grew, like gravity pressing between us. Maeve's defiance smoldered in her eyes. Every part of me wanted to look away—to blink, to breathe, to hide.

My eyes stung. Water pooled at my lower lid until Maeve's face shimmered.

I blinked.

Click.

The stopwatch sliced through the silence.

"Brynn Cole." Uncle Dunn's voice was calm and cold. "Only thirty-seven seconds. I'm surprised at you."

Maeve stepped back, triumphant.

Uncle Dunn tilted his head, eyes narrowing as if he could see through me. "What are you hiding, Brynn? Do you know who's been stealing food? Is it you? Maeve?"

My mouth went dry. "No—sir, I don't—"

"Lies rot the soul," Melissa sang from the sideline. "That's why we play. To see who's holding on to secrets."

The room seemed to shrink. The other girls watched, waiting to see if I'd break. I crossed my arms over my chest, covering the flesh spilling out of my ill-fitting bra.

"I don't know who's stealing food." I darted my gaze between Uncle Dunn and Melissa. "I swear I don't."

Uncle Dunn stepped toward me. "Are you protecting your friend? Are you protecting Maeve?"

"I'm not protecting anyone."

"She's lying," Melissa pronounced. "I can tell."

"I'm not!"

"Lesson Room Two," Melissa said finally, her tone bright and final.

I wanted to protest—that it wasn't fair, that I hadn't even had a chance—but no one argued once a "lesson" was assigned. Lessons were supposed to make us better. More loyal. Better potential employees and community servants.

I only knew about lesson rooms through others who'd spent time in them. They could be anywhere. A basement, an attic, the yard. Lesson rooms were designed for thinking, for contemplating how to make good choices. At least it was a lesson room and not the Think Tank. We were all terrified of the Think Tank.

I made my way down the corridor, arms clutched around myself. My legs felt bloodless. Uncle Dunn stayed behind me, his shoes clicking in an even rhythm. He didn't touch me. He didn't have to. The sound of him was enough —a reminder that there was no escape. Entering the Think Tank was always presented as a choice, but lesson rooms were mandatory.

The hall narrowed, bulbs flickering. He stopped before a door that was cracked open to a blade of blackness.

"Inside," he said.

I hesitated. The space beyond looked too small to be a classroom, but I stepped in anyway. Not a classroom. Shelves crowded with boxes, buckets, stacks of Astra Cynthia's books. A supply closet.

The door slammed. The latch caught.

I pressed my palm against the wood and jerked the doorknob. It didn't give.

Then, the retreating tap of Uncle Dunn's shoes sounded along the tile.

The dark was absolute, with only a thin sliver of light under the door. Somewhere above me, a drip echoed. *Plop. Plop.* I sank against the wall beside me, knees pulled tight to my chest. The concrete floor leached the warmth from my skin, leaving a chill in my bones.

Time stretched. Minutes or hours—I couldn't tell. I counted heartbeats, shivers until they blurred together, until the stillness itself became a sound.

The doorknob rattled.

A soft scrape followed, cautious, like someone trying not to be caught.

I hugged my knees tighter. Was I being released, or was I about to face something worse?

The door eased open, spilling a shard of yellow light. A

silhouette filled the frame—tall, lean—then a flash of white from a flashlight.

I lurched to my feet, shoulder blades hitting the shelves. A box toppled and hit the floor, cracking like a gunshot.

"Who's in here?" The voice was low, male, rough-edged.

I shrank into the corner, arms across my chest.

A clicking sounded as he tried the useless wall switch. Then the light widened with the glow of his flashlight. He stepped in. The beam slid across the shelves, the floor, and then me.

"What the hell?"

For a suspended second, neither of us moved. His breath hitched, and the light trembled before dipping toward the ground.

"Shit," he muttered, turning the beam toward himself.

Tousled dark blond hair. A sharp jaw.

"Sullivan?"

The flashlight lifted again, catching my face. "Brynn?"

"I didn't know anyone was—" He stopped, glancing behind him as if someone might appear. "I was … never mind." He stepped inside, closed the door. "What are you doing in here?"

"I blinked." The words sounded ridiculous.

"You blinked?"

"We were playing the Eye Game, and I—I blinked."

Heat flooded my face. Standing there in panties and a thin bra that no longer fit, I felt flayed open. Every nerve burned.

Sullivan stepped back, as if distance could undo what he'd seen. "You—uh—should … here." He pulled his sweater over his head, leaving only the T-shirt underneath, and held it out between us. "Take it. Please." He turned toward the wall.

I hesitated, then slipped it over my head. The fabric was soft and warm, smelling of soap and earth.

"Thank you."

He remained facing the wall. "I didn't mean to … I was looking for supplies. I didn't expect to find—"

"It's OK. I'm glad you're here." The warmth of his sweater made my body shake harder.

He crouched by the shelves, setting the flashlight on the floor, careful not to aim it at me. Shadows carved his face into planes of light and dark. We sat opposite each other, knees drawn up. I wasn't alone. Somehow, that was both worse and better.

Sullivan's brows knit. "You shouldn't be in here."

"Neither should you." Another chill wracked me.

He angled the flashlight toward me again. "You're shaking."

"I'm freezing."

He hesitated, then grabbed the flashlight, crawled across the space between us, and sat beside me, his shoulder brushing mine. "I don't want to leave you like this." The ball of light bounced along the walls. "Do you want me to get you out of here?"

"No. It'll be worse. You'd be in trouble too."

"I'll stay with you for a while."

Suddenly, I was aware of every sensation—the space between our arms, the cool air licking my bare legs, the press of concrete against my skin.

I tugged at the hem of his sweater, pulling it down over my thighs. A tremor rose in my chest, unfamiliar, frightening, alive.

Astra Cynthia told us, teenagers, that we weren't supposed to feel our bodies, our temporary shells, distractions from our path. Right then, I was so very, very far away from not feeling. Every inch of me *felt* something. Sullivan felt too real.

He finally spoke. "Why did they put you in here?"

I looked at my knees, pale in the weak light. "I told you. I blinked."

"That's all?"

"I didn't mean to. It just … happened."

He leaned his head back against the wall, eyes on the ceiling. "You can't control everything. Blinking, breathing…"

The light beneath the door flickered. Was someone outside? Listening in? We both froze.

When no footsteps followed, he leaned forward, forearms on his knees. "Have they ever locked you in here before?"

"No. I didn't even know this room existed."

"Yeah." His voice dropped. "They don't talk about the rooms they use for punishment."

The way he said *punishment* seemed to come from memory, not rumor.

"They said someone's stealing supplies. They accused me of knowing who it is. But I don't."

"You don't have to tell me the rest."

"There isn't any rest. Just this." I gestured at the dark—the walls, the air, the nothing.

My shame hovered, but Sullivan's presence was forgiving, like he'd seen me at my worst and wasn't repulsed.

I studied him in the glow of the flashlight—the glint of his lashes, the slope of his cheekbones. His pale blue eyes looked older than his eighteen years.

"You haven't come to our house in a while," I said.

He shrugged. "Been working a lot."

"Sometimes I see you at The Collective. You're training for management now?"

"Yeah."

"Do you like it? Management?"

He gave me a sidelong glance. "Brynn, you *know* I hate it."

Of course I did. I knew what his dream was.

He bowed his head. "Ever since I first came here, I've been determined never to let them change who I am. But they keep trying. Little by little, they carve your old beliefs out of you, replace them with theirs."

"How do you hold on to what's true?"

He huffed out a half-laugh, half-sigh. "Well, to begin with, you stop believing their version of truth. Have you ever noticed how it keeps changing? Astra Cynthia says one thing one day, another the next, and everyone pretends it makes sense. You can't build a life on that."

His words were like thunder in my head. "You shouldn't say things like that out loud." As soon as the words came out of my mouth, I shuddered. How many times had I heard those words of warning? From Astra Cynthia, from Honey, from my own mother. Now here I was—repeating them.

"I know," he said. "But I can't stop thinking them."

"Don't forget about Jason."

He met my gaze. "I haven't."

"Why would you risk that happening to you?"

"Because I already have risked it," he said. "And because I can't stay here forever."

His words were thrilling—and terrifying.

"Please don't tell anyone, Brynn."

I shook my head. "I won't. I promise."

The small ache inside me widened. I didn't want him to

go. I wanted him to stay in Crystal Cliffs—with me. His own mother wanted that … but only because she wanted him to stay.

His gaze shifted to the door. "I've been planning it. Waiting for the right time. There's a world out there that doesn't belong to her."

"The Gray."

"Right. Except it's not gray—it's bright and colorful. Crystal Cliffs is the real Gray."

Pipes vibrated and clanged overhead.

"Maybe…" His voice was barely above a whisper. "You could come with me someday."

I thought I'd misheard him. "What?"

"When you're ready."

The idea tore through me, wild and impossible. Leave? I couldn't even picture it. And yet … I could. An image painted itself behind my eyes—open sky, no supercenter, no rules, no Friday night community center gatherings. Just wind, sunlight, music.

"I wouldn't know how to leave," I said.

"You'll figure it out. You're smart. Those carvings you do, those figurines. You still making them?"

"Yeah. When I have time."

He smiled. "I've still got the one you made of me."

"Really?"

"Really. That thing is so cool. I'll always keep it."

My face heated.

"You're really talented, Brynn."

I wanted to believe him. I wanted to believe everything he said.

He reached behind a crate. "You hungry?"

"Hm?" My mind still hadn't trailed away from his compliment.

"Hungry." His mouth tilted in a faint smile. "Turns out this isn't just a junk closet."

He dragged a box across the floor, the cardboard scraping the concrete. "Go on."

I peeled back the flaps. Inside were juice boxes and sealed bags of trail mix, the kind we got on reward days in lower school, all stamped with The Collective emblem—a "C" surrounded by yellow stars.

My breath caught. "How did you know those were in there?"

He jerked his chin toward the shelves above us. "There's more. Overflow from The Collective, what they bring to the dormitories. Peanut butter, noodles, sauce." A tinge of pride flickered through his voice. "This isn't my first time closet creeping."

I smacked my hand over my mouth. "You're the one stealing supplies."

He didn't deny it.

"I try to spread it out—alternate between the supply closets in the boys' and girls' dorms. I've been locked in here once or twice too." He shrugged. "Once I realized what was stashed here, I started coming back. Grabbed a few extras when I could. Figure I'll need them when I finally make my break." He lifted a juice box, shook it, and grinned. "You'd be surprised how far you can get on apple juice and granola."

He handed me a juice box.

I peeled the straw off the side. "How did you even get in here? The door was locked."

"I've gotten pretty good at picking locks." He chuckled softly. "We've got a whole section of doors and doorknobs at The Collective. They all use the same kind of lock. I practice."

I pictured him calmly kneeling at a lock, while the rest of us followed orders and buzzers. It seemed too brave to believe.

He poked his straw through the foil and took a slow sip. "One day soon, I'll use my skills on the front gate."

I was suddenly glad I'd been locked in here. I took a sip of the juice. It was the sweetest I'd ever tasted.

He rested his wrist on his knee. "You still cold?"

I nodded.

He hesitated, then slipped an arm around my shoulders. He didn't look at me, but his warmth seeped through his T-shirt, through the fabric of his sweater that I wore.

We stayed like that, side by side, until the sounds outside—the wind, the pipes, the creak of the building—harmonized. My body finally stopped shaking, but I was afraid to move, afraid the spell would break.

"They'll open the door, let you out in the morning," he said. "I'll need to be gone by then."

He was right. If anyone saw us in here together, there would be a worse punishment than a lesson room. Even so, that night, it seemed as though Sullivan Stonecutter and I were the only humans left in the world.

Chapter Seven

BIG BEND, FLORIDA, 1994

"The Weight of Sound"

Several sunny days passed after the closet encounter. But when the women came for me, the air outside was weighted with humidity and gray light, promising rain. It was laundry day, and I'd been in the living room folding linens and watching *Oprah* when Honey appeared on our front porch. I opened the door, and her shadow spilled inside, all five feet eleven of her stretching across the floorboards.

Her face still held traces of sympathy, though her eyes didn't. They were assessing, accusatory. Honey Barrett was a woman who had long ago learned to quiet her conscience.

"Astra Cynthia wants you." Her voice was flat, void of warmth. "Now."

Something inside me dropped, as if the floor had given way. I knew what this was about—the looks, the whispers that had followed me all week after my time in the closet with Sullivan. What Sullivan and I did not know was that cameras had been installed in the closet to catch "the thief." Not only had they caught their thief, but they'd caught us cuddling like lovers and rummaging through the boxes. Rumors rippled through the community like waste in clean water—slow, inevitable, impossible to hide.

Without a trial, we had been found guilty of "conspiratorial and unseemly behavior." And Sullivan had been identified as the thief pilfering supplies.

I looked beyond Honey, out onto the porch. They were waiting—two women and one of the men from Astra Cynthia's administrative crew—their faces lit by the remaining afternoon glow. Ruthi, who'd braided my hair for a wedding I'd been in a few months ago, and Ashley, who sometimes worked with me at The Collective, as well as Chuck Crow, Astra Cynthia's henchman.

"You shouldn't have touched him." Ashley's voice shook, but not from sympathy.

"I didn't." Not really. Not with the intent they assumed.

"Astra Cynthia will decide what you did." Ruthi lifted her chin. You should have turned him in immediately."

They didn't grab me, but we walked in formation. As we made our way across the yard toward the sidewalk, we passed Mama. She stood at the porch rail. Her eyes, brimming with liquid disappointment, darted to mine and then away again. I wanted to call out to her, "They're wrong! Nothing happened."

But silence was required of the accused on their march to the community center.

"Please." I mouthed the word to her as we passed.

For a moment, she looked as though she might reach out to me, but then she turned away. That was when the fear settled in—like a hand closing over my throat. I'd seen others publicly accused and punished, but that was something that happened to other people. This was really happening. To me.

By the time we reached the community center, the other members were already assembled. Hundreds of them, all waiting to be a part of the process.

The air inside was thick with the scent of damp wood and a dizzying mix of Collective-brand perfumes, colognes, and soaps. Someone had drawn the blackout curtains, leaving the space lit only by rows of low amber bulbs along the ceiling. The light made everyone's faces look hollow, their eyes shadowed and skeletal.

Chairs had been stacked against the walls to make room for the circle. At the center stood Astra Cynthia's podium—white, spare, gleaming beneath the light—and beside it, the portable speaker they used for alignment drills. A buzzing vibrated from it, a single sustained tone that made my teeth ache.

Heads swiveled as I stepped into the open, women and men standing in a line, children pressed to their mothers' sides. The only sound was the shuffle of feet on the polished floor.

Towering over me, Honey slipped her arm through mine, and we stumbled forward until I stood beneath the light.

"Do not fight this, Brynn," she said in a low voice. "It will be so much worse if you do."

My reflection shimmered in the full-length mirror that had been set up beside Astra Cynthia's podium. I glimpsed my bare feet and pale dress, my face outlined with fear.

And then I saw him.

Sullivan stood apart from the rest, hands bound in front of him like a prisoner—symbolism that was a lesson to all, as well as a warning. Dirt streaked his cheek. His hair hung in his eyes, wet with sweat. He didn't look at me, but I felt the pull of him anyway. Our shared pain. We were both accused.

Whispers bounced through the crowd—rumors of his plans to leave, his disbelief in the group's mission. I hadn't breathed a word of his plans to anyone. Had Kristen told them? Had his own mother betrayed his confidence? However the information had been relayed, Sullivan would now feel the weight of his actions as the aggressor, the thief, the traitor.

Astra Cynthia stood in the center, a pale column of control, her arms folded like a teacher waiting for her students to settle. Her appearance was as immaculate as ever. Her hair was sculpted high and lacquered into place, not a single strand daring to fall. The overhead light caught the shimmer of powder dusted along her throat, the gleam of coral lipstick that never smeared, thanks to The Collective's line of smudge-free cosmetics. She wore gray like the rest of them, but hers was a shade lighter, a tailored skirt suit, the fabric crisp and new. The effect was deliberate. She was authority wrapped in beauty, discipline masquerading as grace.

If only the outside world could see you now, Astra Cynthia.

When she lifted her chin, the light hit her sharp cheekbones. She didn't look like a woman leading a community but like someone presenting a product to potential customers.

"Brynn Cole." Her voice echoed against the high ceiling. "Step forward."

My bare feet found the cool grit. The world narrowed to the circle. I kept my eyes on the ground.

"When one member of the community is compromised," Astra said, "the entire ecosystem destabilizes."

A ripple of agreement moved through the crowd.

"She broke the regulation," Astra Cynthia continued. "She allowed impulse to override discipline. The body took command of the mind." Her gaze shifted to Sullivan. "But his crimes are worse. He endangered another. He is a thief, and we have learned that he may carry seditious intent in his heart."

Sullivan lifted his head slightly, enough that I saw the bruise on his jaw.

"Two fractures," Astra said. "But one root cause." Her eyes settled on me. "Weakness. And treachery. Do you understand, Brynn?"

I only nodded. My voice would have betrayed me anyway. As far as the members and Astra Cynthia were concerned, I had been caught on camera with a boy, half-clothed—even though it wasn't my decision to be in that state—locked in a room where we'd stayed all night long.

"You will both undergo correction," Astra Cynthia said.

At her signal, precise, rhythmic bursts of sound surrounded me. Shouts from strained vocal cords, a noise so loud it was like a punch.

"Empty yourself of want and hunger."

"Learn to control yourself!"

"Cast off your weaknesses."

The noise grew, a wall of pressure and sound. My chest vibrated with it. The circle tightened until the air around me was like an anvil, driving me to the ground.

No one touched me, but my eardrums quivered with the high-pitched wails and screams. Last year, Denny Everson suffered a burst eardrum after a stabilizing session. It wasn't unusual for people to faint or be sick.

On my knees, I covered my head and closed my eyes.

Minutes later—maybe ten, maybe fifteen—it was over.

My ears rang as the crowd backed away from me in the formation of a horseshoe, allowing me a full view of Sullivan.

His bound hands were twitching. He raised his head, and his eyes met mine, filled with apology and everything we couldn't say—the memory of the closet's dark air between us, the tiny spark of rebellion we hadn't even known we'd lit.

I thought of his words to me that night. He no longer believed *their* truth. He'd stated it openly. Now, the belief had seemingly drained out of him. There was no fire in his eyes, only surrender. He was already letting go of the part of himself that had dared to reach for something forbidden.

Then, the crowd surrounded him. The screams and shouts were dense and suffocating until I could hardly separate their chants from the blood pounding in my ears.

Finally, Astra Cynthia raised her hand, and the din died down. When she spoke, her voice carried the smooth authority of a verdict. "The two of you will not be allowed in each other's presence again."

Those words rang louder than the shouting. An aching cavern opened in my chest. Separation. The worst possible sentence.

Ever since I'd learned that Sullivan was trying to leave Crystal Cliffs, I'd been prepared for him to exit my life. Now that Astra Cynthia had spoken, there was no chance at all that I'd see him again.

Honey and Ruthi marched me out of the community center. The wind shifted behind me, carrying the scuffle of feet dragging in the dirt.

I glanced over my shoulder. Two men had threaded their arms through Sullivan's. His hands were still bound. They forced him to move his legs.

Jason Hillsdale's name swept through my mind.

"Where are they taking him?" I nearly shouted.

"Don't look back," Ruthi warned.

Sullivan's voice rose once more, a protest, a plea.

My legs felt like melted wax, unable to hold me up. I stopped walking. Honey prodded me in the back and shoved me forward. "Don't look."

I couldn't help myself. I turned my head, caught one glimpse through the trees, the floodlights on the lawn, a figure forced to his knees, the crowd folding in like a tide.

The sound that followed wasn't music or words but rhythm, relentless and mechanical, until even the frogs' songs were eclipsed.

Somewhere beyond the marsh, the river widened into the sea. I stared toward it, barely breathing. Even then, still carrying the weight of their voices, I knew what freedom looked like. It looked exactly like that horizon.

I was put on duty in the basement cafeteria of The Collective.

On Fridays, the cafeteria was practically full, and even though I was in the back washing dishes, the window into the dining hall allowed everyone a clear view of me. The steamy kitchen air hung thick with unspoken questions. The cooks and wait staff whispered, then stopped when I passed by, their eyes curious but wary, afraid that proximity to me might mean they were next.

We weren't supposed to talk about the ones who disappeared into the Think Tank. Not for a day. Not for a week. Not ever, if they didn't come back. Like Jason. And now, like Sullivan. It wasn't formally announced, but I knew that's where he'd been sent.

What had happened to him? I had no one to ask.

But one morning, as I moved along the path leading from the classrooms to the girls' dormitory, separated only by a row of dying camellia bushes and a wire fence, I saw him again.

Sullivan was in the field with the construction crew. He was shirtless, streaked with mud and sweat, the skin across his back mottled red from the sun. The young workers stood in a line and shoveled dirt from one trench to another under the supervision of two elders.

A chain gang. Almost literally. Comprised of wayward and rebellious men and boys who had to be brought in line.

I stopped, scooted behind a hedgerow, and watched. Frozen. Transfixed.

Sullivan moved more slowly than the rest, his body trembling with every lift of the shovel. When the whistle blew, the men froze in place.

Astra Cynthia stood at the edge of the field, her hair pinned high and glossy even in the heat. She appeared completely out of place in her pink sweatshirt and white jeans, motioning to the guards. She probably got off on this —watching shirtless men sweat and toil in the sun. She was middle-aged, married with three children, but there were plenty of rumors about her affairs with younger men.

Her calm, instructive voice carried across the field. "When the body rebels, the mind must correct it."

Then she went down the line from one to the next. When she reached Sullivan, he nodded to her, his eyes electric blue, flashing in the late afternoon sun.

"Recite the sixteenth tenet, please."

Sullivan hesitated, his breath ragged, his voice hoarse.

"Giving up something cherished proves devotion and accelerates awakening."

"Good." Astra smiled. "You are learning."

My body shook as I slowly rose from behind the bushes. The smell of mud and sweat and rusted metal burned into me, the same metallic tang as blood. I wanted to call out to Sullivan, to tell him to remember who he was. Instead, I stayed there, standing in the dirt, watching the rhythm of his arms as he shoveled.

By the end of the week, Sullivan was gone. His name disappeared from the duty rosters. The other boys said that his bunk had been stripped bare, his belongings boxed and taken away.

Astra Cynthia told the congregation that he had been "reassigned to the men's satellite group in another state." Somehow, I knew that wasn't true.

One day after math class, Maeve found me at the lockers. Her headphones worn like a backward necklace, her hair unbraided, her silver eyes flashing, she spoke in hushed, excited tones. "Did you hear what happened?"

I shoved my math book onto the top shelf of my locker. "No, what?"

She glanced over her shoulder. "I overheard Melissa talking. Sullivan wasn't reassigned to the satellite group. He ran. He's gone, Brynn. He got out of Crystal Cliffs."

He'd finally done it. He'd made it out. Like he said he would.

It would be four more years before Maeve and I followed him.

Chapter Eight

NOW

I agreed to meet Ivy at a small café tucked inside the courtyard of an old downtown hotel, all whitewashed brick and creeping vines and wrought-iron tables. Pure Charleston charm. Old world flavor, southern manners. No one talks too loudly, everyone remembers to put their napkins in their laps, and plenty of tea drinking with pinky fingers extended.

Ivy is already there when I arrive.

She stands as soon as she sees me, smiling like we've known each other for years. She's pretty in a composed, unfussy way, with dark hair like mine used to be, a pale green linen dress, understated jewelry. But holy crap, is she even thirty?

"Brynn." She leans forward, delicate fingers pressing into the tabletop. "I'm so glad you could make it."

"Of course." I return her smile and hope my face doesn't betray my surprise at her youth. "It's nice to finally meet you in person."

We shake hands. Sit. Order coffee. The ritual is comforting.

"You must love living in Charleston," she says.

"Yes, I do. I've lived here for…" I start to say exactly how long but stop myself. "… a long, long time."

Her eyes are enormous and a perfect chestnut brown. "I always forget how beautiful it is here. It feels so … like, movie set-ish."

Movie set-ish. Interesting terminology.

"I like it. It's home."

She nods, as if that confirms something she already believed. "I wanted to thank you again for meeting me. I know this couldn't have been the easiest situation for you."

I glance around for the server. I might need more than a coffee. Maybe I should have ordered an Irish one. "Life has a way of circling back on us."

Her smile tightens a fraction, then smooths again. "Yes. It does." She reaches over her shoulder and pulls her purse onto her lap. "Will you sign your book for me?" She yanks my book out of her bag and hands it across the table.

I cringe a little as I take the hardcopy with its original dust jacket and set it to the right of my place setting. The book is in its third reprinting and now has a different cover. She must have gotten this copy from a third-party vendor on Amazon. Was she even born when this came out?

"I know it's strange, asking someone to sign a book that's so … like, personal."

"It's fine," I say. My fingers linger on the edge of the cover, which stares back at me like an artifact from another life.

She exhales audibly. "I've read the book several times." Then—almost casually—adds, "I even underlined a few passages, and one really stayed with me."

I glance up. "Yeah?"

She quotes—not verbatim—but close enough that I recognize my own words.

"You wrote that after you left, freedom didn't feel like relief at first," she says. "That it felt like standing in an open field with no markers, no directions, just space. And that sometimes you wished someone would tell you where to stand so you wouldn't disappear."

I'm impressed. That was a good line.

Her eyes lift to mine. "That passage about how certainty can feel safer than choice. I think about that a lot."

I remember that feeling when I first got out. The late nights were so unlike my regimented bedtime in Crystal Cliffs, and the fear crept in that if no one was watching or timing me anymore, I might spin out of control. "I was still pretty raw then."

"I can imagine." The brightness in Ivy's eyes dims a little. "Reading your book also helped me, like, understand him better."

Him.

She doesn't even need to say Sullivan's name.

"I think that's why your work matters so much," she continues gently. "You articulate things people don't always have language for. Especially people who've built their lives around survival."

Why do I feel like she's blowing smoke up my ass?

I pick up a pen from my bag and do a baton routine with it between my fingers. "Do you spell your name I-V-Y?"

"Yes."

As I write, my hand feels unsteady, like I'm signing a document instead of a book.

To Ivy—

With thanks for reading, and for understanding.
—Brynn Cole

Those words seem appropriate. I slide it back to her.

She beams and seems genuinely pleased. "Thank you. That means more than you know."

I nod, but my senses are all on alert. This isn't only a girl wanting an autograph. This is a woman who has read my past closely enough to understand my vulnerabilities. She knows everything I felt for Sullivan, and that slow realization drips through my veins. She hasn't come here just to meet me. She's come to remind me—politely, beautifully— that she already knows how the story goes.

Or at least, how she intends for it to go.

Ivy closes the book, tucks it back into her bag, and then wraps both hands around her mug. "Sullivan was relieved when I told him we were meeting. I think part of him has been afraid of things staying unresolved forever."

"So, you told him we were meeting?"

"Oh, yeah. We talk almost every night. I couldn't not tell him we were meeting." She giggles, and her dark eyes flash. "I mean, come on! This is a big, big deal."

There it is. She's not threatened by me.

"That makes sense." I sip my coffee. I'm definitely going to need a little extra pop in this mug.

"He's spent so much of his life carrying things he didn't know how to put down," she continues. "I've learned that sometimes the best way to love someone like that is to give their past some room, without, like, letting it take over *your* present."

The words are minted straight from a self-help book. Or a therapist's office. Reasonable. And unmistakably strategic.

I study her. The calm confidence. The lack of urgency.

"That takes a lot of grace," I say.

She smiles. "It takes honesty. On everyone's part."

I clear my throat. "Where did you go to college, Ivy?"

Ivy's smile doesn't falter. "Wellesley."

Of course. "Are you a therapist, by chance?"

She laughs. "No, oh no, not at all. I majored in marketing."

I raise my eyebrows. Surprising.

"My parents were very… intentional about education. Structure. Stability." She gives a small, self-aware laugh. "I think they believed if you planned carefully enough, nothing bad could really happen."

"And did it work?"

She considers the question, her gaze darting toward the cloudless sky. "It worked in the sense that I graduated from college, got a job. But like, I didn't plan for Sullivan." She bites her lip. "He was a bonus. And a challenge."

My stomach rolls. "I'll bet."

She glances off. "I'm only now realizing how people function inside systems. Your book helped me with that. Understanding how people, like, justify them. Protect them. Stay loyal to them even when they're no longer serving anyone." Her gaze meets mine, open and steady.

"That must be helpful to Sullivan."

Her smile widens if that's possible. "I hope so. I really do." She lifts her cup, takes a sip. "What about you? Did you ever imagine yourself in college back then?"

Back then.

She appears to have caught her error and amends it. "I mean, when you first left the community?"

"No," I say honestly. "I couldn't imagine anything that far ahead. I didn't go to college until several years later."

She nods, not surprised or judgmental.

"And then graduate school in my thirties," I add for good measure.

Our server, a waif probably no older than Ivy, with a pixie haircut and a horseshoe nose ring, stops by and checks on us. "More coffee?"

I hold up my hand. "Can I get an Irish coffee this time?"

"Of course." Then she glances at Ivy. "You?"

Ivy giggles. "Oh, not for me. I'll have another coffee, but keep it American." Then she turns to me. "I don't drink."

Of course she doesn't.

I hesitate, then ask the question that's been hovering between us since we sat down. "How did you and Sullivan meet?"

"At a fundraiser in Nashville, actually. One of those small, quiet ones, no press, no performances. He was there with a friend. I was on a planning committee."

Her teeth are perfectly shaped, perfectly white.

"He wasn't what I expected," she continues. "Very reserved. Almost watchful. But kind. He listened more than he spoke."

I realize I'm clasping my hands under the table.

"We ended up talking about music," she says. "Not the industry—just the parts that still matter to him. Lyrics. Influences. What's next for him." She folds her hands on the table. "We kept, like, running into each other after that. That whole week." She laughs. "So, we ended up getting together for some coffee. Dinners. Nothing dramatic."

Nothing dramatic.

"And when did it become … more?" I keep my voice neutral.

She quirks her mouth, considering. "Slowly. Slowly felt right for him—for both of us, really. He was very upfront about you, from the beginning. About what you shared in the book. What he lost all those years ago. I appreciated that. It told me he wasn't pretending the past didn't exist."

"And you were OK with that?" I take a sip of the lukewarm dregs in my cup.

"I was," she says simply. "I don't need to be the only chapter in someone's life to be the one they're living now."

I nearly spew my coffee. I'm sure she doesn't mean to sound pretentious, but as I look at Ivy—so young and so achingly in love with the same man I adored at twenty—her words poke that old bruise inside me.

The server brings my Irish coffee, and I risk the burn at the back of my throat to put down several swallows. Then I cough a little. "He's lucky to have you."

Ivy's dark eyes flash. "I won't pretend I don't know why you matter to him. You shared something formative. That doesn't disappear just because time passes."

"No, it doesn't." I take another sip.

"But I believe people can carry more than one truth at a time," she says.

Damn, this girl could start her own cult.

I interrupt her philosophical onslaught. "You mentioned Pawley's Island on the call. Do you live there?"

Ivy's face brightens. "Yes. We do—I mean, Sullivan is only there part of the year, but he loves it. The quiet. The water."

We.

She smiles again. "He says it's one of the few places where his nervous system, like, actually settles down."

My fingernails tap a rhythm against my mug.

"I can see why," I manage. "It's a special place. As you know from my book."

She nods. "It really is. There's something about it—like,

time behaves differently. We have a little cottage near the marsh. Nothing fancy. It was supposed to be temporary at first, but…" She trails off with a soft laugh. "You know how that goes."

The cottage. Our cottage? I picture it instantly—the creak of floorboards, the salt-wet air, the way the light used to slant through the windows in the late afternoon. I remember the way Sullivan laughed there, unguarded and stunned by happiness.

"That sounds lovely," I say, because that's the polite thing. Then I drain the remainder of my drink, not caring that the temperature and the whiskey scald and burn simultaneously.

"It is," Ivy agrees. "It feels like a beginning."

A beginning.

Her smile evaporates. "I'm sorry. I know you and Sullivan spent time there. I don't mean to be insensitive. I don't think he bought that cottage by accident. Some part of him must have wanted to try to—I don't know—rewrite history, maybe?"

And Ivy—gracious, intelligent, perfectly composed Ivy —is making sure she's in every version of that revision.

She looks up at me. "Can I ask you something?"

"Of course."

"You probably know him better than anyone. At least who he was then. What advice would you give me in helping him deal with the past?"

I take a breath and speak slowly, choosing each word. "I think Sullivan learned very early that survival meant never looking too closely at what hurt him. He's good at keeping things functional. Stable. But that doesn't mean they're resolved."

She nods, absorbing this without interruption.

"So I'd say—don't rush him toward closure," I continue. "And don't assume time does the work for you. Some things don't fade just because years pass."

Her expression deepens, brow furrowing, chin jutting. "OK."

"He needs space to acknowledge what happened then without feeling like it threatens what he has now." I meet her gaze. "If he feels like he has to choose between past and present, he'll shut down."

Ivy exhales slowly. "Once, I was sitting in the room when he shut down. I didn't know what had happened. He wouldn't talk. For several days, he wouldn't eat or sleep. He went mute. I told him I couldn't help him if he wouldn't tell me what had happened to him all those years ago."

Her words hit with the force of a physical blow. Those were the same words I'd spoken to him so many years before.

"Do you know what happened to him, Brynn?"

I shake my head. "I don't. He never told me."

Gratitude blooms in her eyes. "Well, I appreciate your honesty. I want to help him any way I can."

Ivy finishes her coffee. I take care of the bill. Then we sling our purses over our shoulders with synchronized grace.

"I'll be in town for a few more days," Ivy says as we make our way into the parking lot. "If you want to get together again before I head back…"

I almost smile at that. "Sure. You have my number."

Chapter Nine

BIG BEND, FLORIDA, FEBRUARY 1999

"The Flight"

"Hurry up, Maeve!" I called.

We had less than ten minutes to clear out of the subdivision. If we weren't climbing into Teddy's van as everyone gathered for Astra Cynthia's Friday evening community meeting, we would be caught. Security would scream through the neighborhood. Cars would swarm our driveways. They would send out all the resources.

"I can't leave without my driver's license, Brynn." Maeve ran back into her house while I waited outside, shivering in the late February cold. I shook more from fear than from the frigid temperatures.

Were we doing the right thing? After all, our whole life existed inside the safety of the gated community—home, college, work, friends, even curated entertainment. What would it be like once we were out there—in the Gray?

Standing by the hedgerow, I comforted myself by softly singing the lyrics of Cutter's song, "Meet Me at the Bridge."

I'd be in nearly as much trouble for singing that song as I would be for trying to run away. We had all been forbidden to listen to Cutter's music once Sullivan had left Crystal Cliffs.

I scanned the dark landscape around me, slapping my leg to the rhythm in my head. "Come on, Maeve. Come on," I whispered under my breath. I glanced down at my watch, the tool I had lived and breathed by for the last eight years.

Maeve had often been punished for lagging, showing up late for classes, and pushing the boundaries. If she ever needed to be on time, it was now.

I repositioned my backpack on my shoulder and raised my eyes to the large, glowing clock that shone over Crystal Cliffs from its stone tower, staring down at me as though it saw what we were doing.

Everyone should be at the community center by now, and no doubt Chuck Crow and Uncle Dunn were doing a headcount right this second. They would know who was missing. They would look for us if we weren't there.

Maeve finally blasted from the door of her house, holding up the strap of her purse. "Got it."

"Let's go!" I grabbed her arm and towed her forward. Our feet swished through the sand, breath huffing like racing thoroughbreds as we dodged fences and shrubbery, bent at the waist, trying to avoid being seen.

My sneakered feet were already cold as we exited the neighborhood and entered the woods, still running as hard as we had at the starting line. Going through the woods meant we could avoid the front gate and security cameras. Branches grabbed at our clothes, trying to apprehend us. We kept going. Nothing mattered but emerging on the other side at the highway's edge. I glanced down at my watch. We were two minutes late to meet Teddy, an outsider. Maeve had gotten to know him a year earlier, when she started sneaking out at night and walking down to the all-night gas station where he worked.

"What if he's not there?" I panted.

"He'll be there," Maeve answered breathlessly. "He'll wait for us."

A dog barked. I whipped my head around but could see nothing in the darkness. Security?

Fear spurred me on, and I pushed myself to run faster, leaving Maeve several feet behind.

"Wait, Brynn!"

Ahead, lights flashed—cars on the road ahead. I waited at the edge of the asphalt for Maeve to catch up. Finally, she plunged through the remaining rows of trees.

Teddy waited where the road narrowed, the RV tucked far enough off the shoulder to be camouflaged by the trees. Only the hazards were visible, blinking. Pine trunks rose behind it like a wall, pale and straight.

Clasping hands, Maeve and I bolted forward. I could hardly believe it. It was almost too good to be true. We'd done it. We'd escaped.

Maeve jerked open the pinstriped passenger door, and we clambered inside.

Life in the Gray was about to begin.

My heart raced as we drove along the highway. I couldn't stop glancing out the back window every few minutes, checking for headlights or some car that might be following us.

"It's OK," Teddy said. "Relax."

Maeve sat up front in the passenger seat. I perched on the couch behind them, gripping the edge of the cushions, my eyes fixed on the dark palette of sky ahead.

Teddy handed Maeve a pack of cigarettes. She took one, lit up, and extended the pack toward me. "Want one? It'll calm you down."

I shook my head. I'd never smoked, and now wasn't the time to start. My stomach was already twisting. "No, thanks."

Teddy caught my eye in the rearview mirror. "Got a bunch of beer in the fridge. You can grab one if you want."

"No, thanks. Not right now."

He shrugged and looked back at the road. "When we stop for the night, we'll pop a few."

Maybe I was hungry. "Can we stop somewhere for food?"

"Yeah, but let's get to Valdosta. We'll go through a drive-thru."

A drive-thru. I hadn't been through one of those since I was a kid. Since before we came to Crystal Cliffs.

A Cutter CD played on the stereo. Maeve rolled down the window and blew out smoke. Her bare feet went up on the dashboard as she hummed along to one of the songs.

The sound and lyrics reached inside me, revealing the bits and pieces of Sullivan I'd never gotten to know until I'd heard his music. When the chorus rose, Maeve sang with it. My throat was too tight to join her. My lips moved without sound. *Inside my mind, I'm free.* The line echoed long after the song ended, buzzing in my ears.

Teddy laughed. "Maeve, babe, you are many awesome things, but a singer is not one of them."

She smacked him on the arm. "Shut up!"

I turned back to the window, hiding the sting in my eyes.

What was Mama doing right now? Had she realized I was gone?

This escape had been months in the making. The planning, the saving, the covert messages passed between Maeve and me at school. Sullivan would be so proud. We'd done it.

"Is this RV yours, Teddy?" I asked.

He ran a hand through his curly brown hair. "Nah. It belongs to my parents. This is a 1997 Tiffin Allegro. My dad bought it brand new. They're not using it right now, so when I told them I wanted to take a gap year and travel, they said I could take ole Theodora here."

Maeve glanced at him. "Theodora?"

"The van's name." His voice lilted with mock seriousness. "Every RV has to have a name, right?"

"I guess so." Maeve laughed, smoke curling from her lips.

I still wasn't sure how the three of us were going to live in this space for the next six to eight months—our projected timeframe to hit the concert venues in various states, including Woodstock's reunion in New York. After that, there was no specific plan. We would see where the road took us.

Maeve's shadowed profile was silhouetted in the headlights of oncoming cars in the other lane. "What did your parents say when you told them you'd be traveling with two runaways?"

His voice dropped. "I … didn't … actually … tell them."

"What?" Maeve trilled, her feet sliding off the dashboard.

He raised one hand off the wheel. "Look, my mom nearly had a shit fit when I told her I was following a band up north. I wasn't about to make it worse by saying I had two girls with me. My dad was cool, though. Said he followed the Dead around when he was my age."

I wrinkled my nose. "The dead?"

He laughed. "The Grateful Dead—the band."

"Oh." I'd never heard of them.

I didn't know much about Teddy except that his father was an ophthalmologist and his mother a pediatrician. All of them were Gray Ones. Rich Gray Ones. Maeve said they weren't extravagant people, despite their wealth. They expected Teddy to pull his own weight.

"What are you going to do after this, Teddy?" I asked. "Like, when the trip's over? Do you know what kind of job you want?"

Maeve twisted around, mock horror distorting her face. "Brynn, stop being weird. We just got on the road. We're going to see the greatest band in the world, with a lead singer that sprang from our midst!" She threw her hands up dramatically, claws in the air. "The last thing Teddy wants to think about is what comes after."

Maybe I was already having second thoughts. It felt like we were driving into space, with nothing tethering us to Earth. Mama and I hadn't been getting along recently. She'd always been all-in with Astra Cynthia's philosophies, but ever since she was named a member of The Collective's board of advisers, she'd been especially serious, scrutinizing my every move. Suddenly, I couldn't stop thinking about her. She must be terrified, wondering what happened to me.

Teddy glanced at me in the mirror. "It's OK, Brynn. To answer your question, I'm thinking of moving to the Pacific Northwest. There's a big music scene there. Maybe I could be in a band too. I'm a decent guitarist."

Maeve shot him a glance. "I didn't know that, Teddy."

He grinned. "I have many hidden talents."

"No, I mean that you were thinking of Seattle."

His voice lowered. "We'll have to settle somewhere. We'll need to work. You know, for money?"

"I have three hundred dollars," I announced. It had taken me a couple of years to save that, from what little I made at The Collective.

Teddy met my eyes in the rearview. "I brought some of my savings too. Don't worry. This is all part of the adventure."

Maeve leaned over, rummaging through her huge black nylon purse, a knock-off brand name she'd gotten from The Collective. When she raised her hand again, she was holding a thick wad of cash, maybe six inches high, bound by a rubber band.

I coughed. "What is that?"

She waved the bundle back and forth like a puppet, her voice dipping into Astra Cynthia's southern drawl. "Looky what I have here, girls and boys. What does this look like to youuuu? Can you say *munney*?"

All the air deserted my lungs. "Maeve, are you kidding? Where did you get that?"

"Where do you think I got it?"

My body burned from the inside. "How much is that?"

Her chin lifted. "Five thousand."

Teddy and I shouted in unison, "What?"

Teddy stared at her for too long and swerved to move back in his lane. "Five thousand dollars? Shit, Maeve. How did you get that kind of money?"

Maeve jabbed him playfully in the arm. "Don't worry about it. Keep your eyes on the road." She craned her neck to look back at me. "And you don't question it either. It's my money. Ours now."

Something cold opened in my chest. Maeve had worked

for Astra Cynthia for the past two years, counting member dues—all cash. She knew where it was kept. She had the combination to the safe.

"Maeve…" My voice shook. "You didn't steal that from Astra Cynthia's safe, did you?"

Maeve faced forward again.

The lights from passing cars streaked across the ceiling like search beams. For the first time since we'd left Crystal Cliffs, I felt less like we'd escaped and more like we'd run headlong into a trap.

A little later, I jolted awake with a gasp, sitting up and pawing at my eyes, listening to the low drone of tires on asphalt. I'd dozed off. Where was I? Panic surged through me, with an instinctive need to be somewhere, to report to someone.

I was sleeping on a couch. My confusion ebbed as I focused on the huge pane of glass in front of me. Outside, the road slipped beneath the vehicle like a slow-moving ribbon. Oh yeah, I was in an RV with Maeve and Teddy headed to Ohio to see Cutter.

"What time is it?" I croaked.

"It's about three," Teddy said.

Three in the morning. I didn't think I'd ever been awake that late. In The Collective, lights went out by ten, and everyone was up by six.

"Where are we?"

"Near Chattanooga. We're stopping at an RV park for the night."

Teddy turned the wheel, and we veered onto a gravel road. The headlights caught a wooden sign, its letters peeling and yellow. *ALLMAN'S RV PARK.*

We passed other RVs in varying stages of decay, some rusted and caved in, others patched with duct tape and hope. The ache in my chest sank lower, settling in my stomach, as my mind reviewed the previous day. I was so far from everything familiar, my narrow bed, my mother arriving home late from The Collective, turning on the television in her room next to mine. The sound of her voice as she talked to someone on the phone.

Homesick. That was the word.

But how could I miss a place I'd prayed to escape?

And Maeve was a thief. She'd stolen $5,000 from Astra Cynthia. The police were probably looking for us.

The thought circled my mind like a vulture, picking at my peace. Would I be arrested too, even though I hadn't had anything to do with taking it?

Our first Cutter concert was the day after tomorrow. I needed to focus on seeing Sullivan again after four years. Even if it was only on stage. The excitement flickered inside me, weaker than I expected. Maybe anticipation was better than reality.

Teddy parked beside a smaller RV that looked like it had been through a war, with rust along the seams, one window covered with cardboard. Through the side blinds, I glimpsed frost crystallizing on the other vehicles, lacquering them in silver.

He killed the engine. Silence fell. "Well, we're here."

Maeve stretched her arms, yawning. Teddy opened the door, and a blast of frigid air punched through the cabin.

With Teddy out of the vehicle, I leaned forward. "Maeve, what were you thinking—taking that money?"

She sighed. "I said, don't worry about it."

"I am worried about it. What if the police are looking

for us? Worse, what if Chuck Crow and Uncle Dunn are looking for us?"

Maeve grabbed the headrest of her seat, twisting around to face me. "They won't find us. Anyway, it'll be ages before Astra Cynthia notices the money's gone."

Astra Cynthia's office flashed through my mind—lavender walls, gold-framed paintings, fake serenity meant to disguise greed. I'd never seen the safe, but Maeve knew exactly where it was. After high school, she'd become Astra Cynthia's personal assistant, a position "bestowed" out of generosity, though rumor said she had a soft spot for Maeve's father.

"She knows you're gone now," I said. "You don't think she'll check her safe? Count her money? Queen Midas?"

Maeve scoffed. "You worry too much." Then she straightened in her seat. "Remember Astra Cynthia's song about worrying?"

I groaned. "Ugh, yes. How could anyone forget that?"

Maeve raised her hands as if she were holding puppet strings and sang in a high, syrupy voice.

"Don't fear, don't fret,

faithful friends do not forget.

When you're in want or need,

We are here as friends indeed."

A shiver bolted through me. "Please don't *ever* sing that again."

Maeve giggled. "I hated all her stupid songs."

"She thought she was such a great singer too."

We both laughed. It was good to laugh. No matter how frightened I was.

Then silence again and the tapping of something loose outside, maybe the wind brushing the metal siding.

I squinted at the dark windows. "What's Teddy doing?"

"Plugging in the RV, so we can get heat."

I rubbed my eyes. "I'm so tired. I need to sleep."

Everything would be better in the morning. Astra Cynthia always said so.

Maeve tilted her head. "Are you missing it yet? Crystal Cliffs?"

"What? No way."

That was obviously the right answer.

"Brynn, this is our big adventure. We're free. Away from all the control and abuse."

She was right. I needed reminding. Still, the feeling lingered, that sense of being unmoored. We'd done the unforgivable. No turning back. Like Sullivan.

The door opened again, blowing a frigid blast of air inside, and Teddy stepped in, hugging his arms against the cold.

"Brrr." He moved to the small electric heater and switched it on. "Let's warm this place up."

Maeve grabbed a blanket off the couch. "What time is it?"

Habit. Both of us searching for the anchor of time, routine.

"Three-thirty." Teddy opened the cooler and pulled out a brown bottle. "You want a beer?"

"Sure." Maeve yawned. "But we should sleep. I've usually had six hours by now."

Teddy popped the cap, handed her the bottle.

Maeve stood and stretched. "Hey, Brynn, do you mind if Teddy and I take the bed and you sleep on the couch?"

I blinked at her, the pieces falling into place. How naïve could I have been? Teddy and Maeve. Of course.

"Oh. OK," I stammered.

"Thanks." Maeve grasped Teddy's outstretched hand,

and together they disappeared into the narrow bedroom stall.

I watched, stunned, until the accordion door slid shut, sealing me off from their laughter and the low murmur of their voices.

The couch creaked beneath me. Frost glittered on the outside of the windshield. I lay back, staring at the dark ceiling. Somewhere in the whirr of the heater, I almost heard Astra Cynthia's voice again, singing her sugary little song about fear and forgetting.

I sat up and wrapped my arms around myself. I'd never been so cold indoors. The temperature was always perfect in the houses at Crystal Cliffs—68 degrees in winter, 70 in summer. Electric bills were monitored. Water. Groceries. Every variable was managed. We were never too cold or too hot, never hungry or thirsty.

The space heater had clicked off, leaving the air cold enough that my breath showed in the orange light flickering across the window, where the glow danced … like fire.

I moved closer to the glass.

Outside, flames reached upward, orange tentacles clawing at the dark. My heart hammering, I jumped up, flung open the door, and dropped onto the frozen ground.

A few feet away, fire burned inside a metal barrel. Behind it stood a man with a balding head and chiseled white cheekbones. He stared at me through the fire, eyes half-moons, mouth sliding into a smile that raised those sharp cheeks.

I backed into the RV and slammed the door. The fire wasn't the danger; the watcher was. His smile had chilled me to the marrow.

Why had we done this? The Gray was just like Astra Cynthia said—danger at every turn.

And now Maeve was in the back with Teddy, becoming one of the women Astra Cynthia used to warn us about. One who gave her body to men and veered off the path of enlightenment. A wasted woman.

———

The morning of the concert, I felt better. The panic from before must have been a side effect of waking at the wrong hour, being off my schedule, and listening to my brain spin. My spirit felt lighter, what Astra Cynthia used to call *gravitationally resistant,* a state we were urged to maintain.

"Hey, if we arrive early enough, we might see the tour bus pull in," Teddy called out over the music.

"Once we get there, I want to find an internet café," Maeve said. "See if Sullivan responded to my email."

Teddy scoffed. "You think he's going to write you back?"

"Why wouldn't he?"

"He's crazy-famous. He doesn't have time. He's touring, writing songs, probably having sex with like twenty girls a night."

The thought of it turned my stomach.

Maeve stared him down. "Brynn and I are his *people*. We all came from the same place."

Teddy gave a high-pitched laugh. "So? You think a guy like that cares? He's probably tried hard to leave that life behind and forget about it."

Maeve flung herself against the seat back.

Teddy was probably right. It had been four years since Sullivan left Crystal Cliffs. Why would he want to see us? We were walking reminders of what he'd escaped.

Tired of watching the highway, I lay back on the couch that had become my bed, my car seat, my lounge chair, and flipped through the magazine Maeve had bought yesterday at one of the rest stops—*Smash Up*. Cutter was on the cover, their name in huge lettering, other bands' logos stacked around it. Sullivan stood in the center, shirtless beneath a white blazer studded with metal. The photo centered on his lean, defined abdomen, every muscle drawn tight beneath the skin. The guitarist and bassist flanked him. The drummer stood in the background. No question who the star was.

How was it possible he'd gotten even better looking since I last saw him?

If his mother had gotten her way, I could've been married to him now. But he'd been destined for something else.

"Oh, shit!" Teddy's gaze frantically sought the rearview mirror.

Maeve's feet slid from the dash. She ripped off her seatbelt, bolted for the back bedroom of the RV, and pulled the accordion door closed behind her.

I sat up. "What's going on?"

"Police," Teddy said. "We're being pulled over."

Gravel growled under us. A red light strobed across the opposite window.

I gripped the couch cushion, my heart thudding in my palms. What did this mean? Were they here to arrest Maeve and me?

Teddy rolled down the window, and the officer's voice drifted in, broken by passing cars that shuddered the RV.

"Is everything OK, officer?"

Astra Cynthia's rule unfurled in my head like a banner across the beach sky: *If the police ever come to Crystal Cliffs to question you, keep your eyes on theirs. Don't look left or right. You can*

*answer their questions, unless doing so harms a Collective employee—
including you. If it does, you say, "I don't know."*

Over the past two years, the police had come. They'd
asked some of the kids if we were mistreated, if we were
beaten by Astra Cynthia or made to do unspeakable things.
Stand in the basement with a mouthful of dirt? Sit outside
nearly naked in the cold?

I wished I'd been able to coach Teddy on what to do
before this happened. What if he didn't know how to
handle the police? What if Maeve and I were arrested?

Through the open window, the officer said, "You made
an illegal turn back there. Authorized vehicles only.
Dangerous move in a rig this size."

"Sorry, sir," Teddy said. "I realized I was going the
wrong way and tried to turn around fast so I didn't get more
off course."

Silence.

"This registration says Matthew Graff."

"That's my father, sir."

"Does he know you're driving his RV?"

"Yes, sir."

"Where you headed?"

"Downtown. The arena. We're seeing a concert tonight."

"What concert?"

"Cutter."

More silence. Then: "I love Cutter."

Teddy laughed, nervous relief spilling out. "Yeah, we do
too."

"I'd be there if I wasn't on duty."

Not how I thought this would go. The two men
discussed favorite albums. The newest radio single. The
Cutter concert that the officer had seen last year.

A minute later, Teddy restarted the engine and waved. "Thank you, officer."

"Be careful," the man called. "But enjoy the concert."

I sank into the couch cushions as my adrenaline ebbed.

"Wow," Teddy said. "What do you know? Officer Smiley's a big Cutter fan."

I clutched my neckline. "That was really scary."

The accordion door scraped open, and Maeve reappeared, frowning.

My head twisted toward her. "Did you hear all that?"

"Yeah. Through the wall." She stalked past and dropped into the passenger seat.

"I guess cops like rock music too." Teddy laughed.

"Yeah? Well, stop driving like a maniac," Maeve snapped.

Teddy's knuckles whitened on the wheel. "I'm not driving like a maniac. I made one wrong turn."

"You've been reckless," she fired back. "You're going to get us all arrested if you're not careful."

The air in the RV seemed to vanish. From where I sat, I had an angle on the muscle in Teddy's jaw. It was jumping.

"The only person who's going to get us arrested is you, Maeve," he said. "Where's the money?"

"It's under the seat."

Teddy shook his head, running a hand through his hair. "Damn. Why did you do that?"

My thoughts exactly, but I was surprised he finally said it.

"Technically, it's my money," Maeve shot back. "Astra Cynthia hasn't paid me in a month. She said I was late getting copies for that big meeting, and she had to use the overhead projector. Anyway, she's been stealing from our families for years. Five thousand is a drop in the bucket."

Teddy huffed out a laugh. "Police won't see it like that. You put us in danger." He flung a hand toward me. "Brynn and I are accomplices."

He was right. Who would believe we hadn't helped take the money for a road trip?

I pictured a cop sitting across a table, interrogating us.

What do you know about your friend taking $5,000 from Astra Cynthia's safe?

Me: *I don't know anything.*

Even in my head, it didn't sound convincing.

Chapter Ten

COLUMBUS, OHIO, 1999

"Inside My Mind"

Smash Up Magazine, February 1999
Stonecut Truths: Sullivan Stonecutter on the new Cutter
album, *Den of Vipers*

Smash Up: You've said the lyrics of the band's new album,
Den of Vipers, pull a lot from your upbringing. Can you
elaborate?

Sullivan: I haven't really talked about it much before, but
yeah, my upbringing wasn't like most. I was raised in … I
guess you'd call it a commune.

Smash Up: A commune?

Sullivan: My mom joined when I was a kid. After that, we
lived in a community with all these people who worked at

the same place. The owners controlled pretty much every-thing. By nineteen, I just had to get the hell away. So, a lot of the lyrics deal with freedom, individuality, and forging your own way. And I'm the primary lyric writer, so yeah [laughs], I guess all that influences it.

Smash Up: This is one of Cutter's biggest years. You have a huge tour, and then Woodstock in July.

Sullivan: Yeah, that's pretty cool, man.

Smash Up: How's the road, fans, big venues?

Sullivan: It's an adjustment. I lived life to a timer for a long time. Funny thing is, I still answer to a lot of people. The rock star myth says you can do whatever you want. Nah, that's not true. But the fans have been amazing.

Smash Up: In Atlanta, a massive crowd showed for your video shoot.

Sullivan: [laughs] Police showed up too. Crazy. We didn't expect that many people in the street.

Smash Up: Thoughts on the name people use for your die-hards—the stoneheads? Folks following you around the country.

Sullivan: I don't know. It's weird. It's my name, you know. Sometimes it feels like I traded one cult for another.

Maeve and Teddy were fighting. They'd been fighting since we pulled into the Value City Arena lot.

Teddy faced forward, staring out the windshield. "I'm just saying you weren't thinking about me or the kind of trouble you could bring on my parents and me."

"What did you want us to live on?" Maeve's voice had reached screech-level.

"I thought we agreed we'd stop and get jobs when we needed to." Teddy's voice stayed low but tight.

How did he stay so calm?

"Look," he said. "I'm all for skimming off the top here and there, but you grabbed a wad of cash and ran. That was stupid, Maeve. Stupid."

Maeve shrieked a string of unintelligible sounds the same way the community used to when someone was under discipline.

"You are an idiot!" she bellowed. "You don't know what you're talking about! Maybe I'll leave, and you'll never see me again!"

Teddy rocked back, looking at her now, eyes wide. "Hey, you're free to go anytime. I'm not holding you hostage."

During those days, anyone screaming made me freeze, made my stomach hurt, made me fold into myself. I grabbed my coat, shoved my arms through the sleeves, and slipped out the door. The parking lot greeted me with quiet. Almost. Their raised voices still leaked through the thin walls.

I wove between a few RVs at the back of the lot and hugged myself. I had to pee, but I wasn't getting back in that vehicle until they stopped yelling. Maybe the concert venue was open, and I could use the bathrooms.

The tires of passing cars hissed on the wet road. A couple of people chatted nearby. In one corner, green dumpsters steamed in the cold. Sour rot and cigarette smoke lifted from behind them.

"Hey!" a voice called from near the dumpsters.

I kept walking.

"Hey! You here for the Cutter concert?"

I turned.

The girl looked about my age or a little older, tottering toward me on bare, spindly legs beneath a red leather skirt, a size too big. Frizzy blond hair spilled out over a jacket. Cigarette held aloft as if suspended from a string.

"Yes," I said.

Why else would I be here?

As she moved toward me, cigarette ash trailed behind her. "You got any aspirin or ibuprofen? I've got a shitty hangover."

"No, sorry." I started to move away.

"Hey, got a quarter then?"

I pivoted again.

She jerked a thumb behind her. "For the pay phone. We partied with some guys last night, and the dickheads stole our money. I gotta call my dad to wire me some." Smoke rings mixed with her expelled breath.

I dug in my pocket and pulled out a one-dollar bill. "I've got a dollar." I had more in my purse, but I wasn't about to tell her that.

"Great. Come inside with me. We'll break it, and I'll give you the change."

I sliced my hand through the air. "Keep the whole dollar."

She caught up with me, and we walked together toward the building.

"Where are you going?" she asked.

"Inside. To use the restroom."

"Oh, shit, yeah, I gotta piss too." She flicked the cigarette onto the sidewalk and trotted along beside me. "So, who's your favorite band member?"

"Um, well, I guess…" I pretended to think.

"Mine's Sullivan."

My heart dipped—a reaction that seemed stupid. Every girl in America loved him.

"Although every time we've gone backstage, he's usually not around," she added.

We reached the glass doors. Maybe once we were in the building, she'd head for the phones, and I could find a bathroom.

As we walked inside, she kept talking. "When we met the boys in Philly at the end of last year, Sullivan was always off somewhere else, so we hung out with Nate, Cutter's guitarist. Oh, and Primal from the opening act. Really nice guys."

"Oh." I pulled the door open. "So, you've already met the band?"

"Yeah, a couple times." She glanced back, smiling. "My friend Amy got to give Primal a blow job."

I was pretty sure I'd heard Maeve use that term, but I didn't really know what it meant.

"Hey, Twinkie! We're over here."

Two girls waved; one looked part Asian, with long dark hair and wearing ripped jeans. The other one was in a black miniskirt.

Twinkie brandished the dollar bill. "She gave me a dollar. Either of you have change?"

The dark-haired one planted a hand on her hip. "If we had change, we wouldn't be looking for a quarter, would we?"

Twinkie laughed. "Yeah, you're right." She swung her gaze toward me. "That's Delia. What's your name?"

"Brynn."

"Yeah, I gotta give Brynn seventy-five cents."

I lifted a hand. "No, really, you don't."

The dark-haired girl whom Twinkie had introduced as Delia pointed toward a line of pay phones. "Twinkie, call your dad."

"OK, OK." Twinkie tottered in the direction of the phones.

I bee-lined to the restroom and barely made it. The wall of phones lingered in my head. I could call home. Leave a message. Tell Mama I was OK. She must be so worried.

No. I'd go back to the RV. If we were lucky, the tour bus would pull in, and maybe we'd see Sullivan.

When I came out of the bathroom, all three girls huddled by the water fountain, whispering.

Twinkie looked up. "Hey, Brynn. Can I ask another favor?"

"Um, what?"

"My dad can't get the money to us until later, and we were hoping to buy some beer. Do you have any more money? Or could you loan us a little so we can get some?"

Teddy had beer in the RV.

Twinkie tilted her head. "I can't promise anything, but if you help us out, I can try to get you backstage to meet the band."

I led Twinkie, Delia, and Kelly across the lot to the RV. I rehearsed what I'd say to Teddy. It was his beer. Did we even have enough for all of them? I didn't know how any of this worked, but the hope of easy access to Sullivan dangled before me like a warm blanket and a good night's sleep.

Maeve stood outside the RV, smoking. Her face was pink and mottled, her eyes watery. She'd obviously been crying. When she saw me, she lowered the cigarette and knit her brows.

I started babbling before I was ten feet away. "Hey, Maeve, this is Twinkie, Delia, and Kelly. They know the guys in Cutter, and if we share some of Teddy's beer, they'll try to get us backstage."

"Try," Delia emphasized. "We'll try."

Maeve's tiger eyes raked over them. "Y'all are groupies?"

They laughed.

"We like to think of ourselves as fans," Delia said. "A support system for the band."

"We're big fans too," I said, hoping Maeve wasn't going to screw this up with her snark. "We'd love to meet them."

Maeve chewed the side of her mouth, then looked at me. "Ask Teddy. It's his beer. I don't care."

"Ask Teddy what?" Teddy rounded the RV, his red coat collar up and his face matching it.

I rushed through introductions and the pitch.

Kelly smiled at him. "We can show you where the bands come and go around back. There's a door just for them."

A small smile tugged at Teddy's mouth. "Sure. Sounds great. I can always get more beer."

Maeve's face pinched as she put the cigarette to her lips. Teddy stepped inside, and the three girls giggled and streamed in after him.

Maeve narrowed her eyes at me. "Why did you bring them here?"

My blood drained to my feet. It was the same feeling I

used to get when Astra Cynthia walked into class and yelled about rules we didn't know we'd broken. "I thought you'd be excited. They can introduce us to the band. We want to meet up with Sullivan, right?"

Maeve crossed her arms, shaking her head. "You're unbelievable. Sometimes you can be so stupid, Brynn."

The words stung and confused me. What had I done? Why was she being like this? Before I could ask, she stomped up the steps into the RV.

―――――――――

"Primal is the best!" Kelly howled after her third beer. "Funniest guy. You sit and talk with him for a few minutes. You'll laugh your ass off."

It was three in the afternoon. We hadn't left the RV in two hours. A sweet, heavy smoke hung in the air from the marijuana cigarettes Teddy had produced from the pocket of his jeans. My insides churned with nervous energy and a million questions. What if we were caught? Was the tour bus here yet? Shouldn't we be checking? I didn't want to miss the bus as it pulled in.

I'd tried one beer. It tasted sour, so I switched to a soda. A soda was rebellious enough for me since non-Collective beverages were forbidden in Crystal Cliffs.

Twinkie and Delia sat on the floor, laughing so hard they tipped over. Teddy and Maeve passed the cigarette around. They offered it to me twice. I shook my head, coughing, waving away the dizzying haze.

Delia eyed me up and down. "So you're a good girl, Brynn. No beer, no weed."

Maeve took another drag from the joint and then sang,

"Oh yes, Brynn is a very good girl. And pure as spring water."

Astra Cynthia's "Good Girl" song slipped into my mind:
Be a good girl, be a good girl,
Never let them steal your pearl.
Always close your legs real tight,
And you will live a life that's right."

Ugh. It had taken me years to figure out what she'd meant by that one, but now it seemed like the dumbest song ever. Astra Cynthia—the queen of hypocrisy. Telling us all to keep our legs closed while she slept with every man in Crystal Cliffs who struck her fancy. At least I recognized that now.

I glared at Maeve.

"Brynn never does anything wrong," she trilled.

"That's not true," I snapped. "I left Crystal Cliffs with you."

Her face fell. "You're saying you regret it?"

I shrugged. "I don't know."

"What's Crystal Falls?" Kelly asked.

"Crystal Cliffs," Maeve corrected. She pushed down on Teddy's shoulder as she struggled to stand. "It's a *c-ul-t.*" She popped the C and T.

"A cult?" Delia beamed. "Really?"

"Yep." Maeve popped the *p*. She wobbled to the kitchen, opened a cabinet, and pulled down orange cheese curls.

Twinkie raised onto her knees. "You guys are in a cult?"

"It's not really a cult," I said. "More like a community." I searched my brain for the word Sullivan had used. "A *commune*. But we left."

"Like Sullivan!" Delia jabbed a finger in the air. "He said he grew up in a commune."

"Same one," Maeve said, mouth full of cheese dust. She pointed between us. "Brynn and I both knew Sullivan. Before he split."

Their mouths fell open.

"Are you shitting me?" Delia laughed like this was the funniest thing she'd heard in years.

"Nope." Maeve waved the bag at me. "Brynn over there was supposed to marry Sullivan. Arranged stuff."

Now all eyes were on me. I shrank.

"Bullshit," Kelly said, the word coming out like a sneeze.

Delia sat up straighter. "Wait—you and Sullivan Stonecutter had an arranged marriage?"

"No, no, no." I cleared my throat. "He lived next door, and his mom sometimes joked about us getting married. It was just a joke."

Twinkie got up and sauntered toward me, loose-limbed, and put her hands on my shoulders. "Tell us everything. Did you guys have sex?"

"No." I pulled back. "I was only fifteen the last time I saw him."

They exchanged glances and then burst into cackles.

"That's old enough!" Twinkie howled. She let her hands slip from my shoulders as she turned toward Delia. "How old were you your first time?"

Delia's mouth twitched into a smile. "Fourteen, I think."

Twinkie nodded. "Yeah, fifteen for me."

"I waited until I was seventeen," Maeve announced, casting a gaze in Teddy's direction.

A little jolt went through me. Seventeen? I'd never heard her talk about it out loud before. Somehow, it made her seem older than me in a way that had nothing to do with age.

Kelly's eyes were on me. "Did you and Sullivan at least make out?"

"No."

"Kiss?"

"No."

"Have you talked since he left?" Delia wiped orange cheese dust onto her jeans.

I shook my head. "No. He left, and that was that. We didn't even know what had happened to him until we heard he'd joined a band and was famous." I glanced up at Maeve. "That's when we started sneaking out, getting the CDs, finding magazines."

Kelly looked at Delia. "This is ah-mazing. We have to make sure she meets Sullivan—tonight. After the show."

Delia's face didn't change. "Good luck. I've never even seen Sullivan after a show. He's always gone by the time I get there."

"Yeah," Twinkie said. "He's not really into the groupie scene."

When the other girls went back to comparing "first times," the relief hit hard. They were off me. Finally.

Delia went quiet, but the air in the RV shifted. Maybe it was the smoke and beer, but I could feel her eyes on me— moving up and down, like I was a strange specimen on a tray—almost like being back at school, or under Astra Cynthia's scrutiny.

Chapter Eleven

NOW

It's my birthday.

Paul tells me he wants to take me out and do something special, so I indulge him. He doesn't tell me where we're going, but we drive a few miles outside Charleston to a place that looks like an old general store.

After I get out of the car, he takes my hand, and we walk up to the front of the place with its wooden steps and a sign that reads "Mini Mart."

"What is this place?"

He smiles. "You'll see."

He holds the door open for me, and we step inside. One side of the store is an old ice cream shop with a real soda fountain counter and vintage décor.

At the other end of the store, shelves hold all manner of grab-and-go items. Dishwashing detergent, laundry soap, cereal, local eggs in cartons, a freezer full of frozen meats from nearby farms. But it's what lines the walls that immediately catches my attention.

Glass cases filled with small rooms and scenes—just like

the ones I make. Tiny kitchens with copper pots no bigger than thumbnails, dollhouse libraries with spines you can almost read, little shops frozen mid-moment. A miniature bakery. A train station. A perfectly scaled living room, complete with a throw blanket folded over a couch the size of my pinky.

I stop short.

"Oh," I breathe.

Paul watches my face instead of the displays. "You make all those memory boxes. So, I figured…" He shrugs and suddenly seems a little self-conscious. "This place might speak your language."

Heat spreads through me, catches in my chest. His thoughtfulness is startling.

"It does speak my language," I whisper. "It really does."

He motions me forward, and we wander slowly. I stand in front of one case and let my eyes tick over each room, finally landing on a tiny bedroom scene with an unmade bed, light spilling through a window no bigger than a chicklet.

"How did you find this place?" I ask.

"I did a little research," Paul says. "Did a little reconnaissance before I brought you here."

I'm moved. I really am. I hardly know what to say.

His smile produces deep lines in his cheeks. He's proud of himself. "Are you impressed?"

I nod. "I am more than impressed."

We move along in silence. Paul doesn't rush me. He asks questions. Listens and lets me talk about scale and measurement and how some of the rooms must have been incredibly difficult to make.

"They're all for sale," the voice comes from behind us.

A woman drifts over from behind the counter. She's

older—sixties, maybe—with silver hair pulled into a low knot. Her fingertips are smudged with paint. She's tiny too. Probably less than five feet tall. "I make the rooms."

Paul smiles politely. "They're incredible."

"Thank you." She gestures to the display cases. "Like I said, they're all for sale."

I blink. "All of them?"

She nods. "Every room. I build them, live with them for a while, then let them go."

I point to the bedroom scene with the unmade bed. "They're based on real places?"

"Sometimes," she says. "Sometimes they're memories. Sometimes they're images that pop into my head." She smiles. "People always assume I'm recreating the past. But not always."

Paul glances at me. "And once they're sold? Do you miss them?"

She shrugs lightly. "They belong to someone else. They get a new context." Then, almost as an afterthought: "That's how you know they're finished."

Paul jerks his thumb toward me. "She makes them too."

Her blue eyes widen. "Oh, do you?"

My face burns. "Well, I don't have nearly as many as you do." Although I've probably made as many over the course of my life. "I've only kept about twenty-five of my most important ones."

She raises bony hands to her hips, nodding. "If you ever need miniatures, I sell a bunch in the back—little things, you know—tiny books and lamps and tables, basic stuff. Sometimes people buy them for their dollhouses and things." She holds out her hand to me. "I'm Debra, by the way."

I introduce myself and Paul.

"It's her birthday," Paul announces.

I shoot him a look of death.

Debra beams. "Well, happy birthday. Hey, tell them that when you go over to the soda fountain. They'll give you a free ice cream."

We thank her, and she drifts away again.

Paul slips his hand into mine.

I don't pull away. I like the way it feels. It's been a long time since I've wanted to hold a man's hand.

We trail over to the soda fountain counter and its red-vinyl-seated stools. I pull myself onto an empty one and read the chalkboard menu hanging on the wall.

Paul doesn't sit right away but stands beside me. "What flavor are you going to get?"

I smirk. "Birthday cake, of course."

He gets a two-scooper with vanilla and sea-salt caramel.

Once we both have ice cream, he finally sits, and we shovel in several bites.

My tongue quickly freezes. "This was perfect. Thank you."

"Good. I wanted it to be," he says. "I wanted today to feel good for you."

It does. That's the problem. It feels really, really good.

I take another bite, then set my cup aside, suddenly aware that I'm full of emotion. Like, I could cry. "There's something I should probably tell you."

Paul's expression doesn't change much, but I see the shift in his eyes. It's like he's trying to get ahead of whatever story I'm about to give him.

He twists his stool toward me. "Before you do, can I ask you something?"

"Sure."

He takes a breath. "How are *you* feeling about *us*? Do we

need to keep telling the staff we're having founders' meetings three times a week?"

The question doesn't seem to demand anything of me, but I tense a little anyway. I'd hoped to keep everything light today. But after absorbing all the trouble he went to in finding a place that was perfect for me, my heart is in a different position.

I look at my hands, sticky with melted ice cream. "I like being with you," I say honestly. "A lot. I like you."

He nods. "That matters to me."

My tongue moves slowly, still stiff from the cold of the ice cream. "I don't want to pretend I'm not carrying a lot right now."

He dips his chin a little. "I wouldn't want you to."

Paul leans toward me, near enough that I can feel his warmth. "I … really care about you, Brynn. More than a casual birthday dinner kind of way. I know there's history in your life that doesn't evaporate. I'm not asking you to be finished with anything you're not finished with."

My throat tightens.

"But I also don't want to be invisible to you," he continues. "Or provisional. And if I am, I'd greatly appreciate it if you'd tell me that straight up. I promise you we'll still have a great birthday dinner later. And we'll still be friends."

"You're not invisible or provisional," I say quickly.

His shoulders seem to release a little. "OK. Then that's enough for me … at least for tonight."

I nod, grateful. I'm overwhelmed in a way. I'm thankful we don't need to label this tonight, but I'm also resolved suddenly not to tell him about Ivy. I don't want to cloud out the little light that we've shed on this relationship.

I pick up my ice cream again, though it's mostly melted

now. "For what it's worth, this is the best birthday I've had in a long time."

"Good." He bumps his shoulder gently into mine. "OK, what was it you were going to tell me?"

"Oh, um …" I close my eyes for a couple of seconds. "I forgot. Doesn't matter."

We sit there a while longer, sharing stories about past birthdays, and somewhere in the back of my mind, Ivy and my unfinished past with Sullivan wait their turn.

Paul pulls up in front of my building and puts the car in park. The engine drones beneath us.

"Thank you," I say, even though the words feel inadequate. "For today, for tonight. For all of it."

He turns toward me, one hand resting on the steering wheel, the other loose in his lap. "You're welcome." Then, after a beat, "I meant what I said, Brynn. About how I feel about you, but I'm not going to rush you. I know things are complicated because of our business relationship."

When are things not complicated in relationships?

I stay a moment longer than necessary, resisting reaching for the door handle. The air in the car feels electrical, like we're both aware of how easily the charge could spark.

Paul lifts his hand, hesitates, then tucks a strand of my newly red hair behind my ear.

"Happy birthday," he says softly before leaning in.

It isn't the first time we've kissed, but it's the first time there's been so much passion between us. Heavy breathing, hands, open mouths that are eager but unhurried. I sense that Paul's giving me time to decide whether I want this.

I do.

But even as I kiss him back, something inside me stays oddly alert, like I'm listening for a sound or waiting for a feeling that doesn't belong here.

When we finally pull apart, Paul lets his hand drift from my face down my arm. "Good night, Brynn, and happy birthday."

"Good night," I reply.

I get out of the car, wave once, then close the door. He waits until I'm inside before driving off.

I feel a little high as I enter my dark and quiet home. Elation pumps through my veins at the care Paul took in crafting a day that so perfectly checked all my boxes.

I kick off my shoes, set my bag down, lean against the door, and recall the details. The general store with its miniatures. The vintage ice cream counter. A steak dinner at—

My phone buzzes in my hand.

I look down at the incoming call and don't recognize the number, but I recognize the town it's coming from.

Nashville, TN

Chapter Twelve

COLUMBUS, OHIO, FEBRUARY 1999

"The Sound of Salvation"

Blinding, searing light.

A lot like the flicker of the overhead bulbs that used to buzz through the nights at Crystal Cliffs.

Then the sound hit.

Drums. Guitars. A roar like thunder.

When I lifted my head, I was nearly struck to the ground with awe.

I'm in an arena. Seeing Sullivan Stonecutter for the first time since I was fifteen. This is happening.

The man who'd once been my next-door neighbor and friend stood yards away on a platform of flashing lights and shattering sound. Dressed in a white shirt and baggy pants, he prowled across the stage, every movement magnetic. He gave everything to every song, the veins in his neck corded with effort, his voice scraping the ceiling of the arena.

I couldn't remember exactly what it felt like to look into his eyes that night we spent locked in a closet together, but this was something else entirely. I was nowhere near him. He seemed miles away, a vision glimpsed through smoke and starlight. He was beautiful. Untouchable. Like some rare bird that crossed the sky only once a year, too fleeting ever to capture.

There was no chance of reaching him. No chance of speaking to him.

In that vast sea of people, Delia and the others had vanished, and their promises of getting us backstage felt hollow now.

Beside me, Maeve screamed, her hair slapping her cheeks as Teddy head-banged. He showed us how to form the proper hand signs—pointer and pinkie extended in rock-and-roll solidarity—or we could stretch our arms toward the stage, palms open.

The gesture felt too familiar. The same one we used to give Astra Cynthia when she entered the community hall— a sign of loyalty.

For an hour and a half, we worshiped Cutter's raging guitars and thrashing drums wrapped around Sullivan's rasp and growl. When his shirt clung, soaked through, it outlined the sharp cut of his chest and shoulders. He was no longer the boy I'd known, but a man who belonged to the world.

What had I expected? That he'd see me in the crowd and remember? That he'd look down, through the haze and the lights, and find the girl he left behind?

Was I in love with him, or was this the emotion Astra Cynthia had warned against? The one that would make me a wasted woman if I let it consume me?

I didn't know. I couldn't think. I didn't care.

All I could see was Sullivan. Strands of golden hair

hanging in his eyes, his voice, the life that could have been mine.

When the final note faded, he stepped back, breathless. "Thank you, and good night!" The words echoed like a benediction.

The lights dimmed, and the crowd began to chant his name. Hundreds of flames from cigarette lighters arose from the audience.

I held my breath. The sound was oceanic. Alive. Holy.

Then the stage glowed again as the band returned. Sullivan strode back to the mic, dressed now in black, his damp hair slicked away from his face, and the room exploded.

It was too much. Too much joy. Too much longing. I wanted to cry, scream, kneel, tear at my hair because I didn't know what else to do with this feeling. How did people live through this kind of emotion? How did they survive it?

Cutter played three of their biggest songs, the crowd screaming every word. I sang too, shouting until my throat was raw, until my tears stung, until I could barely see the stage through the blur.

It felt intimate. Sacred. Like salvation.

When the lights blazed again, the band bowed low, their arms linked. Then they were gone. This time for good.

The arena exhaled—thousands of sighs at once—and I was left spent, trembling.

Maeve let out a shriek beside me. "That was awesome!"

Teddy grinned, his hair plastered to his forehead with sweat.

The three of us followed the human tide toward the exits, where the air threatened, cold and biting. Bodies spilled through the glass doors, still singing, still high on the aftershock.

I didn't want to leave this place, where Sullivan's voice still echoed in the walls.

I closed my fingers around Maeve's arm. "Aren't we going to the backstage door? Delia said they'd be there."

Maeve blinked. "Oh, yeah—we told them we'd meet them after the show."

Teddy groaned. "Come on. There'll be other shows. Do you really want to wait around all night in the freezing cold?"

Maeve and I exchanged a glance.

I knew I did.

"Yes," Maeve said flatly. "We do."

Teddy huffed out a cloud of white air. "Fine."

Maeve looped her arm through mine. "Let's go. Teddy's just stoned, and he's being a dick."

We cut through the waves of people like fish fighting the current. My pulse throbbed in my neck. What if we actually saw him? What if, for even one moment, he saw us?

By the time we rounded the arena's back corridor, I was sweating under my coat. The night air was charged with anticipation, possibility, hope.

Dozens of fans had already gathered near the backstage door—thirty, maybe forty of them—wrapped in black leather and denim, faces flushed, breath forming clouds in the air. The sight jolted me. The press of bodies, the expectancy, it was exactly like the gatherings before Friday community meetings, when the faithful waited for Astra Cynthia to appear.

Maeve squeezed my hand. "There they are."

Delia, Twinkie, and Kelly stood near the front, their

excitement obviously fraying into impatience, their weight shifting, their glances darting toward the doors.

We pushed forward through the cluster of people, earning a chorus of annoyed groans.

The metal door opened. A man in a Cutter T-shirt and black puffer coat stepped out, and the crowd surged toward him, shouting out the names of the band members.

"Jared!" someone screamed.

"Sullivan!"

The man in the black puffer coat lifted his hands, trying to be heard, but the words dissolved in the chaos. I caught only fragments—"band … can't … tonight…"—before the groans began.

Delia swung around, her face twisted with frustration. "They're not letting anyone in."

Maeve leaned close. "Why not?"

"Something about a death threat."

My stomach dropped. The noise of disappointment rolled through the crowd, followed by a slow unraveling, people breaking away in twos and threes, heading for their cars, their voices dulling in the cold.

Delia drifted toward the lot. "Come on. It's over."

We walked the long stretch back to the RV. The music still rang in my ears, but its power was fading like a dream I was already forgetting.

Up ahead, Maeve and Teddy argued in low, cutting tones.

"I don't feel good about this," Teddy said. "I'm really pissed off, Maeve."

I hung back, their voices obscured by the sound of engines as cars poured out of the lot.

The night stretched before me, endlessly gray, smeared with exhaust and disappointment.

Delia and the others stood near their car, heads bowed in a private conversation. They didn't look up when I passed. I didn't call out to them. I kept walking.

By the time I reached the RV, Maeve and Teddy were standing near the rear bumper, their faces lit by the taillights of cars waiting to exit the parking lot. Their voices rose again, Maeve's shrill and defensive.

I slipped inside the vehicle and closed the door behind me. I shrugged off my jacket, grabbed a bottle of water from the tiny fridge, and sank onto the couch. Then, I stared at the condensation forming on the window and traced the lines with my fingertip.

I had just seen Sullivan, yet he might as well have been a star in the sky. I couldn't reach him. He probably wouldn't even remember me. What was I doing here? Suddenly, this experience—this life—felt borrowed. Like I was living someone else's dream.

The door squealed open and then slammed shut. Maeve's voice sliced through the night, sharp as a siren. "I'm leaving." Her eyes were dry. Determined.

She thrust a hand under the passenger seat and dragged out the sack of money. "You can stay if you want, but I'm done."

"Why?"

She shoved the money into her backpack. "Because Teddy is an asshole."

I shot to my feet. I couldn't stay with Teddy alone.

"Where are we going?"

Her fingers bit down hard on my forearm. "We'll find our own way. We can rent a car. I've got money."

Yeah. Stolen money.

She wiped at her face, smearing what was left of her

eyeliner. "But you have to decide now. I'm not staying another minute."

What choice did I have? I grabbed my backpack, shoved my things inside, and swung it over my shoulder. "OK. Let's go."

Maeve and I exited the RV and speed-walked away, our breath puffing in the freezing air.

"What happened?" I asked as we hurried through the parking lot, dodging departing cars, the headlights flashing into our eyes.

"I'll tell you later," she said. "I can't talk about it right now."

Delia, Kelly, and Twinkie still huddled by their baby-blue car, where I'd passed them minutes earlier.

Maeve strode up to them, her backpack thudding against her hip. "You guys have room for two more?"

They stared, caught off guard.

"Why? Where's Teddy?" Delia asked.

Maeve waved a hand. "We're done. I can't sit in that RV with him another minute."

Twinkie's eyes ballooned. "Wow. You guys broke up at a Cutter concert?"

Maeve crossed her arms, staring at the pavement. "Yeah, I guess so."

Twinkie leaned against the car, its paint peeling like old sunburn. "You should come with us. We met this guy. He's got a rental house nearby, and he said we could crash there instead of wasting money on a hotel."

I looked at Maeve. Was that something we wanted to do?

Maeve's eyes flicked between them. "Really? You'd let us stay?"

Delia shrugged. "Sure. What's two more? Anyway, it's not our house."

Maeve turned to me. "What do you think?"

The cold gnawed at my fingers through the fabric of my coat. "Yeah," I murmured. "OK."

Kelly held up a slip of paper. "He drew us a map. It's close."

We piled into the car. Kelly drove, Delia beside her, and Maeve and I crammed into the back with Twinkie. The heater wheezed warm air as we inched through the slow-moving line of cars leaving the lot. The others chattered about the show, how hot the guys looked, how loud the music was, but their voices drifted like the fog floating beneath the headlights. My eyelids dipped as my adrenaline subsided. The world slid in and out of focus.

Later, when the emergency brake cranked, I jerked awake.

"We're here," Delia said.

We were parked at the curb. The house loomed behind a curtain of overgrown bushes and trees, its windows black. We all got out of the car, and Kelly and Twinkie hauled three sleeping bags and a comforter from the trunk.

Then we made our way down a long driveway. The concrete rose in places, with inflamed cracks zigzagging across the surface. Once we stepped onto the front porch, the darkness of the place struck me. No outside light, no way to even see the street because of the overgrowth.

Delia grabbed the doorknob. "He said he'd leave the door unlocked." She shouldered the wood, and it groaned before giving way. The porch light stayed dead, but she reached in and flipped the light switch. An overhead bulb flickered to life.

The front room was bare except for two tall umbrellas on tripods.

The girls dropped the sleeping bags and blankets on the floor. I took off my coat and laid it on top of them.

Maeve pulled her backpack close to her. "What are those?"

"Light stands," Delia said. "Photographers use them. I've seen them all over the studios where I took my modeling photos." She walked up and touched one, sliding her fingers across the silvery inner surface. "These are pretty nice."

It didn't surprise me that Delia had been a model. With her long, black, silky hair and exotic face, I could easily imagine her on a magazine cover.

Twinkie tossed her purse against the back wall. "Delia was in a music video last year."

"Really?" Maeve said. "Which one?"

Delia flipped her hair over her shoulder. "Ever heard of Pudding Face?"

Maeve and I both shook our heads.

Delia shrugged. "Yeah, he's kind of new, does like white rapper stuff. I was one of the girls who danced in the video."

Maeve beamed. "Cool."

I glanced around. No furniture. No couch. No chairs. Nothing but an echo.

Kelly crossed through the room and disappeared into a hallway. "Here's the kitchen," she called. "The guy said he had a bottle of vodka in here."

Still clutching her backpack, Maeve followed Kelly. "I need to find a bathroom."

Twinkie made a slow turn in the center of the room.

"Where is all the furniture? How can he rent this place with no couch or anything?"

Delia peered out the picture window. "Maybe people bring their own. Those bushes make it impossible to see the street. Wait—hang on. Looks like headlights outside." She pressed her forehead against the glass. "I think there's a car in the driveway."

"Probably just someone turning around," Twinkie said.

Kelly reappeared, holding up a half-empty bottle. "Found the vodka!"

Delia kept her post at the window. "You drink. I'm going to sleep. Once this car pulls away."

Kelly shrugged, unscrewed the top, and took a long pull from the bottle.

I checked my watch—2:43 a.m.—and leaned against the wall, fighting exhaustion. Would my body adjust to this new sleepless schedule? Astra Cynthia would say a few more nights like this would surely kill me.

Delia rolled out the sleeping bags, side by side.

"No pillows," she said, "but plenty of room."

"I need to find a phone," Twinkie said. "I told my dad I'd check in."

We scattered to search for a phone. In one bedroom, I found a phone jack but no phone—just a black tarp spread over half the carpet. Maybe photographers used tarps for something?

When I returned to the main living area, Maeve burst from the hallway, breathing hard. "There are no curtains in the bathroom. You can see straight out to the driveway." Her voice trembled. "Delia's right. Someone is sitting in a car out there."

Delia, Kelly, and I rushed down the hall and into the

bathroom, where we all crowded into the tiny space. "Where?"

Twinkie soon joined us, sweeping her hand across the light switch. A white fluorescent glow bloomed over the room.

Delia screamed. "Leave the light off!"

The room plunged into darkness again.

Soon, five of us were pressed shoulder to shoulder. Through the pane, the streetlight glinted off a black car parked in the drive. A shadowy figure sat perfectly still behind the wheel.

"Shit," Delia said. "His headlights are off now. He's just sitting there."

"Is that him?" Maeve asked. "The guy who owns this place?"

"I don't know," Kelly said.

"What is he doing?" Delia whispered.

"Probably waiting for us to go to sleep so he can kill us," Kelly muttered, fogging the glass.

"Maybe he's making sure we got here safe," Twinkie offered.

Maeve backed away. "Y'all, we've got to get out of here. Now."

Delia nodded, her face a mask of fear. "She's right. This is too creepy."

My chest tightened, and my breathing came in short gasps.

Twinkie hesitated. "What about our stuff?"

"Leave it," Delia said.

My backpack still dangled from my shoulder, but I had to leave my coat behind as we tore through the dark house, the floorboards complaining under our weight.

"Stay low," Delia directed. "Go along the far side of the house until we get to the car."

My heart jogged and then broke into a sprint before my feet did. Out the back door, the yard opened into a snarl of weeds and beer cans. A rusted car crouched in the moonlight like an animal's skeleton.

Then we ran—past the side yard, down to the curb, breath coming in gasps—until we reached the car. My bladder was perilously close to dumping its contents as we piled in on top of each other, Maeve and I in the backseat with Twinkie.

Kelly swung inside and jammed the key into the ignition. The engine coughed to life, and the tires squealed as we pulled away.

The empty house vanished behind us, swallowed by the dark.

None of us spoke. I stared out the window at the passing trees, their limbs like hands reaching toward our headlights.

Once again, we were headed for nowhere.

Chapter Thirteen

COLUMBUS, OHIO, FEBRUARY 1999

"Dead of Morning"

We stopped at an all-night diner somewhere off the interstate at 3:35 in the morning. The sign out front buzzed blue, casting a cold halo over the parking lot. The aroma of coffee and the nauseating smell of fried oil filled my nostrils.

Delirious from lack of sleep and hunger, I slid into the booth beside Maeve and across from the trio. Their faces were streaked with day-old mascara, eyes rimmed with exhaustion as they devoured their before-dawn breakfasts of eggs and toast.

"I can't believe we left all our shit there," Twinkie said around a mouthful of bread.

Out of the corner of my eye, I glimpsed Maeve clutch at her backpack.

Delia chewed, her gaze drifting toward the ceiling tiles as if the answer might be hiding among the grease stains. "We can get more sleeping bags."

Twinkie let her fork clatter to her plate. "Yo, those were expensive."

Delia peered around Kelly at her. "You want to go back for them?"

Twinkie quirked her mouth. "No."

"That was freaky as shit," Kelly said. "We could've ended up on the news—girls murdered in serial killer's house."

I finished my biscuits, gravy, and sausage links in exactly two minutes and twenty-two seconds—beating my previous record of two twenty-five. Five minutes was the absolute limit for any meal, usually reserved for leisurely lunches.

Delia watched me as I ate, her chin propped in her hand. When I finally set down my fork, I wiped my mouth and met her stare.

"You inhaled that," she said. "Did you even taste it?"

Maeve answered for me. "In Crystal Cliffs, all our meals were timed. We learned to eat fast."

Twinkie talked with a bite of scrambled egg in her mouth. "Why were your meals timed?"

I knew this answer by heart. It was written on page twenty-nine of *Living an Interstellar Life*, the book Astra Cynthia wrote and sold by the thousands:

"A clock mimics the heartbeat of the Earth. Living life to the ticking of a clock ensures you remain mindful that you are only given a certain number of seconds to live, and every one of them must be counted, used properly, and never wasted."

"Shit," Kelly said in her monotone voice. "I couldn't live like that."

Out of habit, my eyes found the nearest clock above the register, red digits glowing through the haze. "You could if it's all you knew. Anyway, I've always found timekeeping comforting. It grounds me in the world."

Kelly shrugged, her green eyes drifting. "Whatever."

The waitress cleared our plates, moving with the weary rhythm of someone who'd been awake too long. She refilled our coffee cups, and I sipped mine greedily, grateful for the little pulse of warmth that crawled through my veins.

Kelly gestured toward the mugs. "But you guys can drink coffee?"

"Yeah," Maeve said. "We're not Mormons. Coffee was like a sacrament when I worked at the supercenter. Astra Cynthia owns her own coffee field somewhere."

Delia stretched her arms out in front of her. "So what'll you do now? Still head on to Wisconsin?"

I glanced at Maeve. Maybe it was the fatigue—or the adrenaline crash after running from a potential serial killer—but a part of me wanted to give up, go home, stop chasing a freedom that felt more dangerous than the captivity. Or maybe I was tired. Home wasn't safe either.

Maeve straightened. "Yeah, of course. We came all this way. We're not going back now."

She was right. Going back meant punishment through the lower house or even the Think Tank. Add stolen money on top of that, and we'd be arrested before we reached the front gate.

"We'll rent a car," Maeve said. "We'll get a hotel room in Milwaukee."

Twinkie tossed her napkin onto the table. "Hotels are expensive. You have money for that?"

Maeve hesitated for half a beat. "Yeah. We've got money."

Three pairs of eyes flicked toward the backpack at Maeve's side. My pulse quickened. We didn't really know these girls. They weren't like us. What if they tried to take Maeve's backpack?

We stood in line at the register. I rechecked the clock—4:22. Maeve slipped a twenty from her backpack, the green bill flashing between her fingers. I pulled a ten from my change purse.

Overhead, a TV broadcast some early-morning news show for insomniacs and truckers. A man in a gray suit spoke about Y2K, warning viewers to stock up on food and water. "We recommend at least a year's supply per household."

So, Astra Cynthia wasn't the only one preaching the apocalypse. Even out here in the Gray, the end of the world was a shared gospel.

Then the news anchor's tone shifted. "Police in Florida are asking for the public's help in locating two women reported missing by their families."

I turned toward the screen. My face stared back at me —next to Maeve's. A rush of heat flooded my chest and neck.

I yanked the sleeve of Maeve's coat.

She spun, frowning. "What?"

Keeping my hand low, I pointed at the TV. Her eyes followed my finger and widened.

"Authorities say the women may be traveling together and could be heading out of state. Police stress there is no indication of foul play at this time. Anyone with information is urged to contact the Florida Department of Law Enforcement or their local police department."

All the blood in my body seemed to drain toward my feet. The edges of my vision pulsed. Around us, the scrape of cutlery and the soft murmur of conversation faded to nothing.

A man at the counter turned slightly, his gaze sliding across the room until it landed on me.

I looked away, heart battering my ribs, and nudged Maeve forward. "Pay," I whispered. "Now."

She moved up to the register, keeping her head bowed as she handed over her bill.

I felt the man's eyes on me, heavy as a hand between my shoulder blades. I shoved my ten-dollar bill across the counter and turned for the exit before the cashier could hand me change. The bell above the door gave a dull jangle as I stepped into the cold predawn air.

I knew they'd be looking for us, but somehow, I hadn't thought they'd use the media, the local police. That must have meant that Astra Cynthia knew. She must have discovered the theft, and now they were looking for us. It could only be a matter of time before someone recognized and reported us.

***

We were back under the bruise-blue sky of almost-morning. My mouth was full of the taste of biscuits and sausage and the edge of panic.

Delia, Twinkie, and Kelly were driving east to Pennsylvania, the opposite of where we had to go. And after seeing our faces on the television, it was clear we couldn't stick with the same people. We needed a hole to crawl into for a few days until the next show. Right then, our main problem was getting anywhere.

From the driver's seat, Delia's eyes found mine in the rearview mirror. "Do you guys have a credit card?"

"No," Maeve and I said in unison.

"Just cash," Maeve added.

I flinched at the word.

Sitting in the backseat with us, Twinkie aimed her eyes toward our bags in the floorboard by our feet.

"Then you won't be able to rent a car," Delia said. "They require credit cards."

"You could come with us to Pittsburgh," Twinkie offered.

"Thanks," Maeve said. "But we want to stick to the plan. Get to Milwaukee. Or at least part of the way there. Maybe Chicago."

"I've got a cousin in Chicago," Twinkie said. "He and his girlfriend could maybe let you crash. I'll call him."

"How would we even get there?" I asked.

"Bus might be your best bet," she said.

At a gas station, Delia pumped while Twinkie fed quarters into a payphone and Kelly went inside to get us all coffees.

Maeve and I remained in the backseat.

With the others out of the car, she organized some of her money into an envelope and thrust it into the backpack's front pocket. "Brynn, are you alive? Why are you so quiet?"

I shivered. I'd have to get a coat at the first possible opportunity. "I'm cold. And scared. Aren't you?"

She stared ahead. "I'm too tired to feel anything. I just want to get on the bus and sleep."

Kelly approached the car window, balancing coffees. I stared east, where an orange flare lifted over the next hill. Where would we land in a few hours? With whom? Another empty house? Another man lying in wait behind a locked door? Astra Cynthia always said the Gray was full of threats. The thought needled me, and suddenly, I wanted my bed, the prepackaged bland meat casserole from The

Collective, Mama snoring in front of the TV. The safe, small cruelty of a schedule.

Delia finished pumping gas and slid into the driver's seat.

Seconds later, Twinkie yanked open the car door and got in. "I talked to my cousin, and they'll take you in," she said. "We'll drop you at the Greyhound bus station. My cousin will pick you up in Chicago."

Kelly handed out the coffees. Warmth seeped into my hands from the cardboard cup.

"Does your cousin have a name?" Maeve asked.

Twinkie popped her lid. "Oh, yeah, everyone calls him Pitt. He even kinda looks like Brad Pitt."

At the bus station, Maeve and I climbed out of the car and shouldered our backpacks. Without a coat, the frigid air cut right through me. I wrapped my arms around myself and dipped my head back inside. "Thanks for the ride."

"Maybe we'll see you in Wisconsin!" Twinkie formed the rock-and-roll hand sign as they rolled off.

A police cruiser idled at the curb. I bumped Maeve's elbow and nodded toward the car.

"Don't act weird," she said.

I didn't know how not to. I was visibly shivering. People clustered in coats and blankets, smoke curling from their mouths. A tattooed man leaned on a pillar and stared at us. I looked away. Had he seen the news, or did we look lost?

Inside, we bought two one-way tickets to Chicago and sat in a row of orange plastic chairs. Thankful to be indoors, I clamped my backpack to my chest and dug out my toboggan.

Then I pulled the wool cap over my head. "What if someone recognizes us?"

Maeve tugged the front of the toboggan over my fore-head. "Keep it pulled low, and don't make eye contact."

When the bus boarded, we filed on with the others, keeping our heads bowed until we collapsed into a stained fabric seat. I pulled the cap over my eyebrows and closed my eyes. Six hours from then, we would arrive in another city, with more strangers. Strangers, I prayed, who didn't watch the news.

Without opening my eyes, I asked, "Do you miss Teddy?"

No answer. I rolled my head toward Maeve. She was already asleep.

A kick to the back of the seat snapped me awake.

"Hey," a man whispered, leaning over the headrest. "Hey, girl."

Dark eyes, a narrow smile with a missing tooth, a faded blue star on his cheek. His hand dropped over the seat. His nails were black with grime.

"What's your name?" he rasped.

My mind scrambled. *Not Brynn.* "Bea," I said.

He nodded like we'd made a pact. "Where ya headed, Bea?"

"Chicago." The answer spilled before I could stop it. Weren't we all headed to the same place on this bus?

"Yeah, me too." His breath was sour and warm.

I glanced at Maeve, her head against the window, her mouth hanging open.

His eyes darted toward her. "Is that your friend? What's her name?"

"Em," I said.

Bea and Em.

He tasted the names. "You wanna buy some Molly? Got good stuff."

I stared. What was he talking about?

"Ecstasy," he said, patient as a tutor. "Or liquid. Or a little blow."

Drugs. I might not know the terms, but I understood the intent.

"No, thanks." I faced forward, my hands folding into fists in my lap.

He slithered back into his seat. I soon dropped into a dream in which I was running, jumping barricades while Crystal Cliffs security wailed behind me.

Then, the bus bumped over something, and I woke to Maeve's open eyes staring at me.

Behind us, low voices traded numbers. "How much you got? I can sell you a bag."

I whispered to Maeve, "He's dealing drugs."

Maeve nodded. "I get it."

I looked at my watch. Three hours down. Three to go. Maeve tilted her head back and slept again. The bus droned forward through a tunnel of gray.

It was like being alone, even with her next to me. The trip we'd planned—the RV, Teddy, that lumpy vinyl couch—felt like a different planet. Now we were two missing persons on the run with a backpack of stolen cash.

When I opened my eyes again, we were inching into the Chicago station. Maeve was turned around, chatting lightly over the seatback with the guy behind me.

"Look, honey," the man said, "if you need anything— car, place to stay—I know people."

My skin prickled as the brakes squealed and the coach

lurched. The doors folded open with a gasp of cold air. I stood, gripped my backpack, and started down the aisle.

"Yeah, thanks for your number," Maeve said.

I wrenched my head around in time to see the man wiggle his fingers. "Don't be shy, baby."

I hurried outside the bus, scanning the strange faces all around me. Twinkie had said her cousin would meet us, but what if he didn't? Then it was Doug the Drug Dealer and the rest of the world.

Maeve jogged to catch up to me.

"What were you doing?" My voice took on a shrill edge.

"What?"

"Talking to that guy. He's a drug dealer."

She planted a hand on her hip. "You think I didn't know that?"

"They're dangerous."

"He wasn't," she said.

"How do you know?"

She patted her pocket. "Bought us some Molly."

The pavement tilted. "You what?"

"Ecstasy," she said, like she'd bought chewing gum. "People take it at raves. Delia told me."

I had no words. Who was this person I'd trusted to run with?

Maeve's eyes moved past me, and she shot out a finger. "Look."

A young woman with freckles and a waterfall of strawberry blond curls spilling out from under a periwinkle beret stood off to the side. She held up a square of white poster board with our names written on it.

My mouth went instantly dry. It hadn't occurred to me how we would find Twinkie's cousin and girlfriend, or how they would find us. Our names—not common ones to begin with—looked like a blaring neon sign pointing out our whereabouts.

The woman stepped forward and smiled at us. "Hi! I'm Renee." She hooked a thumb toward the man behind her. "This is Gerry, but everyone calls him Pitt."

Pitt was tall, blond, bright-eyed. They looked like a billboard couple, clean and gorgeous.

We fell into step behind them as we made our way through the parking lot.

"From Florida, right?" Renee chirped. "Where's your coat, girl?"

"Lost it in Ohio." I tried to keep my face tipped, turned toward the ground. *Please don't let them recognize us.*

"You'll freeze," she said. "You can borrow one of mine until you get one." Renee dropped back, walking beside us. "You're stoneheads too?"

"Stoneheads?" I asked.

"Cutter fans who follow the tour," she said. "Twinkie and them are hardcore, going all around the country. Pitt and I've got tickets to see the band in October here in Chicago."

October felt like a foreign country. Eight months away. We'd only survived one show.

We stopped beside a black Audi. For a second, I was back in Crystal Cliffs, where half the cars were Audis.

"Nice car," Maeve said flatly.

Renee opened the back door for us. "Oh, thanks. It's Pitt's. It drives like a dream, but if something goes wrong, look out. You'll be dropping two thousand dollars for repairs."

Two thousand dollars. A little less than half of what Maeve had stolen from Astra Cynthia.

In the floorboard of the back seat sat a cardboard box filled with bottles.

"Oh, sorry, I'll put those in the trunk." Pitt ducked inside and lifted the box.

Renee climbed into the passenger seat, and Maeve and I sank into the back.

"Pitt works for a liquor store," Renee said. "He gets all sorts of free samples."

He closed the trunk, moved back to the driver's seat, and we were off.

It was late afternoon, and the road was thick with vehicles. While we waited behind a line of cars to get onto the highway, Renee chattered away.

"I'm from this tiny little town," she said. "Normal, Illinois? You ever heard of it?"

Maeve and I shook our heads.

"Coming to the big city was a shock. But I've learned to love it. There's so much to do here, shows to see, and galleries."

"The weather sucks, though," Pitt interjected.

"Yeah, that's true," Renee continued. "You guys are here at a bad time of year. But the summer is beautiful."

As Renee talked about on-ramps and galleries and summers on the lake, some of the dread pooling in my stomach began to seep away. My fear of being recognized was usurped by Renee's friendliness. It was almost like she'd known us forever.

A brief image of our faces on the diner's TV passed through my head before I let myself unclench my hands.

Chapter Fourteen

NOW

My breath catches, sharply, painfully.

I stare at the number on the screen of my phone, the Nashville location. Would Sullivan really be calling me? I did give him my number the first time we emailed. Ivy has it too.

For a moment, I don't move, don't think. I stand there, phone vibrating against my palm. The timing is almost cruel.

I swipe to answer before I can talk myself out of it. "Hello?"

There's a pause on the other end. His voice is older, deeper, but unmistakably his.

"Brynn? I hope I'm not calling too late."

I push off the door and cross the room. My hands shake as I turn on a lamp. The soft light fills the space, and I glance at the dark window, my own reflection staring back at me—stunned eyes, mouth slack.

"No, it's fine."

"It's good to hear your voice," Sullivan says. "Hope you

don't mind me calling. You gave me your number in your email, so I figured—"

"Oh, it's fine, it's fine." My heart is pounding. "It's good to hear from you."

I sink onto the couch, the echo of Paul's kiss still warm on my mouth.

Another pause. I can hear Sullivan breathing.

"Ivy told me you two met," he says. "She said it went well."

I close my eyes. "It did. I like her. She's nice." I feel obligated to say it.

"Ivy is a nice girl."

Girl. *Exactly*.

"Damn, I can't believe I'm talking to you, Brynn," he says.

I imagine him sliding his hand through his hair—a familiar move. I wonder if it's still as thick as it once was.

"I know. I'm a little shocked too." I laugh nervously.

There's so much hanging between us that I barely know where to start.

He coughs.

Wonder if he's still a smoker…

"It's your birthday, right? Happy Birthday."

He remembered.

"Yeah, thanks."

"Did you have a good birthday? What did you do? Or maybe you haven't even gone out yet."

I snort. "I'm kind of a wuss these days. Asleep by ten o'clock and all that."

He laughs. "Oh, well, you know, I'm out playing music most nights, so…" A sharp exhale. "Damn, Brynn, it's great to hear your voice."

He's already said that. Is he drunk?

"You know," he continues, "I meant what I said in the email—about the regrets and all that."

A rock lodges in my throat. "I think we both have our regrets."

He groans loudly. "Twenty-five years, Brynn. There's so much to say, you know? Too much to say over the phone."

My eyes fill. "A lot of time has passed."

Another pause. "Would you—would you ever be willing to meet? Like, you could come here, or I could come there?"

I press my palm to my sternum. My chest is so tight I can barely breathe.

Images collide in my mind—Paul's hands, the warmth of his kiss, the way he waited until I was inside before driving away. Then, just as sharply, another picture overlays it. Sullivan on stage, on the beach, in bed…

"I don't think I want you to come here." I'm surprised by how clearly I say it.

"OK, I understand."

"And what about Ivy?"

Silence. Then, "Well, I mean, Ivy and I aren't married."

"She really cares about you."

"I care about her."

"There are people here I care about too," I say.

"I understand."

I sit forward, my fingers tapping out a rhythm on my coffee table as I let out a breath. "I'll think about Nashville. It might be easier for me to come to you."

His voice brightens. "That would be great, Brynn."

"But," I add, before the momentum carries me somewhere I'm not ready to go. "I need time to think. To make sure this isn't a really bad idea."

"I get that."

Does he really? Does he understand how much of my heart and head is at stake? Still, right now, I'd give anything to see him.

"This isn't me saying no," I tell him. "It's me saying I want to be careful. I've worked really hard to build something stable."

"I wouldn't want to be the thing that knocks it down." His voice is sincere.

"I know, and I appreciate that."

Neither of us is ready to end the call, but both of us breathe with an awareness that something irreversible has already been set in motion.

"Think about it," he says finally. "No pressure."

"I will." And I mean it.

We finally end the call, promising to talk next week. I sit in my living room, staring at the opposite wall, my insides twisting with one thought.

If I go to Nashville, it won't be to revisit the past. It will be to take a good, hard look at my future.

Chapter Fifteen

CHICAGO, FEBRUARY 1999

"Cold Morning, Bright Lies"

Renee and Pitt lived on the third floor of a brick building that leaned a little, at least that's how Renee excused the floors, which had a slant that made you feel like your equilibrium was off. The architecture was boxy and unattractive but seemed to pay homage to a different decade. The stairwell was dingy and brown, smelling of cooking onions and unfamiliar spices.

Pitt carried my backpack and offered to put Maeve's over his other shoulder, but she held it close to her body.

Every step felt like a hurdle. I hadn't slept in years. Or since before Ohio. Same thing.

Inside, the apartment was a collage of a thrift-store couch with the stuffing trying to escape at the seams, a low coffee table with scattered magazines, plants hanging in the windows, their vines draping down like green curtains. A string of tiny white bulbs looped around a bookshelf.

Someone had tucked a dried sunflower into the corner of a poster for a band I didn't recognize.

"Shoes off wherever." Renee dropped her coat on a hook and tossed her keys into a bowl on an entryway table. "Bathroom's down the hall, towels under the sink. You guys hungry? We're a little low on groceries at the moment. We've got eggs, cereal, probably some soup."

Pitt lifted his wrist and stared at his watch. "We've also got a bed," he said. "You both look wrecked." He walked straight into the living room, picked up a remote, and pointed it at the TV across the room.

The screen woke up. The sound of a sportscaster talking about last night's basketball game put me on alert. Any minute now, they could broadcast our faces—thieves on the run. I glanced over at Maeve. Was she thinking the same thing?

Pitt flipped through channels, stopping on a woman with a shiny black bob and a bright blue suit, talking about the weather. Then he dropped the remote on the arm of the couch.

Renee called out from the kitchen. "Leave it on Channel 5. *The X-Files* will be on soon."

Maeve swayed, catching herself on the arm of the couch. Her eyes were wide, fixed. She hadn't said much since the bus, but suddenly, she wouldn't shut up.

She began to dance in place, swinging her arms like pendulums. "I love *The X-Files!*" She tilted her head back, staring at the colored string lights hanging from the book-shelf as if they were new constellations. "Do you ever think about how everything's connected? Like—lights and people and thoughts?" She reached out and brushed her fingers over the colored bulbs. "This place feels warm. Like it's breathing." She laughed loudly then leaned into me, pressing her forehead briefly to my shoulder. "I'm just really happy."

Pitt looked at me, a smirk pulling at his lips. "Is she high?"

I didn't answer. What was happening to her?

Renee emerged from the kitchen. "I think she needs some food. Then you both probably need some sleep."

It was less of a directive than I was used to, but her voice held authority, like she was aware of something I wasn't. I appreciated that.

Maeve and I sat at their kitchen table, which was barely bigger than a nightstand. There wasn't even enough room for four plates.

Renee took items from the refrigerator. A carton of eggs, a stick of butter. She cracked the eggs into a chipped blue bowl—the soft tap of shells on the counter oddly soothing—and used a fork to scramble them.

"Hope you don't mind eggs for dinner. Like I said, we haven't had a chance to get to the grocery this week."

"No problem." I wasn't picky—just glad to be eating something.

My mouth dropped open a little as she cut off a block of butter—more than I'd ever seen added to a pan—and poured the egg mix on top of it. The savory smell filtered into the air as she slid the pan onto the burner.

"We could order pizza," Maeve said. "I've got money."

My breath caught. *Shut up, Maeve.*

"Maybe we can order pizza tomorrow night if you want," Renee said. "Twinkie said you guys are staying a couple of nights. Is that right?"

I tensed. "If that's OK."

"Sure. Pitt and I both work in the morning, but there's plenty you can do in the city. Museums, stores, cafés."

Maeve stood and drifted to the kitchen window, her hands gripping the sill like she was afraid she might float away. Her breath fogged the glass, and she drew a little circle in it with her fingertip, staring through the smear at the street below. She began to move, gyrate, singing the words of a song I didn't recognize.

"Are you OK?" I asked softly.

"Yeah." Her eyes stayed on the window. "Watching the snow melt."

But there was no snow, only patches of gray slush dissolving into the gutter. Her reflection looked ghost-thin against the glass.

She spun around, flitted over to the counter, and propped herself against it, kicking her legs into the air. "I love the smell of eggs. My mom used to make them on Sundays—she'd always ask me what kind I wanted, scrambled or poached or fried—but I liked it when the edges got crispy."

Renee smiled kindly without pausing her stirring. "You'll like these then. They're gonna be crispy as hell."

"And toast? Will we have toast too? I love toast, with a lot of butter." Maeve laughed, the sound bouncing off the tile. When she caught me looking at her, she pressed her lips together, sat down, and wrapped her arms around herself. Still, her legs jackhammered in place.

As if in reply to her question, Renee grabbed a plastic bag of bread off the counter and popped two slices into a silver toaster.

Maeve's knee kept bouncing under the table. *Tap, tap, tap.* Her fingers drummed on the wood. It wasn't the normal fidgeting of tiredness. It was jittery, electric.

"Maeve." I mouthed the words more than spoke them. "Stop."

The butter crackled in the pan, and Renee scraped the eggs from the bottom. I looked around at the orange window curtain, the sunflower oven mitts, and the blue plates. This small, warm kitchen was probably a happy place for Renee and Pitt.

Pitt entered the room, opened a cabinet, and took down a jar of something red. A soft pop sounded when he twisted the lid.

"Burned the toast!" Renee announced without apology.

"Nothing new." Pitt set out four plates in front of Renee.

The bread clattered as she threw it onto the ceramic. Soon there was a plate of food in front of me—eggs, brown-black toast with a sunburst of yellow in the center, and a blob of something red from Pitt's jar that tasted like summer tomatoes and basil. The plates were chipped, but the food was edible. I was so hungry and weak and tired that I'd have eaten dirt.

Pitt was quiet, his eyes on his food as he shoveled it into his mouth.

He was nice to look at. His blond hair was long in the front, neatly cut in the back. Two floppy bits kept sliding into his eyes, which were the color of the window glass that used to be in my room—palest blue—a lot like Sullivan's.

Maeve took a careful bite, chewed slowly, then smiled to herself. A minute later, the food sat cooling in front of her, untouched. She dragged the spoon through the eggs. "It smells nice," she said, distracted. "Everything feels really nice."

Pitt made eye contact with me and chuckled. "That girl is so damn high right now."

Renee seemed to silence him with her eyes, and he

turned back to his plate. Renee must have recognized Maeve's bizarre behavior too.

I'd already pieced it together. The ecstasy she'd bought on the bus. She'd taken it. Maeve *was* high. Who knew how Pitt and Renee felt about that, but an intense desire swelled within me to protect them from this knowledge.

"We're both so tired," I reiterated, my eyes darting to Maeve. "I think delirium has set in."

I kept checking the microwave clock. The numbers shifted in neat jumps, and I breathed easier every time they did. Time was passing. Soon, within two days, we would be on our way to Milwaukee.

On TV, a newswoman was interviewing someone on a busy street corner.

I felt Renee's eyes on me.

This night was unraveling. Maeve was on another planet, and I was waiting for my face to show up on Renee and Pitt's TV. Or for an officer to knock on the door and herd me back into a life I'd fled.

After we ate, Pitt slung some folded sheets and a blanket on the couch.

I hovered at the edge of the room. My skin felt coated with road grime. How many days since I'd showered? Two? I must have stunk. I cleared my throat. "Would it be all right if I used your shower?"

Pitt straightened. "Yeah, sure." He pointed me toward the bathroom. "Towels under the sink."

The bathroom was small, about the size of my closet at home. White tile ran from halfway down the wall to the floor. The rest was painted a dingy white, the coat thick and shiny, like it had been painted and repainted, covering mold, dents, and dirt.

I turned both knobs until the water wasn't scalding, then

pulled the lever, and the water screamed through a pipe. I jerked the clear shower curtain across and stood under the stabbing spray.

The water surged hot again, and I let it burn my skin, the needles leaving pink trails. On the other side of the clear curtain, the mirror steamed, erasing any reflection of my naked body behind the plastic. I used Pitt and Renee's peppermint shampoo, which tingled my scalp. When I was done, I stepped out and wrapped the soft gray towel around me. The feeling was glorious. Like Astra Cynthia always said, cleanliness was the next most important thing to timeliness.

I wrapped the towel tighter around my body and reached for the clothes Renee had loaned me, folded neatly and left on the edge of the sink. An oversized T-shirt and sweatpants.

The doorknob turned.

I froze. Who…?

Then the door cracked open, and a slice of cool hallway air cut through the steam.

"Oh—sorry." Pitt's voice.

He was halfway through the door before he seemed to register me standing there, hair dripping, clutching the towel to my chest.

"Didn't know anyone was in here."

He didn't step farther in, but he didn't back out immediately either. His eyes flicked up—just once—and then down to the floor.

"It's fine," I managed, though my voice caught on the word. "I'm done." And thankfully covered.

"Yeah." He hesitated another second, then nodded toward the counter. "Needed to grab my razor. Forgot it this morning."

He reached in, his arm brushing the humid air near my shoulder. The razor clattered against the sink, surfing back and forth in the basin. He fished for it. Then he was gone, the door clicking softly shut behind him.

I stood there for a long moment, pulse in my throat. The air felt colder now, the steam thinning into patches. He knew I was taking a shower in here. And there seemed to be only one bathroom in the apartment, so why would he need his razor now?

At boarding school, privacy didn't exist—rooms were inspected, showers timed, doors never locked—but somehow this felt worse.

I dressed quickly, dragging the borrowed T-shirt over my damp skin. Then I stared at the mirror until my reflection sharpened through the fog.

For a heartbeat, I saw Astra Cynthia's face behind mine, smiling that knowing grin. *Told you. The Gray is dangerous.*

I turned away before the image of her face, her exacting eyes, her mocking mouth, could finish forming.

Back in the living room, Maeve was curled in the corner of the couch, knees to her chest, staring straight ahead. I followed her gaze to a framed photo of Renee and Pitt on a beach. She didn't blink for a long time.

Renee sat on the other end of the couch and looked up as I entered. "You two can take the bedroom if you want, and we'll take the couch and the foam fold-out mattress. Your call."

I glanced over at Pitt, his eyes glued to the television.

"The foam is fine," I said.

I'd feel weird sleeping in someone else's bed.

Renee unfolded the mat in a corner by the bookshelves. Pitt dragged over an extra quilt and then perched on a chair in the corner to watch TV.

"Laundry day is tomorrow," Renee said. "We can throw your stuff in with ours."

Laundry day. Just like Crystal Cliffs, when every household washed every cloth thing they owned. You could smell the laundry soap all over the neighborhood—musky, sometimes with a hint of lemon.

On the TV, the news looped between infomercials and weather. The anchor smiled with too many teeth and said something about delays at O'Hare. Then there was a segment on the "new millennium," with someone standing beside buckets of rice—more talk of stockpiling food for the coming global crisis.

"I guess Pitt and I will be sunk come January." Renee picked up the remote and lowered the volume. "It's not like we have anywhere to store anything." She stood and popped her back. "Anyway, I'm sure you two want to sleep."

Maeve sank onto the foam, pulling the quilt over her, but her movements were restless. She fluffed the corner of the blanket, then immediately tossed the pillow aside.

"Lavender." She buried her face in the fabric of the sheet. "Smells clean."

Renee smiled. "My mom sends sachets from the farmers' market. Keeps the moths away too."

Maeve nodded, still clutching the blanket. "Must be nice. Having a mom who mails you things." She said it softly, but I caught the dark edge in her tone. Neither of us would ever know what that was like.

My anger toward Mama was fading now after a few days away from her. In fact, my heart ached for her. Her own must have been broken.

Pitt finally pushed out of his chair and grabbed his coat from the hook in the hall, while mumbling something about a delivery. The door opened and closed again.

Maeve's eyes darted toward the hallway where Pitt had disappeared and then to the front door. Was she measuring escape routes like I was?

She rubbed at her arms, fingernails dragging white lines over her skin. "I can't get warm."

"You're tired," I said quickly.

"Yeah. Tired." She started folding and refolding the socks Renee had given us. The motion was methodical, almost frantic.

I nudged her arm. "Why don't you put the socks on? If your feet are warm, the rest of you will be too."

I stretched out on the foam and covered myself to the chin. The radiator clicked in the corner. Someone's dog barked outside, then stopped.

Maeve finally settled. She must have been coming down off her high.

"I can't stop seeing our faces on that TV," she said.

"Me either."

"You think Teddy's seen it?"

"I don't know."

"I hope he saw it. Maybe he'll find us."

I rolled onto my back and stared at the ceiling, surprised at her words. She'd been missing Teddy after all.

"Do you think we'll make it to Wisconsin?" she asked.

"I don't know."

She was quiet for a long time. Then, "I can't go back, Brynn." Her voice was thick with fear, the first hint of it I'd heard from Maeve.

"I know."

"I mean it. Even if it kills me."

I folded my hands over my ribs. "It's the same for me." And I meant it. No matter what, I couldn't go back.

I closed my eyes. When sleep finally came, it felt like

falling through warm water. I didn't fight it. I let it drown the clocks in my head.

Astra Cynthia was waiting behind them. She always was. Her voice braided with Sullivan's, command and song layered until I couldn't tell which one was calling me.

Chapter Sixteen

CHICAGO, FEBRUARY 1999

"Chains of Time"

Renee and Pitt both worked during the day, so Maeve and I had to find somewhere to hang out until they came home. Killing time was a skill I was unfamiliar with. Where did you go when you had nowhere to be?

"We could move on to Milwaukee," I suggested to Maeve. "Grab a bus today. Stay at a hotel." That seemed the sensible thing to do. Especially after last night and Pitt walking in on me in the bathroom.

"When's the next time we'll have the chance to see Chicago?" Maeve said. "Come on. Isn't this part of the adventure?"

We ended up at a coffee shop a few blocks from the apartment, where we sat at a sticky table in the back corner under low lighting, the heater blowing stale dry air onto our heads. At least there were no TVs running news cycles showing our missing faces.

"Pitt is so hot." Maeve stirred her latte with a straw.

"Yeah. But he's kind of a creeper."

"What do you mean?"

I told her what had happened. The shower, the unannounced entrance.

Maeve wrinkled her nose. "Sounds like an accident."

My shoulders sank. "He knew I was in there, Maeve."

She shrugged. "Well, at least he's not hideous like Uncle Dunn."

Did it really make a difference what he looked like? What if he'd done something to me? To either of us?

"We don't know these people, Maeve. They're Gray Ones."

She ballooned her eyes at me. "Listen to you. You still sound like them."

I raised my voice. "We can't blindly trust people."

Maeve seemed distracted. Her brow was furrowed as she stared off into the café. "Well, they don't trust *us*, at least not to stay alone in their apartment. They probably think we'll rob them and disappear."

I glanced down at her backpack. "Which, in your case, isn't entirely off base."

She gasped in mock offense. "Excuse me? I would never."

"No." My voice came out darker than I intended. "Not unless they've got thousands of dollars lying around."

Maeve's eyes narrowed, and she straightened. "Wow, Brynn. That's really what you think of me?"

I shrugged. Even if I did, I probably shouldn't have said it.

Her expression hardened. "Thanks, Brynn. Thanks a lot."

I stared into my cup, watching the milk and espresso swirl together. "Seriously, what are we going to do, Maeve?"

My hands shook from too much caffeine—or maybe nerves. "We should've stayed on Teddy's RV. How are we supposed to get to all these Cutter shows without transportation? We can't keep taking chances like this, staying with complete strangers."

Her gaze flicked to the window, restless, impatient. "We'll figure it out. You should try being a little more grateful to be out of that place."

"I'm sorry, but it's a little hard when we're so totally off our plan. Not when we're on the run. I never wanted this—being *fugitives*."

She laughed under her breath. "We're not fugitives. You need to frickin' relax, Brynn." Her expression shifted. She reached into her bag, and her face lit up as if she'd remembered something miraculous. "Hey, you wanna try ecstasy? I told you I bought some yesterday—"

"No!" I yelled, and a few heads turned. "You were on that stuff last night, I could tell. And so could Renee and Pitt. We need to be thinking, Maeve." I pressed my palm against my forehead. "We don't need to be out of our minds. We'll get caught for sure."

Maeve drained the rest of her coffee, set the cup down too hard, and stood. "You're on your own for a while."

I blinked up at her. "What?"

"I need some space. I'll meet you back at the apartment at five. Renee said they'll be home by then."

"Wait, Maeve. You're going to leave me here alone?"

She slung her coat over her arm. "You'll be fine."

Was she serious? Should I go with her? I stood up and reached for my backpack, but Maeve was already on her way out the door.

I slowly sank back into my seat. For a while, I sat there, staring at her abandoned cup. The hiss of the espresso machine, the scrape of chairs, the soft murmur of strangers closed in around me.

Without Maeve, the city felt like a whale, waiting to swallow me.

I'd spent the last few years of my life being told when to sit, when to stand, when to sleep. Even the escape had been initiated by Maeve. I'd simply ridden her current. Being alone meant no one was guiding me anymore. That terrified me more than being caught.

Stay put, Brynn—give her time to cool off. The truth was, I didn't know what to do with time anymore. I was a rudderless ship.

I looked out the window. Snow drifted sideways across the street, catching in the light like ash. People passed by in heavy coats, laughing, touching, belonging.

"I don't even have my coat," I whispered to myself, envisioning the abandoned article in that empty house in Ohio.

Freedom wasn't supposed to feel this lonely. Should I call Mama? Would they even let her speak to me?

I finished what was left of my latte, threw the cup away, and stepped outside into the cold. The wind bit through my sweater. The city whirred around me, with cars, sirens, fragments of music leaking from bars.

I started walking without thinking, arms wrapped around myself, slush underfoot, shivering, past bookstores and secondhand shops, until I spotted the bright red-and-yellow sign on Clark Street.

Tower Records.

The windows glowed like stained glass. I ducked inside, welcoming the dry, hot flow of air and the too-bright fluorescent lights buzzing, music blaring something by Stone Temple Pilots, a song I'd heard in Teddy's RV only a couple of days ago. It already felt like a painful, distant memory.

I drifted through the aisles, running my fingertips along the jewel cases. Aerosmith. Bush. The Cranberries. Every band name felt familiar and comforting. On the sidewalk outside the store, a man with spiky black hair talked to a girl with electric-blue hair who was selling paintings on the street. He told her he was a drummer and had once opened for the Smashing Pumpkins.

One hour successfully wasted at Tower Records. Only six more to go.

I bought a cheap pleather coat at a thrift store and drifted through the city, walking in and out of stores, trying to keep track of where I was going and how far it was back to the apartment.

I took a tour bus. I ate lunch at McDonald's. Later, I had more coffee in a café. Somehow, I'd found a way to kill the day.

Finally, it was time to go back to the apartment and face the terror of the unknown. What if Maeve didn't show up? What if she'd hitched a ride on her own, leaving me stranded in Chicago?

When I reached the apartment, she was already there, in the kitchen with Renee, who was doling out spaghetti onto plates.

"Hey, you made it!" Renee said brightly. "Grab a plate."

Maeve sat cross-legged on the counter, twirling noodles around her fork. There was only room for two at the table, and tonight that was Pitt and me. Renee drifted in and out of the kitchen, humming along to a Cranberries song playing on the living room stereo.

The three of us ate quietly. Pitt finished first, beating my three-minute spaghetti consumption before wordlessly pushing his chair back and carrying his plate to the sink. Then he left the room.

I looked up at Maeve. She didn't move from her perch.

"So, where did you go today?"

She shrugged. "Just walked. Went down Michigan Avenue. Some museums."

"The whole day?"

"Yeah."

She didn't ask what I'd done.

I chewed at the corner of my mouth. "I wasn't sure if you were coming back."

Her face turned serious. "No matter what you think of me, I wouldn't do that."

"OK." I wanted to believe her. I really did.

She dropped her legs off the counter, slid down, and put her plate in the sink. "Tomorrow morning, we'll head to the bus station."

I nodded. This was only the second Cutter concert, and we were already getting on each other's nerves.

Renee floated back into the kitchen, leaned her hip against the sink, and darted her gaze between us. "So, we didn't have a chance to talk much last night, but are you two really planning on going to every Cutter concert this year?"

Maeve sipped from a glass of water. "Yeah. As many as we can."

Renee laughed a little. "That's got to be expensive, not to mention the hotels and food and everything. Are you guys independently wealthy or something?"

I shot Maeve a glance, warning her not to answer that.

"Long story," Maeve said. "But the road is our home now."

Renee raised a brow. "You two on the run or something?"

My heart seized.

Maeve didn't even hesitate. "That's it. We're fugitives. On the run from a mountain mafia."

I wanted to smack her.

Renee snickered and then turned to me. "You running from the same thing?"

My voice squeaked out. "We're just following the band."

She studied me a moment longer. *Did* she suspect something? I held my breath, and when I didn't offer any other explanation, she shrugged and tossed her dish towel onto the counter. "Everybody's running from something, I guess. Everybody's being chased by something."

I wondered what was chasing Renee.

Pitt wandered back into the kitchen, opened the fridge, and pulled out another beer. The cap clinked against the counter. "Nothing's chasing me." He winked at Maeve.

I really didn't like this guy.

I picked up my plate and put it in the sink with Maeve's and Pitt's.

Renee poured herself another glass of wine and raised it in my direction. "You'll figure it out. Whatever you girls are looking for."

I didn't know what that was anymore. Maeve seemed to fit into the world so much better than I did. Or at least, she could put on a better act. She laughed easily and leaned close when Pitt or Renee spoke to her. Later, in the living room, she danced to the music on the stereo, the lights flashing off her hair, and she looked like she belonged there, with regular people, out in the Gray.

I hovered near the wall and watched Pitt watching Maeve dance. His eyes were fixed and wide, the same stare he'd given me when he'd entered the bathroom accidentally on purpose.

That night, Maeve slept on the couch while I tossed and

turned on the foam mat, my mind spinning. Tomorrow we'd catch another bus to Milwaukee, then figure out where to sleep after the concert. Or maybe we'd go straight to the station after the concert and catch another Greyhound to Anywhere. At least we had Maeve's money. We could get a hotel like we should have done in Chicago, instead of staying with strangers.

After lying awake for an hour, I got up and went into the kitchen for a glass of water. Pitt was there, barefoot, bent at the waist, the refrigerator light cutting across his face. An empty beer bottle sat on the counter, and he was grabbing another—his third, maybe fourth.

I froze.

He closed the refrigerator, and the light went out. He faced me, his silhouette hovering like a tall, creepy shadow. "You're up late."

"I just came in for some water."

"Want a beer?"

"No, thanks."

I grabbed a glass from the drying rack and filled it with tap water. When I turned again, he was blocking the doorway.

His face was cloaked in shadow, but I could feel his eyes sliding over me.

"You and your friend have a fight?"

"No. We're OK."

"So, you girls are like, groupies, right? Like my cousin? I mean, that's why you're following Cutter across the country?"

A strange vibe radiated from him, making my skin flush hot.

"Not really groupies," I said. "We're fans."

He stepped toward me. "Yeah, but I mean, you sleep

with the band members and all that. Right? I know my cousin does."

Twinkie.

I shook my head. "No. It's not like that for us. We go to the concerts, listen to the music, then we leave."

He reached by my ear and flipped on the light over the sink. Illumination flashed across his face. A smirk tipped his full lips. "Where's the fun in that? What's the point of shlepping all over the place if you're not gonna get some at the end of it?"

I took a step back. He took another step forward.

My voice seemed to have drained out of me. "No, we're just about the music."

He closed the space between us and cupped my elbow. "Come on. I'll bet those guys go crazy over you two."

I flinched. "Pitt," I said evenly. "It's late. You should go to bed."

He grinned, teeth flashing in the dim light. "You telling me what to do?"

The way he said it—almost teasing—twisted my stomach. Astra Cynthia's voice flickered through my mind, sweet as maple syrup right before she handed down punishment.

I gripped the glass harder. Water sloshed onto my wrist.

Pitt drifted closer until the stale heat of his breath brushed my face.

"You don't have to be nervous," he said. "I'm not gonna hurt you."

I kept my gaze on the kitchen's yellow linoleum flooring. I knew better than to look a predator in the eye. "Renee's asleep," I managed. "If she hears you in here—"

"She sleeps like the dead." His laugh was a low sound that curled through the dark. "Relax, Brynn. You're wound too tight."

There was nowhere to go. The counter dug into my spine. The glass knocked against the sink's edge.

"You should stop." My voice was firm.

For a second, I thought he might. His smile faltered. Then his eyes flicked downward—over my shoulder, my neck.

Take control of this situation, Brynn. Otherwise, he will.

I set the glass down on the counter. "I'm going back to bed." An announcement. Not a question.

Pitt didn't move.

I slid sideways, shoulders tight, breath shallow, and slipped past him into the living room.

Maeve was sprawled on the couch, dead asleep. Her mouth hung open slightly, her hair tangled across her face.

I crouched beside her, shaking. I wanted to wake her, to tell her we needed to leave right then.

The hall floorboards creaked. Pitt was moving away, toward his own bedroom. Soon after, the bedroom door clicked shut.

Heaving a sigh, I lay down on the mat, pulled the quilt up to my neck, and stared into the dark.

Every sound was amplified. The click of the refrigerator making ice, a thump from next door. I waited for the return of his footsteps. They never came.

Chapter Seventeen

FEBRUARY 1999

"The One Who Ran"

The interior of the Greyhound bus was almost as cold as the outside. Maeve and I sat near the back, hunkered down in our coats. Nearly every seat was full, vibrating with motion, with other people's stories. Maeve's knees bounced, headphones in place, a hiss of staticky sound coming from her earphones.

"What are you listening to?" I pointed to my ear as I asked.

She pulled off her headphones off and let them hang around her neck. "'The One Who Ran.'"

"Oh, I love that one." Even though the lyrics broadcast Sullivan's pain.

Bondage, prison, chains so tight,
Hands are tied, I lost the fight.
I knew exactly what he was singing about in that song.
The bus lurched forward.

"Here we go." Maeve grinned. "Milwaukee, here we come. Stop number two. Third row seats. Aren't you excited?"

The third row meant closer to Sullivan.

"What about Teddy? You think he'll be there—in the third row with us?"

Maeve's face tensed. "I don't know. Maybe. I'll deal with that when the time comes."

"Don't you feel anything for him? I mean, after what you guys did together?"

Her face was lined with amusement. "You mean that we had sex?"

The admission slipped from her mouth so easily.

"Don't you feel like that bonds you somehow?"

She shrugged, a glimmer of moisture in her eyes. "It's not always like that. Think about all the relationships that ended in Crystal Cliffs. Sometimes things don't work out."

Through the window, the world slid past. Frozen fields, truck stops, neon signs that promised coffee and maybe a honey bun wrapped in a sticky plastic wrapper like the one I'd bought from a bakery in Chicago.

I put my head against the bus window and fantasized about Sullivan on the stage, covered in sweat, his hair dripping. Something simmered in my lower abdomen, accompanied by a spark of excitement at the memory of his face.

"When did you and Teddy first have … sex?" The word felt strange in my mouth.

Maeve pulled her backpack onto her lap and rested her arms on it like a pillow. "A year and a half ago. It was after that night at the bonfire. Remember the one in front of The Collective's warehouse? They'd invited all the normies in for happy hour and discounted goods. Remember? All the tents were set up everywhere?"

I remembered. Recruitment day. Bring outsiders in, let them shop at The Collective at bargain-basement prices, and let them see our perfect community. That was the night my mom and Kristen got super-drunk. I'd never seen them like that, falling in the street. I thought I'd even seen them kiss, but I'd probably just imagined it.

"Teddy snuck in too," Maeve said. "We'd planned everything, of course, but no one even noticed him coming back to the house with me. Mom and Dad were volunteering at the bonfire, so they never knew."

"You did it in your house?"

"In my bedroom."

I dropped my jaw.

She lifted and dropped her shoulders. "No one's ever home at my house. Anyway, I thought I loved him then."

I leaned back against the headrest. "If Teddy's at the concert, I think you'll feel something for him again. Maybe we can even get back on the RV." *Oh, please, please.*

"I don't know if he can forgive me. I wouldn't be surprised if he turned me in."

Her words froze my insides.

Maeve ran her fingers over her mouth. "This cold weather is making my lips peel off my face."

"You have any ChapStick?"

"Yeah, in my pack." She unzipped the front pocket of her backpack and reached a hand in. Her whole body went unnaturally still, like she'd been unplugged.

"What?" I asked.

She dug both hands into the backpack, pulling out clothes and letting them drop onto the seat and the floor. A tangled cord of headphones came next.

"What?" I said louder.

She turned the bag upside down and emptied the rest of

its contents into her lap—leggings, a crumpled hoodie, a granola bar. Nothing else.

Something was very absent—conspicuously so.

Her eyes flicked up to mine, wide and glassy with panic. "It's gone."

"What's gone?" I already knew the answer.

"The money." Her voice cracked on the word. "Brynn—it's gone. It was right here. I had it right in here."

The air around us seemed to shrink. For a second, all I could hear was the drone of the bus engine, the wet sound of tires on the road, my own pulse thudding in my temples.

"Check again." Even though I knew she already had.

Desperate, frantic, her fingers unzipped and dove into pockets again and again. "It's gone," she repeated, louder.

A couple of passengers in front of us turned around.

I grabbed her wrist. "Maeve—stop. Don't draw attention." That's all we needed. Someone to think we *had* money. Someone to realize we didn't have it anymore.

She leaned close, her breath shaking. "Renee or Pitt took it. They had to. I had it the whole time we were there. I even checked the envelope last night."

I swallowed hard. Last night's images flickered: Pitt, in the kitchen, coming onto me. Renee, watching TV in the den. Pitt was constantly moving around the place. He could easily have taken the money.

This was bad.

"They stole it." Her voice was raw and broken. "They stole everything. Brynn! What are we going to do? That was our only hope—all we had to keep us going." Panic tightened her voice until she sounded like a child.

I felt the world tilt, cold dread pooling in my stomach. Without that money, we weren't just broke—we were trapped. I still had a bit of cash, but was it enough for a hotel room in Milwaukee? We couldn't get to the next concert in New York. We couldn't even go back to Crystal Cliffs. We couldn't go or do anything.

Somehow, Pitt must have known about the money. Maybe he even recognized our faces from the news. I had a hard time believing Renee would have taken it, but Pitt? There'd been something a little sketchy about him all along. Had he overheard our late-night conversations? Realized that there'd be no repercussions for taking the money because we had taken it from someone else?

"We'll figure it out." My tongue felt thick, my mouth dry. "We'll figure something out."

Maeve's breathing came hard and fast. Gasping, hyperventilating. "What if—what if they knew about us, about the money?"

I grabbed her hand under the pile of clothes and squeezed. "Listen to me. Stay calm. Stop being so loud. We don't tell anyone. We don't let anyone know we're scared." I turned my eyes toward the others peering over the bus seats, and whispered, "It's dangerous to look scared."

Her chin trembled. "I can't believe—after everything—how could we have trusted them?"

The bus carried on through the gray slices of landscape, but it suddenly felt like we were suspended above nothing, drifting in a direction we hadn't chosen.

Maeve stared down at the empty backpack as if it had betrayed her. Then she pulled it close, hugging it to her chest. "We're dead. The money's gone. How are we going to eat? Pay for a place to stay?"

I didn't have an answer. The real one was too terrifying to speak. I held her hand tighter and hoped she couldn't feel the tremor in mine.

I didn't know what would happen after. I only knew we

had to make it to Milwaukee. We had to get to the Cutter concert.

Chapter Eighteen

NOW

Ivy asks to meet me again before she goes back to Pawley's Island—this time for after-work drinks—a step up from our tea at Lulu's.

She suggests Twist, a wine bar downtown with tall windows and soft lighting.

Wait, I text back. *I thought you didn't drink.*

I don't, she writes. *But I thought I'd make it easy for you. It's near your work.*

How martyr-ly of her. I'm not even sure why she wants to meet me again, or why I'm agreeing to it.

Women who are acquaintances don't usually request second meetings unless there's something unfinished. Makes me think she still wants answers. Maybe I do too.

I've been to Twist a few times on my way home from work. I recognize the bartender as I enter and give her a wave.

Ivy isn't here yet, so I grab a seat at the bar and put my purse on the stool next to me to save it. A few minutes later, she arrives, and she isn't alone. The woman beside her is visibly pregnant—third trimester, maybe—with a calm, self-possessed air. She wears a navy wrap dress and low heels, one hand resting casually at the small of her back. She looks like someone who is comfortable in her life and knows exactly where she fits.

Ivy's eyes meet mine, and she waves her arm wildly in the air.

I slide off the stool. Obviously, the bar is not the right seating arrangement in this instance. As I walk toward her, I note the straw bag, the button-down shirt over a hot-pink top, her dark hair spilling over her shoulders. She looks as though she's headed to the beach after this.

She lunges forward and hugs me. "I hope it's OK. I brought my sister. This is Matilde."

Her sister smiles warmly. "Mattie. It's really nice to meet you."

"Of course," I echo. "Nice to meet you too."

Where is this going?

We sit at a table in the corner. I order wine—Mattie and Ivy abstain, of course, refusing it with amused smiles—and we settle into the dark, narrow space of the wine bar. Ivy's broad smile suggests that she's pleased, as if the evening has already gone exactly as planned.

Mattie reaches a well-manicured hand toward me. Pale pink gel fingernails. "Ivy's told me so much about you. Your work. Your podcast. I listened to an episode on the drive down."

I force a smile. "Which one?"

"The one about afterlives," she says. "After leaving. The adjustment and the reversal of all the…" She seems to search for the word. "…brainwashing that went on before. That was really powerful, hearing that woman describe her 'detoxing' process."

My mouth curves a little more despite myself.

Ivy watches us, relaxed. "Brynn is really good at that. Putting language to things people feel but can't articulate."

I inhale and try to keep my gaze from floating condescendingly toward the ceiling. "What do you do, Mattie?"

Mattie rests her hand on her belly as she speaks. "I work in a nonprofit too. In an administrative capacity. A lot of transitional housing. People rebuilding."

"That must be rewarding work. Takes a lot of inner strength, I'm sure."

She slides her hand up to her chest. "Or a certain stubbornness."

The conversation flows easily. That's the weird part. Ivy has chosen her proxy well—someone unthreatening, empathetic, grounded. Older. Someone who represents continuity.

At some point, Ivy leans back, swirling her club soda. "Sullivan's been in a reflective mood lately. I think talking to you helped with that."

She knows we talked. I don't respond immediately.

"Closure can be a gift," Mattie says gently. "Even when it doesn't look like we expect it to."

Ivy nods. "Exactly."

I drain what's left in my glass and manage to flag down a server. "Another, please."

Mattie leans forward, her elbows on the table. "I'm sorry, Brynn. Ivy didn't say. Do you have children?"

"No."

She sits back in her chair as if her suspicions were confirmed.

"I guess all the people you've helped are like your children," Ivy says.

Mattie's brow furrows. "Does revisiting their pain help

you heal yours? Give you some closure from what you've been through?"

Oh, what an elegant segue.

Now I get it. This is a tag-team operation with barely masked intent.

"Sometimes," I say carefully. "Closure isn't really about finishing something. It's about understanding it honestly. Sometimes you have to revisit what you lost."

Both women look at me, nodding.

"I guess that's true," Mattie says. "But understanding doesn't always require revisiting. Does it?"

"No." The smile on my face is tense. "But sometimes it does."

Ivy smiles. "I think Sullivan's like, finally learning that the past can exist without disrupting the present."

The words are delivered with a firm certainty. Maybe she thinks she has already won.

This isn't a competition, Brynn.

Oh, but it is.

I'm relieved when the server brings a refreshed glass of wine.

The conversation veers off from there. We talk about Charleston, about travel, about how strange it is to feel your body changing without your permission. I tell them that the brink of menopause gives you more surprises than you want. Something for them both to look forward to. Mattie gives us details about kicking babies and stretch marks.

This whole encounter has been wildly awkward, yet strangely normal.

Finally, Mattie excuses herself early, fatigue edging her smile. "You ladies will have to excuse me. My husband is picking me up. We've got to do some shopping tonight." She turns her eyes toward Ivy. "See you back at the house?"

Ivy nods.

Mattie meets my gaze. "I'm really glad we met," she says sincerely. "It's been interesting talking to you."

When Ivy and I finally head outside, the streetlamps are beginning to glow. She reaches out and touches my arm in a brief, friendly, proprietary way that she probably doesn't even register.

"Thank you again," she says. "This meant a lot. To meet. To get to know you."

"It was good to meet you too." Truth.

We part with a polite warmth that suggests something has been settled.

It hasn't.

But Ivy doesn't need to know that.

I walk a few blocks to where my car is parked.

The night air is cool, the city settling into itself. Restaurants, traffic, and the sidewalk are all coming to life.

I slide into the driver's seat and rest my hands on the wheel. Ivy believes she's handled this. Smoothed the edges. Introduced context and reframed me into something safe.

She's wrong.

Because what tonight clarified for me is that no one gets to decide what this means except me. Not Ivy and her sister with her cheerful, rehearsed kindness. Not Paul with his steadiness. Not even Sullivan with his regrets.

I've made a decision. I will go to him.

A solo road trip to Nashville. No witnesses or accomplices. Just asphalt and time and the truth waiting at the end of it.

The decision is fully formed. I pull out my phone and text Sullivan before I let second thoughts dilute it.

I've thought about it. I can come to Nashville next week, if that works.

I stare at the screen for a beat.

Then I hit *Send*.

The message whooshes away, seemingly small and ordinary, but carrying a choice big enough to rearrange everything in my life. And his.

Chapter Nineteen

MILWAUKEE, WISCONSIN, MARCH 1999

"All for You"

Maeve and I used some of what little money I had to catch a cab. The driver dropped us off across the street from the Eagles Ballroom. For a second, I stared up at it, my breath fogging in the freezing air. The building looked old, with huge arched windows and ornamented stonework that made it seem as if it belonged to another century. I probably would've thought it was beautiful if my stomach wasn't tied in one giant knot.

People streamed toward the entrance in thick lines, bundled in coats, some smoking, some laughing.

Maeve held her backpack tight against her chest even though there was no longer anything in it of value. She hadn't spoken much since the bus. Every few minutes, she'd check the zipper like the money might magically appear again. A light had gone out in her. The loss of the money somehow equaled a loss of the freedom we thought we had.

Inside, the venue was warm, crowded. The pre-show

music thumped through the floors. My ribs felt tight, like the sound was squeezing me from the inside. The noise, the heat, the density of people. It was a lot to take in.

The ceiling arched above us, painted with faded clouds I barely glimpsed through the haze. Bright stage lights flashed from the far end of the room, bouncing off the old wooden floor.

Maeve popped something into her mouth. Her throat constricted as she swallowed it.

I grabbed her arm. "What did you take?"

She shot forward and walked in front of me, beelining through the crowd.

"Maeve!" I followed her, weaving through clusters of kids in oversized hoodies and glittery eyeliner.

The closer we got to the stage, the noise pressed into my chest. The smell changed too, with more sweat, more smoke, as if we'd stepped deeper into the lungs of the building.

We found our seats in the third row and let the minutes tick by.

As the house lights dropped for the opening band, a cheer rolled through the ballroom, rising from the back and crashing against the stage. Maeve flinched at the sound, then laughed a loud, horsey guffaw.

Her pupils were enormous, swallowing the color of her irises. She tugged at the neck of her shirt as if she were suddenly too warm.

I leaned in. "Maeve, what did you take?"

She shrugged. "Just a little something. To … you know. Feel better."

This was all I needed. "Are you serious?"

She smiled. "It's fine, Brynn. Just chill."

I whirled toward her. "I need *you* right now. I need you to be with me. Not off with the fairies somewhere."

But my words were too late.

The stage lights strobed across the crowd. Reds, then whites, then an icy blue. The band hit their first chord, a vibrating wall of sound.

Maeve gasped, and her eyes flew wide open like someone had dropped something beautiful and unexpected in her hands.

She jumped up and down and grabbed my hand. "Do you feel that? It's like—like it's under my skin."

I didn't feel anything except the cold edge of panic rising.

I wanted to scream at her. Why had she done this? What would I do with her after the show? Especially if I was dealing with someone halfway to another planet.

People around us shouted, danced, shoved closer to the front.

Maeve's palm turned damp in mine, and she seemed entranced by the lights. It reminded me of a fairy tale my mother had read to me when I was a kid, in which the girl followed a ball of light up the stairs and then pricked her finger on the spindle of a spinning wheel. She'd fallen into a deep sleep for years, losing all the safety measures she'd had until then.

I held on to Maeve's hand for as long as I could, as though trying to keep her from floating away. After some time, she pulled her hand free and turned to the strangers standing next to her. "Everything feels like it's glowing."

I didn't want to leave her, but she seemed happy to dance with her new friends, and we both needed to eat something. My stomach had been growling since we stepped off the bus. I glanced over my shoulder at the exits, where concession stands waited. I still had a bit of cash, enough to buy us rubbery hot dogs or pretzels with salt grains that would stick in our teeth.

"I'm gonna get some food," I yelled into her ear. "You need anything?"

She shook her head, grinning. "I'm fantastic."

Fantastic. Yeah, right.

I made my way toward the lobby, praying that Maeve wouldn't do something stupid while I was gone. At least there, amid thousands of people, it was easy to be invisible.

For me, the smell of popcorn and soda syrup was irresistible. I pushed my way to the concession stand, bought two pretzels, and then stood there while I downed them, not even bothering to time my consumption. People were still streaming into the place, drenched from the drizzle outside, faces shining with expectation.

"Brynn?"

For a second, I couldn't place him. He looked different out of the RV, out of that dim, endless highway light. His hair was shorter than it had been a few days ago, his jacket cleaner. He was holding a beer, half-smiling like he wasn't sure if he should be happy or worried to see me.

I lunged toward him. "Teddy! We weren't sure if you'd come or not."

He laughed, shifting his weight. "Yeah, I figured I can't pass up third-row seats." His gaze flicked toward the doors, then back to me. "Is Maeve here?"

"She's inside. She'll freak when she sees you."

He winced. "Yeah, that's kinda what I'm worried about."

I hesitated, the pretzel salt turning to paste in my mouth. This wasn't exactly something you dropped casually, but Teddy deserved to know.

"She's—" I glanced toward the ballroom doors.

Teddy's brows pulled together. "What?"

I used the word I'd heard from Delia and Twinkie. "She's *rolling*."

He blinked at me. "Rolling? Maeve?"

"She took something on the way to our seats. Ecstasy, I think. She's with some people now. She seems OK, but … it's hitting her."

Teddy stared past me, jaw working. Then he swore under his breath, set his beer bottle on the corner of the concession stand. "Maeve doesn't do well when she can't read people. She's too trusting."

"I know. And there's more, Teddy." I bit my lip.

His eyes were wide. "What?"

"The money? It's gone. It was stolen in Chicago."

"Shit." He swept his hand over his mouth. "I shouldn't have left her."

I didn't know what to say to that.

He grabbed his beer again, took a sip, his eyes scanning the crowd. "She said some pretty rough things when she left. But that's all water under the bridge now."

"She'll be glad to see you." I prayed that was true.

He huffed a quiet laugh. "Guess I'll take my chances."

"We should get in there."

Teddy nodded. "Lead the way."

He fell into step beside me, weaving through the concession crowd toward the ballroom doors. The opening band was already nearing the end of their set.

I led Teddy toward Maeve, who was spinning under the glowing lights, eyes closed. We slid past five or six others with their fists in the air. I stepped on some guy's shoe and then yelled an apology.

"Aw, you're good, babe," he bellowed back.

Maeve's eyes flew open as Teddy brushed past and positioned himself on the other side of her. Then she draped her arms around his shoulders, grabbed his face, and kissed him.

He slid his arm around her, easy, familiar. Smiling, she yelled something into his ear. His hand tangled in her hair before they kissed again. Seemed like they were back together. Maybe we could return to the RV, have somewhere to stay the night. A fragile thought.

The set ended in a storm of feedback and applause. The house lights flared halfway. It was the intermission before Cutter came on. People surged toward the aisles, spilling beer, shouting over each other.

Maeve and Teddy stayed put, their heads close together. Her hand slid up his arm as she said something that made him grin.

With my nerves sparking and my bladder flooding after drinking a tumbler of soda, I made a quick visit to the restroom. The hallway was filled with security men in yellow vests, holding CB radios.

As I exited the bathroom, something caught my eye. Across the hordes of people, near the merch table, a man stood with his hands clasped behind his back. Heavyset, straight spine. Shoulders squared. His head was covered with a dark cap. He scanned the crowd, watchful.

My stomach dropped.

Chuck Crow.

No, it couldn't be.

I squinted. He stood too far away for me to be absolutely sure. He was talking to someone, half-turned, but the angle of his jaw, the way he tilted his head when listening—it was him. It had to be.

He glanced up and our eyes almost met. I jerked back,

heart thudding, and bumped into someone carrying a tray of drinks.

"Hey, watch out!" the woman snapped as beer sloshed over her sleeve.

"Sorry," I muttered, backing away.

When I looked again, the spot by the merch table was empty. I quickly overhanded my way through the waves of people, propelling myself out of the lobby.

Maybe it wasn't him. Maybe it never had been. My brain was playing tricks on me.

I took a shaky breath and returned to my seat before the lights dimmed again and screams filled the place. A single white beam cut through the haze, blinding. The stage erupted in sound, with drums pounding as if war were imminent.

The first time I saw Sullivan at the show in Ohio, it felt like watching a movie. We were so far from him, he didn't seem real. But seated in the third row, I was close enough to see his facial expressions change, to catch the glint of light in his eyes.

He stepped forward, guitar slung low, head bowed for a beat as the crowd screamed his name. His hair brushed the tops of his shoulders. Under the stage lights, it looked almost golden, catching fire every time he moved.

He closed his eyes as he sang, voice thick with grit and ache. The sound was bigger than the room. His voice hit low and rough, the same tone that had once whispered my name in that dark closet. Every word dragged something out of me—memory, guilt, want.

The audience mirrored him, arms lifted, mouths open, shouting his lyrics back at him.

Feedback hummed through the amps. Sullivan stepped

away from the mic, breathing hard, his chest rising and falling under the lights.

"Thank you." He glanced toward the wings, raked his wet hair back from his forehead. "This next one's about finding a way through life, when you don't know who you are anymore. This one's called 'The One Who Ran.'"

He was telling our story, but no one else there knew that. To them, it was just another song about survival.

And then, it happened. His eyes swept the first few rows, and for one impossible second, they landed on me. The moment was gone in a blink.

It felt like a minute later, but I knew another forty-five of them had passed. The notes of the last song trembled against the rafters, and Sullivan stood with his face tilted toward the lights until the sound finally died.

The band waved and jogged from the stage, and the house lights flared.

It was over.

Maeve and Teddy still jumped and whooped, but I stood where I was, half deaf, my pulse syncing to the bass that wouldn't stop vibrating in my bones. For a moment, our eyes had met. For a moment, I thought he had recognized me.

The throngs of people started to move, everyone talking about the music, the encore, the voice, the feeling. I didn't even notice the man coming down the aisle until he stopped in front of me.

My eyes met his two-way radio first, then the laminated badge with his picture, then his angular face. Some sort of security. Black shirt, earpiece.

My mind swam with horrifying possibilities. Were we about to be arrested?

He scanned the thinning crowd before bending at the

waist. "Mr. Stonecutter asked if you'd be willing to wait a few minutes. He'd like to talk to you, wants to know if you want to come backstage."

I couldn't form words. My mouth opened, but nothing came out.

The man straightened, glancing toward the side door near the stage. "You can say no, of course, but if you're willing, he said he'd send someone to walk you back."

I nodded slowly. "I'll wait."

He gave a curt smile. "All right. Stay put. Someone will come get you."

Sullivan wanted to see me.

After all this time.

Chapter Twenty

NOW

The rain starts again somewhere between my apartment and West Ashley on my drive to Paul's place. He lives on a narrow street in Ansonborough, where the houses sit close together, muted in color—soft gray, pale cream, weathered blue—their shutters closed like half-lidded eyes. I push the low wrought-iron gate, and it opens without a sound. A brick path curves toward the side of the house, shaded by a crepe myrtle whose branches skim the windows.

His apartment is on the second floor. With water still clinging to my hair, dampening the shoulders of my sweater, I knock on the door. It's probably unlocked. He's expecting me, but I wait.

A muffled voice calls out: "Come on in!"

I step into a warm, dry world of rosemary and garlic.

"Hope you're hungry," he calls from the kitchen.

The floors are original heart pine, their warm grain grounding the room. Tall windows line one wall, dressed in simple linen curtains that let in the late-afternoon light. The furniture is solid, nothing trendy or fragile. Bookshelves are built into the walls.

Paul appears. He's barefoot, his jeans and shirt covered with a dark blue apron. He wields a wooden spoon half-covered in something red. "Come on back," he says breezily. "I'm in the kitchen."

I follow him. "You didn't have to cook."

"I wanted to."

The kitchen opens off the main room without ceremony, narrow and galley-style.

Everything is where it should be. A knife block with only the knives he actually uses. A cutting board scarred with shallow grooves. A kettle on the stove, old but clean.

His sleeves are rolled up, his forearms dusted with flour. "Besides, after all the takeout we've had at the office, I owe you a real meal."

The sight of him like this—casual, domestic—throws me a little. I can't remember the last time a man cooked for me.

He gestures toward the open bottle on the counter. "Wine?"

"Sure." He doesn't know I've already had two at the wine bar.

He pours. I take the glass and swirl it once. "Whatever is cooking smells amazing. You're like a real chef."

"It's my one good dish. Don't get used to this."

I scan the counter, scattered with flour, the pasta maker sitting nearby. "You made pasta from scratch?"

He smiles, shrugs. "I prefer it that way."

I sit on the stool at the island, watching him drain noodles, the steam rising around him like fog.

How can I not be impressed?

We talk about the next conference he's helping organize.

The intern who double-booked studio time. Ways to keep supply costs down.

When we finally sit down to eat, I fall into a concentrated quiet, focusing on each bite of food. Tangy tomato sauce, perfectly al dente pasta, seasoned to perfection with basil and rosemary.

I have to tell him. I can't *not* tell him.

He sets his fork down first. "So…" He watches me for a beat. "What's new?"

There's nothing to do but blurt it out. "Paul, I told you Sullivan had emailed me."

He doesn't flinch, doesn't sigh or lean back or ask me to clarify. He nods once, like this is information he's been waiting for me to tell him.

"Well, I've also talked to him on the phone."

"I figured something was up," he says quietly.

"You did?"

"Yeah." His eyes darken. "You've had that look all week. Like part of you was somewhere else, checking the exits."

"I'm not checking the exits," I say emphatically. "We just talked. He asked if we could get together—here or in Nashville." I bounce my eyes away from him and force myself to say the rest. "And I've decided I'm going to Nashville. To see him. Next week."

He folds his hands together on the table. "OK."

Why does he have to be so damn calm?

I rush on. "I'm not doing this impulsively. I'm not chasing anything. I just—" My voice wobbles despite my best efforts. "I can't let other people manage this for me. Ivy, or the past, or even you."

"Ivy is the girl who called in—"

"To the show, yeah.

"And she's connected with him, how?"

"Girlfriend, I think." Cringe.

He nods. "I see."

"Anyway, I need to look at this situation straight on."

"OK," he says again.

"I wanted to tell you before I go," I add. "I didn't want it to feel like I was sneaking around."

Paul nods again. "I appreciate that."

A weighted silence settles between us. The kitchen clock ticks.

I expect him to ask me what I think I'll gain from meeting Sullivan.

Instead, he leans forward. "Can I say something?"

"Please."

"You know I care about you. And I won't pretend this doesn't hurt—a lot. But I also know what it's like to live with unanswered questions."

I swallow. "I need a few days."

"I know," he says gently. "I'm not going to ask you not to go. That wouldn't be fair to either of us."

I meet his eyes. "This doesn't detract from my feelings for you. This is separate." Even as I say the words, I'm not sure that's quite true. "When I come back—"

"When you come back." He lifts a hand. "We'll see where things are."

I want to cry. For him, for me. "Thank you. For not making this harder."

He stands, reaches for my empty plate, then pauses. "Brynn?"

"Yeah?"

"Whatever happens in Nashville," he says, "Don't lose the person you worked so hard to be."

"I won't."

He takes my plate to the sink, rinses it, sets it in the rack. When he turns back to me, his forehead is lined.

"You're welcome to stay tonight," he says. "If you want. No expectations. I'd like you to stay, really. You've been drinking."

I consider it. The warmth of his apartment, the safety of him, the road now stretching invisibly ahead of me—it all makes me want to take him up on his offer. "Not tonight. But thank you."

He walks me to the door.

Outside, the rain has thinned to a mist, and the street-lamp casts a dull halo around us.

"Drive safe." His voice is a little distant, almost professional.

"I will."

He doesn't kiss me. He touches my arm and then lets me go.

As I step back into the night, the clarity in my heart and mind feels almost painful.

Here I go again.

And this time, it's a road trip on my own.

Chapter Twenty-One

MILWAUKEE, WISCONSIN, MARCH 1999

"When the Lights Go Out"

I stayed in my seat and waited for the security guard or someone else to come for me. Maeve and Teddy were a few rows up, talking to people who had wandered over. Teddy seemed to know them. Maeve was laughing.

"Maeve!" I called, pushing through a few lingering people.

She turned, hair sticking to her damp cheeks. "What's up?"

"Sullivan asked for me."

Maeve blinked, then grinned. "What? You're kidding." She hung on Teddy's arm. "Teddy, did you hear? Brynn is going backstage! Sullivan invited her!"

Teddy raised his eyebrows, skeptical. "You sure it's legit? Could be some creep trying to score with you backstage."

I shook my head. "The security guy said Sullivan asked for me specifically."

Maeve's eyes were shining. "Oh, Brynn, that's insane! You have to go!"

Teddy frowned. "You want me to come with you? Make sure it's on the level?"

"No. They said to wait here. Someone's coming to get me."

Maeve squeezed my hand. "I wanna know everything he says."

"Yeah. I'll come back out once we've talked. Maybe you guys can come backstage too."

Maeve pointed at the ground. "We'll meet you right here after, OK?"

The lights above us flickered as stagehands started clearing the set. Stragglers drifted toward the exits.

A door creaked. The same security guard appeared at the front of the stage, tilting his head toward the door behind him. "You ready?"

I waved to Teddy and Maeve and followed him through the door marked *AUTHORIZED PERSONNEL ONLY.* The hallway beyond was narrow and dim, lined with posters of bands long gone. The cinderblock hallway reverberated with voices.

The guard stopped beside a black curtain. "He's in there. You've got a few minutes."

I wiped my palms on my jeans, nodded once, and slipped inside.

The backstage world felt like another dimension of half shadow, half gold. Light spilled from an open dressing room door, catching on cables, bottles of water, sweat-stained towels.

Sullivan sat on a flight case near the far wall, a towel draped around his neck. His hair was damp, falling into his eyes.

He looked a little older than when I'd known him in Crystal Cliffs, but still impossibly, heartbreakingly beautiful. His hands rested loosely on his knees, and he glanced up as I stepped closer, sea-glass eyes narrowing like he was trying to bring me into focus.

"Brynn. It *is* you."

"It's me."

"I wasn't sure." His voice was roughened from two hours of singing. "From the stage, I thought … but I couldn't believe it was you." He exhaled, like he had been holding his breath. "I took a chance. Told security that if I was wrong, then I just ended up with a pretty girl backstage. But I had to know."

My heart felt like it had detached from its rightful place in my chest and was rattling around in my throat. "I can't believe you recognized me."

He gave a tired smile. "I remember your face. We spent some time together, didn't we? And you don't forget someone who got to witness your world burning down."

"Or was responsible for setting the fire."

He slid off the case. "I never blamed you for that. You were as much a victim as I was." He took a step toward me. "Is it all right if I hug you?"

I managed a nod. He closed the space between us. My head fit under his chin. His skin smelled of soap, but his shirt held a hint of cigarette smoke.

"I used to wonder what happened to you." His voice rumbled. So low it was more like a vibration. "Whether you made it out—"

"I did," I cut in. "Barely."

We pulled apart. He obviously hadn't seen any of the news reports about Maeve and me as missing persons.

His expression was shadowed. "Yeah. Me too. Barely, I mean."

"I always wondered how you got out."

He huffed out a dark laugh. "One day, I'll tell you." He dragged a hand through his hair. "You look ... the same. How old *are* you now?"

"I'll be twenty in March."

He nodded. "You look great, actually."

"You look..." I tilted my head. Did I tell him that he looked incredible? Too many girls probably said that to him. "Different. But not really."

Then, as if the main point of this whole thing had just occurred to him, a smile danced across his lips. "How did you even get here?" He glanced toward the door. "You didn't come alone, did you?"

"No, I came with Maeve—Maeve Robbins. Remember her?"

He sucked air through his teeth. "I think so. Honestly, I've blotted out a lot of faces, a lot of names." His eyes were haunted. "I try not to think about that time."

"We came with Maeve's boyfriend in an RV. We were in Ohio too. And next, New York." I beamed. "We're stoneheads."

He laughed. "Oh, don't say that. It makes me cringe every time." He hung his hands from the back of his neck. "Where are you staying?"

"I'm supposed to leave with Maeve and her boyfriend in the RV, right after this. Whenever we finish talking."

"Good. Don't go anywhere alone." His tone carried the quiet, protective edge I remembered from before.

"It's really you," he said again, almost to himself. "You said you're going to New York?"

"Yes."

"Meet me backstage after that show. I'll put your name on the list. We'll spend some time together. I won't be in such a rush then. We can really talk."

"OK."

Someone called his name from the hallway, and he held up a hand. "Be there in a sec." Then he moved toward me again, placed his hands on my arms. "Be careful, Brynn."

"I will."

Sullivan signaled to a man in a black fitted polo and tactical pants. "Hey, Dart, make sure she gets where she needs to go." He glanced at me once more over his shoulder. "See you in New York."

The seats were a ghost town of empty cups, wadded paper, and even someone's sneaker lying like roadkill as a janitor pushed the discarded items into a bin.

I glanced out of the corner of my eye at the man Sullivan had called "Dart." He had a massive physique, with closely shorn hair and a neatly trimmed goatee. A clear coil descended from behind his ear and disappeared into the collar of his shirt. His small, dark eyes were fixed in front of him, constantly shifting left, then right. He seemed to be monitoring our surroundings with the precision of a hawk and reminded me a little of the man who ran security for Astra Cynthia.

"You see your friends here?" Dart dipped a hand toward the brick-like radio holstered at his side.

I panned the rows of seats from one end to the other. Maeve and Teddy were nowhere.

"No."

It was like being in the community center after everyone had cleared out, all the noise sucked away.

Dart pressed a finger to his earpiece, listening.

"They were supposed to meet me here. Maybe they're in the lobby?"

Dart walked slightly ahead of me and to the side as we traveled into the lobby, past the dark concession counters. I checked the corridor to the restrooms—nothing. No sign of them.

Where were they? Of course, they had just reunited. Would they have slipped out to the RV to spend a moment alone? I'd been backstage for a while.

"Maybe they went to the RV." The fizzy beginnings of fear bubbled in my chest.

Dart nodded. "I'll accompany you out there."

We began walking toward the exit. "Are you the only security guard still here?"

"I'm actually a bodyguard, ma'am. I travel with the band."

Oh. I hadn't considered that. But with Sullivan's past— and everything that had come after—it fit.

The parking lot was nearly empty, just iced-over puddles gleaming under streetlights and the line of cars still making their way out of the lot. It was freezing cold, and my breath puffed out in clouds of condensation.

"The RVs usually park over here, ma'am," he said, pointing toward the exit gate.

But the lot was empty. No headlights. No engines running. No sign the RV had ever been there.

The panic started small—a candle flame in my stomach —but spread fast.

Maybe they went to get gas. Maybe they thought I'd already left. Maybe…

Even as the excuses formed, I knew better. Maeve wouldn't leave without me. Not unless something had gone really wrong.

Chuck Crow. I'd thought I'd seen him earlier in the lobby, except I'd decided it couldn't have been him. Could it?

I spun toward Dart, breath catching in the frigid air. "They're not here."

He studied my face, then let out a slow breath and glanced toward the dark stretch of highway beyond the fence. "All right, ma'am. We're not staying out here. Let's take another look inside, and I'll notify the principal."

The principal? What, or who, was that?

His shoulder mic chirped. Dart pressed a thumb to the push-to-talk button clipped near his collar. "Copy. Returning the guest."

As we moved back toward the arena, Dart stayed close behind. I felt the controlled pressure of his presence steering me. He pulled open the heavy side door, and the blast of stale heat inside wrapped around me like a blanket, buffering the cold that had sunk its claws into my ribs.

We swept the lobby again. Nothing. No one. I glanced at the spot where I thought I'd seen Chuck Crow. Now the booth was only a folding table with a cardboard box.

Dart keyed his mic. "Lobby's clear." A beat later, he touched his earpiece, listening. "Understood."

He turned to me. "Ma'am, the principal requests you be returned to him."

"The principal?"

Dart nodded.

"Sullivan?"

He nodded again.

A different kind of panic pricked at me, spearheaded by

embarrassment and dread at being a problem. "Oh, I don't want to bother him."

Dart stopped, fixing me with an unwavering, professional stare. "I've been given my instructions."

My pulse thudded in my ears as we moved down the corridor. At the far end, Sullivan was talking with one of the techs. He turned at the sound of our footsteps, and his expression shifted instantly, fatigue disappearing, concern taking its place.

"What's going on?" he asked.

"The RV lot's empty," Dart reported. "No sign of her friends."

The sting behind my eyes surprised me. "I'm sorry, Sullivan. I didn't mean to drag you into this. If someone can just take me to the bus station, I'll—"

"No." His gaze swung back to me. "You're sure you didn't have a different meeting spot? You don't have a cell phone?"

I shook my head, clenching my fists until my nails bit into my palms. "No."

Something unspoken passed between us. He must have guessed the thoughts coursing through my brain.

He jerked his chin toward the back doors. "All right. Bring her out."

"Out where?" I asked.

He hesitated, then met my eyes. "We'll figure this out in the morning. You're coming with us tonight. To New York."

"I can't—"

"Yes, you can." His voice was calm but firm. "I'm not letting you wander around Milwaukee in the dark, in the freezing cold."

Dart gestured toward the loading dock. "Transport is ready."

I followed them, half in a daze.

Part of me wanted to argue that I didn't need help, I'd find my own way, but the words wouldn't form. My mind was sluggish with fatigue and distress. Because, really, he was right. Where was I going to go?

Every sound rattled in my ears—the shuffle of my feet against concrete, the swish of Sullivan's leather jacket as he walked. As we stepped out into the cold night air, wet against my face, the city lights blurred in the mist. The band's tour bus idled under the streetlamp, black and chrome, windows tinted, engine purring.

Sullivan stepped aside to let me climb on first.

Inside it was warm and heavy with the unfamiliar smell of beer, boys, and an extra layer of smoke. I gripped the edge of the nearest seat as I propelled myself along.

The other three band members and two women all looked up, their eyes startled, curious. They were scattered through the narrow aisle, half-packed duffel bags and open pizza boxes between them.

Jared, the drummer—wiry and tattooed to the elbows—chomped on a burger. "Uh, we're picking up strays now?" he asked with a full mouth.

"Long story," Sullivan said. "This is Brynn. She's a friend."

The words hung in the air. *A friend.*

Someone snorted.

Sullivan moved into the center of the group, gesturing to each one. "Brynn, this is Jared—drums. Nate, guitarist extraordinaire. And that's Red back there on bass."

Jared gave a lazy salute with two fingers. "Hey."

Nate, blond and sharp-featured, nodded once, cautious but not unkind. "Hey there." A raven-haired woman sitting beside him squinted at me.

Red—older, quiet, half-hidden behind a curtain of graying hair—lifted a hand in greeting before turning back to the open fridge. "You two hungry? There's plenty of pizza."

"I'll eat in a while." Sullivan handed me a bottle of water.

Red spoke in a low drawl. "Aw, you're gonna give her water, Sullivan? Shit, we got some stronger stuff in the fridge, and…" He eyed me. "She looks like she might need some of that right now."

I shook my head, clutching the water bottle. "I'm fine, thanks."

"She's had a long night," Sullivan said.

Red closed the fridge with a soft thud.

Sullivan motioned to the couch along the wall. "You can sit if you want."

I lowered myself carefully onto the soft fabric. Red clicked a lighter and lit a cigarette. Jared wadded up his empty hamburger wrapper.

The bus vibrated, and we were on the move.

Sullivan stood in the aisle, one hand braced on a seat-back, his presence filling the narrow space. "These guys can sometimes be assholes," he said. "But no one is going to touch you." He leaned over and made deliberate eye contact with Jared. "Right?" Then he straightened and looked at me. "You're safe here."

Safe. The word was too unfamiliar to be trusted.

Chapter Twenty-Two

FEBRUARY 1999

"Songs for Ghosts"

Nate brushed past Sullivan with a guitar case. "Bunks are full up tonight."

I glanced toward the narrow hallway where the sleeping compartments lined both sides—six cubbies, curtains already drawn shut. A soft laugh came from one of them, a woman's voice.

The other woman sat next to Nate on the front couch, glossy hair as dark as mine spilling over her shoulder, her bare feet tucked under her. Nate didn't even seem to notice her as he positioned his headphones over his ears.

The woman's eyes flicked to me, no doubt assessing "the stray" Sullivan had picked up after a show.

After a while, she climbed into a bunk. Nate followed her a few minutes later.

Sullivan's voice came from behind me. "That's Brooke. She's with us for a few weeks. Crew support." He laughed at his own description. "Anyway, don't mind her. She can be a little prickly, but she's basically a nice person."

I had no reason to mind anything or anyone. I wasn't even supposed to be here.

Sullivan sat at the table in the front and pulled out a notebook. Every so often, he glanced over at me. It was strange. Once, we'd been so close when we lived at Crystal Cliffs. We'd talked about all sorts of things. Now there was an awkwardness between us that seemed to preclude conversation.

I put my head against the window and felt the cold air flowing through the seams. Every time the bus hit a bump, the walls creaked like an old ship shifting on open water. I should have slept, but the bus's rhythm kept me awake. Headlights passed in a blur, sending a strobe across the narrow aisle. The world outside was all shadow and motion —gas stations, truck stops, towns that existed only for a blink before dissolving back into the dark.

I closed my eyes for a few minutes at a time but finally gave up on sleep. My mind churned with fears and confusion. How had I ended up here?

The lounge area was dim, lit only by the faint blue glow from the dashboard up front. Sullivan moved his pen in short bursts, occasionally looking up, as if trying to remember something or hear music in his head.

His gaze landed on me, watching him. "Can't sleep either?"

I pulled my knees up onto the seat. "Not really."

"You get used to sleeping on the road. Mostly. Although sometimes I still wake up thinking I'm somewhere else."

I slid out of my seat and moved to sit opposite him. "What are you writing?"

He glanced down at the notebook. "Trying to finish a

song. Every time I think I've got the words, I look at them again, and it's like they vanish, or they don't sound right." He leaned back, eyes flicking toward the dark window. He pushed the notebook away. "I can't believe you're here." He shook his head a little. "I never thought I'd see you again."

"After you left, I didn't think I'd see you again either."

"That whole world seems like a lifetime ago." He clasped his hands on the table. "How are you feeling about all of that, where we came from. I mean, where's your head at?"

I passed a hand across my eyes. "Right now, my head is everywhere."

"I'll bet."

I leaned forward. "How does it feel to be famous? You broke away, and you got everything you wanted."

Sullivan ran a thumb along the notebook's edge. "When I left, I thought this world…" He held out his hands, motioned to the walls of the tour bus. "I thought the music would drown that place out of my head, you know? Her voice, everything that happened there. The forced obedience." He sat back. "But sometimes I think fame's just another version of that. Different master, same leash."

"Aren't you happy?"

"I'm not unhappy," he said.

Someone was snoring loudly in a bunk, keeping time with the bus engine.

"You made something out of all of it," I said. "That's what matters."

His eyes were wide, luminescent. "You did too. You got out. Like me."

Why, then, didn't I feel freer? Instead, there was a weight to where I was right then, of the bus gliding through the night, carrying us somewhere between the past and the next town, of how I didn't know where I'd be in another day or two.

But I was with Sullivan.

His voice drifted through the twilight of my brain. "You should try to sleep. Tomorrow's a long day."

"I can't really sleep sitting up."

He stood and motioned with his head toward the back of the bus. "Come on."

I followed him along the narrow corridor. "You can take the lounge. Couch folds out. It's the best we've got."

"But where will you sleep?"

He shrugged. "There's another couch up front, and I don't really sleep much."

The gesture—giving me his bed—was so like how I remembered him. Always generous, always sacrificial.

He pushed the door open. A folded blanket rested on a couch, a pile of notebooks stacked near the window.

I hovered in the doorway. "Are you sure? I don't want to displace you."

He chuckled. "Displace me? No, you're not displacing me, Brynn. You'll be more comfortable back here."

I stepped inside, fingers brushing the edge of the couch as I turned to look at him. "Thank you."

He hesitated a second longer, like he might say something else, but he didn't.

"Sleep well." The door scraped shut as he pulled it closed behind him.

I stretched out on the couch and pulled the blanket to my chin. Through the thin wall, I heard a man's laughter, a woman making sounds of pleasure.

Then, quieter, a sound from the front of the bus. Guitar strings. Sullivan, playing his unfinished song.

Morning. Light slanted through the narrow windows as the bus came to a stop. I nestled close to the wall and looked out. We were parked at a rest area. Outside, the band milled around, stretching, smoking, leaning against the guardrail, hugging themselves, shivering in the cold.

I emerged from the lounge area and found Sullivan sitting near the open door of the bus, guitar in hand, quietly tuning.

He glanced up. "Morning."

"Morning."

"You hungry?"

I shook my head. "Not yet."

He strummed the strings once and then stopped the sound with his hand. "We'll hit New York in a few hours."

The morning air snapped with a cold bite as I stepped down from the bus. Beyond the trees and the gray fog stretching over the hills, cars zipped by on the highway.

Red crouched by the curb, tying his boots. Jared leaned against the guardrail, cigarette secured between two fingers. The woman with long, straight black hair lit a cigarette off his. Nate paced, phone pressed to his ear, nodding at something being said on the other line.

No one seemed surprised to see me anymore. Just another face in the revolving door of tour life, I supposed.

Sullivan descended the bus steps, holding his heavy leather jacket closed. The morning light caught in his eyes, turning them to liquid glass. "You need coffee?"

"I'm good," I lied.

I didn't want Sullivan to assume he needed to do one thing for me beyond what was absolutely necessary. Coffee felt like a luxury right now. One I couldn't afford.

He arched his back and stretched, his long torso lifting the fabric of his shirt until skin was exposed—the tops of his hipbones. "Next stop's in Jersey for fuel and breakfast. You can grab whatever you want there."

I shoved my hands into the pockets of my thin jacket. "I probably shouldn't keep tagging along, Sullivan. I mean— this is *your* life."

He blinked. "It's just a bus, Brynn. You're not taking anyone's place."

"I don't want to be a problem."

"You're not." His gaze drifted toward the line of trees behind the restrooms, his voice quieter. "And don't mind these guys—if they say anything to you. You're just … new."

"New?" I laughed a little. "What does that mean?"

Even though the lower half of his face was covered in probably a week's worth of stubble, I could see the creases appearing at the sides of his mouth. He glanced up at me and then quickly darted his eyes toward Nate and Jared. "You know, women sometimes get on the bus. But it's usually for pretty specific reasons."

My face burned off the cold that had settled there. "You mean, they think—"

"Who knows what they think," he cut in, rubbing the back of his neck. "I haven't told them who you are. Or that I knew you in Crystal Cliffs. They're probably wondering why we aren't—"

"Sharing a bed," I finished.

"Yeah." He snickered. "Welcome to the road, Brynn."

I shifted my eyes toward Nate, who had his arm around the waist of the girl Sullivan had called Brooke. She put her arms around his neck and hung there while the two of them exchanged laughter and low chatter.

"You should get to know Brooke. She'll watch out for you too."

"Are you going to tell them how we know each other?" I asked.

"Maybe." The corner of his mouth lifted. "Hey, remember when Astra Cynthia said the world outside—the Gray—would eat us up? Like the big scary monster she used to tell the kids was waiting in the closet for them if they were bad?"

"She told you that?"

He chuckled, pushed his hair off his forehead. "Yeah. She didn't tell you that?"

I shook my head. "No. But after that time in the closet with you, Astra Cynthia told me that if I'd done anything with you that I shouldn't have, one night, when I was sleeping, the floor in my bedroom would open up, and the earth would swallow me."

He ballooned his eyes. "Wow. Shit. You win. I'll deal with the monster any day."

I smiled. "I didn't believe it, though. I was past believing her at that point."

A blast of wind swept through, cutting through my thin coat as if I weren't wearing one at all.

Sullivan visibly shivered too. "Come on. Let's get back on the bus. It's frickin' freezing out here."

His long legs took the steps in two bounds. Then he turned, reached out a hand for me to grab. I did, even though I didn't need it.

Back inside, I swung onto the couch, hugging myself, my teeth knocking against each other. "Maybe Astra Cynthia wasn't wrong."

He stood in front of me, a giant looking down on me with diamond eyes. "About what?"

"Maybe that monster, the world, has eaten us both."

He tilted his head back, like he was thinking about that. "Yeah, well, I'd rather be eaten by a monster than live in her horror show."

He shrugged out of his coat and tossed it over my shoulders. "What's with that jacket you're wearing. That is not the kind of thing you wear in the north. Why don't you have a real coat?"

"I had one. I lost it in Ohio."

And then we lost $5,000 of Astra Cynthia's money in Chicago. I still hadn't told him about that.

"Keep the coat," he said.

I started to protest, but he quickly moved on to another subject. "We're playing a small venue tonight. You can stay on the bus during sound check if you want."

"I'll be fine. I want to watch you play. I already have tickets. Maeve and I saved enough to buy tickets for the first three shows before we left."

Maeve. I couldn't stop thinking about where she was. What had happened to her? To Teddy?

Sullivan cocked his head. "Well, you can leave those seats to some other interloper. I got a way better place for you to sit."

"No, I probably should take my ticketed seat—in case Maeve and Teddy show up. I want to be there if they do."

His gaze lingered, searching. "You sure?"

"I'm sure."

I pulled his coat tighter around me and looked out the vast bus window at the highway beyond. The horizon felt endless, but I knew it wasn't. This couldn't last. Eventually, I would have to step off this bus. At some point, the past would catch up. And then what?

Chapter Twenty-Three

NOW

It's been a while since I've done a road trip. I've forgotten how much I love the drive, the solitude.

The highway opens up. Charleston slips behind me in pieces, marsh grass dark with morning dew, the low sweep of bridges, the last familiar exit numbers.

I drive with the windows cracked, the spring air cool, the sky still undecided about what kind of day it wants to be.

And of course, there's music.

I alternate between streaming the 90s and the 2000s, the era when Cutter's music was most prominent. A song I haven't heard in years comes on, bringing with it some of the things I've worked hard at switching off. I almost switch the song off, but then I don't. I let it play all the way through, even as memory flickers at the edges of my vision. Cheap motel rooms, late nights at Denny's, early mornings at rest stops.

I have to stay clear-headed. I'm not that girl anymore. But I also can't pretend she never existed. Whatever waits for me in Nashville—I'm ready for it. Whatever the outcome, I'll accept it.

Traffic thickens, then thins. I count exits. Time stretches and collapses. Somewhere between one mile marker and the next, I talk to myself, rehearse what I'll say when I see him.

The road bends west, sunlight breaking fully through the clouds now, bright enough to make me squint. I stop once for coffee at a place that Sullivan would have loved, where the waitress calls me "hon" and my booth backs up to a couple on their honeymoon, a fact I learn through overhearing snippets of their conversation.

My phone buzzes against the tabletop, and I grab it, expecting to see Sullivan's name on the screen. Instead, it's a text from Paul.

Text me when you get there so I know you arrived safely.

I sit back. I had to tell Paul about this trip, of course. We're business partners, and my absence affects the nonprofit. Possibly, we're something else as well … just not sure what yet. I love that he's concerned, but there's a part of me that wants this trip Paul-free.

Even so, I type back. *I will. Thank you.*

I set the phone face down again and sip my coffee, watching the couple in the next booth lean close, their laughter hushed and private. It's a warm and fuzzy kind of moment that makes me feel a little squishy inside because I know what that feels like.

The television mounted in the corner above the counter plays some news show, the volume low but not muted. I'm only half paying attention, but then I hear her name.

"Astra Cynthia…"

My whole body jerks, and I slosh coffee over the rim of the mug.

Her face fills the screen. She's older now, her silver-streaked hair pulled back, her expression neutral as she's escorted up the steps of a courthouse. The chyron reads *Group leader arrested in multi-state investigation.* Words like *fraud, coercion, financial abuse* scroll beneath her image, clinical and incomplete.

The reporter keeps talking. Former members. Ongoing inquiries. More arrests expected.

I parse through all the emotions hitting me at once—relief, vindication, triumph. I never thought any of those people would be brought to justice.

I nearly call Paul, but then I stop myself.

No, the first person I should discuss this news with is Sullivan.

Chapter Twenty-Four

NEW YORK CITY, MARCH 1999

"Glass and Fire"

I'd always wanted to go to New York City. The books I'd read, TV shows I'd watched, painted it as a glamorous and fun place. But as the bus rose onto a bridge, high enough to make my stomach dip, and the whole skyline opened in front of me, a jagged wall of towers stabbing up into a sky, New York didn't seem as much like a city as another planet.

Down below the bridge, the water churned, dark and restless, tugging at the pylons. Ahead of us—lights. Even in daylight, some windows were already glowing. It looked like every star I'd never been allowed to wish on had fallen into this one place.

Yellow taxis swarmed the lanes like bright insects, darting and cutting between cars with seemingly no fear of dying. Horns screamed sharp bursts of sound. Everywhere, people rushed along sidewalks in business suits, wearing backpacks, carrying shopping bags.

I rested my forehead against the window glass as the bus

turned onto a narrower street where the buildings leaned in, blocking out the sky. I replayed my conversation with Sullivan from earlier, while still holding his coat around me.

He was in a different headspace altogether by then, talking to his manager, his bandmates, and sound techs. This was his world. I was just standing in it for a moment. And I wasn't prepared for any of it.

From the outside, Le Hall Heureux resembled any other anonymous Manhattan doorway on a street full of them. The moment I stepped inside, I fell through a trapdoor into another world that didn't care who I was or where I came from.

The ceilings were vaulted and shadowed, the inside of an old cathedral someone had turned into a nightclub.

I'd agreed to watch the first part of the concert from backstage.

"I'd really rather you stay backstage the whole time," Sullivan said. "It's safer for you."

"I know, but I have to see if Maeve and Teddy show up. I have to know if something happened to them."

Sullivan nodded. "Promise me you'll come right back as soon as you've got confirmation one way or the other." He shot a glance toward Dart, standing sentinel near the emergency exit. "I'll put Dart on the door. He'll let you back in."

Someone called Sullivan's name, and he was gone again.

Brooke perched beside me on a folding chair. She wore a black crop top and a denim jacket covered in Sharpie signatures, a patch that read *Faithless and Free* sewn above the pocket.

"You ever been to one of these before?" she yelled loud enough to cut through the pre-show noise.

"This'll be my third show. But I've never watched from backstage before."

She grinned, tugging at the hem of her sleeve. "Watching the band from here, standing on the stage with them, it'll eat you alive in the best way. It's like … a religious experience." Brooke popped a piece of gum into her mouth and chewed. "You knew Sullivan from before?"

Before. "Yes. We sort of grew up together."

She nodded. "Thought so. In the cult, right?"

"Yeah." Even then, knowing what I did about Crystal Cliffs and Astra Cynthia and her methods of control, I still flinched whenever anyone used the word *cult*. "Did he tell you that he knew me before?"

"Well, I knew he *knew* you." She shrugged. "The way he looked at you earlier. I had a feeling. That's all." She swiveled toward me. "How old are you, anyway?"

"I'll be twenty in a week."

She rolled her eyes. "Damn, girl. What I wouldn't give to be twenty again."

"How old are you?"

She lifted her chin. "Twenty-eight. Two years away from my life being over."

"Your life being over? Why?"

"Thirty, honey. The beginning of the end." She waved a hand and shifted toward the stage. "It's all downhill after that. Everything dries up. You're just old."

"You don't look old."

She gave me a sidelong glance. "I've got pretty good genes. I figure I gotta get all of this in before that." She circled her hands in the air, palms down. "By the time I'm thirty, I'll have to stop hanging out with rockers, find a real guy, start popping out kids." She grabbed a chunk of her hair, pulled it forward, started braiding it. "What are your plans? I mean, after the tour?"

Plans? Like I had any. Mercifully, before I had a chance to answer, the lights dropped and the crowd exploded.

The band rushed the dark stage, and the sound hit like a bomb. Bass, drums, and a wall of guitar shook the floor. Blue light projected the band's logo on the back wall.

Sullivan seemed to have materialized out of nowhere. He put his hand on my shoulder. "Wish me luck."

"Good luck."

"Break a leg," Brooke added.

Sullivan strode into the spotlight and raised his arms to the crowd.

Brooke stood, clapping her hands over her head.

At the mezzanine level, people leaned over the railing with their drinks, watching like royalty surveying a feast. Down on the floor, bodies swayed and collided.

Sullivan leaned into the mic and then yanked it from its stand. He was just a silhouette in red light. Between songs, he moved to the edge of the platform, sweat shining along his jaw, his eyes scanning the audience.

It was an odd feeling to watch someone you know become something the whole world wanted a piece of. Once upon a time, I had been Sullivan Stonecutter's friend. If his mother had gotten her way, we might have been married. Then came the thought that ripped through me like the scream of Nate's guitar: *It's not too late.*

The riff of "Den of Vipers" coiled through the air, the words twisting in my chest. "The den is dark and deep, and your soul is never yours to keep..."

Maeve and Teddy! I had almost forgotten. I yelled in Brooke's ear that I'd be back in a minute and made my way to the backstage exit, to Dart's station. He nodded as I approached, already walking as he adjusted his earpiece. He ushered me in front of him.

By the time I reached the corridor leading to the seating, some of the crowd was already spilling out—waves of people leaving before the curtain call, talking, laughing, buzzing with the afterglow of sound.

Maeve would be there. She had to be, her head thrown back in laughter, waving from the row where we were supposed to sit. She wouldn't miss this concert.

But when I reached the seats we'd bought months before, they were occupied by only one person. Teddy did a double-take, our eyes meeting as his face broke into disbelief. Then he fought his way across the other people in the row.

When he reached me, I threw my arms around him. "Where's Maeve?" I funneled my words directly into his ear canal. "I've been trying to—"

He pulled back, shaking his head. "She's gone, Brynn."

I cupped my hand to my ear. "What?"

He aimed his eyes toward the exit to the lobby. It was too loud to talk in here. Teddy grasped my hand as we descended the concrete steps, and Dart followed us all the way as we curved into the lobby and stopped next to a concession stand.

Teddy faced me. "I've been waiting here since sound check. I wasn't even sure you'd come."

"What happened to Maeve?"

His voice dropped. "They took her, Brynn. In Milwaukee. They got her."

My heart jolted. "What?"

"At the last show—we were waiting for you while you were backstage with Sullivan. They appeared out of nowhere. Pulled her away. Two guys dressed like everyone else. I never saw 'em coming. I tried to stop them, but—" He broke off, breath shuddering. "She didn't even fight them, Brynn. She just … went. Looked over her shoulder at me once, and that was it. Like she was walking to the merch tables instead of being dragged away. I tried to follow them in the RV, but…" He shook his head. "I mean, there was no way." He flapped his arms. "They took her back to Florida."

The world narrowed, the din of voices and music around us turning into a single sharp tone in my ears. "Did you call the police?"

"Yeah. They went to her house, talked to her. She told them everything was fine. That she had just gone home." He squinted. "At least I know she's still alive." He passed a hand over his mouth. "I tried to call her house—the number I had for her. Phone's been disconnected."

I braced a hand against the concessions counter, my mind thrashing. "She wouldn't go back there, Teddy. She said she'd never go back."

"Well, she did." Teddy's eyes were bloodshot, desperate. "They got to her, Brynn."

The words settled like cold iron in my stomach. The music inside the arena had stopped, replaced by the screaming crowd.

Teddy put his hand on my arm. "I was thinking maybe I should go there—to Crystal Cliffs."

"No, Teddy, don't, they'll—"

"Just to know she's all right."

I shook my head. "Please don't. They are dangerous, Teddy. They've made people disappear."

"I know. People like Maeve."

My mind leapt to what could be happening to her. The

torment they could be putting her through. It would be worse than anything I endured.

Did he want me to say I'd go with him? "I can't go back there."

He nodded. "Where are you going to go?"

People began spilling into the lobby. Dart stood behind me, waiting for my next move. I glanced toward the glass doors leading out to the street. Somewhere out there, the Cutter bus waited.

"I don't know where I'm going to go."

Chapter Twenty-Five

MARCH 1999

"Emotional Hangover"

The tour bus waited. Windows fogged, music leaking through the thin metal walls. Dart walked me across the slick pavement. All the while, Teddy's words replayed in my head. *They took her. She didn't fight.*

Why hadn't she fought? Was it the drugs? Or was there some old track in her brain that was reactivated when she saw them? A voice that whispered into her psyche that she couldn't say no.

Aboard the bus, Jared and Nate were on opposite couches, shouting over each other, half-empty bottles in hand. Brooke leaned against the counter, grinning at something Red had said.

A girl I'd never seen before was dancing in the aisle—head tipped back, hair a burnished copper under the overhead lights. She moved like she was underwater, slow and unbothered, the guys cheering her on.

"Excuse me." Dart's low voice cut through the noise. "Coming through."

They all stopped, looked up, their faces straightening. Dart was obviously a man who commanded immediate attention and respect.

Brooke pushed away from the counter with some effort. "You're back. Did you find what you were looking for?" Her words were slurred.

Jared gave a lazy salute. "Dart, my man! Bring us more recruits?"

Then Nate's voice: "It's just Sullivan's girl."

"Oh, yeah."

Sullivan's girl?

I kept my head down, clutching Sullivan's coat around me as we wove through the chaos. Someone's laughter burst too close to my ear.

Sullivan sat at the back of the lounge, half in shadow. He was drinking a beer, leaning close to the blond sitting beside him. His hand rested lightly on her shoulder as she said something in his ear. Whatever it was made him smile.

He didn't see me at first. His arm was around her shoulders, and he stared into her eyes, seemingly engaged with every word she said. He brushed a strand of hair away from her face and looked like he might lean in to kiss her.

I felt like all the oxygen had been siphoned out of my lungs.

Dart cleared his throat softly. "All secure, sir," he said.

Sullivan jerked his head up. The change in his face was immediate, and his expression flickered through a reel of emotions as he jolted out of his seat, his head smacking the overhang. Wincing, he put a hand to his temple. "Brynn, this is uh…" He looked over at the girl, blinking, rubbing the back of his head.

"Sheila," she answered for him.

"Yeah. Sheila."

The woman glanced between us, reading the shift in the air. "I should check on Jared." She stood and squeezed Sullivan's arm once before slipping past me, perfume trailing.

Sullivan watched her go, then turned back to me. "You made it."

"Yeah." My voice came out raw.

He nodded. "Everything all right?"

I almost laughed. *All right.* The word felt meaningless now. "I found Teddy. Alone. He said they took Maeve."

That got his attention. His posture stiffened, the color draining from his face. "What do you mean they took her?"

"At the Milwaukee show. He said she didn't even fight them."

He shoved a hand into his hair and held it there. "And he's sure it was them?"

"He said two men. Looked like any other concertgoers."

"Why would she go with them?"

The noise from the front lounge swelled—Brooke's laughter, a bottle clinking against the counter, someone shouting lyrics over the music.

"Shut up!" Sullivan bellowed.

The volume dropped slightly, punctuated with expletives and mutterings.

"Maeve stole money," I blurted.

"What?"

"She stole $5,000 from Astra Cynthia."

His shoulders dropped. "Shit, Brynn. That's serious."

"I know."

"They'll crucify her." He swept a hand over his mouth,

and the sound was like sandpaper across wood. "And you, if they catch you."

I nodded. "I know."

"Come on." He reached for my hand, and the warm, secure grasp of his fingers sent a charge up my arm as he led me toward the back lounge, where the lights were low. The small space was a haven of quiet compared to the chaos up front. He closed the door behind us.

For a moment, neither of us spoke.

His blue eyes bored into me. "I'll make some calls in the morning. See what I can find out. But you need to rest, Brynn. You look more tired than I feel."

Of course Sullivan was exhausted. He had just finished a two-hour set. The rush of adrenaline must have been subsiding.

Questions pounded in my brain. What had they done to Maeve? Were they still looking for me? And who was the blond girl Sullivan had been with?

He walked to the waist-high fridge on the opposite wall, opened it, and pulled out two beers.

He held them up. "You want one?"

I stared at the brown bottle.

"Or would you rather have something stronger?"

"I'll have a beer." Right then, I'd have welcomed anything to calm my heart, my head.

He used a bottle opener to pop the tops on both and handed me one. I took it, tipped it up, and let the fizzy, bitter beverage slide down my throat.

Outside the thin wall, someone cranked up the music.

I motioned toward the door with the bottle. "Do they know anything yet? Have you told them?"

"No one knows anything right now. And we'll keep it that way."

I turned the bottle, watching condensation bead and slide. "That time they caught us in the closet…"

His eyes flicked up, but he didn't interrupt.

"They took you to the Think Tank. Didn't they?"

A muscle in his jaw pulsed. "Yeah."

My voice barely carried over the hum of the bus. "What did they do to you in there?"

He stared past me.

"I need to know, Sullivan. I need to know what they're doing to Maeve."

His voice was low. "They make you sit. For a long time. No windows. No clock. They ask you a lot of questions." His Adam's apple bobbed. "They don't touch you at first. That's the worst part. They want you afraid of what *might* happen."

My stomach curled in on itself.

"They tell you who you are. Who you belong to. What you owe." His eyes came back to mine. "And they don't let you leave until you agree."

"Agree to what?"

"To whatever version of the truth they decide you need."

I hugged Sullivan's coat tighter around myself. "How can I help her?"

"You can't." He put the beer to his lips with one hand and grabbed the remote from the table with the other, clicking the TV on. "You want to watch something?" He settled next to me on the couch. "Or would you rather sleep?"

The blue light washed over the room.

The way he skirted the subject planted dread deep in my chest. "You don't think anything can be done to help her now, do you?"

He shook his head slowly.

Red's voice carried through the thin door. "Brooke, grab that bottle. Give me a refill."

I looked over at Sullivan. "Doesn't seem like they're going to bed anytime soon."

He blinked. "You can sleep in here again."

"What about you?"

A small smile tugged at his lips. "This is where I usually sleep, so … if you don't mind, I'll join you."

I took another swallow of beer.

He stretched his arm along the back of the couch, not quite touching me, but close enough that the warmth radiated from his skin.

I turned back to the TV. It was on a news station. The image was familiar—black iron gates, a security shelter monitoring the comings and goings. And then, the face of a woman I'd known all my life.

Mama.

The headline crawled across the bottom: *Missing Girl Returns Home. Authorities Continue to Seek Information on Second Missing Woman.*

My breath caught. My own face stared back at me, smiling that practiced, obedient smile from another life.

Sullivan set his bottle down slowly. "Shit."

The female reporter's voice was animated as she held out a microphone toward my mother. "What would you like to say to your daughter, if she's listening?"

Mama's face was void of makeup, only a little lipstick. Maybe it was the camera lighting, but the lines around her eyes were pronounced, and gray roots defined the part in her hair. She looked like she'd just rolled out of bed.

"Brynn," Mama said, "please come home. We all love

you. We're worried about you. We want to know you're OK. That's all."

The reporter turned to the camera, holding the microphone and speaking into it. "Twenty-year-old Maeve Robbins has been found and safely returned to her home in Florida. But the search continues for nineteen-year-old Brynn Cole, who, according to Robbins, is staying with friends and avoiding contact."

Sullivan inhaled sharply through his nose. "She said you're avoiding contact. They're twisting it already."

The reporter's voice droned on in the background, polished and detached.

I looked up at the screen, my mother's face. I couldn't stand it anymore. I reached for the remote, but Sullivan got there first. He clicked the TV off, the screen collapsing into a dark reflection of us both—two ghosts staring back.

The silence that followed echoed with my mother's voice: *We all love you. We want to know you're OK.*

Sullivan cradled the remote. "When I left, they tried the same thing with me. Letters to my parents, press statements."

The heater kicked on, blowing warm air across my face, but it didn't touch the chill that had settled deep inside me. "Sullivan, what am I going to do?" I choked on the words.

"You'll keep moving with us. Moving is safer for you, harder for them to find you. And if they come for you…" He gave a quick shake of his head. "I'll make them wish they never laid eyes on either one of us."

He reached for me, pulled me against him. This was only the second time he'd hugged me—the first time when we'd met backstage. But this time was different. His embrace lingered, and his words hung in the air between us.

I knew he meant them, but no one defied Astra Cynthia without paying for it. Sullivan knew that too.

His hand moved up and down my back in slow, absent strokes, like he was trying to calm both of us. The heat seeped through my skin, and the tears I'd been holding finally fell—silent, unstoppable.

It was the first time in weeks I'd felt anything that resembled safety. Even so, I recognized a similar feeling to the one I'd experienced in the closet with Sullivan all those years ago. Desire. A longing to be close to him in a way I'd never been with anyone else.

Finally, he pulled away. "All right. Listen to me. We don't say a word about this to anyone. None of the guys, not the crew. Not yet. Not until we have to."

I nodded. "OK."

"We've got one more concert and then we've got some time off before the Woodstock reunion. You could come with me. We'll go somewhere and hide out for a few weeks." He was talking fast, seemingly speaking whatever thought came into his head.

"Why—why would you do that? For me? I mean, I'm just some girl who used to live next door."

"Brynn," he said, his voice quiet but steely, "you were never just the girl next door."

Chapter Twenty-Six

NOW

I stop in Greenville, South Carolina, for the night. I've already booked my stay at a basic chain hotel off the highway. Next to it is a restaurant with a bar called Shorty's.

I shower, change clothes, sit on the edge of the bed for a minute to watch the news. There's more information about Astra Cynthia's impending arrest. She's not the only one. Apparently, Chuck Crow is holed up with her too, along with a couple of other community officers I don't recognize, and a dozen or so Crystal Cliffs inhabitants.

I switch the channel off the news before it cycles back on. I don't need to see Astra Cynthia's face again. Ever. I hope the police drive her and Chuck Crow out of their bunker. I hope she's convicted and spends the rest of her life in jail to make up for all the years and people she imprisoned, tortured, and murdered in Crystal Cliffs. Because yes, I fervently believe she's responsible for many deaths. I'm just thankful my mother is finally out of that place. Even though I don't actually know where she is these days.

The restaurant next door has a sports bar vibe.

Several games are playing on four separate screens hanging over the bar, and the fifth screen plays the news on a loop. I grab one of the only seats available and order a cabernet.

The bartender is an older man with graying hair and a little paunch around the middle and under his eyes. His cheeks bear the ruddy coloring of a drinker, and he chats up several of the customers. Probably a regular.

Above us, the news cuts back in with grainy footage of Crystal Cliffs from the air, a live feed. *Crystal Cliffs standoff enters second day.*

The familiar layout of the communal hall, the gardens, the houses, flashes across the screen. I shudder. I'd know that place anywhere, could draw it from memory.

The camera lens is dotted with raindrops but shows the community center from a distance, with police cruisers angled across the drive, yellow tape fluttering in the wind. The building looks smaller than I remember, less imposing. The front doors are closed, apparently barricaded from the inside.

A female reporter stands in a yellow rain jacket, hood pulled up, blinking against the precipitation.

"Authorities say Astra Cynthia and senior administrator Chuck Crow remain inside the main hall along with fifteen others, and have refused all attempts at negotiation…"

Someone at the bar lets out a sharp laugh. "You gotta be kidding me."

A man two stools down leans forward, elbows on the bar. "They're holed up in there? Like a damn Waco situation?"

Another voice pipes up from a young guy sitting beside me, wearing a Clemson baseball cap. "Why don't they just go in and drag 'em out?"

The bartender cranes his neck to watch the TV. "Because they're afraid of a PR nightmare."

The guy a couple of stools down has the heavy-lidded eyes and slurred speech that suggest he's been here for a while. Mid-forties, maybe. Lean with sunken cheeks. His work shirt is untucked, with a logo stitched over the pocket —something industrial, HVAC, or electrical.

He shakes his head. "I still don't get how anyone falls for this stuff. Barricaded leader, end-of-the-world bullshit. How stupid do you have to be?"

I drink my drink, peruse the menu, let the images flicker overhead and the debate flare beside me.

"Idiots, all of them. I mean, how stupid do you have to be to fall for something like that?" The drunk guy asks again.

I set down my drink, lean forward, and make eye contact with him. "People don't usually fall for *cults*. They fall for belonging."

He stretches his neck to talk around the guy sitting between us. "Same difference."

"No," I say. "Belonging is feeling like you mean something to someone. And these groups are good at making you feel special. Later, the locks and the control come in. By the time you realize the door only opens one way, it's too late to leave."

That seems to quiet him. He turns his face back to the television.

Now the news is showing an aerial shot again. Officers clustered. Negotiators waiting. The building sealed like a tomb.

The man squints at the screen. "Still. You'd think at some point you'd wake up."

"Some people do," I say. "And some people are afraid,

or they're brainwashed into thinking that the outside world is the real danger."

The drunk guy huffs. "Well. They chose it. I stand by what I said."

I pick up my glass, finish it slowly. "Some of them did choose. Others were born into it."

The bartender is watching me now, seemingly interested in how this conversation will go.

The man frowns. "Still seems obvious when it gets that extreme."

"Only in hindsight," I reply. "When you're inside, it doesn't feel extreme. It feels… incremental. Like boiling water, you don't notice until it's too hot to stay."

"I'd notice."

I meet his eyes. "Most people think that."

"Blow 'em all up, I say. They deserve whatever's coming to 'em," the man mutters. Then he drains his glass.

The guy in the Clemson hat turns toward me and anchors his arm on the bar. "You sound like you know a lot about this kind of thing."

I motion toward the TV. "I grew up near there." Not a lie. Just not the whole truth.

He nods, apparently satisfied. "Crazy world."

The bartender slides my check over. I pay, tip him well, and step back into the night air.

I don't replay the drunk man's words as much as the ease with which he said them.

How stupid do you have to be?

It's a sentence said with the comfort of knowing you'll never have to imagine yourself on the other side of it.

A few years ago, his words would've sent me spiraling with shame, the old reflex to defend, to explain, to justify. I would've cataloged every decision I'd ever made, every rule

I'd followed, every punishment I'd endured, and then I'd ask myself why I didn't run before I did. Why didn't Mama leave before she did?

It still hurts, but after years of podcasting and shadowing Paul in his interventions, I finally see it for what it is. People want to believe that danger will announce itself. They want to think manipulation wears a uniform, and that having a supposedly sound mind will give you armor against all such threats. They want to believe no such thing could ever happen to them.

I step into the elevator and watch the doors close on my reflection. Right now—on this road, between what I escaped and what I'm choosing—I don't need anyone to understand where I've been. I'm the only one who needs to do that.

Chapter Twenty-Seven

MARCH 1999

"Songs for Ghosts Part II"

When I woke, the bus was still moving. Pale light seeped through the blinds in thin lines, painting the walls in motion. Sullivan no longer lay next to me on the couch.

I quickly dressed and slid the accordion door aside, stepping out into the hallway. The bus creaked and shifted on its path toward Virginia—the last show for that leg of the tour.

The others were still asleep—or passed out. Empty bottles rolled in the aisle. A half-eaten sandwich sat on the counter beside an overturned ashtray. Someone's denim jacket lay across a table.

Brooke was curled under a blanket on one of the couches, mouth slightly open, eyeliner smudged like bruises beneath her eyes. Her bare shoulders hinted that she wasn't wearing anything else under the cover. Nate's legs spilled into the aisle, one hand still clutching the neck of a whiskey bottle. A thin haze of last night's cigarette smoke hung in the air, tinted gold by the weak morning light.

The whole place smelled like stale beer and cigarette smoke and something worse, like maybe someone had gotten sick.

Sullivan sat near the small table by the window. His head was bent, the pen moving fast, tapping the edge of the page every few seconds. There was a mug beside him and a guitar across his lap. As I approached him, I glimpsed the page filled with scrawled lines, crossed-out words, little arrows pointing to fragments of lyrics.

He looked up when I dropped onto the edge of the leather couch.

His eyes were heavy with exhaustion, his hair flattened at the crown. "Hey. Did you sleep?"

"A little." I wrapped my hands around my knees. "You?"

He gave a small shake of his head. "I don't sleep much after shows. It's hard to come down from the adrenaline."

I nodded toward the notebook. "New song?"

He glanced down at the page. "Yeah."

"What's it called?"

"Songs for Ghosts."

"Who's the ghost?"

He strummed a chord. "Sometimes I think every song I've written since I left that place has been about her—Astra Cynthia. But this one's about me."

I watched him, not sure if I was supposed to answer. The name—her name—still made something in me recoil.

He exhaled loudly. "After I left, I spent the first year touring. Spent the next two years kissing up to industry people, doing exactly what they wanted me to do, trying to become exactly who they wanted me to be." He slowly drew his eyes up to mine. "This life is hardly mine, Brynn." His hand raised to his chest. "I'm the ghost."

Outside, the sun burned through the haze, streaking the

window with light. The road curved, and the reflection of the sky slid across his face, blue, then gold, then gone.

He gave me a small, tired smile. "You ever think about what could have happened? Us, I mean, like if we'd been together the way my mom always wanted?" He tapped his pen on the paper.

My face burned. The question hung there, suspended. "I used to," I admitted. "But it always felt like one of those things I shouldn't imagine. I know it's irrational, but I used to think Astra Cynthia could see right into my thoughts. I was afraid she'd know I was thinking about it."

The corner of his mouth lifted. "That's exactly why I thought about it all the time."

A thrill ran through me. "You're terrible."

"Probably." He leaned back in his seat, eyes drifting to the window. "But when everything was rules and punishment, thinking about you was the one thing that felt kind of normal."

I didn't know what to say to that, his bald honesty. Every nerve ending in my body was sparking.

He blinked. "You, that day in the closet. Scared and shivering."

"And half naked," I reminded him.

He shot both hands into his hair and scraped it back from his forehead. "Maybe I shouldn't have been thinking that way. You were just a kid, really—"

"I was fifteen."

"Right. A kid."

"So were you. You're only three years older than me."

He shook his head a little. "I remember sitting with you in the closet that night and thinking—how damn lucky am I to get to hang out with this girl—without anyone knowing?"

His words knocked the air out of me. Everything else faded away.

He anchored his hands behind his head. "You know what else?"

"What?"

"Remember that carving you made? The one of me?"

"Yeah."

He grinned. "I still have it."

"Liar. You do not."

He raised his eyebrows. "I swear I do." He reached down into his guitar case, opened a black velvet compartment, and withdrew the figure. The red and blue paint I'd used for his shirt and jeans were as vibrant as ever. The face was unchipped, still perfectly formed.

I made a noise between a laugh and a gasp. "I cannot believe you kept that."

He tossed it gently and caught it again. "I keep it in my case for luck. It was important to me. I wanted to forget most things from that place, but there were a few I wanted to remember. You were one of them."

I stared at him in disbelief. I wanted so badly to touch him, to slide my hand along his jaw, into his thicket of hair.

Instead, I shifted my gaze to the thin line of highway sliding past the window. The world looked so normal out there—gas stations, truck stops, trees.

"I want to forget all of it too," I said. "All of it. Except you."

His hand twitched against his leg, like he wanted to reach for me but thought better of it.

"If I ever seriously thought of marrying anyone, Brynn —" He stopped himself. Shook his head. "Forget it."

But I didn't.

Long after he turned back to his notebook, his unfinished sentence replayed in my head.

Chapter Twenty-Eight

VIRGINIA, MARCH 1999

"In the Afterglow"

The crowd was packed shoulder to shoulder, screaming Sullivan's name before the lights even dimmed. I watched from the side stage, half hidden behind a stack of speakers.

Brooke was there too, wearing huge sunglasses even though it was dark in the wings. Sullivan had told me I should make friends with her, but I wasn't sure why or even how. Our conversations had been stilted and polite. It was hard to imagine us becoming besties or anything.

She positioned a folding chair beside me and straddled it backward. "How are you?" she yelled over the din of voices.

I forced a smile and gave her a thumbs-up.

"I saw your picture, you know. On the news." She tilted her head, her mouth curving around a half-smile. "People are looking for you."

The lights from the stage spilled past the curtain in flashes—white, then red, then blue—and each one hit me like a punch. Sullivan had told me not to say anything. "You must've seen someone else."

She studied me for a beat, one manicured nail tracing the metal edge of the chair. "Maybe." A small shrug. "But it looked a lot like you. And I don't know many other people who've escaped from a cult named Brynn."

My pulse throbbed behind my eyes. The noise of the crowd swelled. The first chord of the set shook the floor.

Brooke leaned closer. "Don't worry," she yelled. "Your secret's safe. I didn't tell anyone." She cut her hand through the air as though already tired of the subject. "You're not the first person to run from something. Definitely not the first to hide something." She lowered her sunglasses, revealing puffy purple and red skin around her eye.

I drew in a sharp breath. "What happened?"

She shrugged. "Sometimes Nate gets a little edgy."

For a moment, I couldn't find words. Wasn't even sure I'd heard her correctly. The sound from the stage—Sullivan's voice, the crush of guitars—was suddenly muffled, like someone had thrown a blanket over us.

"Edgy?" I echoed. "Brooke, he hit you?"

She flipped her sunglasses back into place and tipped her chin toward the stage. "I'm not exactly innocent. I know how to push him."

My insides went cold. "Don't say that," I shouted back at her.

Brooke crossed one leg over the other, her boot tapping in time with the music. "What?"

"You didn't make him do that." My voice broke.

Standing, she brushed invisible dust from her jeans and patted me on the shoulder. She put her mouth close to my ear. "It's fine. I have ways of punishing him too. Don't worry about me or anyone else. You worry about you. Keep your head down. The more people around here who know something, the less control you've got over it."

Before I could respond, she melted into the noise and light, absorbed by the movement of the stage crew.

I watched the rest of the concert, trying not to think about the things Brooke had said. I'd seen more than a few black eyes and split lips in Crystal Cliffs. Abuse was common and never talked about. I didn't know much about relationships, but I knew hitting wasn't a normal part of it.

Backstage after the show, a makeshift bar appeared near the dressing rooms. A line of fans snaked down the hallway, mainly comprised of women in crop tops and leather jackets, their eyes wide and hopeful.

Sullivan moved among them easily, letting them touch his arm, signing shirts, whispering jokes that made them laugh. He held a brown bottle and sipped from it before saying something to one of the women whose hand brushed his chest and lingered there. He didn't pull away. He seemed to like being worshiped and wanted.

Brooke was there too, pressed strangely close not to Nate but to Red, who barely looked at her. When he sat, she sat beside him. Her sunglasses still in place, she rocked her head to the side, resting it on his shoulder, a smile pulling at her lips.

I glanced across the room. Nate stood in the corner between two women. His eyes darted toward Brooke and then away again.

I tried to stay invisible while waiting for Sullivan to tell me what to do. The version of him from that morning—the quiet man with a notebook, the one who'd said he thought about me in that closet—felt like someone I'd dreamed up.

This Sullivan glowed under the backstage lights, a cigarette clutched in his fingers, a halo of smoke surrounding him. Maybe forty-five minutes or an hour later, when he finally found me, his pupils were wide, the shine of alcohol in his eyes.

"There you are." He smiled a loose grin. "You vanish faster than my stage techs."

"I wasn't far."

He leaned in close enough for me to smell the beer on his breath. "You ready to head out, go back to the hotel?"

"Yes." My voice was lost in the rush of sound as he guided me through the maze of people holding cameras and snapping pictures. Someone called his name, and he raised his hand without looking.

Minutes later, we were in a limousine, along with Red and another random girl.

I stayed quiet, listened to Sullivan and Red chat about the set, Jared's flub on the third song, the problems with the lighting, and the fight that had broken out in the second row.

By the time we reached the hotel, it was after midnight. The lobby buzzed with road crew, fans, and journalists who had gotten wind of the band's stay. I took Brooke's advice—kept my head down, hair forward, hanging like curtains on either side of my face. Hopefully, it was enough to hide my identity. The overhead lights were bright, and every camera flash felt like it was aimed at me.

A group of reporters loitered by the bar, badges clipped to their coats, talking in low voices, scanning faces. One of them had a notepad, a camera slung across his chest. They might as well have been holding guns. Each one of them was a danger to my anonymity.

Sullivan's hand landed lightly on my back as we crossed the lobby.

"You OK?"

"Yeah," I lied. My legs felt like boneless, rubbery tentacles.

He gave me a quick glance, brow furrowed. "We're almost there."

Almost where?

"Hey, Sullivan, who's your friend?" one of the reporters called out.

All of them wanted to know who the girl was with Sullivan Stonecutter.

Except the reporters weren't really looking at me. They were staring at the blond on the other side of him. She'd seemingly appeared out of nowhere, and now her arm was entwined with his.

Sullivan moved ahead of me, clutching the other girl's arm as the cameras continued to flash.

"You people really never sleep, do you?" He held up a hand. "Not tonight, thanks."

The elevator was ahead of us, the doors open, waiting, and we ducked inside. Even before the metal panels began to close, the paparazzi's attention pivoted to Red, and they shouted questions about tour dates and the upcoming album.

The doors shut, sealing the three of us off from the rest of them.

Sullivan exhaled through his nose. "So damn annoying."

For a long, awkward moment, none of us spoke. The blond and I shot gazes across Sullivan, eyeing each other.

She had a flawless look, waist-length wavy hair, perfectly applied red lipstick, and a sequined top that might have served well at a dinner party.

I looked away first, pretending to study the glowing numbers on the panel. Sullivan's arm brushed mine as the elevator shot upward.

When the doors opened, the girl stepped forward, her hand sliding along Sullivan's arm as if it belonged there, like she'd expected him to move with her and leave me behind in the elevator.

When he didn't, she leaned against the door, keeping it from closing. "You should come on up. Room 918. We'll celebrate." Again, her eyes rested on me. "She can come too."

Ew.

Sullivan's grin wavered. "Appreciate the invite, but I think I'm calling it a night."

Her sultry smile faded. Clearly, she wasn't used to being turned down. "You sure?"

"Yeah." His tone was easy, final. "Long day. Maybe another time." Sullivan put his arm around my shoulders.

I worked to keep my lips closed, but the edges twisted upward anyway. I felt chosen, and I liked it.

The doors slid closed again. The weight of his arm remained, warm through my coat.

I tilted my head back, looked up at the mirrored ceiling. "She seems nice."

He made a chuffing sound. "She's persistent."

"You didn't have to send her away because of me."

"I didn't," he said. "I sent her away because I don't want a headline tomorrow broadcasting the threesome I had at the Hyatt in Alexandria." The corner of his mouth lifted enough to break the tension.

"A threesome?"

He gazed down at me. "You don't know what a three-some is?"

The elevator stopped again.

"I can guess," I muttered.

He chuckled. "Come on, innocent girl. Let's find our room."

I followed him down the carpeted corridor, my mind reeling with exhaustion, the excitement of the prospect of sleeping in a bed, and the terror of sharing a room with Sullivan.

He swayed slightly, catching himself with one hand on the wall. "I overdid it. You'd think I'd know my limits by now."

"Your limits?"

"Yeah. There's a sweet spot between loose and useless. I blew right past it about two beers ago."

We stopped outside the double doors at the end of the hallway. He fished through his pocket for the keycard, missed once, swore under his breath, tried again. This time, it worked.

"Home sweet Hyatt." He pushed the door open.

The suite was dimly lit, with one lamp on the far night-stand, a king-sized bed, sheets half-pulled back by house-keeping. Floor-to-ceiling windows offered a glimpse into the darkness, overlooking the city.

The furniture was sleek and modern. Black leather, brushed steel. A bottle of champagne chilled in a silver bucket on the coffee table beside a bowl of fruit.

All I could see was the bed. The first bed I'd slept in in two weeks. White, cloud-like, heavenly.

Sullivan sighed. "I hate hotel rooms."

I moved further into the room. "Why? This is beautiful."

He dropped his wallet and sunglasses on the dresser. "Yeah. Well, tomorrow we'll be in Pawley's Island, in a place that makes this look like a trailer."

I set my bag down by the chair. My pulse hadn't slowed since the elevator. I was very aware that we were alone—really alone—for the first time. No voices or tour bus noise from the next room. No sound at all.

"Pawley's Island? Is that one of your houses?"

"No, it belongs to a friend, but he's never there, so he lets me stay whenever I want." Sullivan crossed to the coffee table, loosened the wire cage on the champagne bottle, and eased the cork free with a soft pop. Bubbles spilled over his hand as he poured two glasses. "I like it because it's away from all of this." He swept his eyes across the ceiling as if "this" existed there. "It's quiet. Beautiful. Peaceful." He held the glass toward me.

I shook my head. "I don't really—"

"House rules." He pushed the glass into my hand. "Every hotel room comes with overpriced guilt. And I don't like to drink alone."

We clinked glasses, and I put the rim to my lips. I'd never had champagne before. It fizzed against my tongue.

"It's not bad."

"Careful." He laughed. "Drink a couple of glasses, and I'll be scraping you up off the carpet."

I turned the stem of the glass between my fingers, watching the bubbles climb. "Those reporters tonight ... I thought they were going to recognize me."

He leaned one shoulder against the window, city light sliding across his face. "No. They see what they want to see

—in this case, they saw the blond hanging on my arm, a story they could print. They never saw you. Not really."

I took another sip. "Geez, am I that plain?"

"You're hardly plain." He turned back to the window. "But she was loud, she wanted to be seen. You'll learn. The paparazzi are a funny bunch. Sometimes they don't want to know the things you think they do."

My insides were beginning to fizz right along with the champagne. I joined him by the window and watched the red taillights drift through the fog.

"You want another?" he asked.

I held out my glass and allowed him to top it up. Then he refilled his own and shot it like whiskey.

Stretching his legs, he toed off his boots, sauntered over to the bed, and sank onto the edge. "You've got to be shattered, Brynn."

I shrugged. "I was until we started drinking champagne."

He rubbed his face with both hands. "Uh-oh. I've created a lush."

I nervously toyed with the ends of my hair, twisting it around my free hand.

Sullivan leaned back on his elbows, and the lamplight caught the veins on his forearms. "I should get in the shower."

I sat on the edge of the bed beside him. This night could have gone differently for him. Maybe it usually did. Blondie could have just as easily been in this room with him now, drinking champagne.

The champagne seemed to be doing its work, bubbling away my shyness. I closed my eyes. "If I weren't here, would you have gone with that girl to her room?"

He bit his lip, wincing. "Probably."

I'd hoped for a different answer, even though the one he gave me didn't surprise me.

"At least you're honest."

He collapsed back onto the bed. "I'm too tired to lie to you."

I traced a seam in the bedspread. "It's just—" I stopped, searching for the right word. "Strange. Hearing you say it out loud."

"It doesn't mean anything, Brynn. That stuff—it just fills the hours. None of it lasts."

"Maybe that's worse."

He touched my leg with one finger. "Why?"

"It's not real." I lay back on the bed beside him, the duvet pillowing around me, the champagne buzzing in my veins. "So, what do you do with girls like that?"

He sat up, his face incredulous. "Are you really asking me this right now?"

"Yes. I want to know."

He sighed, cranked his head back, and stared at the ceiling. "Mostly I disappoint them."

"What do you mean?"

"I mean they expect me to be something that … well, like they want the stage persona, you know? I have to put on a show all over again to uphold the fantasy."

"So why keep doing it?"

He looked at me as if trying to decide how much he should say. "Shit, if I know."

I balanced my empty glass on my stomach. "That's not a good answer."

He glanced back at me and offered a lazy smile. "I'm not Superman, you know? I just try to do what they want."

"I want you to kiss me." The words rolled off my tongue.

He lingered another moment, his eyes darting back and forth. Then he stood. "Probably not a good idea."

I pushed up onto my elbows. "Why?"

He raised his hands to his hips. "Have you ever been kissed, Brynn?"

My gaze dropped. "No."

He nodded, hooked his hand behind his neck. "That's what I thought."

I pushed off the bed and moved toward him. When I swayed a little, he caught my elbow.

"Whoa. See? I told you. Two glasses and you're staggering."

I faced him, smiling, my eyes wide. "I want you to be the first to do it. To kiss me."

His brow furrowed. "Brynn, it's late. I don't want to get into this tonight."

"I just … I want to know what it's like."

He dropped his gaze to my mouth briefly before returning it to my eyes. "I'll disappoint you too."

I didn't look away. "Only if you don't kiss me."

He sucked in a slow, deep breath and slid his hand from my elbow up my arm. With his other hand, he brushed the side of my face.

"Is this what you do with them? The other girls? The groupies?"

"Sometimes." He smiled but his expression seemed sad.

The hand resting on my arm joined the other until both framed my face. A surge of panic flowed through me, spurring on the beats of my heart. But then he lowered his face toward mine. I closed my eyes and felt his lips, so light and brief, it was more like a brush than a kiss.

It was a start, but that wasn't what I was looking for.

When he pulled back, I wrapped my hands around his

and backed toward the bed until the backs of my legs touched the mattress. Then I sat, still holding his hands, looking up at him.

Sullivan pulled against me. "Brynn…"

I let go of his hands, lay back on the bed, and waited.

He stood for a heartbeat too long, staring down at me. Then he sat on the edge of the bed, and the mattress dipped beneath his weight. His hand found the blanket near my arm, but he didn't touch me.

"This isn't how it's supposed to happen," he said.

I stared up at the ceiling, fighting the sudden burn behind my eyes, the flutter in my stomach. "What's supposed to happen, then?"

"It's supposed to happen naturally."

"Nothing has ever happened between us naturally. Nothing in my life has ever happened naturally."

He seemed to consider this, the corners of his mouth pulling a little. Then he took my hands, placed them around his neck, and forced me to sit up next to him.

I slid one hand down, near his collar. "Is this what you do with them? The others?"

He nodded. "Yes."

His brushed his thumb across my cheek, tracing the edge of my jaw. Then he kissed me again, and it was nothing like the first one. The world went quiet. I slid my arms over his shoulders, and the kiss hardened, his mouth pressing mine until I opened my lips and allowed his tongue inside, tasting champagne, salt.

His breathing picked up, loud against my skin. Then he leaned back, and his eyes bored into mine.

My first kiss had been Sullivan Stonecutter. But I already knew that one kiss would never, ever be enough.

I smiled. "Don't stop."

He blinked. "I think I should. You have no idea what's going through my head right now."

I wanted to pull him on top of me, feel his weight pressing me into the bed. I wanted him to keep kissing me. I wanted him to touch me.

"I want you to keep going."

He flattened his mouth. "No."

"Why not?"

He breathed in sharply, his eyes searching the ceiling. "Because the one thing that always happens with the others is that I never see them again. And I don't want that to happen with you."

"It won't." But I didn't know that. For all I knew, I'd be off the tour bus in a couple of days, and this would all be a memory.

Sullivan leaned down and kissed me quickly on the forehead. When he spoke, his voice was rough. "I think that's enough for one night."

The air between us was electrified. I could still feel the imprint of his hand against my skin, the memory of his mouth on mine. He rubbed the back of his neck and then crossed to the window, where the city lights painted him in silver and shadow.

I'd remember this for what it was: a moment I'd fantasized about for years. No matter what happened, I would never stop wanting more.

Chapter Twenty-Nine

NOW

I stop for gas somewhere outside Knoxville. I swipe my card, start the pump, and lean against the car while it fills. The highway roars steadily behind me. A Tennessee Volunteer flag snaps in the wind near the pumps, orange bright against the gray Tennessee sky.

My phone buzzes in my pocket. Maybe from Sullivan, checking my progress down the road or confirming that we're meeting at that comedy club tonight. I finish pumping, climb back into my car, and check my phone.

The message is from Ivy.

I hesitate before opening it, my thumb hovering over the screen before swiping.

Hey! I wanted to say thank you again. I talked to Sullivan last night, and I actually used some of what you said about how to do more listening than anything. I think it really helped.

I stare at the bubble and finally give it a thumbs up. Acknowledged.

Three dots show on the screen. She's still writing. A few seconds later, another bubble pops up.

It was one of the most honest conversations we've ever had. He opened up about Crystal Cliffs. He also told me about some of the trauma that happened to him years ago, including some pretty grisly stuff that I'm probably not at liberty to say. I feel like I finally understand him better, and I think he understands how much I care about him.

As I stare at the words, something shifts and unfurls inside me: jealousy. It's ugly and silly, I know it is. Sullivan and I haven't been in touch in years. And does it really matter who he shared his secrets with as long as he did? The resounding answer is *yes*. I wanted it to be me. Not her.

I look down at the third installment of the message.

Anyway, I wanted you to know. I really appreciate your generosity, transparency, and friendship. I'm headed back to Pawley's Island today. Hope we chat again soon.

Generosity. Friendship?

The pump on the other side of mine shuts off with a hard *thunk*.

Cars are waiting. I focus on a man in a ball cap carrying a ream of lottery tickets back to his truck while I mentally craft my reply.

Ivy believes she's building something solid with Sullivan, and maybe she is.

What she doesn't realize—what she *can't* realize—is that the conversation she's so proud of is only possible because Sullivan already knows how to speak this language. Because he learned it once, a long time ago, in the dark, with someone who didn't have the luxury of distance. With me.

Except the secret he told her is most likely the one he's never told me.

I talk-text my reply.

"I'm glad it helped. It sounds like a meaningful step for both of you."

Grinding my teeth, I hit send. The message goes through. A small, polite punctuation mark on something much larger.

I start the engine and then pull out of the gas station, onto the highway again. Nashville is hours away. No matter what Ivy believes she's secured, Sullivan is still waiting. For me.

I'm not changing what I plan to do.

Chapter Thirty

PAWLEY'S ISLAND, SOUTH CAROLINA, MARCH 1999

"The Detour"

We left the tour bus behind and rented a car. Dart remained with us for the course of the trip—he and Sullivan in the front, me in the back.

"I never travel anywhere without him," Sullivan said from the passenger seat as he whomped Dart on the shoulder. "He's peace of mind in a six-foot-six frame of muscle and fury."

Dart laughed and caught my eye in the rearview mirror. "I'm only going as far as Pawley's Island. Then I'll take the car back to Virginia."

Sullivan grasped Dart's shoulder harder and tried to shake him. "But then you'll be right back with us on the second leg of the tour. Aren't you excited?"

"Exceedingly," Dart deadpanned.

For me, Dart's presence offered a bit of reassurance that no Chuck Crows or Uncle Dunns would grab me from a hallway the way they had Maeve. "We won't need him in South Carolina?"

Sullivan chuckled. "Wait'll you see this place we're staying. It's hard to find, even if you have directions."

We drove south for hours, the landscape uncoiling in shades of gold and green. The farther we traveled from the interstate, the trees closed in, air thickening with salt and pine.

By the time we turned off the main road, the sky was a kaleidoscope of colors from the sunset. The dirt drive curved through a tunnel of live oaks, their branches laced with Spanish moss. The house appeared at the end like something forgotten by time, a low, weathered place with a wraparound porch and peeling paint, light glimmering from a few upstairs windows.

Dart parked the SUV and got out first, scanning the treeline before moving toward the house. He was inside for a minute, maybe two. Then he came back out. "Looks clear."

Sullivan glanced at me over his shoulder. "Welcome to the Low Country."

The interior was white beadboard, high ceilings, mismatched furniture, wall hangings of fake starfish and netting. A stereo sat against the far wall, stacks of vinyl beside it, and a baby grand partially covered with a dust cloth.

"This place is..." I trailed off, looking around. "Something."

"Yeah." Sullivan set his bag down. "Harlan built this house after his wife died. Like I said, he's rarely here. Just keeps it for the few weeks out of the year he comes."

I ran a finger along the uncovered edge of the piano, leaving a clean streak in the dust. "Where is he now?"

"Overseas." He gave a half-smile. "So we've got the place to ourselves. Well, us and Dart."

Dart almost smiled. "I'll be out of your hair tomorrow."

I wandered toward the screened porch. The night air pressed close, thick with the sound of frogs and distant thunder. Out past the grass, the marsh glowed under the rising moon—water silvering between the reeds. The last time I'd seen beauty like this was in Crystal Cliffs. *A beautiful trap.*

Sullivan joined me on the porch, leaning against the rail. "Feels strange, doesn't it? Being here after the craziness of the road."

"How long are we going to stay?"

He studied the horizon. "We'll stay for a while. I mean, unless you don't like it here."

"I love it. It's so peaceful. What about the rest of the band? Where do they go?"

"They scatter for the break," he said. "Nate to Charleston. Red home to Atlanta. Jared—shit, who knows? And Brooke..." He hesitated. "Brooke's wherever she wants to be."

Funny that he considered Brooke part of "the band."

Somewhere in the distance, something splashed in the water.

I leaned against the railing. "Brooke had a black eye." I raised my hand to my eye to emphasize my point. "From Nate."

Sullivan's face hardened. The easy calm he'd worn since we arrived drained away, replaced by a cold steeliness in his eyes. "Yeah," he said finally. "I saw it."

"And you didn't do anything?"

"Like what?"

"I don't know. Confront Nate? Just—I don't know—do *something*."

His gaze shifted, jaw tight. "You don't always get to do something in this business, Brynn. Not without it blowing up in your face."

"That's not an excuse."

He turned back to me, his eyes shadowed. "No, it's not. But it's the truth. Nate's been with me since before Cutter was anything. He's a little volatile, like so many other musicians, I guess."

I crossed my arms, wondering if he really felt as nonchalant about this as his attitude suggested. "He's hitting a woman. That's not cool. You don't ask questions?"

After a long silence, Sullivan scrubbed a hand over his face. "You think I don't want to fix it, Brynn? Every time one of them screws up, I feel like it's my fault. Like I built a house with a bunch of ghosts and now I'm surprised it's haunted." His tone was tired, deflated.

"I just don't like watching people pretend it's normal," I said. "Not after what we've lived through."

He stared out at the marsh. "Neither do I."

We'd opened the bottle of champagne the owner had left chilling in the fridge. Sullivan claimed it was criminal to let it go to waste. I told him champagne must be our current theme. He'd smirked at that, and I'd poured myself another glass anyway because the last time I'd had champagne, he'd kissed me, and maybe the beverage was the way to make it happen again.

The night softened after that. The air through the open windows carried the scent of marsh grass as we sat cross-legged on the floor with the bottle between us, talking about nothing and everything. Once Sullivan had consumed a couple of glasses, he became a philosopher, explaining the mysteries of the universe and how we all fit into them.

I finished the last of my champagne. "You could take over for Astra Cynthia when she retires."

Sullivan rocked back, his long torso braced against the couch, and he closed his eyes. "Maybe I'll start my own cult."

I giggled. "I think you've done that. I've seen the way the crowds worship you."

He opened his eyes again, and his smile filtered away. "I don't get to keep things, Brynn."

I stilled. "What?"

"I don't have a house, don't live anywhere. The people around me, I mean, I never know if they're really my friends or if they're just using me." He sat up again. "Schedules change every five minutes. The label decides what we sound like. Management decides where we sleep. Half the time I don't even know what day it is."

I set down my empty glass and crawled over to him, putting my back against the couch too.

He took a deep breath. "Everything moves. All the time." He swallowed. "And if something breaks, they replace it." His gaze shifted to me, his eyes were almost fierce. "I don't want this to be like that. You and me. I want this to be real."

The admission hovered, fragile as blown glass.

My breath caught. I started to reply but his lips were suddenly on mine, his hands sliding up my arms, over my shoulders, and into my hair. He pulled my bottom lip into his mouth, and I grasped his face, figuring out exactly how to anchor him in place so I could intensify the kiss.

I wanted to crawl under his skin, but I settled for shoving my hands under his shirt, raking my fingers over his collarbone, the light hair of his chest, his ribs, down to his hips.

"I've been thinking of our kiss last night every minute of today," I breathed.

He smiled against my mouth. "Me too."

I pulled back a little. "What are you thinking now?"

He closed his eyes like he was deciding whether to tell me the truth. "I'm thinking we're already in trouble." He used the couch to push up and stand. Then he reached down, grabbed my hand, and pulled me to my feet.

There were only two bedrooms. Dart was occupying one of them.

Sullivan paused in front of the room with the open door and gestured me in. "Guess this one's ours."

A ceiling fan turned lazily above a king-sized bed draped in white linens. There was a lamp on the nightstand, a single painting of the marsh at low tide, and nothing else.

Sullivan stood by the door a beat longer than he needed to, hand on the frame, like he was still deciding whether to walk in.

He looked at me. "If this gets weird, I'm blaming you."

"Weird?" I managed a small laugh. "I think we passed weird about two states ago."

Then I ducked into the bathroom and did what I knew to do, shrugged out of my clothes and into my pajamas before returning to the room, where Sullivan was already under the covers.

When I climbed in beside him, he rolled over and fingered a lock of my hair. "Don't disappear, Brynn," he murmured. "Stay with me."

"I'm here," I whispered.

He reached over and turned the lights off, and I lay there, listening to the thrum of the fan and the pounding of my heart.

My fingers curled against the sheet, inches from his. I could feel the heat of him. The memory of his kiss coursed through me, bringing back the way my body had responded.

I wanted that again. And again.

He shifted slightly, turning onto his side. His hand brushed mine, accidental, but neither of us pulled away. He left his hand there for a moment, not moving. His fingers threaded through mine, tentative at first, like he was testing whether I would let him. When I didn't pull back, his hand traveled slowly, carefully up my leg, over my hip, as if memorizing me.

"Mm, that's nice." I coaxed.

His hand stopped moving.

"It's OK," I said. "You can touch me."

"Are you sure?" he whispered.

"Yes. I want you to."

He slid his fingers over my thigh and between my legs.

I gasped, and my hips bucked a little with the surprise and the sensation. When I closed my eyes and allowed a moan to slip from my throat, he shifted the material of my panties, and I felt the naked skin of his fingertips as they moved against me. Then the pressure of his finger as he pushed it inside me. I groaned, and my hips moved involuntarily as waves of intense pleasure rolled through me.

As the tremor faded, something else rose in its place. It wasn't relief exactly, or even satisfaction. It was something more dangerous. Not only did I want Sullivan more than anything, but I suddenly felt a cataclysmic fear that I might lose him.

In that moment, I was willing to do anything he wanted. I waited for him to climb on top of me and complete what we'd started.

Instead, he leaned over me, his mouth near my ear, his hand in my hair. His forehead rested against my shoulder. For a moment, he was very still. "I'm so tired of everything being temporary," he said in a rough voice. "Songs. Hotels. People."

His fingers tightened slightly, like he was afraid I might slip through them.

"I need something that's mine. Something that doesn't get scheduled or sold or replaced." He lifted his head and looked down at me. "I think we should get married."

I raised my head. "What?"

He couldn't be serious. Things like that didn't happen, not in the real world.

He lay his head in the space between my neck and shoulder, his breath warm on my arm, and whispered, "Yeah, I really think we should."

My first instinct was to laugh. Blame the champagne. Blame the dark. Blame the fact that we had shared a childhood.

Sullivan wasn't smiling.

His expression wasn't reckless. His eyes were serious. Maybe a little afraid and searching. But marriage?

In Crystal Cliffs, marriages had rarely been about love. They'd been alliances, business relationships, permanence you didn't choose.

This felt different. It was as if he was reaching for solid ground in a world that wouldn't stop moving.

And the terrifying part was that I wanted to be that ground.

Chapter Thirty-One

"The Real Thing"

Dart left the next day.

After that, it was just Sullivan and me. And a cold, sunny day in March on an island, which, from where we were sitting, felt deserted.

We'd been on the beach all morning and drinking beer since noon. A red-and-white cooler sat between our beach chairs. Bundled in sweatshirts and jackets, our heads covered with baseball caps, we dug the heels of our shoes into the sand, leaving half-moon marks that served as holders for our beer bottles.

All morning, I'd been dreamily replaying the scene from last night in my head, how easily it had happened, how natural his touch felt. His words.

Then my euphoric thoughts darkened, turned to Wisconsin, and the last time I'd seen Maeve and Teddy on the floor of the arena, on the brink of reconciliation, on the edge of freedom.

"I keep thinking of Maeve," I said.

Sullivan yanked off his baseball cap, and the wind blew his hair across his eyes. He brushed it away, squinting toward the water. "Me too."

"What do you think happened to her?"

He grimaced. "Honestly? They probably sent her to the Think Tank."

He had been there. He knew what that place was like. I was almost afraid to ask.

"How bad was it?"

He looked off toward the water. "It was bad."

I waited, gauging how far into the weeds I should wade. "How long were you there?"

"About a week. Maybe more." He passed a hand over his mouth and chin, where the beginnings of a red-gold beard were forming. "It's hard to remember." He rolled his head toward me. "They try to make you forget everything, including how much time is passing. It's a complete reset of your mind in there."

I wrinkled my nose. "How do they do that?"

He pointed two fingers at his temple, like he was holding a gun to his head. "They mess with your head, break you down, sometimes they use drugs too. It's reprogramming."

"They used drugs on you?"

"Some, yeah."

I shivered, suddenly feeling colder than I had all morning. "So, you don't really remember what happened while you were in there."

"I remember trying to hold on to whatever bits of myself I could," he said. "I remember feeling foggy when I finally got out, but all I could think about was doubling down on getting away from Crystal Cliffs."

I pulled my coat closer around me. Even the mention of that place darkened my mood.

He raised his eyebrows. "The only good thing that came out of that place was you."

I breathed in, allowing a brief tide of happiness to wash over me.

He smiled. "That place was hell, but you and I had some fun times together, hanging out, watching TV at your mom's house. *90210*."

"Oh yeah. Good times with Brandon and Brenda."

He laughed. "And my mom trying to arrange our marriage." He dug his hands into his coat pockets and stood. "Come on. Let's walk."

We walked along the edge of the water. Gulls circled overhead, sharp and loud.

He grabbed my hand, intertwined our fingers. "You know, I meant what I said last night."

I laughed—a reflexive reaction. "Yeah, right."

"I'm serious."

"You'd been drinking."

"So had you."

He stopped walking then and turned toward me, wind pushing his hair back from his face.

"I wasn't kidding, Brynn."

The words were calm. No grin. No edge.

"I know how it sounded," he continued. "Like some rock-star-impulse thing. But I've been thinking about it for a day or so."

I laughed. "A *whole* day?"

He didn't laugh. "The band could implode tomorrow." He gestured vaguely toward the horizon. The wind lifted his shirt slightly at the hem. "But I can choose you. That's not temporary. That's not someone else's decision."

My throat tightened. Was this real? How could I even be sure?

"Sullivan…"

"I'm not talking about some Vegas stunt. I mean real. Papers. Rings. The whole thing." His voice softened. "I want you, Brynn."

Was wanting the same as loving?

I wrapped my arms around myself. "In Crystal Cliffs, marriages rarely lasted."

He nodded. "We're not them."

"I know," I answered. "And maybe I'm just scared. I've only ever seen permanence used as control. You're offering it as safety."

"It is," he said, almost fiercely. "It's me saying I'm not going anywhere."

"But you do go," I said gently. "You leave every week. Every month. Your whole life moves."

"That's exactly why I want something that doesn't."

We stood there with the wind pressing against us, the tide beginning its slow return.

"What if we ruin it?" I asked.

He stepped closer. "We're already in trouble. Remember?"

Despite myself, I smiled.

"I'm serious," he added. "I don't want this to be something we look back on and say it was just part of the tour. *You're* not part of the tour."

The tide crept closer to our feet. I reached for his hand. His thumb brushed over my knuckles.

"South Carolina doesn't make it hard," he continued. "You get a license, and you do it." He gazed at the ocean. "Your birthday is the day after tomorrow, right? Seems like the perfect day to get married."

I waited for the panic. It didn't come.

"I know what I'm saying, Brynn." His wry smile deepened. "You're considering it, aren't you?"

"Is this your way of proposing?"

His blue eyes flashed. "What if it is? What would your answer be?"

I knew my answer. Why would I ever say no? I loved him in ways I never knew were possible, but admitting to that seemed like the dumbest idea ever.

"Do you really want to marry *me*, Sullivan?"

He didn't answer right away but pushed the toe of his right shoe deep into the sand. "Yeah," he said finally. "I do."

I wrenched my head back and looked up at the sky. "This is crazy."

He looked down at the ground and dropped onto his knees in front of me. Then he stared up at me. "Brynn, will you marry me?"

His hair was salt-stiff hair, and his eyes reflected the cloudless blue sky above us.

"Yes."

The answer seemed to surprise us both.

The parenthetical creases appeared on either side of his mouth as it slid into the widest smile he'd ever given me. "Then let's do it."

Chapter Thirty-Two

"Gold"

Marrying Sullivan wasn't something I'd planned when I'd run off in an RV weeks before. The wedding wasn't anything like what I'd expected either.

The events of getting a marriage license and the twenty-four-hour wait passed in a strange, suspended time warp. It gave us both time to change our minds, which we didn't. It gave us time to talk about the future, which we didn't. It gave me time to buy a yellow sundress, for Sullivan to buy a shirt, and for us to purchase gold bands at a local jeweler.

It was my birthday—and my wedding day. The sun was shining, deceiving us into believing it was warmer than it was. March on Pawley's Island was cold and bright.

We walked down to the beach where the officiant was to meet us. The island was off-season quiet. There were no umbrellas, no children, no music drifting from rental houses. Just sand and sea and wind moving steadily in from the horizon.

I wore a white sweater over my sundress, and Sullivan wore jeans and a button-down shirt, the sleeves rolled to his forearms. He looked nervous in a way I'd never seen before, his eyes alert, his limbs restless.

The officiant met us near the waterline, a local man with a weathered face and kind eyes. His wife was the photographer. Dressed in a pale pink suit, she looked like she'd spent a lot of time on the beach or in tanning beds. Two cameras hung from her neck. One a more professional model, the other a Polaroid.

Farther down the beach, a couple walked with a black Labrador. Their presence was distant, their features indistinct, but they stopped and watched as we kicked off our shoes and walked over the sand to stand under the wedding arbor, its white ribbons and tulle blowing in the breeze.

Sullivan took my hands. His fingers felt as cold as mine, and his thumbs brushed my knuckles in small movements.

"You OK?" he mouthed to me.

"Yes." And I was. Mostly.

The wind picked up, tugging at my hair, ruffling the hem of my dress. The ocean was within reach, but the tide stayed at bay, allowing us this moment.

The officiant gave us the words to speak. Repeating them was easy. Vows to love one another, to make a future together, to forsake all others for this union.

When I said *I do*, I was really only claiming something that already existed in my heart.

When Sullivan said it, his voice cracked slightly, and his grip on my hands tightened.

"You may kiss your bride," the officiant said.

Sullivan and I leaned toward one another. His mouth was warm and sure against mine, the kiss unhurried, a little less passionate than the ones we'd previously shared. The click and buzz of the Polaroid camera signaled the immortalization of the moment.

When we pulled apart, Sullivan laughed. "We did it."

"We did," I said.

We shook hands with the officiant, took his wife's business card to order the rest of the pictures, and walked to the car hand in hand. I looked back once, at the stretch of beach where it happened. Our footprints were already fading behind us as the tide crept closer.

The officiant and his wife were no longer standing there. They'd disappeared like ghosts. The arbor was the only evidence of what had taken place moments before, but the white tulle had blown off and was probably tumbling down the beach somewhere.

Sullivan looked at me. "Let's go home."

Home.

A word that hadn't meant anything to me in a long time.

I nodded, holding the Polaroid photo against my chest.

We drove back to the cottage along the same route we'd taken to the chapel, the morning light slanting through the trees, the radio turned on low. Sullivan kept one hand on the steering wheel and the other resting on my knee, his thumb moving in a slow circle that ignited something deep in my belly.

My ring felt too light to be real, like it might float off my finger if I didn't keep checking it. Several times, Sullivan lifted our joined hands to his lips, kissed my knuckles, and grinned.

Not long after, we returned to the cottage. Sullivan shut the door with his foot, then faced me. His smile faded, replaced by anticipation.

I stood awkwardly in the middle of the living room,

waiting. He dropped his keys onto the side table by the door and walked toward me.

"Come here," he whispered and tugged me to him. "You looked so beautiful out there. Even under that stupid arch with those plastic roses." His hands framed my face. "I kept thinking—I get to have this. I get to have you."

He kissed the corner of my mouth, then my jaw, tracing a slow path down my neck. I curled my fingers into the back of his shirt, pulling him closer, and the whole world narrowed to the sound of his breath.

Sullivan backwalked me into the bedroom. There, with a kind of agonized gentleness, he reached down and pulled my skirt up to my hips. Then he lifted me—one leg on either side of his hips—and carried me to the bed. My arms wrapped around his shoulders, and his grip tightened like he didn't want to let go, even long enough to set me down.

When he lay me on the mattress, he stayed above me for a moment, braced on his elbows.

"What?" I whispered.

"I want to remember this," he said. "Every second. I want to remember what you looked like the day we … married each other."

He slid a hand along my ribcage, upward, pausing as if asking permission without words. His touch was warm and deliberate, electricity under the skin. The heat built between us, a storm gathering.

"Sullivan…" I whispered.

"Happy Birthday, Brynn." He kissed the place where my heartbeat pulsed beneath my collarbone. "I've never wanted anyone the way I want you," he spoke the words against my skin. "Not ever. Not like this. No groupie. No girlfriend."

For all his swagger on stage, he was vulnerable too.

And I loved him for it.

He rose up, yanked his shirt over his head, stepped out of his pants, and lay on the bed beside me.

All my nerve endings felt like they were on fire as his fingers brushed the skin above my underwear, over my bare hip. My eyes searched his serious, questioning ones. I helped him, wrestling my panties the rest of the way over my knees and kicking them off until they slid over the end of the bed.

When he finally moved over me, slow at first, both of us breathing hard, he kept his fingers knotted with mine.

And for a little while—minutes or hours—there was no band, no tour, no history of life in Crystal Cliffs, no past at all. Nothing except the two of us. The kaleidoscope that was our life, individually and collectively, seemed to have fatefully culminated in this moment.

When it was over, he collapsed beside me, pulling me against his chest. I rested my head over his heart, still beating wildly.

He kissed the top of my head. "I love you, Brynn."

I tilted my head and looked up at him. I'd never said the words to anyone—not even Mama. And they sounded foreign then as they poured from my lips. "I love you too, Sullivan."

Eventually, he drifted to sleep, his hand loosely holding my fingers.

I lay awake long after, listening to the distant crash of the ocean and thinking about that Polaroid—proof that this had really happened. That we had chosen each other.

Finally, I belonged somewhere.

To someone.

For now.

Chapter Thirty-Three

NOW

It's the last stretch before Nashville, and I've chosen a podcast episode from my library, one I bookmarked weeks ago. One I've been avoiding for some time. *The Cutter Years: Fame, Fallout, and the Man Behind the Voice.*

This is totally reconnaissance. If I'm going to walk into his present life, I need to review his past. After all, I haven't seen the man in twenty-five years.

The host is a country-singer-turned-podcaster who knows a lot about the industry and a little about an era of music that was popular before she was born. She references her "dad's music," falling in love with Cutter during long drives to visit her mother in Michigan, and a childhood spent listening to songs that suggested the world was about to end. The reference makes my stomach churn a little.

Her voice is polished, confident, and perfect for podcasting. She recaps the early days of Cutter's music—first the club scene, then the breakout album, and finally, the sudden velocity of success. I keep my eyes on the road, the

Tennessee landscape leveling, the mountains giving way to long stretches of highway.

I open a packet of potato chips with my teeth and shovel several into my mouth.

The podcaster's tone shifts. "Early Cutter years were volatile. A lot of people forget that Sullivan Stonecutter left the band altogether in 2001. A brief rehab stint never made the press. It was kept quiet, handled internally. There's been a lot of speculation about that period after the second album," she says. "Not the touring or the band tension, but you. People close to you have described a kind of … disappearance. Can you talk about that?"

There's a pause.

"I don't talk about this much." Sullivan's low, sultry voice cuts in. "Mostly because it doesn't fit the story people want."

My hands tighten on the wheel. *Damn it.* Even though I talked with him on the phone a few days ago, his voice still affects me. Twenty-five years of managing, forgetting, and trying to heal are wiped out in one second. I shove the bag of chips between my knees, put another handful into my mouth, and wipe my greasy fingers on my jeans.

"I wasn't disappearing because of drugs," he continues. "Or burnout. I didn't have anything else to give. I was a mess."

In the distance, the sky is a bright, burnished orange. The horizon. The future. In a little while, I'll see Sullivan in the flesh. This man, who says he wants a new beginning. We'll talk about all of this then.

"I came from a place where obedience was survival," he says. "Where you learned very early that having your own wants—your own voice—was dangerous. And then suddenly, I was in a band where everyone wanted something from me. My sound. My anger. My pain." A breath. "It felt familiar in a way that scared me."

The host doesn't interrupt.

"I didn't realize it at the time," he says, quieter now. "But I was repeating a pattern. Letting other people decide who I was allowed to be, because that felt safer than choosing it myself."

My throat clogs with salt and fried potatoes.

"I used to freeze," he admits. "On stage. Off stage. I'd go somewhere else in my head. Dissociate. Sometimes for days." A short, humorless laugh. "I didn't even have language for it back then. I thought something was wrong with me."

I stare straight ahead, the lane markers blurring slightly.

"I had people around me. People who cared. But I didn't know how to let them see it. I didn't know how to say this isn't pressure, this is old wiring coming back online."

"Because you were in a cult earlier in your life, right?" she asks.

He exhales loudly. "Yeah, I was, and that's old news. Everyone knows about that. I wasn't ready to face the world when I came out. I lost a lot, including people who mattered to me. Including someone I loved very much."

Thump.

A loud one. Under my car.

Once. Then again.

I frown, easing off the accelerator. The sound repeats, rhythmic but irregular, like something loose but determined to be heard.

"Shit," I mutter, flicking the podcast off and pulling onto the next exit.

Another gas station. I park in front of the store.

The car idles as I step out, wind pressing against my

jacket. Tractor-trailers pull into the diesel lots a few feet away, their vibration rattling me.

I crouch, peer beneath the car. Everything looks intact—tires solid, nothing dragging. Somewhere under the chassis, a thin sheet of metal ticks and cools.

I straighten, brushing my hands on my jeans, a little unsettled. I'm about to get back in my car when voices carry across the pavement from a few yards away.

"I said, give it to me."

"I didn't do anything wrong."

A young couple stands near the ice chest. Early twenties, maybe. The girl's arms are crossed, clutching her purse like armor.

The guy looms too close, his hand out, palm up, impatient. "Damn it, Belle, give me your phone. Stop making this a thing. You're embarrassing yourself."

Something about the girl holding her purse against her chest—or maybe it's her wavy brown hair—reminds me of Maeve.

I don't rush or shout. I leverage my age—at least twenty years on them—and I walk over as if I know them.

"Hey," I say to the girl, keeping my voice light, familiar. "Sorry, but do you know if the bathroom's open? The one inside was closed."

She looks at me, startled. Then relief filters through her expression. Just enough.

"Uh—yeah," she says. "I think so."

The guy scowls at me. "We're in the middle of something."

"Cool," I reply easily. "I won't interrupt long." I meet the girl's eyes again. Hazel—almost silver. Like Maeve's. "You want to show me, like, where the bathroom is?"

I know and she knows that this is staged, meant to

defuse the situation. Hell, he knows it too. I can tell by the tension in his cheeks.

She hesitates for half a second. Then she nods.

We take three steps together before the guy scoffs. "Seriously?"

I stop and glare at him. "She's fine. Right? We don't need to call anyone? Like the police?"

The question hangs there, quiet but loaded.

He drops his hand. Shrugs. "Whatever."

The girl doesn't look back as we walk toward the restroom. Inside, fluorescent lights buzz overhead. She breathes out shakily.

"Thank you," she says. "He just—he gets intense. He wouldn't hurt me."

"Really?"

"Really."

I nod. "You don't owe anyone your phone. Or your time."

Her mouth tightens. "I know."

"Good." I offer a small smile. "Trust that."

"I'm really OK."

I don't stay or ask questions. She's not Maeve, and I have to remember that.

Back in the car, I sit for a moment, hands resting on the wheel. That came too easily. Paul says I'm too comfortable these days, butting into other people's business, but my past dictates intervention. A long time ago, I was blessed with a safe landing space. I can't look away from someone else who might need the same.

I start the engine and the podcast crackles back on, mid-sentence, Sullivan's voice threaded through archival audio. There are still things I don't know. There are also things I do.

I know what control sounds like when it raises its voice. I know how easily people mistake intensity for love. And I know that whatever version of Sullivan waits for me in Nashville, he isn't the myth people talk about on podcasts.

He's just a human who survived something.

So am I.

Chapter Thirty-Four

"Hiding From Reality"

The days after the wedding slid together quietly. Sullivan and I stayed tucked away in the cottage most mornings, rising late. He couldn't have been more attentive, more giving. He fulfilled my every fantasy on so many levels.

Sometimes his hand found mine in the dark. Sometimes he woke before me and slipped out quietly, returning with coffee.

"Morning, Mrs. Stonecutter," he'd say, as though reminding me who I was.

Maybe I should have thought it was too much, but I liked the way it sounded. I liked the way he said it.

We learned each other's ways and mannerisms. Sullivan paced when he talked on the phone—management calls, studio rumors, someone always needing something from him.

I learned which silences meant he was thinking and which ones meant he was somewhere else entirely.

Most of our days were spent in the cottage or on the beach. Other days, we took short trips to Charleston or to Myrtle Beach. Charleston was beautiful and idyllic. Myrtle in March was still a busy place. The boardwalk may have been less crowded, but there were plenty of people around, which made me feel like we were still part of the world, not hiding from it or suspended outside of it.

I liked that.

Sometimes Sullivan was recognized, his six-foot-two height and golden-blond hair giving him away. A second look. A whisper. A nudge between strangers. Most of the time, he wore a beanie pulled low over his forehead and dark sunglasses, blending with the rest of humanity.

I liked that more.

There was something peaceful about walking beside him without cameras or backstage passes or someone telling us where to be next. We bought greasy fries in paper baskets. We stood in line like everyone else. We argued about which arcade game to play. Ordinary things. I'd never realized how much I wanted ordinary.

At night, we frequented the Comedy Cabana to see stand-up comedians. Usually, we arrived once the place went dark and sat in the back, leaving before the end of the show.

In the dark of the club, I could lean into him without wondering who was watching. I could laugh without thinking about who might disapprove. The ring on my finger caught the stage lights sometimes when I lifted my drink, a quiet flash of gold that startled me every time.

Wife.

The word still felt strange in my mouth, not quite real.

Blissful as the time was, some small part of me kept

waiting for the tide to shift, for someone to tell us it was time to move again.

The news no longer mentioned my name, but the silence was in some ways worse than the televised acknowledgment that Astra Cynthia and my mother were looking for me. Where were they now? Did they have any idea where I was? Did they even care? Maybe they'd given up. Maybe having Maeve back was enough.

Poor Maeve. We'd had no idea when we started on this journey that I would end up as Sullivan's wife and she would end up back in Crystal Cliffs. This new life had been her idea; she had done all the planning. Were it not for her, I wouldn't have found myself here—with the man I'd always dreamed of marrying. Now I was the one living this life for both of us. We'd thought we'd be touring the country, following Cutter in an RV. Instead, I would be traveling the country with Cutter in a tour bus.

"What are you thinking about?" I asked Sullivan one afternoon while we were walking on the beach.

He stooped down to pick up a shell. "Everything."

"That sounds ominous."

We resumed our pace.

He scanned the horizon. "I was just, you know, thinking about the band. The second leg of the tour. Some set changes I want to make."

Something inside me pinched. Not jealousy, really, but in a few weeks, we'd be back out there. At least … he would. Who knew where I'd be.

"Did you talk to Fletch?" I asked.

He frowned. "No. I'm tired of talking to those people. I'll have to talk to them soon enough when we go back out on tour."

That was a subject I hadn't breached yet. Our days of solitude had been so happy, I didn't want to spoil them with reality. "When you go back out on the road, will I come with you?"

He looked over at me, and a slow smile spread his lips. "Of course. Where else would you be?"

"I ... didn't know."

"You think I'd just turn you loose? 'Good luck, Brynn. Check in with me and let me know where you are.'" He stopped walking and reached for me. "Did you think I'd drop you off at the nearest airport or bus station?" His hands found my sides, digging into my rib cage until I squirmed and jerked.

"Stop!" I half-screamed, half-giggled.

"You are so ticklish." He laughed.

"Yeah, I am. And you'll make me pee all over myself."

His smile slid away, and his face turned serious as he intertwined his fingers through mine. "Are you scared I'll leave you, Brynn?"

"I—"

"Are you afraid I won't be able to handle marriage *and* the band?"

I looked away from him as I spoke the words. "I guess I'm scared that eventually you'll feel like you have to give up this—" I gestured between us "—to have that."

"I need both." He squinted toward the water. "I need everything."

I'd hoped his answer would assure me. Instead, it confused me. Over the past few months, I'd learned to adapt my expectations. Sullivan had expanded his.

He traced the outline of my spine with his fingers. "Of course you'll come with me, Brynn. I want you with me everywhere. If you want to be with me."

I kissed his shoulder, and we started to walk again. "I don't want to be anywhere else."

The days slipped into a rhythm. The nights felt like dreams. I had never been happier. It was like I'd tried on someone else's life, and I never wanted to take it off. But as April gave way to May, management called his cell phone more often. He ignored most of the calls, tossing his phone onto the couch, laughing when it buzzed again.

The messages on his phone became more frequent until one night after we'd been out celebrating Cinco de Mayo, we came home to a message on the cottage's answering machine.

The voice was low, crackly, and immediately recognizable.

"Hey, Sullivan, this is Red. Look, man, we hit the road again in two weeks. We need to rehearse. Where the hell are you? You need to call Fletch, OK? We play at Universal Studios at the end of this month. I don't know what's going on, dude, but you need to get your shit together and call us. Call *me* at least."

After the message ended, Sullivan stared at the machine. He shot a hand through his hair, wrenching it back from his forehead. "How the hell did he get the number here?"

It was the first time I realized that the phone calls he'd been receiving weren't routine. Bandmates, managers, they were angry.

"They don't know where you are?"

Sullivan didn't look at me. "Hell, no. You think I would have been avoiding their calls if I'd wanted them to know where I was?"

I lowered myself onto the couch. All these months, I hadn't been the only one hiding. "Why? Why didn't you want them to know?"

He swiveled toward me then, his eyes skimming mine. "I needed a break. From all of them. Everyone. That's all."

I lay my hands on my knees, palms up. "Are you going to let them know?" My voice was small. "Are you going to call Red back? Tell him where you are?"

Several seconds ticked by. Suddenly, the old Sullivan surfaced, the one who never wanted to disappoint his band or risk losing momentum. The man who feared being replaceable.

He lunged forward, grabbing his mobile phone from its charger on the kitchen bar. "I guess so. Otherwise, they'll say I'm off somewhere having a breakdown or a drinking binge. That I can't hack it. They've said that before, you know."

"Who?"

"People who thought I wouldn't make it this far."

He called Red and moved to the porch to talk to him out of my earshot. Still, I heard his raised voice, the defensive tone. After that, he came back inside and phoned Fletch, the band's manager. He spoke to him behind a closed bedroom door.

Sullivan emerged an hour later. His face seemed to have aged during the call. His eyebrows formed a sharp ridge over his bloodshot eyes. The lines around his mouth were pronounced.

"We're leaving here on Wednesday."

That was in two days.

"Dart will meet us here," he said, his voice monotone. "We'll catch a plane to Orlando."

I put down the pot I'd been drying. "Do they know about me?"

He nodded, and his eyes reflected a moroseness I'd never seen before. "And they're not happy about it."

Of course. Why hadn't I considered this outcome? Why had I assumed it wouldn't matter? Sullivan was a twenty-three-year-old rock star. A wife was not part of the record label's marketing plan.

Sullivan moved to the kitchen counter and poured bourbon into two shot glasses. "Want one?"

"No, thanks." I covered his hand with mine. "Is there anything I can do?"

"No." He drained one glass, then the other, slamming the second glass on the counter. "I'm going to bed."

Then he turned off the kitchen light and left me standing in the dark.

That was the first night since we'd been married that we didn't make love.

The night before we left Pawley's Island, we fought for the first time.

It started over something stupid—laundry, of all things.

I swept through the living area, gathering up our belongings, which had simply become part of the fabric of this cottage over the past two months. The slatted double doors to the closet that housed the washer and dryer were open. Sullivan stood there, shirtless, pulling clothes from the dryer.

As I moved through the kitchen, he appeared on the other side of the door, holding up a white button-down.

"You shrank my only good shirt," he snapped.

At first, I wasn't sure he was being serious. I nearly laughed, but as I gauged the fire in his eyes, heat rushed through me. He was actually angry.

"I'm sorry," I said. "I didn't mean—"

"It's the only one I didn't look like a kid in." Wadding the shirt into a ball, he tossed it across the room. The fabric snapped as it flew through the air and landed on the couch in the den.

"I'm sorry." My eyes stung.

Sullivan dropped his gaze. He seemed to have caught himself, and guilt flooded his face.

"No, I'm sorry." He took three steps to close the space between us and pulled me close.

I clung to him. My face pressed against his chest, my hands clutching at his ribcage. I didn't know what that was —that flash of anger—but it had rattled me. The sudden, unexpected nature of the accusation.

His breath was hot against the top of my head. "I'm scared I'm screwing things up. With the band. With everything. You didn't do anything wrong."

Later that night, a storm blew in. As the rain pelted the windows, we sat on the couch for our last night in our honeymoon cottage. We finished off our last bottle of champagne and watched *That '70s Show*. Just as it was about to end, his phone lit up with a number he must have recognized. He went completely still. Then his hand flexed, hovered over the device.

"Who is it?" I asked.

He stared at the phone as if it were a venomous snake. "Nobody."

He answered anyway, turning away from me, shoulders tense as he stood and moved into the kitchen. "No. No, don't—I told you I'm with my wife." His voice dropped too low for me to hear over the TV.

My skin prickled. I shifted my gaze from the TV and watched him travel from the kitchen to the sliding glass door. He stepped out into the pouring rain as lightning flashed in the distance.

"I said stop calling... No, I'm not—"

He slid the glass door shut.

I turned back to the TV, but my breathing had picked up along with my heart rate. Over the last two months, I'd watched enough soap operas to understand that I should be suspicious of this conversation. He'd never given me cause until now. Was he talking to another woman?

Minutes later, he came back inside, scraping his wet hair back from his forehead. His phone bleeped with the sound it made whenever he turned it off, and he tossed it on the counter. I didn't ask him about the phone call. He didn't explain.

Instead, he stripped off his wet shirt and marched down the hall toward the bathroom. The hiss of the shower followed.

The room's dim lighting suddenly seemed even darker. Maybe it was the panic I'd seen in his eyes or the anxiety that infiltrated his voice that was all too familiar, but I sensed that something or someone had a hold on him. And he didn't want me to know about it.

Chapter Thirty-Five

MAY 1999

"Stark Daylight"

Departure day. Sullivan stood by the car, hands in his pockets, staring at the cottage door.

Some new security guy loaded our stuff into the back of a rented black van while Dart kept watch, speaking into his mobile phone every few minutes.

I put my hand on Sullivan's arm. "You ready?"

"I don't want to go back." His jaw tightened. "But don't worry. I will. I just … I liked who I was here." He reached for my hand and squeezed it. "Don't let me become someone else out there."

My heart twisted. "You won't."

He didn't argue, but his silence said he didn't believe that either.

We drove toward the airport, Dart and the new guy in the front, Sullivan and me in the back.

Something was off. Tension radiated from Sullivan like radioactive material. He was keyed up, eyes wide, fidgety, and wired. I glanced over at the bottle of bourbon anchored in his lap. Every few minutes, he put it to his lips and tipped it. This wasn't like him. Was this the way he was going to handle things? Silence? Drinking?

His cell phone buzzed nonstop. Someone named Paz called with questions about backstage accommodations. Someone else called with an itinerary for once he arrived in Florida.

"I'll never remember all of that, Marcy," he said. "Email it to me."

Red called with instructions on rehearsals for the next day.

"Yeah, I've reworked the lyrics for that," Sullivan assured him. "We'll go over that tomorrow."

An executive from the record company called. His name was Jim, I would soon learn. Jim called about me.

Sullivan stared out the window. "Well, like I said, Jim, we're married. And that's that." He announced it with confidence. With defiance. Like it was the best decision he'd ever made. It was his life, after all. He wanted to marry, and that was his business, not the record company's.

But then came the blast of fury through the receiver, shouting, expletives.

Sullivan's face hardened. "Why the hell not? Why can't people know?"

Jim's voice crackled through the line.

Sullivan's face crumpled. "What do you mean it'll ruin my image? You've got to be kidding me." He slumped down into the seat, rubbing his forehead. Another shot from the bottle of bourbon. "So what—you want me to pretend I'm single? Lie about my life?" He slammed his hand against the side of the door. "No, I'm not doing that. I'm not hiding her."

Whatever was said next—whatever threat or leverage they used—broke his resolve. His eyes closed.

"Fine. We won't announce it, but I'm not pretending she doesn't exist."

After he disconnected the call, his eyes watered. Shame and rage wrestled across his face.

"They want me to appear single. Like I would do that to you."

The force of his admission cut into me. No one was congratulating Sullivan on his wedding. That much was clear.

He dragged a hand through his hair. "Do you know what that asshole said? That a married frontman doesn't sell. That it'll 'confuse the target demographic.'" He mimicked the phrase, his voice dripping with sarcasm. "Like I'm supposed to flirt with women from the stage? Let girls scream and think I'm going home with one of them?"

I didn't know what to say.

He flailed his hands. "Anyway, you heard me. I told them no. I told them I wasn't hiding you. They want me packaged. A product. A fantasy. They want me to look attainable." His expression shifted—anger collapsing into vulnerability. "Well, I'm not doing that."

"Good," I said. "Stand up to them."

He stared hard at the seat back. "Brynn, they can make things ... difficult."

"What do you mean?"

He hesitated. "They could cut me out of decisions, out of promo. Bring in people who will 'get with the program.' And if the band goes along with it..." He exhaled shakily. "I could lose everything."

This was the real threat. Sullivan wasn't worried about his public image. This was the old slithering terror finding its way back into his brain. That he would end up where he started—with nothing.

I reached for him. "You won't lose everything."

His eyes flicked to mine. "You don't know that."

"You won't lose me," I said.

He shook his head. "I can't let them control me." He seemed to be reassuring himself. "They make me feel like I'm still trapped. Like, no matter how far I run, someone's going to decide the rest of my life for me."

I stroked his jaw with the back of my hand. "You're not trapped. They can't tell you what to do like that."

"They just did."

"Tell them to go to hell." I had to fight for him. I hadn't come this far, run from my own prison, just to let a new set of wardens take him from me. "They don't own you, Sullivan."

He swiveled his head toward me again, and his eyes were full of something tragic. "Yes, Brynn, they do."

It was the first crack splitting the beautiful, fragile world we'd built—a fracture that would only widen in the days ahead.

Chapter Thirty-Six

JUNE-JULY 1999

"The Shift"

Somehow, we made it through the Orlando concert. Then on to Philadelphia, New Jersey, Massachusetts, and three more dates in New York. Woodstock loomed large. It would be the largest crowd the band had ever performed for. Then back down South, and soon after, we would be on our way out West. Texas, Missouri, Colorado, Arizona, Nevada, and California after the new year—if there was one. The dates kept coming like balls in a batting cage.

Over the next few weeks, as we spent more time on the tour trail, Sullivan began to change. He grew quieter. More tightly wound. More easily irritated.

He drank, smoked, and slept more. Between nights crammed in the lounge of the tour bus or crashing into hard beds at roadside hotels and motels, I felt like the pendulum in a metronome.

At least for now, Brooke was the only other woman traveling with the band. She'd rejoined the bus in Philly, walking up to the wide windows, carrying a duffel bag and wearing a smile that didn't show one iota of fear or anxiety.

Despite my confusion at her willingness to forgive Nate's abuse, I envied her confidence and how loosely she held to her tenuous position. If this all ended tomorrow for her, she would probably land on her feet. She didn't hover. She didn't apologize for anything. She perched cross-legged on the bus seats, wandered around backstage with a beer in hand, laughed easily with the crew. No one questioned why she was there.

As her tall, willowy form sashayed down the aisle of the tour bus, she made eye contact with me, shot out a fist, and gently punched me in the arm. "Good to see you, girl." Then she bent down and whispered in my ear. "Congratulations."

It was good to see her too. No one but Brooke and Sullivan even talked to me. I was Pariah—the reason why the record company was monitoring so closely, breathing down all their necks. Even though I didn't really understand how, I threatened their position on the Billboard charts. The other band members ignored me, the managers scowled at me, and if Sullivan didn't ask me if I wanted coffee and an Egg McMuffin most mornings, I would have assumed I was completely invisible.

One afternoon outside a venue in New Jersey, while the band was inside doing sound check, Brooke slid into the seat across the aisle from me.

Propping her feet up on the seatback in front of her, she popped the tab on a soda. "So, how's married life?"

I rolled my head toward her. "It was great until we got back on the bus."

She shrugged. "Screw 'em. You know? You love him, he loves you. Who cares what anyone's saying?"

What were they saying, exactly? It was as if I were living in a soundproof bubble.

I focused on her cheekbone, right by her eye. No more bruises. "What made you come back?"

She furrowed her eyebrows. "Come back? Oh, honey. I'll always come back. Are you kidding?" She pulled a packet of cigarettes from her pocket and held it out to me. "Want one?"

I shook my head while simultaneously pulling one from the pack. She poked hers into her mouth, lit the end of it, and puffed.

"You act like you're surprised I came back." She held out the lighter to me.

I froze, the cigarette poised in midair. "I don't really know how to—"

"Here, let me do it." She took the stick back from me, lit it in her own mouth, and then returned it.

I held it, blinking against the smoke. "I guess after the way things ended last time, I figured I wouldn't see you again."

She took a drag and blew out a foggy stream. "Are you talking about that thing with Nate?"

I nodded. It had seemed like more than just a "thing."

She faced forward, her voice dipping into a near monotone. "Just part of the territory. You learn what you can put up with. And what you can't. You learn when and how long to stay on board, and when to jump ship, to push back." She took another puff. "You learn when to look the other way."

I stared at her profile. "Yeah, that's not … that's not something I can deal with. I came from a life of that kind of shit. Looking the other way. Not asking questions. I can't do that anymore."

"Like I said, you learn what you can and can't put up with. At least you know." She turned her head slowly until her eyes met mine. "Are you going to smoke that thing or let the ash burn your hand?"

I stared at the glowing end of the stick, licked my lips, and then put the filter against my tongue. I sucked in a little, and the smoke hit the back of my throat and then fast-tracked to my lungs. There was nothing I could do but cough.

"Burns so good, right?" Brooke smiled a little as she took a sip of her drink.

I continued to sputter, choke, and pound my chest.

"Anyway," she said. "This isn't the rest of my life. This is just a chapter."

Later that night, after the show, I found Brooke sitting on the steps behind the venue, her feet dangling off the loading dock. Nate sat beside her, his arm slung loosely around her shoulders. They were talking low, their faces close together.

I quickly swung away from them, pulled out a cigarette lodged in my pocket, and stuck it in my mouth. Brooke had given me a few of hers "to practice" with after my pathetic attempt that morning. I'd decided that I would take up smoking. Not that I liked it. Not that I stood a chance of finding myself popular with the other band members, but maybe, by sharing a vice, I could rise to something more than extra-terrestrial in their eyes.

I stood there, sucking on the unlit cigarette, while I patted down my pockets, pretending to look for a lighter I didn't have.

I hadn't seen Sullivan in hours. He was in a huddle with

management, or going over some rhythms with Red and Jared, or pacing alone, his mind always three steps ahead of wherever we actually were. I was here with him, but he wasn't here with me. Not really.

Now, I didn't even have a damn lighter for my cigarette.

"Hey, Brynn? You want a light?" Brooke called out to me.

I spun around.

She was already holding up a lighter, its flame dancing in the breeze.

With a shrug, I joined them, mindful of Nate's half-hooded gaze, his upturned chin, his hands clasped between his knees. His hatred for me oozed from his pores, and I made sure to shoot flaming frequencies back at him. Brooke might have forgiven him for hitting her, but I hadn't.

I leaned forward, allowed Brooke to light my cigarette, then I sucked in and immediately coughed as the smoke burned my larynx. My vision blurred.

"You all right?" She smacked me on the back.

I nodded, but the hacks continued.

Nate held out his bottle of diet soda. "Here. Take a swig."

I tipped it up and drank the cold, fizzy cola. "Thank you," I gasped, beating one side of my fist against my sternum. "I'm not very good at this."

"Obviously," he deadpanned.

I handed him back the soda and wiped my mouth immediately.

"You get used to the burn," he said.

I finally managed to take a drag that didn't result in emergency intervention. Then I suspended the cigarette in midair like I'd seen Brooke do. I caught a glimpse of myself in the window of a tractor-trailer parked nearby. Unlike

Brooke, who always looked cool holding her cigarette, I looked like I was hailing a cab, my arm raised too high, fingers extended.

I dropped my arm. "So, Woodstock on Sunday?"

Nate lit his own cigarette, pulled smoke into his mouth, and blew it out again. "Yep."

"I hear it's going to be a huge crowd—like, they're expecting around 250,000."

Nate blew a smoke ring. "Yep." He turned to Brooke as if remembering something. "Hey, I heard that Mark Byron is flying out. Fletch said he's coming specifically to hear us play."

Brooke wrapped her hands around her throat and pretended to be choking.

Nate's eyebrows met. "What?"

"You know he's a slimeball, right?"

"What do you mean?"

Brooke raised her hand to her hips. "Come on, Nate. You must have heard the stories about him. I have, and I'm not even a musician."

"What stories? The guy's a brilliant producer."

Brooke tapped ash onto the ground. "Watch yourself. Don't go anywhere alone with him. Don't say yes to anything."

Nate scoffed and gave her a *you crazy, girl* look.

Someone called Nate's name from inside the building. He pushed to his feet. "Be back in a minute," he said to Brooke. Then he disappeared through the concrete entrance.

"Who is this guy you're talking about?" I asked.

Brooke threw her cigarette on the ground and squashed it with her foot. "Just another sleazy music industry asshole."

She draped her arm around me, wrapping me in a scented shawl of smoke and what I had come to learn was patchouli. "Hey, listen, I know you're trying, but you don't have to be *on* all the time. No one expects that."

I licked my lips and took another drag. I didn't even know what she meant by "on." I hadn't felt *on* since Sullivan and I left Pawley's Island weeks ago. All I knew was that somehow, I had to hold everything together. I had to be the wife, the anchor, the reason he didn't drift. Or spiral.

"Thanks for the tip."

She squeezed my shoulder. "Hang tough, girl." She let her arm slide away. "I gotta go find my man."

Later that night, I joined Sullivan inside the van that would take us back to our hotel. When I arrived, he was already inside. His face in shadows, he stared straight ahead.

Something was wrong. Sullivan's breathing was overly pronounced, his chest rising and falling too fast. His hair was still wet from the shower he'd taken after the show, and the water had dripped down his neck, making water marks on his shirt.

He ran both hands through his hair, breathing hard.

I put my hand on his leg. "What's wrong?"

He squeezed his eyes shut, shook his head.

Fletch, the band's manager, climbed into the van and stalked toward us. His crow-like eyes fixed on Sullivan, then tracked to me. "Sullivan's a little keyed up. He's been given a sedative. He should be feeling much better in the next minute or so."

What a minute. What? He'd been *given* a sedative? As in, this was something that had already happened.

My mouth dropped open. "A sedative? Really? Why?"

Fletch sank into a seat behind us. "Woodstock is going

to make or break us," he said to me or someone else, it hardly seemed to matter. "Tomorrow may be the most important gig we ever play."

A beat later, Sullivan whispered, "You mean make or break me."

Fletch answered. "No, Sullivan. Make or break the band. Not everything is about you. Or, at least, it shouldn't be."

After that, the van was quiet. We pulled out of the lot and moved toward the hotel like we were the first car in a funeral dirge.

We were heading toward the weekend that would change everything.

But none of us knew that yet.

Chapter Thirty-Seven

NOW

I arrive at the hotel a little early for check-in, but my room is ready. I take a shower and get dressed. Of course, I'm going to spend extra time on my makeup and straightening my hair.

Even after all of that, I still have three hours before I meet Sullivan at the comedy club.

The hotel has a bar, so I head down there. It's half-full, with a mixture of people sitting at tables and at the bar itself. I perch on an empty stool at the end and order a bourbon, just to take the edge off. The bartender looks like she's around my age, with long braids and a bright blue butterfly tattoo on her hand that matches her eyes. She pours generously, slides the glass toward me, and moves on to the next customer.

Most people here seem like business travelers, dressed in suits or business casual. A couple sitting a few stools over tells the bartender they're killing time before seeing a show at the Grand Ole Opry. A man in a corner booth sits with his feet propped on his suitcase, head tipped back, mouth open.

I take two slow sips, feel the warmth settle behind my ribs. With no food in my stomach, this could hit me fast.

I wave to the bartender. "Can I also get a coffee?"

She nods and returns to her computer screen to enter my newest order.

A guy sitting next to me turns slightly, and I feel his eyes on me. "Bold move," he says. "Mixing the depressants and the stimulants."

I glance over. He's probably mid-forties, with a lean face, dark hair starting to retreat at the temples. He's wearing a black hoodie with the sleeves pushed up.

"Midlife compromise," I say. "I've got somewhere to be tonight, so I can't fall asleep."

He grins. "Respectable strategy."

He lifts his glass. Looks like he might be drinking something similar to my bourbon. There's a notebook on the bar in front of him, edges frayed, pen tucked into the spiral.

"You in town for business or punishment?" he asks.

I laugh a little. Interesting choice of words. "Uh, well..."

He holds up a hand. "Wait. Let me guess." He closes his eyes. "You're either here for a conference or, and forgive me for saying this, and please don't be offended, but you could be meeting someone you shouldn't be meeting."

"Wow. Are you psychic?"

He opens one eye. "So, it's the latter."

"Is it that obvious?"

He opens his other eye, sits back, and clasps his glass. "Only because you ordered bourbon and then immediately course corrected. But don't worry. I won't tell anyone."

Seems like this guy might already have had a drink or two. "What about you? Here for business or punishment?"

"I'm here for comedy," he says. "Which is sort of both." He gestures toward the TV above the bar, where muted sports highlights flicker. "This hotel's a short walk from Zanies. Sometimes I come in here to calm my nerves before doing something brave or stupid."

"And which are you contemplating tonight?"

"Brave," he says without hesitation. "Definitely brave." Then, after a beat, "Ask me again after my set."

I shift on my stool to face him. "Oh. So, you're performing tonight?"

"Yep. Later show." He glances at his watch. "Still several hours out. Plenty of time to overthink everything I've ever said into a microphone."

I smile. "I'm going to that show tonight."

"Really? Nah, you're shitting me."

"No, really."

He holds out a hand. "I'm Steve Criss. Steve."

I take his hand. "Brynn."

"Where you from, Brynn?"

"Charleston."

"That's a haul. Damn, girl. You came all this way just to see my show?"

I laugh. "You're funny." I finish my bourbon and swirl my coffee. "I'm actually meeting someone at Zanies."

Steve's eyebrows lift. "Ah. The someone you shouldn't meet."

"Someone I haven't seen in twenty-five years."

He lets out a low whistle. "That's not a meeting. That sounds more like an archaeological dig."

I smile. "Kinda feels that way."

He takes a sip of his drink. "Well. Nashville's a hell of a

place for unresolved history." His mouth quirks. "Hey, I'm a comedian, so I have no filters or boundaries, so I'm just going to ask—ex, old friend, former bandmate, cult leader?"

I laugh hard this time. "Seriously, Steve. Are you psychic?"

"Not that I know of."

I let the coincidences settle around me like falling leaves. "He's a rock singer." I pause. "And my ex."

Steve's eyes light up. "No shit."

"Afraid so."

"OK, now I'm invested." He leans back slightly. "You don't have to tell me details. I'm off the clock emotionally. But I know a few musicians who frequent my shows. I perform at Zanies quite a bit. There are some regulars. I'm just wondering if I'll know this guy."

I tense at his attempt to discover more details. I don't know this man. He could be lying about being a comedian. He could be a psychopath for all I know, trying to nail down my whereabouts for the night.

I don't say anything.

He turns his glass. "It's not Gilbert Tressway, is it?"

I shake my head. "No."

He rubs his chin. "Sullivan Stonecutter shows up at Zanies sometimes," he says casually. "He's friends with a couple of us comics. Comes in, sits in the back."

I jerk like he's poked me with a cattle prod.

Steve clocks the shift immediately. "Oh, damn. That's him."

I draw in my lips and look down at my drink. Either I have stumbled upon the smallest-world town in the United States, or this guy is going to stalk and kill me later tonight.

He sits with the realization for a moment, then says,

"You're Sullivan Stonecutter's ex?" He slaps the bar then freezes, palm still flat, like he's realized he stepped too far into traffic. "Holy sh—really?"

I focus on the condensation sliding down my glass, the way my pulse thuds in my ears.

Steve exhales, and the bravado drains out of him a notch. "I'm not trying to be creepy. I swear."

"Convince me," I say.

He angles his body away from me. "Zanies has a small ecosystem. Comics talk. Musicians talk. Sometimes those circles overlap, especially here. Nashville's not L.A., but it's not a village either—it's more like a big house with thin walls. Look, I don't even live here. I live in Cookeville. I come into town to do shows once or twice a month."

I finally glance at him. "How well do you know Sullivan?"

"I've met Sullivan a few times," Steve continues. "Usually late sets. He sits in the back with a beer and leaves before anyone makes a big deal out of him." He pauses. "I wouldn't have said his name if you hadn't already said rock singer. Mostly, we have country musicians coming in." He slices his hand through the air. "Anyway, none of my business. I'll leave you alone."

Silence stretches between us.

After a moment, he adds, "If it helps at all—and you didn't hear this from me—he's always alone when he comes in. Doesn't bring a crew. Doesn't bring women. Just himself."

The bartender refills my coffee, breaks the spell. Steve lifts his glass in a small, nonintrusive toast.

The bourbon is doing its work, making me feel like I could use one more. I take a sip of coffee instead.

Steve rattles the ice cube in his glass. "How long were you two together?"

I snicker. "I thought you were going to leave me alone?"

"That was a lie," he says. "Come on. I'm a comedian. I use other people's stories to get material. Think of me as your psychoanalyst. You know, comedy's cheaper than therapy."

I flash him a look. "You are *not* using my story. I will sue your ass."

He rests his head on his hand, still smiling. "I never force anyone to talk to me."

I hesitate, order another bourbon. Then I start talking.

Chapter Thirty-Eight

WOODSTOCK, NEW YORK, JULY 1999

"Peace and Love"

The roads leading to Woodstock clogged miles before the site, traffic slowing to a crawl as vans, buses, and battered sedans funneled toward the same inevitable destination.

The closer we got to Griffiss Air Force Base, the more the world changed. Tents. Bare skin. Flags tied to car antennas. People walking along the shoulder of the road, already drunk, even though it was only past noon. Vendors waving handmade signs for water, beer, mushrooms, weed. Heat shimmered off the blacktop, warping everything.

When we finally reached the checkpoint, a staffer with a headset gestured us through with a bored flick of his wrist.

From the window of the tour bus, I stared out at the passing people. Shirtless guys with painted chests. Girls with flowers drawn on their cheeks. Older-something men leered openly as women passed.

As the bus inched along, the air thickened with music drifting from portable speakers, laughter, the bee-like buzz of thousands of voices layering over one another. We had crossed into a place where normal rules no longer applied.

When we finally crested a rise, an endless sea of bodies stretched farther than my eyes could follow, dotted with color and movement. Flags whipped in the breeze. Smoke drifted upward in lazy columns. The sheer scale of it was impossible to process. Biblical. Like standing at the edge of something ancient and otherworldly.

"What the hell?" Nate murmured behind us.

Brooke pressed her fingertips to the window. "That's a shit load of people."

Red let out a low whistle. "This is it, man. This is the one."

Sitting beside me, Sullivan didn't say anything. His fingers flexed against his knee, his mouth trembling slightly. He looked better on the surface than he had yesterday. The sedative last night and the one they gave him this morning had softened the tension in his jaw, the fidgety movements and wild eyes. In fact, Sullivan had been given a sedative twice a day since we left the last show, and although he was calmer, it was like his core persona had been scooped out and left behind at the last arena. All the fire, the anger, the nervousness was gone, replaced with a watery-eyed zombie stare.

The bus rolled forward, swallowed by the perimeter of the festival. Crew members jogged alongside us, shouting instructions I couldn't hear through the glass.

When we stepped off the bus, the collective noise hit me full force. Thousands of people breathed and shouted and sang as one organism. The ground vibrated. Somewhere in the distance, a band launched into a song and the crowd roared back.

Sullivan's body locked, rigor mortis stiff. I reached for his hand—as much for me as for him.

"You OK?" I asked.

"Yeah. I'm good." But his eyes were glassy, unfocused, as if he were moving inside a dream.

We passed along a maze of barriers and tents, past vendors and medics and clusters of artists. People stared, some recognizing Sullivan, some sensing proximity to someone important. A girl shrieked his name. A shirtless guy bolted out of the crowd and shoved a beer into his hand. Laughter, whistles, and shouts erupted all around us.

Sullivan groaned. "Damn. This is insane. Chaos."

We reached the backstage area, where folding tables sagged under the weight of food and bottles. People moved in loose, frantic orbits—publicists, techs, hangers-on. The energy crackled, electric and volatile. Musicians sprawled on couches, managers barked orders, interns delivered bottled water. A towering fan rattled uselessly in the corner, stirring hot air.

Heads turned when Sullivan walked in. His height always got him some attention anyway, but in here, many of the other artists recognized him. Some sized him up. A few eyed me with open curiosity, trying to figure out my role— girlfriend, groupie, assistant?

A man almost as tall as Sullivan, wearing a headset and a blue T-shirt already soaked through with sweat, clapped him on the shoulder. "There you are," he breathed in a hoarse voice. "You're on schedule for interviews at three, then photo ops, then sound check. Keep your phone on. The label wants to run something by you."

Sullivan barely looked at him. "About what?"

The man had already moved on, calling out orders to Fletch and Nate.

We sat on a beat-up red sofa, the fabric scratchy on the backs of my thighs. Sullivan hunched forward, elbows on his knees, fingers tapping a jittery beat.

"What's wrong?" I asked under my breath.

He exhaled hard. "All I can think is don't screw it up. Don't let them regret putting us on the lineup."

"They won't," I said. "You belong here."

He gave a humorless laugh. "Everyone keeps saying that."

Doubt sparked in his eyes, and I could almost hear his thoughts—that this was bigger than him, an ocean, a momentum that could pull him under.

I put my hand on his back. "You're going to be amazing. Better than…" I tried to think of a band that had played at the original Woodstock. "Better than The Doors."

Sullivan swung his head toward me. "The Doors didn't play at Woodstock."

"They didn't?"

He shook his head. "They were smart." He rubbed a hand over his freshly shaved chin. "This isn't a club show, Brynn. If we tank out here, it's not just a bad set. It's the whole thing. Media sees it. Every radio station hears about."

I squeezed his shoulder. "Then don't tank."

He huffed out a breath, and his lips curved in an almost-smile.

We ventured out near the barricades later to see the stage before sound check. Dart and the new bodyguard stayed close. The crowd was already high on heat and anticipation.

A drunk guy yelled at us as we passed, right before someone shoved him to the ground. A group of boys chanted nonsensical phrases, sloshing warm beer down their chests. The merciless sun hammered down on us.

"This is going to be a disaster," I overheard a security guard yell to another.

I'd never been in a place like this, with so many people. Tension bubbled in my gut. Something was wrong in the atmosphere—like the air before lightning struck.

This didn't feel like peace-and-love nostalgia. This felt like a pressure cooker.

Later that afternoon, Cutter went on.

I found Brooke near the side of the stage, tucked far enough back to avoid the crush. She handed me a bottle of water without asking, and I gripped it like it might be the only one I'd get for days. The heat was oppressive, and there seemed to be no place to escape it.

From where we stood, the audience stretched out in a living mass, bodies pressed together so tightly they seemed to move as one. Heat rose off them, along with the partly sweet, partly pungent incense of sweat, grass, and dirt.

The band swept past us and walked onto the stage, and Sullivan stepped into the version of himself the world demanded.

The crowd's roar surged in a tidal wave of sound, hitting my chest first, then my ears, then my bones, as though I were standing too close to an explosion. Brooke whooped beside me, throwing her hands in the air, and for a while, I danced along with her.

At first, Sullivan looked incredible. Loose. Command-ing. Alive in a way I'd only ever seen flashes of before. He stalked the stage, voice raw and powerful, the band locked in behind him. Red grinned as he bobbed up and down, bass slung low. Nate slammed into his guitar, hair whipping, feeding off the energy.

Brooke shouted into my ear. "Sullivan's on fire!"

He was. Even so, he pushed the tempo a little harder than necessary, and during the third song, he forgot a line. The audience was probably too drunk or high to notice. People were crowd-surfing, bodies passing across a series of hands. A bare-breasted woman sat on a man's shoulders, waving her arms in the air.

Near the end of the set, Sullivan gripped the mic stand and shouted something about tonight mattering, about not wasting the moment, about this generation being the impetus for change, for meaning.

"This is what the first Woodstock was about!" His eyes scanned the crowd. "We have to carry that legacy into the new millennium!"

Cutter's final song detonated the field. Fireworks exploded somewhere overhead. Confetti rained down. The crowd screamed every word back at him, thousands of voices echoing his own—ecstatic, violent, holy.

When it was over, Sullivan stood at the edge of the stage, chest heaving, sweat pouring down his face. He held out his arms, smiling.

The band took their bows and filed backstage, where Sullivan was immediately surrounded and swallowed by a knot of people with headsets, clipboards, and laminated badges swinging from their necks.

"Press," someone shouted.

"MTV first."

"*Spin*'s waiting."

Hands reached for him, steering him without asking. A towel was draped around his shoulders. A bottle of water was shoved into his hand. Someone smacked him on the back and shouted, "Hell of a set, man!"

I tried to follow, tripping along behind the parade like a faithful dog.

I went as far as I could before a security guard stepped sideways, blocking my path with a practiced ease.

"Media only past this point."

I slapped a hand to my chest. "I'm his wife."

He shook his head. "I'm sorry. Artists and press only."

I looked past him. Sullivan was already ten feet away, being guided toward a cluster of white tents.

"Sullivan!" I called.

He turned at the sound of my voice, eyes unfocused but searching. For a split second, relief flashed across his face.

"Stay with Brooke," he yelled.

Dart stood beside him, speaking into a two-way radio, and Sullivan was ushered forward again, the bodies closing around him.

The security guard in front of me stepped fully into my space.

"Ma'am, I need you to move back."

The word *ma'am* stung. I wasn't *ma'am*. I was Sullivan's wife. Why couldn't I be with him?

Sullivan was absorbed into the press area, where boom mics awaited. A woman with a headset positioned Sullivan against a backdrop plastered with logos. A female assistant dried the sweat on his face. A microphone appeared inches from his mouth.

Fletch handed him a beer, and Sullivan's fingers curled around it.

The interviews bled into one another. Between the interviews, there were accolades—people shouting congratulations, steering him toward the next obligation.

No one acknowledged me. I stood outside the tent, invisible and sweating, clutching my arms around myself. Every few minutes, someone brushed past me, laughing, already half-drunk on proximity and adrenaline.

I'd lost Brooke, too. I twisted, looking around for her, hoping she was behind me somewhere nearby, tossing her hair over her shoulder, but all I saw were security guards and people with microphones attached to their heads.

This was Sullivan's job, his life, really, and the cost of the life I'd chosen.

This was the version of him they needed. Not the man I knew when the stage lights were off, the one who loved walks on the beach, football on the television, and comedy clubs. The one who woke up beside me and sometimes whispered my name in the dark.

No, they needed this larger-than-life frontman who'd just demonstrated how he could get a quarter of a million people to worship him.

Later, as we were all ushered toward the bus, Sullivan's beer had been replaced by something stronger, poured into a plastic cup.

I'd lost track of all the people I didn't know who gave the band instructions, telling them what was next. A woman with a tangle of curly hair and glossy lips slid her hand over Sullivan's shoulder as we waited to board the bus. "The after party's at the hotel. A couple of execs rented out a suite. Industry people. Nothing crazy. You should swing by."

A bald man in a tie-dyed shirt chimed in. "You kinda have to."

Sullivan laughed, the sound a little thin. "Yeah. Yeah, OK."

I waited for him to look at me.

He didn't.

Somehow, I knew I wasn't invited.

Fletch appeared out of nowhere, his voice bright and efficient. "It'll be good for visibility. A lot of decision-makers are here."

Sullivan nodded. "Cool."

In the bus on the way back to the hotel, Sullivan turned to me. "I won't be long. At the party. I'll try not to stay more than an hour."

"All right." I was too tired to care. The last place I wanted to be was an after-party. I desperately wanted to wash the sweat off my body and go to bed.

The shuttle dropped us at a hotel thirty minutes outside the festival grounds, a glassy, anonymous building lit up with a downstairs lobby already buzzing with people who looked like they hadn't been anywhere near the heat and turbulence of Woodstock.

As the doors of the elevator slid open and we walked out onto the tenth floor, music thudded. Dart trailed us, staying six feet behind, speaking into his radio every so often.

The tenth floor had been transformed with velvet ropes, temporary lighting rigs, and security stationed everywhere. Clusters of musicians, crew, industry executives, and strangers who somehow always found their way into these things filled the space.

A woman in a silver tank top with hair that seemed like a nod to disco-era perms strode toward us.

"Sullivan Stonecutter!" she said brightly. "That set was unreal. You must still be flying."

He forced a smile. "Thanks."

She touched his arm as if she knew him well. Did she?

"Come meet some people." Her fingers lingered on his

bicep, and she began to lead him away from me. "Every-one's talking about you."

"This is my wife." Sullivan grabbed my hand. "This is Brynn."

The woman blinked. "Oh." Her thinly sculpted eyebrows raised. "Cute." She cupped his elbow and tugged. "Come on. You have to talk to Mark Byron. He's been dying to meet you for months now."

I recognized the name. Brooke had mentioned him at a previous show. Mark Byron. A producer. A powerful one. Brooke had called him a slimeball.

"He doesn't usually fly out unless he's serious," she added lightly. "He's the kind of man who opens doors. Or closes them."

I tightened my grip on Sullivan's hand.

He hesitated. "I'm sorry, Brynn. This guy's a big deal. He flew out here just to see us perform."

The woman yanked a little harder at his arm. Now we were practically playing tug of war with him.

"He asked about you specifically, Sully," she said.

Sully? Ugh. No one called Sullivan *Sully*.

"OK." His eyes were still on mine. "Can Brynn come too?"

Frizzy Hair's smile tightened. "Honey, he wants to meet you, not your whole family. This is very insider, OK?" Her eyes flew wide and shifted to mine. "We won't be long, sweetie. Why don't you plan to meet Sully in the bar? Say, in an hour?"

"It's fine," Sullivan said before I could protest. "I'll meet you in the bar. Like she said."

He squeezed my fingers once. Then let go.

So much for me heading off to shower and bed. I guess I'd be waiting in the bar.

Frizzy Hair led Sullivan through the crowd, behind the velvet rope that blocked off one of the long hallways.

Dart didn't follow but posted himself near the elevators. He stood a little apart from everyone else, arms crossed loosely over his chest, gaze moving in slow, practiced sweeps of the hallway. Calm. Alert. The way he always looked when everything was under control.

Our eyes met briefly across the lobby before Dart turned his attention back to the elevators, scanning the next group of people arriving on the floor.

Knowing he was there eased me somewhat. Dart wouldn't let anything bad happen to Sullivan.

I drifted toward the bar, where I grabbed a high-top table. The room was already fogged with cigarette smoke clinging to the low lights and making everyone's face look slightly unreal. Ram, a young guy from the tech crew, whom I'd gotten to know, bought me a drink and pressed a plastic cup into my hand.

"You look like you could use this," he yelled over the music.

He was a nice enough guy, a little scrawny and gangly with wispy, light-brown hair. Ram paid more attention to me than anyone else on the tour, and Sullivan sometimes joked that he had a crush on me.

"Thanks." I took a sip of the drink. Strong, bitter, but a little fruity too.

He leaned against the table. "What are you doing in here all alone? Where's Sullivan?"

I motioned with my head toward the door. "Partying with the important people."

Ram raised his eyebrows. "Ohhh, I see." He lifted his cup in a half-salute. "Welcome to the glamorous side of rock and roll."

I snorted. "Yeah. I feel very glamorous right now."

"They always peel the lead singer off first. It's like fishing. You hook the biggest one and reel him in."

"That's … comforting."

Ram grimaced. "Sorry. That came out wrong." He scratched his jaw, then tried again. "I just mean, they're going to want a piece of him tonight. Everybody does."

I took another sip, the ice clacking against my teeth. "He doesn't really love this stuff."

Ram took a drink, then leaned in a little closer so I could hear him. "Hey—don't freak out, OK? This is normal. The post-show thing. Execs, producers, hangers-on. It's all just networking."

"Is it?"

He hesitated. "Mostly." He patted his pockets, pulled out a pack of cigarettes, and offered me one.

I took it, put it between my lips.

Ram lit it for me. "You guys just got married, right?"

I blew out smoke. "Yeah."

"That's wild." He smiled. "I mean, good wild, you know?"

I smiled back, then glanced at the hallway again. "He said he'd meet me here."

"He will." Ram tapped his plastic cup lightly against mine. "I'll hang around for a bit, OK? Until he shows."

"Thanks."

Ram returned to the bar for another drink, and I remained at the high top. The music pulsed through the bar, bass-heavy, relentless, vibrating up through the soles of my shoes. Men brushed past me with hands that stayed a beat too long on my arm, my waist, my back.

Hadn't an hour passed yet? I nursed my drink in little

sips while hoping to see Sullivan move into the room any second.

Nothing. Not even Dart.

Ram was embroiled in a conversation at the bar. He didn't notice me slide off the stool and fight my way through a group of drunk and oblivious crew members.

The tenth floor had become a maze with roped-off areas, guarded hallways, and elevators requiring wristbands or nods of recognition. I didn't even know where our hotel room was. On this floor or another one?

My drink was almost gone, and I was beyond tired. If I really wanted to, I could sit on the couch in the corner, beside the golden-skinned girl in the bikini top and the shirtless guy she was making out with. There was enough room for me to rest my head against the wall and fall asleep. But then I might miss Sullivan.

A slow sense of dread dripped through my veins as I wandered, seeking a face I recognized. The lights dimmed. More people vanished into the elevator or behind guarded doors. I slid down the wall and sat on the floor. It must be late. Very late. Sullivan should be here by now. Where the hell was he?

Finally, I pushed myself to my feet and stepped closer to the roped-off hallway, trying to peer past security.

A man who resembled Dart in height and brawn stood on the other side of the barrier. "Sorry," he said. "This is a restricted area,"

"I'm just looking for—"

"If he's down there, he'll come out," he said flatly.

The message was clear. He knew who I was looking for.

"Look, I really need to talk to Sullivan. I'm his wife." Why did I feel the need to keep reiterating that fact?

The man crossed his arms. I wasn't getting through.

On the other side of the rope, near the end of the hall, a man stood talking on a cell phone. His wall-like physique was unmistakable.

I waved frantically. "Dart!" My voice echoed as I called out to him.

He held up a finger, signaling me to wait, and resumed his discussion.

At least Dart was there. Still, my blood was simmering. Sullivan said an hour. Now the party on the tenth floor was basically over, and here I was, still waiting.

I just want to go to the room. I need a shower. A bed.

Dart checked his watch. He stepped forward and rapped hard on the door. "We need to wrap this up," he said as if reminding someone of an agreement he hadn't liked in the first place.

Wrap *what* up? What was happening?

Seconds later, the door yawned open.

My blood stopped its rapid boil and instantly dropped to freezing point.

Voices floated out of the room, low, irritated, overlapping. I couldn't make out words, only the tone, which I matched with Dart's annoyed face. Something transactional was taking place at the other end of the hall.

Dart stepped away from the door and rubbed the back of his neck, his eyes scanning the hallway as though recalibrating. For the first time since I'd met him, his face registered uncertainty, calculation, and his composure seemed fractured.

A few seconds later, Sullivan staggered out of the room, but as he moved up the dimly lit hall, with Dart following and speaking into his radio, the wrongness of the moment intensified.

Sullivan's hair covered his eyes in damp tendrils. His

shirt hung crooked on his shoulders, the collar stretched and wrinkled. There was a dark, oily smudge near his throat that looked like spilled liquor—or blood—I couldn't tell which.

He scraped back his hair and stared straight ahead, but his eyes were glassy, pupils so dilated they swallowed the blue.

"Sullivan?" I whispered.

He didn't look up at the sound of my voice. His face was pained, his eyes blinking as though he'd been living in a cave for a month. When his gaze landed on me, his face registered recognition, then relief, then shame. His lip was red, swollen at the corner.

"I'm fine," he muttered in a voice so low I was sure I'd misheard. The lie was automatic and reflexive. He swayed, caught himself against the wall. Dart moved instantly, a hand hovering near Sullivan's elbow but not quite touching him.

I stepped forward, meeting him, my hand on his chest. "What happened?"

Sullivan's shoulders jerked. "Nothing," he snapped, the edge in his voice unfamiliar. "I just need air." He tried to move past me.

"Sullivan. Look at me."

He couldn't. Or wouldn't. He stared at the elevator like he couldn't wait to get there, the muscle jumping beneath the skin of his jaw.

"Let's go. Please."

Dart reached out and jabbed the elevator button.

As we stood, waiting for the lift, I touched Sullivan's bruised lip.

He recoiled as though I'd burned him with a cigarette.

"Don't," his voice was sharp, the lash of a whip.

Tears blurred my vision. Fear, confusion, and grief for

something I didn't yet have language for cascaded through my brain. What had happened to him?

"OK," I said. "We're going to the room. It's OK."

When we exited the elevator, Sullivan stayed a step behind me, as though he didn't want me to brush against him, as though he were holding himself together by sheer force of will.

Once we reached our room and the door was open, Sullivan stumbled inside.

"Sullivan, should I—should I call someone? A doctor?"

He whirled, his eyes flashing. "Do not call a doctor!" His voice was venomous. "I will *not* see a doctor. Do you hear me?"

I held up a hand. "Yes, yes, I hear you."

He shot into the bathroom and shut the door behind him. The lock clicked.

This was like a bad dream. The worst.

I lingered outside in the hallway with Dart. "What— what happened in that room?" I stammered, as though Dart should know.

Dart's eyes were dark. "He's not right, ma'am."

"I know. But what…"

He shifted his weight, lowering his voice. "I don't know what went on back there. But he's showing signs of being … overstimulated. Maybe mixed substances. Could be shock. Do you want me to call someone?"

Shock.

I pictured Sullivan inside the bathroom, pacing, shaking, shutting down.

"Shit." I shuddered out a breath. "He said not to call anyone."

I was torn between the two decisions. Calling someone

and risking Sullivan having a meltdown, or not calling and possibly dealing with a medical emergency.

Dart exhaled slowly. "I'll be here, ma'am. Just next door. If he gets worse—confusion, vomiting, panic—you call me. Any hour. We'll reassess."

"Thank you." I wanted to cry, but there was no time. Instead, I went back inside and locked the door.

Then I sat on the edge of the bed and waited for Sullivan to come out of the bathroom, while I listened to the patter of water on tile for more than an hour.

Chapter Thirty-Nine

ROME, NEW YORK, JULY 1999

"The Abyss"

I stood by the window and watched the edges of an orange sunset push along the horizon. Pale light crept in around the edges of the curtains. Down below, cars still moved along the highway. The day waited.

Soon, we'd be on the road again, just like the old Willy Nelson song.

Sullivan lay in the bed on his side, covers pulled up to his nose, but I couldn't tell if he was really sleeping. When he'd finally emerged from the bathroom in the early hours of the morning, he'd lain down on the bed, still in his towel, still dripping wet.

I glanced over at our bags by the door. He hadn't even opened his suitcase. I turned on the television and watched the morning news. They were interviewing a computer scientist discussing what would happen once it struck midnight on January 1, 2000.

Blackout. Breakdown. Total chaos.

Didn't seem all that different from what I was dealing with right now.

When the knock—our wake-up call—finally came, Sullivan didn't move. He still lay on his side, eyes closed.

I quietly padded to the door. Before I could open it, another knock followed. Louder this time.

Fletch stood in the hallway with a coffee in one hand and a clipboard tucked under his arm, like Sullivan used to carry in Crystal Cliffs. He appeared freshly showered, awake, ready, as if this were any other morning.

He glanced past me into the room. "We need Sullivan downstairs in twenty. Press thing in the conference room."

My throat was dry. "He didn't sleep."

Fletch gave a tight smile. "None of us did."

I didn't move out of the doorway. "He's not OK." My voice was a plea.

That earned me a look as if he were weighing inconvenience against obligation.

"Sorry," he said. "He doesn't get to be not OK. We have to hit the road soon."

Behind me, the mattress creaked as Sullivan sat up.

"I'm fine," he called out hoarsely.

I turned. He was already pulling on yesterday's jeans, movements jerky and rushed, as though he didn't trust himself to slow down.

Fletch nodded, satisfied. "See? Adrenaline cures a lot."

I wanted to scream.

Sullivan brushed past me and grabbed the coffee from Fletch's hand, downing it in three swallows, wincing like it was medicine.

I stared at him, my mouth hanging open. That coffee had to be scalding his throat.

"Press in the conference room at nine," Fletch continued. "I'll wait here until he's ready, and I'll walk you downstairs."

I closed the door, my mind a painful conglomerate of emotions. I didn't know which to feel first. I wasn't even sure I could extricate one from the other.

Sullivan pulled a clean T-shirt out of his bag and sat on the bed, rubbing his hands together as if trying to warm them.

I moved slowly, keeping a careful distance. I didn't want him to think I expected anything of him—not words, not comfort, not closeness.

Finally, he spoke. "Brynn, I can't…" He shook his head. "I can't talk about it."

"I know. It's OK."

His shoulders sagged a little, like he'd been bracing for an argument that didn't come. He still hadn't met my eyes.

"Let's get ready to go," I said.

A few minutes later, I followed him into the hallway, where Fletch stood against the adjacent wall with Dart.

Fletch stepped forward, obviously expecting to fall into stride beside Sullivan. "Hey, I hear you were a big hit with Mark Byron last night. Early rumblings say the label is absolutely ecstatic."

Scowling, Sullivan shot past Fletch and moved down the hall in front of us. Then, he and Dart got on the elevator and closed the doors before Fletch and I could board with them.

Fletch's keys hung from a loop on his pants, jangling as he walked. "Someone's in a mood today. He hungover or what?"

"He's not well."

Fletch scoffed. "Yeah, he's got something called LSD.

Lead singer's disease. Thinks the world revolves around him."

I felt my heart pounding in my fingertips, rage pumping through me. I stopped walking. "You're not hearing me, Fletch. Sullivan needs a break."

Fletch stopped walking, too, and then stalked forward, his face like concrete. For a flashing second, I thought he might punch me.

The cords in his neck stood out. "Look, this weekend determines a lot of futures. Including his. He doesn't get a break. None of us do. Not until this is behind us."

Behind us.

As if last night and whatever had happened were a hurdle, not an internal wound, the prognosis of which wasn't even clear yet.

* * *

The tour bus idled at the curb while the crew loaded gear into the undercarriage.

The ragtag group moved like zombies, most of them hungover or, like Sullivan and me, completely void of sleep. Nate and Brooke led the way, followed by Jared, Red, and Fletch. Sullivan and I brought up the rear. An assistant stood at the open door, handing paper travel cups of coffee to each of us before we forced ourselves to climb into the vessel that would once again transport us across state lines.

Sullivan moved like his bones hurt, as though every step jarred a tender place inside him. He climbed the steps and took a seat near the front, by the window. I slid in beside him. He pressed his forehead to the glass immediately, his reflection staring back at us both, pale, distorted by the window's curvature, eyes rimmed with darkness.

Finally, the bus lurched forward, rolling away from the hotel, away from the place where our whole world had changed.

"Man." Red stretched his legs into the aisle. "That place was a zoo."

A chorus of agreement followed.

Nate hung a hand over the back of Red's seat; only his eyes were visible over the top. "Yeah, heard it got even wilder after we left."

Red coughed, a crackly, croupy sound. "Wild's one word for it."

"Heard Limp Bizkit's crowd went feral," said Nate.

Sitting behind Sullivan and me, Jared pattered his drumsticks against his thighs. "Cops didn't do shit."

Red pulled a baseball cap over his already flattened bed-head hair. "Yeah, well, people lost their damn minds."

The conversation rolled on, bits and pieces of the previous day's experience drifting through the bus like smoke. Fires, trashed trailers, jokes about how the promoters had lost control.

Sullivan didn't react. He didn't add anything to the conversation. His hands rested in his lap, fingers laced together so tightly his knuckle bones protruded. I watched him out of the corner of my eye, cataloging his responses. He didn't even turn around when Red leaned forward and flicked him in the back of the head.

"Hey, that was one hell of a set yesterday, brother. You crushed it."

Sullivan nodded once. "Thanks."

That was it.

No grin. No deflection. No self-deprecating joke.

Jared stretched his arms above his head. "And then there was that party at the hotel last night. Man, that was *insane*."

A low whistle from Red.

"Absolute madhouse."

"People did some real stupid shit," Jared said.

Laughter followed.

I'd never gotten travel sick before, but the threat of it now was real.

The same thoughts kept going through my mind. The party. Something had happened to Sullivan there. Something terrible. Something he couldn't talk about. And it was tearing him up inside.

Why wouldn't he talk to me? Tell me what happened? Pushing him now would only make him retreat further.

The bus picked up speed. Ahead of us, the road paved the way to another town, another venue, another night. Behind us, Woodstock was already being reshaped into a story they could all brag about and turn into legend later.

Beside me, Sullivan was silent, staring out at the passing trees like he was watching something burn in the distance.

Chapter Forty

FALL 1999

"Undone"

The weeks and months after Woodstock folded in and stretched out accordion-style. Time passed. Highways stitched one venue to the next. Hotels all looked the same and were sometimes worse than spending the night on the tour bus. I'd begun to question what was happening, not only between Sullivan and me but within myself.

I'd started hating the reporters and journalists. I resented Fletch, and nearly everything Brooke said or did irritated me, even though we were in this together. I prayed that everything the news was saying about Y2K was true, and that the grid would go down at the end of the year. The last concert date was slated for New Year's Eve in Florida, just before everything was supposed to go dark. Fitting that it would happen in Florida, the very place where Sullivan's and my history began.

In my mind, if Y2K did happen, then Sullivan wouldn't have to tour anymore. Maybe we could settle, he could get his head back together, and we could start our life as a couple. As it was, Sullivan was changing in subtle ways that soon became unmistakable.

He slept in fragments. An hour here. Forty minutes there. Some nights, not at all. When he did sleep, it was shallow and restless, his body jerking awake as if he'd been called back from somewhere dangerous.

When I reached for him in the dark, he stiffened.

"I'm tired," he'd say. Or, "Not tonight."

Sex between us was practically nonexistent. When it happened, it was distant. Over quickly. He kept his eyes closed. Afterward, he'd roll away and lie rigid beside me, breath shallow, like he was bracing for something else to happen. Like he wanted me to disappear. At least that's how it felt. Sometimes he apologized. Sometimes he didn't.

By late fall, the drinking had crept in quietly, an old friend slipping into the room when no one was watching. Two beers before the show. Two shots afterward. Then three. Then whatever was handed to him.

He only laughed or smiled when he drank. But after too many, he became angry, and sometimes incoherent and out of control.

And Germany. It was looming. Sullivan and I hadn't talked about whether I was going with them. If not, where would I go instead?

I learned not to ask what he was thinking. Not to ask why he flinched when someone touched his shoulder unexpectedly, or why certain rooms escalated his anxiety.

At night, when he paced the length of a hotel room, running his hands through his hair and muttering to himself, I told myself this was temporary. Time would loosen whatever knot had formed inside him. It had to. Because we couldn't go on this way.

Onstage, Sullivan was electric. Charismatic. Untouchable. The crowds were louder every show. The concerts got better, not worse.

Backstage, he unraveled quietly. I became the keeper of his normal routines—water, Advil, cigarettes. Someone else provided him with the other things he needed—sedatives, uppers, shots of things I didn't know the name of.

Every day, my mind circled through the same questions. How much longer? When will he get better? Will he ever talk to me and tell me the truth? I was holding something I couldn't carry forever.

I loved him, but love had become a container that was suffocating us both.

In a hotel outside Charlotte, North Carolina, I finally found out what was to be my fate while the band went abroad. The curtains were half-drawn against the afternoon sun. Sullivan's suitcase lay open on the floor, clothes folded with precision. I had watched him pack and repack and then repack again, a practice that had become part of his routine. The next day, we were headed toward Lancaster, Pennsylvania, the last show before the band left for Germany for two weeks.

I sifted coffee grinds into the hotel coffee maker. "Where do you go first?"

"Berlin first. They want us in Berlin a day before."

Us, but not really us.

"When do you leave?"

"End of the week."

"And me?"

The question hung between us, fragile and exposed.

He paused, then reached for a pair of socks. Rolled, unrolled, rolled again.

I sank onto a chair. "I'm not going with you, am I?"

He rubbed his eyes. "Germany's going to be intense. I thought it might be good if you went back to Pawley's Island for a bit."

"For a bit," I repeated.

"Yeah." He stared down at his hands. "It's just going to be the band traveling. No spouses or girlfriends."

"I see. A boys' trip." I tried to keep the bitterness from my voice, but it was there.

"It's out of my hands, Brynn."

I nodded. "I know."

"Look, the cottage is still available. I talked to my friend. I've arranged everything. It's paid through the month."

Paid. Arranged. Handled.

How was it that I never seemed to make my own decisions? Not in Crystal Cliffs and not with Sullivan. It was like being carried along on a current, while flailing wildly for a rock or a branch, but it kept pushing me downstream toward the falls.

"When will I be going there?"

Again, his eyes darted away from mine. "I thought it would be best if you left in the morning instead of trekking up to Lancaster with us. I've arranged to have someone drive you to Pawley's Island from here."

Had my heart dropped into my stomach? "You want me to leave you tomorrow?"

He exhaled slowly. "It's just for a couple of weeks, Brynn."

Tears stung the back of my eyes. It didn't feel like it would just be a couple of weeks.

"I'll meet you at the cottage as soon as it's over," he said.

"We'll have a day or so to recuperate from the jet lag before the western leg of the tour."

I rubbed my face and swallowed the emotion. Suddenly, all I wanted to do was sleep for two weeks, wake up when this European trip was over, and then everything would be … what? Back to normal? What was that, anyway? What could "normal" ever look like for Sullivan and me?

"Sullivan, am I losing you?"

The honesty of the question seemed to startle him. He put his hand on my leg. "You're not losing me, Brynn. This is my job, you know? This is what I do."

I knew this. But it was so much more than that. Months of strained nothingness between us. Months of living a life in a world in which his name, his face, were everywhere, and I was invisible.

"I just think," he said carefully, "that you shouldn't have to deal with all the mess in Germany. My mess."

That was when I understood. This wasn't about protecting me. It was about creating distance.

"What *is* your mess?" I stared at a dark stain on the carpet shaped like a continent. I'd waited long enough for an answer. "Are you ever going to tell me what happened at Woodstock?"

His gaze moved to the adjacent wall. "I don't know. Let's get through Germany."

A hurricane of anger blew through me. I was over the silence, the walking on the thinnest of eggshells. It wasn't just the trip to Germany. This was a turning. He was slipping away from me, not in anger or cruelty, but in a sort of self-preservation. I was standing still, watching him choose a distance he believed he needed to survive. "And after that?"

"We'll see."

We'll see.

The hurricane in my head was getting louder. I couldn't force him to talk if he didn't want to, just like I couldn't force him to come back to me.

His throat worked, and he seemed to read my thoughts. "I'm not going anywhere."

But I couldn't help the voice in my head telling me he was already gone. Even though neither of us had said the words, it was as though I'd already said goodbye.

Chapter Forty-One

PAWLEY'S ISLAND, SOUTH CAROLINA, FALL 1999

"The Escape"

The cottage was comfortable, familiar, but it wasn't home. Not without Sullivan.

I was stranded there with no car and a cell phone. The first few days, I'd moved through the rooms like I was visiting a museum of our life, touching things, remembering where he'd lain, leaned, where he'd laughed. Inside, traces of us still lingered. The chipped mug he drank his coffee from every morning. A half-empty bottle of olive oil by the stove. A folded throw on the back of the couch that we had bought in Georgetown before we got our marriage license.

After two days of watching television and reading the touristy books on the shelves, I asked the woman who cleaned the cottage to run me to Walmart and to a local craft shop. There, I would find supplies for the one thing I was good at. Something that had gotten me through another tough time in my life.

Once I had my supplies, I spread them out on the dining room table, lining up my tools—tweezers, a craft knife, a few fine brushes, tiny jars of paint, and all the pieces I needed to create miniature worlds.

For two weeks, I carved figures small enough to fit into a tissue box. I shaped their bodies from clay, careful and precise, smoothing shoulders, molding hands. Or I whittled them from pieces of wood I found outside, a dropped oak branch or cedar twig. I painted faces with the thinnest of brushes or drew them with a fine-point pen. Eyebrows no thicker than a human eyelash.

I built rooms for them. Little houses. Little beds. A staircase with glued matchsticks. I even made a version of the cottage itself, with the porch, the crooked screen door, the marsh grass beyond the railing. A memory, a miniature photograph, all inside an empty tissue box.

When I worked, time loosened its grip. In the miniature world, nothing moved unless I moved it. Nothing shouted. Nothing surprised me. I could make the rooms safe. I could decide who stayed and who left. If something felt wrong, I took it out or erased it with the edge of my blade. I could always start again.

Every evening, my back ached and my eyes burned, but I welcomed the discomfort. For the first time in nearly a year, my mind was occupied with something beyond Cutter, the tour bus, and Sullivan. My thoughts were my own.

What if Sullivan didn't come back? Even if he did, what if he didn't want me? What could I do with the rest of my life? Me. Not as an extension of Sullivan Stonecutter, but as someone who maybe had talents and abilities of her own. I'd often thought of going to college. Or maybe I could work at a craft store. Even the possibility of having my own house to decorate and somewhere to put down roots was enticing. People did it every day. Why couldn't I?

One thing I knew for sure. This sort of solitude wasn't for me, and with that realization, a seed of resentment sprang up. With each passing day, it germinated and grew. Sullivan was in Europe, worshiped by the masses and used by the industry. Here I was, hiding away in a secluded backwoods cottage. This was not what I'd wanted when Maeve and I escaped Crystal Cliffs. If this was all there was to look forward to, I might as well have stayed and worked in The Collective.

On my seventh night at the cottage, I sat on the porch steps as the sun bled out over the marsh, listening to the cicada calls. Soon it would be dark again. In a week, Sullivan would return from Germany, and I wasn't even sure if I was looking forward to that.

My cell phone rang out a tune from inside the cottage, and I jolted to my feet. Sullivan had only called me twice since arriving in Germany, and the last time, he'd been drunk out of his mind.

I bolted in through the screen door and snatched my phone off the table. I didn't recognize the number, but he might be calling from someone else's phone.

"Hello?"

There was a pause on the other end. Long enough for cold dread to freeze me.

Not Sullivan. A familiar woman's voice. "Brynn?"

Who else had this number besides Sullivan?

"Hi, Brynn. It's Mama."

I said nothing. Couldn't talk.

There was a pause on the other end. Breathing. "Brynn?"

My spine tightened. "Mama?"

An exhale. "Thank God, I've finally found you! I've been trying to reach you." Her voice sounded thinner than I remembered, hoarse. "It's so good to hear your voice."

I glanced around the cottage, at the bare walls. Did she know where I was? Did any of the other members of Crystal Cliffs know? How had she gotten my number?

"I was afraid I'd never hear your voice again." She sounded as though she were crying.

"How did you find me?"

Silence. Then, "Someone contacted me."

My fingers curled around the phone. "Who?"

"They didn't give a name," she said. "They said they were concerned about you. Thought someone should check on you."

"Concerned" and "check on," words and phrases with a whole other meaning in Crystal Cliffs. Someone was *watching*.

Her voice brightened suddenly. "They said you were traveling. That you were married. That you married Sullivan. Wow, baby. We always knew that was going to happen, didn't we?"

"Man or woman?"

"What, baby?"

"Was it a man or a woman who called you?"

"Oh, I think it was a man."

Who had called my mother?

"He asked if I had your number, said someone should give you a call," she said. "And he gave me this number."

I should hang up. Chuck Crow or Uncle Dunn could be standing outside right now, waiting to take me away like they did Maeve.

"What do you want?" I tried to steady the shake in my voice. "Why are you really calling me?"

Her breath hitched—the smallest fracture in her composure. "We've all been looking for you for so long. I can't even tell you how wonderful it is to have found you, Brynn. Are you all right? Is Sullivan all right?"

Something prickled at the back of my neck as my mind reeled. They could be recording this, tracing my whereabouts. Astra Cynthia could be standing behind her right now, telling her what to say, listening in.

"Mama, I'm hanging up now."

"No, wait—Brynn, please wait! I didn't want you hearing this news from someone else," she said quickly. "It wouldn't be right."

A warning bell went off in my chest.

"Hearing what news?"

"Maeve is dead."

The words, so bluntly flung at me, slipped past, and I couldn't make sense of them. "What?"

"They found her on the kitchen floor at her parents' house," Mama said. "She'd been living with them since she came back to Crystal Cliffs."

No, no, no.

My knees buckled. I sat down hard at the kitchen table.

"The police said it was an accident," she continued. "A fall. She had a lot of drugs in her system."

Of course they said it was an accident.

I stared at the miniature house on the table—the one I'd finished that morning. The tiny door I'd painted so carefully.

"When?" I asked.

"Two days ago."

Two days.

I thought of the calendar on the fridge. The days I'd been crossing off. The careful X's. Day six. Day seven.

"Yes, I'm so sorry, honey," Mama whispered. "Maeve is gone."

I didn't cry. I didn't scream. The room didn't spin. Instead, something inside me went very, very still.

I thought of Maeve laughing in the RV, planning routes on a fold-out map, promising we'd figure out the future together. She'd wanted so much to get free. Now, she was dead.

"They killed her," my voice broke. "Astra Cynthia and all her—her goons. It wasn't an accident!"

"No," Mama said sharply. "That's not true, Brynn."

I pressed a hand to my face, sudden sobs wracking my shoulders as the reality sank in. "Why? Why did they have to kill her?"

"Brynn, I want you to come home. I need my baby girl with me. Please, Brynn, I know you're alone, and I know you're struggling right now. Just come home for a visit."

My chest seized as if someone had cinched a girth around me. That's what all this was about—getting me to come home. Whoever had given out my number was close to Sullivan, had access to all his personal information—and mine. Fletch? Nate? Someone with the record label? Someone who wanted me gone.

"Mama, does anyone at Crystal Cliffs know where I am?"

Another pause. "Well, honey, why don't you give us your address, and we'll send someone to get you, bring you home where you belong."

I disconnected the call. Then I sat there for a long time, eyes darting, breath heaving in and out.

"Maeve," I breathed her name into the room as though summoning her.

When my phone rang again, I didn't pick up. As soon as the ringing stopped, I speed-dialed Sullivan. But he didn't answer.

Instead, a woman did. "'Allo?"

I pushed past the immediate shell-shock of an unknown female answering his phone. "I need to speak to Sullivan, please. Right away. It's very urgent. This is his wife."

Her accent was thick. "Sullivan is not available right now." Then she must have been holding the phone away from her mouth while speaking German. "*Sullivan's Frau ruft an. Was soll ich ihr sagen?*"

The low murmur of another male voice rumbled in the background.

Panic and fury rushed through me. "I want to talk to him right now. Do you understand? This is urgent. Please put him on the phone."

She spoke again. "I'm sorry, *Liebling*. He's just come off stage and … we will have him call you, yes?"

Then a click.

I slapped my hand against my mouth to suppress a scream that tore out anyway. Then I called back. This time, it went straight to voicemail.

My gaze naturally drifted to the clock hanging over the microwave. How long did I have before someone showed up to kidnap me and drag me back to Crystal Cliffs, where I could easily end up like Maeve?

Think, Brynn. I wiped the tears from my face. Whatever my next move, it would be on my own.

I checked the locks twice. I started to turn off my phone, but what if Sullivan called? On the other hand, after what I'd just heard, the chances of Sullivan phoning me were slim. He was surrounded by handlers. And someone, maybe a bandmate or his manager, had leaked this number to my mother. Because I was in the way. With a deep breath, I switched off the phone. Then, I stood at the window watching the drive for headlights that never came.

By the time the birds started their morning chorale, I knew waiting was no longer an option.

Chapter Forty-Two

CHARLESTON, SOUTH CAROLINA, FALL 1999

"Breakaway"

I left the cottage a little before sunrise, as the sky was beginning to thin from black to gray. I couldn't take my room boxes and dioramas with me—no way to transport them. I stood on the threshold, taking one more look at the cottage. Then I closed the door, shouldered my backpack, and started walking. Along the sandy path, I listened for the sounds of a car rolling up, but all I heard were cicadas and the distant rush of water.

At the edge of the road, I waited. A bus station—I had to find one. That was how Maeve and I had gotten around when we were desperate for transportation, and now, I needed a Greyhound again. Where was the closest one, and how would I get there? Hitching a ride with a stranger seemed unfathomable, but what choice did I have?

Twenty minutes later, when the outline of a rusted blue pickup materialized in a cloud of dust, I did the unthinkable. I stuck out my thumb.

The truck slowed and then came to a stop in front of me. An older man with a tanned, wizened face, wearing a baseball cap with Red Man Tobacco embroidered along the front, hung an elbow out the driver's window.

"Where ya headed?"

"The bus terminal?" I said it like a question, hoping I wouldn't have to explain much.

"That's Georgetown. Out of my way." He rubbed a hand across his mouth, the skin around his small eyes wrinkled as he scanned the road ahead. Then he cranked his head to the side, motioning toward the passenger seat. "Hop in. I'll drop you in town."

I hurried around the front of the truck, my heart galloping as I prayed the man wasn't a serial killer. Then I hoisted myself into the cab and perched on the cracked and split vinyl of the dirt-dusted seat.

"Thank you," I breathed, noting the scabs and scratches on the man's arm. The floorboards were littered with hay, a discarded chewing tobacco packet, and a candy bar wrapper.

"You out here on your own?" he asked.

I tensed. "Meeting a friend at the bus station." It was a lie, of course, but the suggestion that someone might be waiting for me at the bus depot was the only measure of self-protection I had.

He nodded. "Where you headed by bus?"

I hadn't thought much about where I was going. Just away. Then, I said the first place that came to mind. "Charleston."

He nodded again.

Somehow, that seemed like all the affirmation I needed. I was going to Charleston.

Boarding a bus for Charleston was one of the first things I'd ever done completely on my own. I sat in a seat by myself. No one asked where I was going. No one cared. No one even spoke to me. No drug dealers were hanging over the seats trying to engage me in conversation.

Behind me, a mother held Crayons while her little girl colored in a coloring book. In front of me, a woman sat alone, wearing a straw hat. Despite the panic of hearing Mama's voice and the sadness of learning of Maeve's death, right then, a sense of safety accompanied me on my travels. No one followed me that I was aware of, and no one, not even Sullivan, knew where I was going.

In Charleston, I found a motel. I asked for a room on the second floor, away from the street.

The room was narrow and clean, if not sparse. A bed. A chair. A window that looked out over a parking lot where people came and went.

The air in Charleston was mild and still. Nothing moved —not the trees, not the clouds—just the sun bathing everything in a wintry glow. I walked. I ate when I remembered to. I sat on a bench near the water and watched boats drift in and out of view, unhurried. I didn't try to call Sullivan right away, didn't leave any messages telling him where I was. I kept the cell phone turned off except to check voicemail, which I only did every couple of hours.

At night, Charleston came alive, and it was easy to get lost in the lights, the sound, the tourists. I stayed in busy areas. I sat at a table alone in the middle of crowded restaurants and cafés. It felt safer that way, like camouflage.

No one here knew my name or cared. I was free to

spend the days walking the city. I even chatted casually with Misty, a homeless lady who sat in Marion Square. Misty kept a collection of Rubik's cubes, all different shapes and sizes. One day, she gave me one on a keychain. "That's for your hope chest," she said with a wry smile.

Maeve's face was imprinted in my mind, but there was no time to let grief settle in. She existed in flashes, her voice in my head, the CDs we'd loved so much and listened to on repeat.

I didn't let myself imagine her last moments. Instead, I focused on what I needed for my survival and what I needed to consider for my future. Within a few days, Sullivan would return from Germany. Who knew what our life would be like then?

On my third day, I used the motel phone and left a simple message on his voicemail. "I'm safe. Call when you can."

Then I waited.

———

For the first time in a few nights, I left my phone turned on.

His call came late, waking me from a twilight sleep. In the background, I heard voices, a drum beating out a wild cadence, and metal clattering. "I've been trying to reach you," he said. "I called the cottage like forty times. I finally asked Harlan to drive over and see if you were OK. He said you'd left."

"Yes."

"Why didn't you tell me where you were going?"

I inhaled slowly. Then I relayed the story to him, Mama's call, my fear of them finding me.

His breathing was loud, uneven. "*What?* How did they get your number?"

"I don't know. She said it was a guy who called and told her he was 'concerned' about me."

"That shouldn't have happened. That's not—" He stopped himself, exhaled hard. "I told them not to share anything. Your number isn't supposed to be floating around like that."

"Told who?" I asked.

"Management," he said. "Security. A couple of people on the road." His voice tightened. "I didn't think anyone would give it to *them*," he snapped, then caught himself. "I mean—I didn't think anyone would give it to anyone."

I sat there, fighting the shock that Sullivan would give my number—my only real connection to him—to *anyone*.

"Brynn." His voice was stripped of edge, threaded with panic. "I'm sorry. I swear to you, I didn't give it to anyone who would hurt you."

I knew he wouldn't. But his instincts were off. He didn't know what he was dealing with when it came to the people close to him.

"You shouldn't have had to run," he said. "Shit, I should be with you right now."

"I'm OK."

"Are you somewhere safe?"

"I think so."

"Where are you?"

I hesitated. "I'm not telling you yet."

Silence. Then, "Why not?"

"Because I don't know who else might hear it, and I can't take that risk."

He didn't argue.

"There's something else," I said.

"What?"

I opened my mouth, then closed it again. The words didn't feel real, even as I said them. "Maeve is dead."

More silence.

My voice sounded flat as I continued. "Mama said it was an accident. A fall. I think they broke her, Sullivan, after she went back. I think—" My throat closed. "I think they killed her."

"I'm sorry, Brynn. I'm so damn sorry."

I imagined him pushing his hand through his hair, pacing the room.

"I just need to get through two more shows," he said. "Once we're back, everything will calm down. We'll talk. We'll fix this. I'm struggling here without you, Brynn. Damn, I want to be with you so bad."

I leaned against the headboard. "Sullivan, I'm not mad at you."

Another voice in the background called his name. He ignored it.

"I feel like you don't trust me," he said.

The words sliced through me.

"It's not you." My voice broke. "I can't risk them finding me like they did Maeve."

"I get it."

He didn't sound like he *got it*. He sounded like he was agreeing because he didn't know what else to do or say.

Someone nearby was speaking in German, maybe the same woman who'd answered his phone the night I'd called him from Pawley's Island.

"I have to go," he said hurriedly. "They're waiting. But Brynn, I'm coming back to you—for us."

"I know."

"I *love* you." The way he emphasized the second word tore at my heart.

I sat for a long time afterward, the phone still warm in my hand.

I hadn't told him that I loved him back.

Chapter Forty-Three

NOVEMBER-DECEMBER 1999

"Who Are We?"

I didn't know what version of myself I was supposed to be when he arrived—his wife, his refuge, the girl he'd left behind, or the one who ran.

I let Sullivan know my whereabouts after he returned from Germany and just before he got on a plane to Myrtle Beach International Airport. Later that day, I opened the hotel room door to a man who was clean-shaven with a duffel bag at his feet, his leather jacket slung over one shoulder, his hair still damp and scraped off his forehead like he'd washed up in the airport bathroom, or maybe the lobby downstairs.

His body was leaner than I'd ever seen it. He was too thin, really, his cheekbones too pronounced, his eyes sunken and red-rimmed.

"Hey, Brynn."

"Hey."

He stepped forward, wrapped his arms around me, and I let myself rest against him, taking in the familiar shape of his chest, the smell of him—cedar and lemon.

"I came straight here like I said I would," he said against the top of my head. "I didn't stop."

When we pulled apart several minutes later, his hands lingered on my arms, like he needed the contact to confirm I was real. I backed away and sat on the edge of the bed. He threw his duffel bag on a chair, but he continued to stand, seemingly unsure if I would let him stay.

"I know it's only been two weeks, but you look different," he said.

"So do you."

He nodded and sat next to me on the bed. "I talked to everyone about the leak. No one will admit to anything. I'm almost positive it was Fletch, though, and he's gone now. Quit while we were in Germany."

I raised my eyebrows. Surprising news.

"Anyway," he continued. "I shut it down. The leaks. It won't happen again."

"I believe you. Why would Fletch do that? Contact my mother?"

Sullivan's face creased with misery. "He was probably doing the record label's bidding. They wanted you out of the picture. They wanted me to be—"

"The single sex god."

He paused, held out his hands. "I should've protected you better. Your number. Your safety. All of it."

I exhaled through my nose. I was just going to say it. "I wish I could've protected you better too. From whatever happened to you at Woodstock."

He flinched with a half-blink. It was still there—the

unhealed open wound. Then he quickly changed the subject. "I can fix this, Brynn. I can slow things down. I don't have to tour the way I am. I don't have to—"

"Sullivan," I said gently. "Listen to yourself."

He stopped.

"You're talking about the future like it's a lever you can pull," I said. "Like everything will miraculously resolve."

His Adam's apple bobbed. "You don't think it will."

"No, I don't." It pained me to say the words. They sounded so final. I tried to soften them by putting a hand to his face. "But let's enjoy your homecoming. Let's enjoy each other tonight."

A lot had changed for Cutter in the two weeks they'd been in Germany. Fletch had quit, and a new manager, Ray, had taken over. Brooke was also conspicuously absent from the tour. When I asked Nate about her, he said she'd gone home to Nebraska—nothing else to explain or add.

"Wasn't she from Texas?" I asked him.

He'd shrugged. "I don't know. Maybe."

Or maybe it was all the same to Nate.

A doctor traveled with the band and was on call backstage at every show. He appeared with the regularity of a stage cue, always at the same time, with the same calm efficiency. Blue button-down shirt. Latex gloves snapped into place.

Before the show, he administered shots to Sullivan offstage, tucked into narrow hallways among the cables and dusty equipment. After the show, he returned, eyes already scanning Sullivan's pupils before a word was exchanged.

Somewhere in between, a small white paper container of pills surfaced, unlabeled, passed hand to hand like a communion wafer.

Every night, Sullivan returned to the tour bus or the hotel room and collapsed.

He'd been lucid when he first came back from Germany. We'd even enjoyed a few weeks together that were a lot like our honeymoon. But once the concerts kicked back into full swing, it was like watching a light slowly dim.

By the time the December shows rolled around, his movements were labored. His reactions lagged. His eyes went glassy at odd moments, watching something far away. Sometimes he'd stare at his hands as if they belonged to someone else.

Before the Nashville show, I stayed with him in the narrow concrete corridor outside the stage. He sat on a bench against the wall, head tipped back, eyes closed. Sweat had already darkened the collar of his shirt. His knees bounced.

The doctor approached, syringe in hand, holding it up to the light, the way someone might inspect a diamond.

"OK, Sullivan," he said easily. "Let's get you prepped."

Don't just stand here, Brynn.

I'd been quiet for months, smiling, nodding, letting them move him around as though he were equipment. Letting them call what they were doing to him "help."

You see what this is. So say it.

I forced my tongue to move. "Hold on."

The doctor paused and drew back the needle, irritation flickering across his face.

"What are you giving him?" I asked.

His eyes narrowed. "It's just a mild sedative. Same as always."

I laughed darkly and jerked my thumb toward Sullivan. "Look at him. Does he look like he needs a sedative? He's like, practically asleep."

Sullivan didn't open his eyes, didn't agree or disagree with what I was saying. It was as though it were happening to someone else.

"It helps take the edge off," the doctor said.

"By knocking him out?" I shot back.

The doctor glanced down the hallway, then back at me. "Ma'am, this is standard."

"No," I said. "What's standard is adrenaline and nerves. Maybe exhaustion. Not this."

Sullivan finally stirred. "Brynn, it's fine."

I stared at him. "No, Sullivan, it's not fine. Do you really want these shots, these sedatives, or whatever they are?"

He shrugged. "Sure."

What scared me most was the resignation in his voice. The words had been handed to him, and he was repeating them out of habit.

The doctor glanced at his watch. "He goes on in twelve minutes."

I crouched in front of Sullivan, my hands on his knees. "Sullivan, do you even know what he's giving you?"

He frowned. "Something to help me focus."

I looked back at the doctor. "What is in that syringe?"

He hesitated. "A benzodiazepine. Short-acting. Out of his system by morning."

I faced Sullivan again. "Don't take it. You don't need it."

Sullivan pushed to standing. "Come on, Brynn. Don't make this harder on me than it already is."

He rolled up his sleeve and held out his arm. Afterward, the doctor shot me a look that spoke clearly. Someone in charge would hear about this.

This wasn't about helping Sullivan. It was about managing him. Making him what they needed him to be. And I was again standing in the way.

Chapter Forty-Four

ORLANDO, FLORIDA, NEW YEAR'S EVE 1999

"Live Wire"

The outdoor stage at CityWalk pulsed with intermittent bursts of fiery light.

Temporary risers had been thrown together at the edge of the plaza, truss lights glaring white and blue against the palms. Neon from the clubs bled into everything—pink, red, electric green—layered over a massive digital countdown clock projected onto the side of a concrete building already slick with humidity.

HAPPY NEW YEAR 2000 blared above it, bold and insistent, as if the future needed convincing to keep moving forward.

The crowd packed in shoulder to shoulder, spilling in from the bars, walkways, or wherever people had been standing when they realized they didn't want to face midnight alone. Especially knowing it might be the last one ever. Party goers brandished their plastic cups and wore silver paper crowns. The anticipation of midnight—of Y2K itself—hung in the air like ozone.

I stood offstage, half hidden by a stack of amps, watching people glance up at the projected numbers.

Ten minutes to midnight. Someone near the front started chanting early—*ten, nine, eight*—and got laughed down, pulled back into the noise. Nobody wanted to rush it.

Cutter hit the stage and the noise doubled. The music was loud enough to rattle the metal barricades, swallow the countdown chants, and make people forget the clock existed.

The band launched into the last song before midnight. One of the older ones that the crowd knew by heart. Sullivan grinned and turned the mic outward, letting the audience carry the chorus.

Ray, the band's new manager, stood beyond the lights, near the edge of the plaza, arms crossed, posture already closed. He wasn't watching the band so much as the situation of the crowd density, the exits, and the clock.

One minute to midnight.

The song crashed to a finish, feedback screaming into the night. The lights cut briefly—on purpose or not, I couldn't tell—and the plaza erupted.

"Ten, nine, eight..."

People climbed onto obliging shoulders. Strangers kissed. Someone screamed as though the world was already ending.

The crowd took over the countdown, voices colliding, rising, unstoppable. "Three, two, one!"

I held my breath ... and the lights stayed on.

Not just the stage lights—the neon too. The clubs. The bars. The glowing red EXIT signs lining the plaza. The countdown clock vanished and reappeared as 12:00.

Nothing even flickered.

People screamed anyway, hugging, laughing, crying into each other's shoulders like they'd survived an alien invasion. Fireworks cracked overhead, bright and loud enough to rattle my ribs.

The world hadn't ended. The ground didn't shift beneath my feet. The air still moved. Music kicked back on from another stage, bass thudding through the concrete, proof of continuity.

I stood there, stunned by how ordinary it all was.

After all that fear. All that waiting. The future arrived without asking permission, without warning, and everything I thought might disappear was still here—lights, noise, breath, heartbeat.

Except for the thing that mattered. The band was still on the stage, playing their instruments in jubilant celebration.

Where was Sullivan?

Fireworks cracked over CityWalk.

I found a quiet corner offstage, a narrow service hallway stacked with cases of water and cardboard boxes, the bass from the plaza still vibrating through the concrete. I sank onto a crate, fighting off an urge to put my head against the wall and sleep. After all the hype, it had been just like any other New Year's Eve.

Cutter's new manager, Ray, stood a few feet away. He was in his mid-forties, an attractive, polished man, with wavy, salt-and-pepper hair and twinkling blue eyes. His demeanor said "unflappable and in control." I imagined him smiling while he fired people.

He cleared his throat and crossed his arms. "Big letdown, huh?"

I shrugged. "I guess if you were looking forward to the end of the world."

He chuckled and stepped closer, his hands in his pockets. "Brynn? It is Brynn, right? Do you have a minute?"

My pulse picked up. The last time someone from Cutter's team asked me if I had a minute was to tell me how bad our marriage was for Sullivan's image.

"Sure," I muttered.

Ray leaned against the wall beside me, his arms still crossed, the smile still tugging at his lips.

"You care about him," he said.

Damn. Here we go again.

"Yes."

"And you know he cares about you."

I nodded slowly.

"Then I'm going to tell you something difficult," he projected his voice. "Because it might be the only thing that saves him." He raised dark eyebrows that didn't quite match his silvery-streaked hair. "He's unraveling. You must be seeing it too, right?"

"Well, I know he's struggling, because you all keep drugging him into oblivion—"

"No," Ray interrupted. "I mean, he's falling apart."

The words landed on me like stones.

He continued, "His performance is slipping. His focus is shot. He's panicking before shows. He can't sleep. He's jumpy as hell. Half the time, he looks like he's about to throw up. The other half, like he's about to run. He's a shipwreck."

I inhaled sharply. "It's all this shit you're injecting into his body."

He held up a hand. "Look, Brynn—is it OK if I call you Brynn?"

"Yeah, Ray. Go ahead."

He placed his fingertips to his temples. "OK, I know the guy's traumatized. He's not choosing this. I'm not blaming him. I'm explaining the reality. If he can't perform consistently, the insurers can pull coverage. If they pull coverage, the tour collapses. The label's asking for reassurances."

My stomach tightened. "Reassurances about what?"

"About sustainability," Ray said. "About whether he can maintain this level."

I raised my chin, staring him down. Ray knew what had happened to Sullivan. He had to. He knew, and I didn't.

Ray eyed me right back. "Now, I know that's not fair. Trauma isn't fair. Love isn't fair." His voice softened, almost kind. "But fame, success, a future—it requires looking past all those things. You've got a chance to do the right thing here."

I sat up a little straighter. "Wait a minute. What do you want me to do?"

Ray didn't answer right away. He glanced down the hallway, then back at me, his tongue surfacing over his lips. "You've been asking questions."

My pulse skipped. "Yeah?"

"About his meds. About why he's being given sedatives before shows. About who's signing off on what."

"Because I'm his wife."

"Yes, well…" He panned his eyes across the ground. "But when he looks at you, he doesn't see the stage. He sees home. That can be a problem."

My mouth dropped open. This was unbelievable. As bad as Astra Cynthia. Worse even.

Ray raised his hands to his hips. "You see him before

and after the stage lights. You see what he's like when the adrenaline wears off. You notice patterns most people don't."

I stared at him. "So what—now I'm a liability because I care?"

"You're an interference point. He doesn't need interference right now," Ray said. "He needs stability. Predictability. A controlled environment."

"I can give him that."

"Not out here on the road, you can't."

"You're drugging him." My voice shook. "That's not stability."

"We're managing him. There's a difference," he corrected. "Sullivan agreed to treatment. There's medical oversight in place."

I slid off the crate and faced him. He was less than a head taller than me. "Is there? He jumps when people touch him, and you're handing him pills like they're mints."

Ray didn't rise to it. He lowered his voice instead. "We're helping him achieve his dream." He gestured vaguely toward the stage beyond the concrete walls. "He walks out there because we make it possible." His gaze settled back on me. "And right now, you're complicating that."

"What do you want from me?"

Ray held my gaze steadily. "I want you to step away … for a while. At least from the tour."

I scoffed. "No."

"I'm talking temporary."

"For how long?"

"For as long as it takes."

I shook my head. "I can't do that."

Ray turned away from me, pinching his bottom lip. "This is a problem."

I was suddenly in freefall. My face heated as blood rushed into my cheeks. "Something happened to him after Woodstock, and no one is letting him deal with it." I took a step forward and pointed a finger at Ray's chest. "And *you* know what happened to him."

Ray's jaw tightened.

"So, tell me, Ray. What the hell happened to my husband in Woodstock?"

He dropped his hands to his sides. "Look. Sullivan's a talented guy, there's no denying that. But this is a business, Brynn. Festivals like that are volatile," Ray said evenly. "You get a hundred thousand people in one place, things go haywire. Nobody leaves untouched. We need stars that can rise above."

His words pierced me. "You're not going to tell me, are you?"

He stared at me, his eyes saying I was right on target, that he knew everything, even as he said, "I don't know what you're talking about."

I threw my head back, stared up at the concrete overhead. "I can't believe this."

"Look, Brynn, you're human," Ray replied. "You're reminding him he's human too. And right now, that's not helpful."

For a second, I couldn't breathe. That was it. That was the whole thing. They didn't want a man. They wanted a machine. A voice. A body that could stand upright under lights and obey.

I was the malfunction.

My eyes filled, and I blinked violently to keep a tear from rolling. "So what—I disappear, and you fix him?"

Ray shook his head slowly. "You give him space. And we make sure he stays standing."

"And if I don't?"

Ray didn't hesitate this time. "If this continues, the tour will be restructured."

"What does that mean?"

"I won't be able to shield him from what happens next."

"You're asking me to abandon him."

"I'm asking you," Ray said evenly, "to stop standing between him and the operation."

Operation. Like Sullivan was a procedure. I pictured him shaking in the hotel room. I envisioned the pills, the silence, the way he flinched when I touched his face.

"He needs me," I said, my voice desperate.

Ray nodded once. "Yes." Then he added, "And that's why you have to go."

I tried to breathe. The concrete walls seemed to press in on me, as a cold understanding slithered through my ribs and into my chest.

They weren't asking me to leave him.

They were asking me to let them have him.

Chapter Forty-Five

ORLANDO, FLORIDA, JANUARY 2000

"Y2K"

I'd been sitting on the bed for hours, staring at the carpet, obsessively replaying Ray's words. *"We make sure he stays standing."*

They were killing him. And no one—including Sullivan—seemed to care.

What choice was left to me? How could we keep pretending this marriage was working? How could it ever work?

It was past three in the morning when Sullivan returned to the hotel. He seemed surprisingly sober. I said nothing as he closed the door behind him softly, as though he didn't want to wake me. But both of us knew we were wide awake.

His face was lined and shadowed, his lanky body loose-limbed. Maybe they'd given him another sedative.

He moved further into the room. "You're still up."

"Yeah."

He rubbed his palms on his jeans. "Long night."

"Yeah."

He tossed his wallet and his phone on the chest of drawers. "Guess that Y2K stuff was all a bunch of bullshit."

I sniffed. "Seems like it. Sort of like all the crap they told us at Crystal Cliffs."

Silence filled the room, dense, painful, choking.

Sullivan stood by the dresser as if he didn't know where to put his hands, his body.

I pushed my hair out of my eyes and stood. "You must be exhausted."

He hesitated. "You too. You've been waiting up for me?"

"Of course. I didn't even get to kiss my husband at the midnight hour, after learning we weren't all going to die."

He hung his head. "Yeah. I'm sorry about that." Then he leaned over and brushed his lips against mine, the way he had the very first time we'd kissed.

I gripped his hands. "After surviving a near-death experience tonight, there's nothing else to do but say it."

"Say what?"

I took a deep breath. "Your life, Sullivan. It's run by managers, bandmates, record companies, and handlers. And they don't want me around."

"*I* want you around." He sounded so sincere that it knocked the breath out of me. "I love you."

"I love you too, Sullivan. I really, really love you."

We both knew that wasn't the point anymore.

He tilted his head back, gazing at the ceiling. "I came here thinking I could fix us. That I could bring you home."

I huffed out a dark laugh. "Where is home, Sullivan? The tour bus?"

His voice was soft. "It would only be for a little while longer."

"You've been saying that for months."

His phone buzzed once on the chest of drawers. He didn't move to answer it.

"Ray told me you were upset earlier. He said you think people are trying to control me."

"They are."

"Brynn…"

"No," I said. "Listen to me. You know this. You've said this to me before. This isn't right—what they're doing. It's just like…" I trailed off, realizing what I was about to say.

He sank onto the edge of the bed. "Just like what?"

"Just like at Crystal Cliffs. You told me that yourself. Months ago."

He rubbed his face with both hands. "I don't know what else to do."

"Stop letting them pump you full of drugs."

He chuffed out a sound of despair.

"I don't know what else to tell you." My eyes blurred with tears. "I think we both may need more help than we can give each other."

"What do *you* want?"

I knew what I didn't want, at least not anymore. I didn't want to spend another week on the road. "I want consistency. Stability."

His face relaxed. "I want that too."

I stood and looked down at him. "No. You want this life *and* stability. You want the stage *and* the quiet. You want both."

He hesitated. "It's my life."

I shook my head. "I can't build a home out of hotel rooms and tour buses. I can't keep waiting for it to calm down."

Silence yawned between us.

"It's not going to, you know," he said finally.

"I know." At least he was admitting it.

He exhaled long and hard. "I don't want to lose you. I can't. The hell with Ray. I don't give a damn what he thinks. I can tell Ray to back off. I can tell them all to back off."

"But you won't." A fact we both knew. "That's the problem. I don't think you understand how deep they have their hooks in you."

His eyes were bright and unfocused, staring at something beyond me. "You think I don't see what they're doing?"

"I think you see it," I said. "And I think you've decided it's the price you have to pay."

He dropped his gaze.

"I'm not judging you," I added. "I get it. This band saved you. It gave you a way out. It gave you a life after Crystal Cliffs. But somewhere along the way, it stopped being a bridge and started being a cage."

He braced his elbows on his knees and put his head in his hands. "I want the same things you want," he spoke the words to the floor. "A home. A routine. A door I can lock at night."

I moved toward him, my heart aching at the desolation in his voice. "I know you do."

He looked up at me. "Then why does it sound like you're telling me goodbye?"

I took a breath, hardly believing what I was about to say. "Just because we want the same thing doesn't mean we can have it together. You want all the rest of this too, and I can't compete with it. I won't."

He lowered his head again. "I can make it work. Just … give me time."

Time. The word evoked an image of Crystal Cliff's clock tower.

"I've given you time," I said as gently as I could. "I've given you miles and nights and buses and hotel rooms. Sometimes I think I can't stand another minute."

The pain was worse than anything I'd ever felt—the knowledge that I was letting go of something precious on purpose. "I want more than a life of setlists and tour dates and recovery times and syringes. Sullivan, I'll lose myself trying to survive your life."

His face crumpled as he stood, crossed the room, and placed his hands on the dresser. Shoulders hunched, he stared down at the scuffed wood.

"You deserve better than what I can give you," he said finally.

Maybe I did. His words gutted me anyway.

"That's not—"

"No." He turned to face me, and his eyes were clear now. "You're not asking for too much. You're asking for a life. All I have right now is this." He gestured at the room, but he meant the invisible machinery grinding outside the walls.

Tears burned at the corners of my eyes. "I hate this."

"So do I."

We stood only a few feet apart, but the space between us seemed unbridgeable. He reached for me, and I clung to him with muscle memory, instinctively, pressing my face into his chest.

"I don't want to let you go," he murmured into my hair.

"I know," I said. "I don't want you to let me go either."

His grip tightened, then loosened, practicing. "I'm not going to ask you to stay."

He finally stepped back, his hands lingered on my arms,

thumbs brushing the inside of my wrists, a signature Sullivan move. Then he bent down and pressed his lips to mine. The kiss was full of everything we couldn't save.

"Stay the night with me," he whispered against my lips. "Don't go until tomorrow."

Every part of me wanted to stay, but if I didn't go then, I'd lose my nerve.

I pulled away from him. Keeping my gaze low, I grabbed my bag, my movements automatic, surreal. Then I stood in the doorway.

"I hope you get the life you want, Brynn," he called to me.

"I hope someday you do too."

I stepped into the hallway and didn't look back.

Chapter Forty-Six

NOW

I dig in my purse for a tissue. Damn it if my eyes aren't watering. Even now, telling a stranger my story dredges up pain as fresh as that plane ride back to Charleston all those years ago, the lonely days I spent searching for an apartment, the monthly checks I received from Sullivan until I told him not to send them anymore.

I finally find a crumpled tissue at the bottom of my purse and dab at the corners of my lids. "So, there you have it." I huff out an old, dark laugh. "My name is Brynn Cole, and I'm a recovering stonehead."

I look up at Steve. His eyes are tearing worse than mine. He smiles a little, but I know he sees right through my protective façade. I once heard that comedians understand pain in a way that would surprise most of us.

"Did you see him again after that?" Steve asks.

"I didn't see him again." I tear open a packet of sugar and dump it into my fresh cup of coffee. "Didn't even really talk to him. After a year, we got divorced. Our lawyers hashed all that out. Not long after, I heard the band had broken up."

"Shew. Complete implosion." Steve shakes his head. "Yeah, I remember when they broke up. Sullivan was blamed for most of that, wasn't he?"

"The record label pushed him too hard. He snapped. Had an all-out breakdown. The label canceled the tour. That was it."

I drop my wadded-up tissue into my empty mug. "Thank you for listening."

He tips his glass toward me, his face resuming a comedic smirk. "Just not sure I can use any of that material. That would be a really unfunny set."

I laugh. "Good. I made it just tragic enough to render it useless."

He pinches his eyes and blinks. "Tragic? I don't know. Your story is real. We all remember what it's like to be chasing devotion, hoping that you'll get it in return."

My phone buzzes against the bar. A text from Sullivan appears in a green bubble.

Are you still good to meet?

I take a long, deep breath and type in my answer: *Yep.*

Three dots and then his response: *I'm on my way.*

I push my phone into my purse and glance up at Steve. "Looks like I've got somewhere to be."

He hesitates, then adds, "For what it's worth? I can see you've got your head on straight these days." His eyes were serious without a trace of humor. "Whether it's a grand reunion and you remarry and live happily ever after, or you walk away with a little closure, you're going to be fine."

I don't think I've really understood that until this moment. "Thanks, Steve. You're right. I will."

My phone buzzes again. Voicemail alert. This time, I've

missed a call from Paul. I can't keep ignoring him. I'll definitely phone him tonight. No matter what happens.

"Well, I've got to go." I push my stool back. "You probably do too."

He stands. "Yep. Gotta head over to the club soon."

I loop my purse over my shoulder. "So, I'll look forward to seeing your show tonight."

He brightens. "Hey, if you and Sullivan want to come backstage, I'll put you both on the list."

I give him a wistful smile. "Thanks. But I've been backstage enough to last a lifetime."

Chapter Forty-Seven

NOW

The neon sign for Zanies Comedy Club buzzes faintly above the door, red and blue bleeding into the damp Tennessee evening. It's tucked into a low brick building, unassuming. You could pass it a dozen times without noticing.

Inside, the ceiling is low. The walls are dark—black paint, black curtains, framed photos of comedians. I pause inside the doorway.

This is it. Neutral ground. No emotional archaeology. No shared memories here. Even though we didn't specifically say it, I'm sure Sullivan understands, as I do, that there are no expectations and that an exit is available if either of us needs it.

I stop at the hostess stand. "I'm meeting someone here. Sullivan?"

She nods and leads me toward a small table along the wall. I slide into the chair, my back to the brick, facing the room.

The stage is low, barely raised. A single microphone waits in the center.

A server brings a glass of water, and I guzzle several gulps. My eyes dart around the place, and my hands are shaking so hard I have to hold them still.

I glance at my phone.

He's late.

Then another thought—what if he doesn't come? On the other hand, what if he does? The lights dim slightly. Someone brushes past my table, and I look up. A tall bald man. Not him.

If he does show, what version of Sullivan Stonecutter will I get? The haunted one? The sober one? The man Ivy loves. The boy I married.

For that matter, which version of *me* will he see?

I swing my head toward the entrance again. It's not his face but his silhouette that I first recognize. Taller than most people who have walked through the door tonight and lean as ever, the shape of him is familiar in a way that maybe shouldn't be after so many years.

He stands inside the entrance, scanning, and there's a subtle change in the room. His every movement is clinically cataloged in my mind. As he approaches, I see that his eyes are the same. Searching, they find me, and he smiles.

I stand, and we move toward each other until we're under a light. His hair is less gold now, and silver is threaded through the strands.

"Hey, Brynn."

"Sullivan."

We hug. There's no rush of music, no swelling emotion. It's a little awkward, but comfortable too. Whatever comes next, we've already crossed the hardest distance.

I stop wondering whether this was a mistake and motion to the table. "Is this your regular spot?"

He nods, still smiling, the familiar grooves creasing either side of his mouth. "Yeah."

"I figured. They knew exactly where to seat me."

We pull out chairs and sit. A server comes right away and takes our drink orders. Still thirty minutes before the first act comes on. Plenty of time to catch up.

I notice his hands first. Sturdier, the veins more prominent than I remember. From across the table, I can feel his adrenaline, the electric undercurrent of his energy.

"You look good," he says more like an announcement than flirtation.

"So do you." Did I say that too quickly? Too emphatically? He does look good. Better than I ever imagined, in fact. Still, I feel the need to qualify it. "I mean, you look the same."

Lines crease his brow. "I've gotten old, Brynn. You can say it."

"You still look like yourself."

He shifts his gaze toward the stage, where the lights are dimming in increments. "So, you still like this kind of thing? Comedy clubs?"

"I do." I almost tell him that Paul and I frequent one in Charleston, but then I stop myself. No point in talking about Paul yet.

His mouth quirks. "Gotta keep laughing, right?"

"Right."

Our server brings our drinks—a beer for Sullivan, wine for me.

His eyes settle on me, clear blue as ever. How is it possible that I still feel that flutter in my stomach?

"I'm glad you came," he says quietly.

"I'm glad you came too. I thought for a minute you might not."

Another smile. "I was definitely not going to back out of seeing you."

I touch my phone, sitting face down on the table. "I still follow you, you know. On all your social media channels."

He chuckles. "I don't even do my own social media. My daughter handles that for me."

This news is a little earthquake. "You have a daughter?"

It's hard to tell in this lighting, but his expression is the same as the one he used to get when he blushed. "Yeah. Uh, Shantel."

Can't say the admission doesn't blindside me. "Did you ever remarry, or—"

He shakes his head. "Nah, she was a—a—"

"A love child?" I laugh as I say it.

His eyes dart away from mine. "Let's just say she was a 'like' child. Her mother and I were never really together." He pauses and then adds, "But I took care of Shantel. I was never one of those deadbeat musician dads. I saw her whenever I could. She's twenty-three now."

He seems to need to tell me that part, as if to let me know it wasn't during the time we were together.

He pushes his hands through his hair like he used to do. "And then, you know Ivy. She handles a lot of my bookings and publicity and stuff."

I force a smile at the mention of Ivy's name. "You're still touring."

"It's still my money-maker." He flicks a hand toward me. "And you—you're a big podcaster now."

I sputter. "Not a 'big' podcaster."

"I've listened to several of your shows. You're really good, talking about important stuff—the people getting out of cults and all. And the guy who's on there with you some-times—what's his name?"

A warmth spreads through my chest. "Paul. Yeah. He's great."

"You guys make a good team."

"We do."

Suddenly, I find myself talking about Paul—how we met, how we got the show going, our plans for its future.

"I'm pretty passionate about the cult and high-control group thing, obviously," I say.

His eyes cloud a little. "Wonder why?"

We echo each other's pained laughs, nervous ones, a wall of protection.

I swirl my wine in the glass. "I guess you've been following the police trying to arrest Astra Cynthia and Chuck Crow on embezzlement charges, finally?"

He nods, his eyebrows raising. "Yeah. You know, they got 'em today. Pulled their asses out of the community center after several days of standoff."

"I thought I saw something on the news that confirmed they'd got them."

He gulps the last of his beer, then shakes his head as he swallows. "It pissed me off, though—no murder charges."

"Yeah, but they got them. More will probably come out during the trial."

Sullivan holds up his empty glass to catch the server's attention. "I guess that'll have to do. It's all we're ever going to get."

The lights dim a little more. Only about ten minutes before the show. I quickly sift through all the information circulating in my brain for the most relevant things to tell him. "Mama's out of there now, you know?"

He sits a little straighter. "Yeah? That's great news. You see her?"

"Not really. It's still a little weird. We've talked on the phone a few times. What about your mom?"

"She's still there. As far as I know."

"I'm sorry." I feel a dip in my gut at the news that Kristen is still part of that warped world. Maybe now, with Astra Cynthia and some of the others in jail, things will change.

After that, Sullivan and I careen from one topic to another, fast, random, trying to beat an invisible clock. Old habits…

The lights are almost showtime dim, and he reaches into his pocket. "Let me show you something." He pulls his hand out and opens it.

A small wooden figure of a young Sullivan rests on his palm. "I've still got it."

The lump swells in my throat, forcing tears into my eyes. "I can't believe it. You kept it all this time?" I take it and inspect my early handiwork. The shoulders are a little too severe, the hair a little too yellow, but the raw talent shows in the carvings of the cheekbones, the chin.

I hand it back to him.

He puts it into his pocket. "You still making the boxes?"

I nod. "Not as much as I used to, but I still make them when there's something I want to remember."

Our eyes collide.

"I've never stopped thinking about you, Brynn."

I inhale slowly. *Here we go.*

Steve Criss steps onto the stage, launching into the opening bit. The room fills with loud laughter, and our conversation collapses into silence.

Sullivan motions with his head at the stage. "This guy. He's hilarious. He performs here a lot."

Steve pivots into a joke about memory, how we rewrite our pasts to survive them. The timing is brutal. Perfect. Did he write that after we talked earlier today?

Sullivan shifts in his seat. Touches my hand. Then he leans over, his mouth next to my ear. "Remember that comedy club in Myrtle?"

I keep my eyes on the stage, my heart jumping painfully. Of course I remember.

His voice vibrates low and deep in my ear. "I want you to know, I blame myself for everything that happened to us."

If only he knew. I'd never stopped blaming myself either.

The room erupts in laughter again. The knot in my chest loosens. We're not going to fix this tonight, and the realization of that relaxes me. We are just two people at a comedy club enjoying some humor and a few memories. We are just two people in the dark.

Steve references a Cutter song and mentions that sometimes Sullivan Stonecutter comes to the shows. The audience hoots and applauds—this is a crowd accustomed to him sitting in the back at a regular table.

Sullivan's smile is electric, and he salutes Steve. "Thanks, man!"

Steve ends his set with a joke that makes us both double over. Then the lights come up. We stand and move along with the tide of people headed for the exit.

Sullivan closes his hand around mine, and we walk together, the choreography of our bodies still familiar enough to be unsettling. How am I supposed to feel? Because right now, the warmth of his hand sends charges of nostalgia and sensation through my arm. I want to embrace him, kiss him, make up for all the time that we've lost. But there's something that we've never resolved, and there's no way to move forward without looking back.

Outside, the night is warm, Broadway spilling music and neon into the street.

We walk past a food truck. Past a group of girls in cowboy boots taking selfies. Past a man arguing with someone on his phone.

At the corner, Sullivan stops and faces me, takes my other hand as well. "Brynn."

"Sullivan."

His thumbs draw circles over my hands. Twenty-five years later, the effect is still intense. "I don't want to avoid this anymore. I didn't come here to reopen wounds, but I also didn't come here to pretend we don't have them."

People sweep past us on the way to somewhere else, but their forms in my peripheral vision might as well be phantoms.

His forehead creases. "I've had a lot of years to think about this, to realize that what broke us wasn't the touring, the bad managers, the pressures, or even the drugs."

I watch his face, afraid to interrupt.

"It was the secret. What happened in Woodstock broke me, but I know that it broke you too."

I hold my breath. Is he actually going to tell me? "When you went to Germany, you tucked me away," I say. "Like you were sparing me something. You came back different. And I knew—" My voice falters, the pain in my chest exploding. "I knew we weren't the same."

He looks off down the street, his eyes glimmering in the lights. "I thought I was protecting you."

"I know," I say. "That's what made it worse."

When he speaks again, his hand slides around my waist. He draws me toward a low stone wall framing some foliage, and we sit, letting crowds buzz past us.

He drags his long legs toward me, and his knee touches mine. "You asked me once if I'd ever tell you what happened." His fingers clutch at his pants. "I didn't tell you, Brynn, because if I named it, it meant I couldn't outrun it anymore."

I don't move. If I do, I might frighten him away, like a rare moth in the light.

His eyes flicker away. "It was a man who had power over my career."

Mark Byron. To this day, I remember the name, but I don't speak it.

"That night after Woodstock, he got me alone, told me everything I'd worked for could disappear with one phone call."

I feel the world tilt.

"I said no many times that night," he continues, his mouth tightening. "But once I was in that hotel room, they *did* drug me. I didn't even know what had happened until I woke up and tried to leave. I found out later, he'd done it to others—other musicians..."

My eyes fill with tears. All these years, I'd suspected so many things, even this—sexual assault—but I'd never been able to give voice to it. I would never have questioned him about it. Now, here it was. The naked truth. And it was as bad as I thought. "Oh, Sullivan."

"They record it. In case they ever need to blackmail you." His hands shake now, openly. "When I came to, I was told that I'd just secured my future. That this was how you earned your place at that level. And if I ever forgot who'd made it possible—if I pushed back on touring, contracts, anything—he had proof. Said no one would believe me anyway. That he'd frame it however he needed to."

It was *worse* than I thought.

"They told me that if I talked about it, I'd be finished. Or that I'd be … handled … as a liability." Sullivan's eyes are dry, filled with a kind of exhausted honesty, as if he's finally laid down something he's carried for too long. "Not that I ever wanted to talk about it. I wanted to forget it. And I didn't tell you because I tried to deny even to myself what had happened. It was the only way I could cope. I didn't trust myself not to fall apart if I did tell you. I was so damn scared of what you would think of me."

I squeeze his hand harder. "I thought I wasn't enough for you. I've blamed myself so many times for leaving."

He flinches as though I've struck him.

"No," he says immediately. "Brynn, no. You did what you had to do, and I never blamed you for one second. I knew I was bad for you. I felt so damaged. Dirty. Disgusting."

"I would never have thought that of you."

"You would've wanted to fight it. And I knew neither of us would have won or survived that."

We sit there, the noise of Nashville swelling and receding around us.

"Sullivan, we can't undo the past," I say. "I just needed to know it wasn't all in my head."

He raises his eyebrows. "It wasn't."

Another pause.

"And for what it's worth," he adds, voice rough, "I never stopped loving you. I just didn't know how to live with myself."

"I didn't come here for that," I say gently. "But thank you for telling me."

We lean in, clasp each other, and stay like that for a long time in the aftermath of truth. When we separate, it's unspoken, mutual. Two people who know exactly when something has reached its natural end.

He pulls back first. "There's something else I should tell you."

"What?"

He clears his throat. "Um, Ivy's pregnant."

Regardless of my resolve from a few moments ago, his words are like a leather strap across my back.

Checkmate, Ivy.

"Oh."

"I only found out yesterday, actually." He turns his eyes toward the streetlight and sighs. "I've been thinking about it, and I think I might do the right thing."

I shudder out a breath. "Of course."

He looks down at his hands. "Our timing has been terrible, hasn't it?"

I nod. "It has."

I had walked back in thinking there were still pieces left to move, but Ivy had secured the board.

The traffic light in front of us turns yellow, then red.

"She loves you, Sullivan."

He shrugs. "This is my chance, I guess. For a real home life."

"You should take it."

He inhales sharply and turns his gaze back to me. "I'm really glad you're doing so well."

"I'm happy for you too. You're still loved by so many."

He studies me for a moment, as if memorizing a version he won't be allowed to keep. "You always were stronger than you thought."

"So were you."

He pinches his temples. "Brynn, you were always way stronger than me."

The night has cooled around us. Laughter spills from the club doors behind us.

"I should go," he says.

"Me too."

He stands and holds out his hand. "I'll walk you to your car."

At my car, he hesitates, then reaches into his pocket for the wooden figure. He holds it up. "I'm never getting rid of this."

I laugh, a thick, sad sound. "I'm glad."

"Take care of yourself, Brynn."

"You too, Sullivan."

I get in my car and watch through the neon-light-streaked windshield until he disappears into the crowd.

Chapter Forty-Eight

NOW

I drive with the windows cracked, letting the cool air clear out the scent of the past. The sky is a pale watercolor blue, streaked with early-evening peach.

Another night in a hotel and an early morning departure will put me in South Carolina before four o'clock in the afternoon. The closer I get to home, the more I settle into realization and relief. Closure feels even better than I expected.

I didn't get Sullivan back.

But I got something else—a glimpse of a version of myself that isn't hardened and angry. Instead, the girl who married a rock singer on a beach, who believed in forever because she didn't know any better, steps aside and makes room for the woman who can hold grief in one hand and growth in the other.

I don't have to be the same forever.

And I can love again.

Even at forty-five.

I call Paul and tell him to have some of his pasta waiting for me. I don't tell him much, only that I'll explain everything once I get home.

When I finally pull into my driveway, his white Tahoe is already there.

He's probably nervous, maybe even bracing himself for the bad news—expecting me to tell him that I'm moving to Nashville, or at least that Sullivan and I are back together.

He doesn't get out of the SUV right away. He sits in the driver's seat, his eyes reflecting in the rearview mirror. When I approach, he steps out and meets me halfway up the walk, clutching a brown carrier bag in his right hand.

"Hey," he says like he's testing the waters.

"Hey." I go to my trunk, pull out my bag. When I close the trunk, he's there, waiting to take it from me.

"How was the drive?" He grabs my bag and puts it over his shoulder.

"Good." We walk together toward my house.

"You doing OK?" he asks.

I breathe out slowly as I put the key in my door. "Yes." I glance up at him. "I'm really good."

There's no jealousy or insecurity in his eyes. "You look lighter."

I shoulder my door open. "I feel lighter."

We step into my living room, and I toss my purse onto a chair and kick off my shoes. Paul sets my overnight bag down, carries the groceries into the kitchen, and begins unpacking them—three large Tupperware containers of pasta and red sauce. I can't see what's in the other one, but I'm pretty sure it's freshly grated Parmesan.

He doesn't look at me as he asks, "Do you want company tonight? I could, you know, leave this and go."

I put my hand on his arm, and he finally raises his gaze to mine.

"Yes," I say. "I want *your* company."

The smile lines spill out from his eyes as he pulls a bottle of wine from the carrier bag and holds it up. "Want some wine?"

I hesitate. "Not right now."

He raises his eyebrows and sets the bottle aside. "How was it?" he asks casually, as if we're talking about a podcast.

"Hard, but necessary."

He glances over his shoulder at me, then begins removing the tops from the containers.

I fill two glasses with water, hand him one, and hold mine up. "To old friends."

He touches his glass to mine, his smile melting away.

We both rest against the counter, drinking our water. Paul stands a few feet away from me, and I sense his question hanging in the air between us.

"You don't have to walk me through it," he says. "Unless you want to."

I nod. "I might. Later."

"OK." He cranks his head back and stares at the ceiling. "How was Sullivan?"

"He was fine." I set my glass down and pivot toward him. "He finally told me the truth, Paul. About what happened all those years ago."

Paul doesn't react beyond a slight tightening of his mouth. He waits.

"I'm so thankful he told me," I add. "But it doesn't change what I need."

Paul studies me. "So, you're not getting back together?"

I shake my head. "No chance."

He gives me a genuine smile. There's relief there, and maybe even a little triumph.

I step closer, longing to reconnect and shore up the breach I've put between us. "You know what I thought about all the way back from Nashville?"

He takes another sip from his water glass before putting it on the counter beside mine. "What?"

"You. Us. Everything you said before I left. About being honest with myself. About dealing with the truth rather than the fear and how that might change things between you and me."

His forehead wreaths. "Yeah?"

"It does change things between you and me."

Paul drops his head a little. "I see."

"In the best possible way."

He raises his eyes to mine from beneath heavy, dark eyebrows.

I put my hand on his chest, right above his heart. "Because … I think we're going to need to stop having founders' meetings."

Paul reaches for me, and his hand rests at my side. "Why's that?"

"I think I might have fallen in love with the founder."

He smirks. "You're not just saying this because I'm easy, right?"

I laugh then—doubled over, hands on knees, comedy-club laughter, and I'm all too aware that it's more of a release than genuine amusement.

"No." I gasp for breath. "You must not know you. You are *so* not easy."

He slides his hand around my waist and draws me to him, forcing me to look up at him.

"I may not be easy, but I am so in love with you." He closes his eyes. "And I'm so glad you chose to come home."

I close my eyes too as we kiss.

Twenty-five years ago, I chose love without knowing what it would cost. This time, I choose it knowing exactly what it's worth.

The Meadows: Prologue

THE MEADOWS

October 1990

"Come on. It'll be fun."

Hunter stared at his friend. "Compared to what?"

Jason made a scoffing sound. "Compared to sitting in the car all night." He shook his head. "Damn, you're such a wimp."

Hunter peered through the windshield and up at the darkened building, its spires reaching toward the moon. Asphodel House. The closest thing to Dracula's Castle in the Western hemisphere.

"I knew you weren't going to be cool about this." Jason shook his head. "Here I am—trying to have a little fun on a Friday night." He pulled a pack of cigarettes from his pocket and patted them against his hand. A thin, white cylinder fell from the packaging into his palm. "Plans foiled by a baby."

"I'm not a baby." The answer was a reflex. It sounded pathetic. "I'm twelve." That sounded even more pathetic.

Jason laughed. "Like I said…"

Hunter opened the car door and climbed out. He'd worked hard for this. Jason was four years older than him, and let's face it—the guy was a bully. But Jason's little sister Laura was thirteen … and the hottest thing Hunter had ever seen. He'd have done anything to get her attention. Even break into an old, abandoned house. "Where's Laura?"

"She rode with a friend. She should be here by now."

"Why not ride with you?"

Jason cast a sidelong glance at Hunter. "'Cuz she wanted to hang out with someone else tonight." His voice crested with irritation.

As the cold air invaded his lungs, Hunter coughed. And then he saw her. She was standing on the porch, her blonde curls glistening like spun gold in the moonlight.

She waved.

Jason got out too, his steps crunching in the gravel.

Hunter jumped at the sound of the slamming car door.

"You know, I hear the couple that lived here just ran … left everything behind," Jason said, striding toward the front porch where his sister stood. His combat boots looked like concrete blocks.

As they approached the porch, Hunter glimpsed someone standing beside Laura. Hunter recognized the boy with the shock of red hair and a wide girth that made him look older than sixteen. "No," Hunter groaned. "Not Zulu Sawyer." The boy's real name was Zuzen, but everyone called him Zulu. Zulu was the same age as Jason and just as much of a shmuck. Worse—because his arm was around Laura's shoulders. "What's he doing here?"

"He's going out with my sister."

"What?" Hunter's voice broke into what sounded like a shriek. "Why? How can you let her date that jerk?"

"*What?*" Jason imitated his cracking voice and broke into peals of laughter. "You're such a little turd, Massabrook. Seriously. The biggest goober I know."

Hunter's face burned.

On the front porch, the foursome exchanged awkward waves. Hunter couldn't help but smile when he looked into Laura's pale blue eyes illuminated over the silver-plated flashlight she held under her chin.

Zulu's stare felt like the touch of an electric prod. "What's *he* doing here?"

Jason shrugged. "Laura wanted him to come."

Hunter looked at Laura.

So did Zulu. "You did? Why?"

She smiled that white-toothed, flawless smile. No braces. She didn't need them. She was perfect. "I'm glad you came, Hunter."

"Come on." Jason waved them forward. He seemed eager to move. "Let's get in there and do this thing. Laura and I gotta be home by midnight before the folks return from the party."

The "thing" Jason spoke of was the very *thing* Hunter did not want to do—break in and see what goods had been left behind by the couple who'd abandoned the house a few months prior.

"I hear the woman was raped by a ghost," said Zulu as they squatted in front of a side window.

Laura gasped. "That's terrible, Zulu. Don't say that."

He laughed a little and shrugged. "Why not? I heard it's the truth."

"Shut up, moron," Jason scolded. "I heard she was an

alcoholic, out of her mind on the sauce. You gotta be pretty perverted to claim you had sex with a ghost."

"It's better than what happened to the people who lived here four years ago."

"Yeah," Zulu agreed. "All of them dead. Except for one. Crystal. That girl was in my seventh-grade math class. After her family was killed, they sent her away somewhere."

"All right, everyone shut up and stop talking shit. Focus." Jason wielded his crowbar and shoved it under the window frame.

"Just break the damn thing," Zulu instructed. "Why the hell you gonna waste our time trying to pry it?"

"What if an alarm goes off?" Laura asked, her blue eyes wide, concerned.

Worse than that, Hunter imagined his parents' expression as he was led up the sidewalk by police escort. His heart skittered at the thought.

But the window wasn't secure, and when Jason cranked it a second time, it burst open.

One by one, they crawled inside.

The house was darker than dark. And so still that Hunter could feel his skin cells regenerating.

"This is so bitchin'," Jason crowed. "Look at this place."

"Where are we?" Laura asked, shining her flashlight over the walls.

It looked like a living room. There was a couch against the far wall and a billiard table in the middle. The former inhabitants had walked off and left all their stuff behind.

"Come on," Jason directed, stalking bravely across the tile floor and into the entrance hall.

Laura shined her flashlight over their heads, and the light refracted off the most enormous chandelier Hunter had ever seen. Little prisms of color danced upon the walls.

"Wow! Look at that thing," Laura gasped. "Can you believe the size of that?"

Hunter pretended to be interested, although his heart was hammering with wicked intensity. He felt a little sick. *God, please don't let me puke in front of them.*

A sound from the next room echoed through the foyer. A voice? Or a whisper?

"What the hell was that?" Zulu asked.

Hunter's fists clenched involuntarily. Now he just needed to leave. Never mind about impressing cute girls or trying to hang out with older friends. He wanted to run. He wanted his home and his bed. And his mommy, if truth be told.

But Jason was unafraid, and his combat boots made muddy tracks on the tile as he strode confidently into the next room.

Hunter shirked behind, trailing the others and holding his breath, as though that would help him. Candlelight cast flickering shadows upon the high walls of the room, and a dining table the size of Texas stretched the length of the floor. But the scene before them stopped all four members from entering the room.

A swirling black mass circulated over the table's surface, just above the naked body of the girl and the cloaked figures standing in a circle around her.

The girl's face was covered by what looked like a Halloween party mask, with hollow eyes and a mouth that was too wide and red. Sores dotted her body—no, not sores—puncture wounds, and from them the figures siphoned rivulets of blood into glass chalices, small vials. One cloaked man knelt on the table beside her and sucked at her arm like an overgrown leech while he gyrated and made obscene sounds.

Laura's scream cut like a hot iron through the unnatural air.

The black mass shot up and disappeared into the ceiling.

Distracted from their task, the hooded humans turned, revealing faces covered in grotesque masks. Slowly, hissing and growling, they slunk forward with animal-like precision—some of them maneuvering their arms and legs inhumanly, like panthers as they prowled toward the group of kids.

Hunter first backed away as though avoiding an approaching tiger, but fear twisted his body. Suddenly, he turned and ran, leading the trio who fell into stride behind him.

He grasped Laura's hand and pulled her, his legs pumping through the entrance hall and into the living room.

But then, he wasn't moving anymore. Something bit down on his shoulder, holding him in place. A hand with the grip of a hawk. He craned his head around and looked into a black mask with a long beak protruding from where the nose should be. He screamed—a sound ripped from his throat that sounded foreign to him. Or was that Laura screaming? Another masked figure held her, their hand clamped over her mouth. Her eyes were wide, straining at the seams with terror.

Hunter fought against the hand that held him, attempting to bite at the fingers and twist away from the vise-like grip.

"Run!" It was Jason's voice from somewhere behind him.

But he couldn't move. Hot, putrid, metallic-tinged breath puffed against the side of his face.

"Let go of her, you bastard!" Zulu flew like a linebacker past Hunter, tackling the cloaked figure who held Laura. Then he straddled them. Even as they held their hands up in self-defense, he delivered blow after blow against the plastic mask.

Hunter's captor let him go, turning to tackle Zulu instead. But Zulu threw the man off as if he were no more than a squirrel.

"Come on!" Laura shrieked, motioning him forward.

Forcing his legs to move, Hunter fell forward and found his footing.

Laura crouched by the open window, preparing to climb through, but Hunter shot past her and clambered out, kicking his legs to wriggle onto the ground.

Laura shrieked as her wrist caught on the windowsill and her hand was wrenched from his.

He popped up again, grabbing her outstretched arm and pulling her head-and-hands-first through the window.

Zulu dove through the opening, rolling and somersaulting on the ground.

But Jason did not emerge.

"Jason? Where's Jason?" Laura screamed.

There was no time to wait. Through the fogged and dusty panes of glass, Hunter could see the hooded figures. Chances were, they were coming around the sides of the house too.

He grabbed Laura's hand, and they ran. Zulu puffed heavy, raspy breaths of air behind them. They ran to Zulu's old, beat-up Monza and piled in, peeling out of the driveway, leaving a wake of gravel behind them.

"What the hell was that?" Zulu panted. "Who were those people? What were they doing?"

"Jason's still in there!" Laura screamed from the passenger seat. "Please, we have to go back for him."

Zulu shook his head. "Sorry, babe." He met Hunter's eyes in the rearview mirror, and his eyes were full of true regret. "Nothing we can do for him now."

As the car joggled and careened across an overgrown meadow and toward the interstate, Hunter couldn't hold it anymore. He fell across the backseat and retched into the floorboard.

The Meadows: Chapter One

NASHVILLE, TENNESSEE

Twenty-eight years later

The woman put her head down on the table. Her shoulders shook. He'd made her cry this time for sure. This was probably it. How much abuse was she going to take before she finally scooted out her chair and left him sitting there? The guy was a dud. Hadn't she figured it out by now?

I looked down into my coffee cup. The almond milk hadn't wholly mixed with the coffee, and the white swirls looked like smoke—or clouds. Wasn't there a song about coffee and clouds?

I glanced again at the couple two tables over from me. The woman's head was still resting on her forearms—she was sobbing. Poor thing.

For the past two weeks, I'd seen the same couple in this café every morning at the same time. They ordered coffee, sat in the corner, and had deep conversations. At least, they looked like they did. I never knew what they were saying, but her forehead was usually wrinkled, and his eyes were usually dead. He felt nothing for her anymore, I could tell. I knew that look too well. They always stayed for half an hour and then left. But today, something was different. Maybe it was the way he looked at her with apologetic eyes. And all of her movements were nervous, fidgety.

My phone buzzed against the table's surface, and I glanced at the screen.

Hey, girl. Didn't hear from you last night. Everything okay this morning?

Corky. My sponsor. I quickly responded. *All good. I went to bed early. At the café this morning. Check in with you later.*

It had only been two and a half weeks since I'd come out of Orange Star Rehabilitation Center for Drugs and Alcohol, so Corky was still super attentive, wanted to make sure I didn't relapse.

I'd heard the whole lecture before leaving the facility. Forty to sixty percent of us would relapse after coming out of the ninety-day program. But I was committed to seeing this through and doing everything they'd told us to do. I stayed accountable and talked to Corky several times a day, keeping out of old haunts and away from old friends.

But I wasn't prepared for how hard it would be. "Hard" sounds doable when you're on a victory high. Before rehab, I hadn't really fought to battle my addiction, but I'd given it all I had fighting against loneliness and depression.

My friends had been the ones who'd organized an intervention for me. On a rainy Friday night, a full-on gathering of concerned loved ones filed into a music studio where I recorded my newest song—the one that would be a hit when sung by an artist whose name was a hundred times more famous than mine. One by one, each friend told me how much they loved me. It was like an episode of *This is Your Life*. But then came the stinger: They would no longer be a part of my life if I didn't get help. So, I'd gone to rehab.

Funny. I'd been out of the center for over two weeks and hadn't heard from one of them. The intervention had been their farewell party to me. I'd cramp their style now. Everyone knew addicts couldn't go to parties and places where drugs and alcohol would be on offer. So, they just didn't invite me now.

Mia hadn't been at the intervention—thought it was a stupid idea—so she still checked in with me every few days. My best friend Stella had been on a cruise for the last three weeks, so I'd gotten a few text messages from her, but somehow, my life had gone from one big party to a series of lonely, episodic, voyeuristic scenes at a coffee shop.

My head was filled with thoughts of escaping Nashville. Corky said I really needed to go. If I wanted to stay clean, I needed to make a clean break. Too many chances to fall back in with the same crowd, the same habits. Anyway, I could write music anywhere. But where would I go? One of my six half-sisters had invited me to visit her in Paris, where she was studying abroad. Tempting? Yes. But something told me I needed to get my life together in some permanent sense—not run off to Paris to escape my lack of a life.

I read a magazine article once about a man who'd been in prison for twenty years and was finally paroled. But once he got out in "the real world," he didn't know what to do with himself. That was me now. New lease on life without the faintest notion what that meant.

I hadn't even been able to write songs, and that had never been a problem before I went into rehab. Maybe because I'd always written music with a tall glass of whiskey looking back at me from the top of the piano, or I'd pop a few lorazepam before strumming chords on my guitar. The last time I'd written a song sober? I'd probably been about fifteen.

Before Will died.

Draining my coffee cup, I glanced at the couple. Her head was still down, and he was beginning to look a little uncomfortable. His hand was on her arm, but his eyes darted around nervously.

My phone buzzed again. An email this time.

I opened it and stared at the name in the address line. Angela Denton. Real estate agent.

Hi, Scarlett,
We talked a few months ago about your search for a "grand estate" in Virginia near where you went to college at Shenandoah University. At the time, I didn't have any listings for the type of grandeur you had in mind, but something just popped up that might interest you. If you're still in the market for a place with bed and breakfast potential, shoot me an email or give me a call at the number below.

A moment of confusion swept over me. Angela Denton must have the wrong person. I hadn't contacted a realtor about a Virginia property. Once upon a time, I'd dreamed about living in the Shenandoah Valley. After all, some of my happiest years were spent at Shenandoah Conservatory, studying music, immersing myself in creativity, surrounded by creatives. Not that there weren't creatives in Nashville, but the stakes were higher now. There was money involved. I had to write commercial music—songs that would sell. Ones that would appeal to prominent artists with bigger labels. Shenandoah had been a different life.

I scrolled down to the bottom of the email and then doubled back. Angela Denton had replied to a previous email that I sent. Yes. My name and email address were there.

Sighing, I shook my head. No doubt I'd written that one night while in a sobbing stupor. One look at the email exchange told me that was exactly the state I'd been in when I'd first written her.

There was a chain of emails, and I followed them to the bottom. The first was dated six months ago.

Hi Angela
I want to know if you can help me find a grand estate in Virginia near Shenndoa unieversty. I used to go there and loved it. I want a house I can trn ino a bed and breakfast. Got anything?
Scarlett DeHaven

I shuddered. It was like reading something that someone else had written. Namely, an eight-year-old.

Her response was simple.

Hi Scarlett,
Virginia is full of beautiful estates. Currently, I know of a few for sale. What price range and type of house are you looking for? We really should schedule a time to speak on the phone, so I can get a better understanding of your requirements. Would there be a time when we can chat briefly?
Angela Denton
Realtor
Passer Johnson Realty
Your dreams are our dreams.

Her name and credentials were flanked by a picture of a well-coiffed blonde woman grinning to rival Miss America. I scrolled down and scanned the following message:

Hi, Scarlett,
I enjoyed our phone chat earlier today.
My stomach dropped. We'd talked on the phone? I had zero memory of that conversation.
Attached, please find several listings that may interest you. If you wish to see any of them and plan a visit to Virginia any time soon, let me know, and we'll schedule a viewing.

I scrolled through the listings—all homes in the one- to two-million price bracket. Not that a price tag like that would be a problem, but the houses looked like they needed a lot of work. I moved on to the message that followed.

Angela,
Nice, but I'm looking for bigger and better. Got anything else? Price is no option.

Great. Angela Denton probably blew a spark plug when she saw that message. Bring on the stately plantations. The next few home listings she'd attached were all in the three- to five-million-dollar category. Stunning places with sprawling acres of land, stables, and even vineyards in some cases.

I was sure none of them were still available. In fact, according to this thread, I'd never responded. The date read April 21. Days before I'd gone into rehab.

She'd never heard back from me, but now she was contacting me again, hoping I might still be in the market. And honestly, it wasn't the craziest idea. Even during my worst binge ever, the kernel of an idea I'd had since I was in my early twenties—to move back to the Shenandoah Valley —had burned through.

My phone buzzed again. A second email from Angela Denton entitled *OOPS!*

Hi Scarlett,
I forgot to attach the listing. I'm doing so now. Let me know what you think.
I scrolled down.
Asphodel Meadows
Waterloo, Virginia
$4,500,000
A Gothic Dream!
The Meadows—historic property and house—has origins c. 1918. Sited on 58 acres. The 15,000+ sq. ft. stone manor house is one of this area's most talked-about locations. Original furnishings include crystal chandeliers from France and hand-carved headboards from Hungary. Fully renovated and furnished caretaker cottage on the property. Asphodel House and Meadows is the perfect abode for a visionary with aspirations to renovate and refurbish. This site could be the perfect bed and breakfast, spa, or family estate home.

Hm. Aspirations to renovate and refurbish? Sounded like what my dad would have termed "a money pit."

But then I scrolled down to the picture.

My breath caught in my throat. Did places like this still exist? A stone mansion, all angles and lines, and jutting triangular rooftops nestled into a bed of trees and foliage and cradled by forest on either side. Magical. A refuge. A sanctuary.

"Hello, Scarlett."

A man stood in front of me. I raised my eyes slowly, scanning the torn jeans, the untucked pink and green plaid shirt that looked too preppy to be paired with jeans in that state. A black satchel slung over his shoulder. A full red beard like a garden gnome's. Beady eyes peered out of a moon-shaped face. Tony Banjo.

No, no, please no.

Unbidden, he pulled out the chair opposite me and sat. "How are you?"

I swallowed. "Fine."

He bobbed his head, his eyes, small and blueberry-blue, shifted and scanned the café. "I heard you were back around. This your new hangout?"

My teeth clenched involuntarily, and I nodded. The less I said to him, the better. A blur of scenes flashed through my mind. Meeting Tony Banjo in the alley behind Bailey's Beer Joint one night when I was especially desperate. I think I'd Ubered there, too drunk to drive, looking for pills. Riding from Brentwood into the city because Tony had texted me that he had a special going on valium. Catching up with him before an award show, where I think I'd even kissed him—shudder—partial payment for a rush order job on a bottle of Ritalin.

"You need anything?" he asked, raising a non-existent eyebrow.

"Nope. I'm good."

He pulled a pack of gum out of his pocket and held it out to me.

I shook my head.

He took out a piece, unwrapped it, popped a green rectangle into his mouth, and chewed for several seconds, his eyes darting around.

I eyed the door.

Tony took a long, full breath. "You know, it's always hard when you lose a good client—a friend, really." He motioned back and forth between us. "I mean, that's what it really amounts to, doesn't it? The loss of a friendship."

I frowned. "We were never friends, Tony. You were my dealer. That was the extent of the relationship."

"And you were a great client. I miss that."

"Sorry. Those days are over for me."

He snickered.

"What?" I allowed irritation to slip into my voice. I just wanted the guy to go. *Leave me alone.*

Shrugging, he pulled a black grocery store bag from his satchel and plunked it on the table between us. I heard pills rattle and jar within.

Tony didn't open it, but he patted the bag. "Lots of people return from where you've been and say those days are over for them." He smacked his gum. "You know how long it usually takes to get that first text?"

I said nothing, grabbed the guitar pick hanging from the chain around my neck, and slid it back and forth.

"Two weeks," he answered. "Sometimes three, but two is the norm." He rattled the bag a little. "You've been around about two weeks now. I got some lightweight stuff. Gold-standard quality. Something told me you might be ready to test the waters again."

"Something told you wrong."

He squirmed in his chair, and his smug grin dropped a little as his gaze shot up to the ceiling. "You know, sometimes I let clients go, but sometimes, I like to see them honor our contract."

I scoffed. "What contract?"

"Well, it's an unspoken one, of course. But like I said, we've been friends a long time. So if you can't fulfill your end of that friendship any longer, then maybe you need to pass my name along to one of your friends or acquaintances. You know, kind of like a business referral."

"Tony, just leave me alone. I'm sure you've got plenty of buyers."

"I don't like to lose *any* of my good clients. See? Not without a replacement."

"Tough." Shifting my gaze to the couple at the next table, I could tell they were getting ready to leave. She was dabbing at her eyes with a napkin, and he was talking in soft words, smiling a little, patting her shoulder. She stood and pulled her blazer off the back of her chair.

I stood. "I gotta go, Tony."

He looked up at me, a mock pout puckering his lips. "I thought we were just having a conversation here."

"Nope. We're done. I'm leaving."

He shook the bag again. "Maybe you're one of the three-week hold-outs." Smirking, he stretched his arms behind his head. "But I'm sure you'll be back. And I'm around. All the time. You know where to find me when you're ready."

My stomach roiled as the memory resurfaced in my brain—his beard pressed against my face, the smell of mint chewing gum and bourbon. His fat hands grasping my shoulders. I turned. "Goodbye, Tony."

"See you soon!" he called after me.

I shouldered the door and followed the broken-up couple. Then I speed-walked down the street and across the bridge to my condo.

Then I dialed Angela Denton's number.

The Meadows: Chapter Two

THE MEADOWS, VIRGINIA

October

Early mornings in Virginia were always my favorite time of day, especially in the fall. The temperature hovered at the crest of warm and cooler weather, producing a substantial low-lying fog that blanketed the reeds in the meadow. As I looked out the cottage window toward the construction site of my new home and business venture, I felt that unmistakable thrill of new beginnings. A charge of excitement had been flowing through me for days now, almost like the nervous energy I used to have when taking methylphenidate or some other stimulant.

The cottage wasn't large, but it would serve for the time being as a place to stay until the renovations at the mansion —known as Asphodel House—were finished.

Intended initially as a caretaker's cottage, the eight-hundred-square-foot space came furnished—fortuitous for me since I'd sold my condo in Brentwood lock and fully stocked bar. I hadn't wanted to keep anything from my old life except my grandmother's headboard, my baby grand piano, and the rest of my instruments, all of which I'd had shipped to Asphodel House. It had been much less of a burden to move a few suitcases rather than an entire truck full of junk.

The furnishings in the cottage weren't really my style. Although new, most of it was outdated and a little too frilly for my contemporary tastes. Basically, it looked like it had been furnished with bargain department or online salvage store furniture.

A plain sofa sat in the living room, some sort of coffee table positioned in front of it. Heavy drapery blocked out too much light, and the bedrooms looked like something out of my grandmother's house. But again, this was only temporary. Eventually, I'd move into the big house and use this cottage as part of the bed and breakfast rental options.

I made a cup of coffee in a travel mug, shrugged into my coat, and headed across the cottage's lawn toward the thick ridge of trees. On the other side was Asphodel House, its triangular, multilevel roof protruding from the forest.

It was still a little hard to believe that the place was mine. I'd only signed the papers a couple of weeks before when I'd arrived in Virginia just in time to close. And most of that time I'd spent in Leesburg, Middleburg, or George-town, hobnobbing with designers and buying furnishings.

Now, I bounced the ring of keys in my pocket to the rhythm of my walk, avoiding mud puddles and fallen branches.

Sunlight reflected off the high, rectangular windows and lit up the face of the mansion. Asphodel House seemed out of place in the Shenandoah Mountains. It should have been located somewhere in England or Wales in some remote, rural setting. Not that Waterloo was a bustling metropolis by any means. Winchester was the closest town, and that was several miles away. From what I'd seen, the most significant establishment in Waterloo was a corner market and an Irish pub called O'Grady's. The isolation would take some getting used to.

Construction crews had been on site for over a week. Although as of that morning, there was no sign of them. I'd gone to some trouble to hire them weeks ago, even though I hadn't closed on the property yet. I'd wanted to make sure the house was livable as soon as possible.

I jangled the ring of keys until I found the one that opened the front door and inserted it into the lock. But shouldering the door quickly reminded me that this door wasn't like most. It opened out, not in. I had to pull, not push. Strange.

It had been disheartening to see the state of the inside when I'd first bought the place. Inches of dust covered everything from the black and white tile floor to the banister of the grand staircase to the furniture left behind from previous owners. From my perspective, I couldn't imagine how any construction company would have this place ready to go in under a year. Still, after only a week, I could see signs of hope. Orlando, the foreman, assured me they were miracle workers. In fact, that concept was embedded in the name of the company: Marvel Construction.

I'd left a few of the downstairs windows open to try and air out the smell. And dear lord, did it ever stink. Angela had told me the house had been abandoned for years, since 1990, which explained why the dining hall looked like Mrs. Havisham had feasted there. Complete place settings had been left behind with plates blackened by decayed food and mold. It also explained why the foyer was littered with cardboard boxes, the flaps flung open as though someone had been packing, and then was called away. The shed out back was full of stuff too. Who just walked away from a house and left all of their belongings?

Angela told me the previous owners had opened Asphodel House as an inn, but they'd encountered some health issues and had to move. Looking at the stuff other people had left behind—remnants of a life interrupted— gave me the creeps. I'd called 1-800-JUNK-NOW the first day, and they'd hauled out several loads, but there was more to go.

I sauntered through my new house, checking out the state of the rooms, shrieking more than once as the odd mouse scurried across my path. One room upstairs with no windows was still smelly, and the ceiling was blackened with mildew from a leak. Had that been there when the home inspector came through?

The only thing in the house that wasn't covered with construction dust was my baby grand piano in the living room, protected with a heavy casing to keep it from damage.

The wing of the house that would eventually be my living space housed a downstairs bedroom and bath. Just off of that was an indoor swimming pool and garden.

As I stepped inside the greenhouse-like building and looked up at the glass ceiling, a chill rushed through me. I passed through the gray and dead vines, all tangled, clinging to the old columns and creeping over the tile floor that cut through the atrium. The indoor swimming pool held only a few feet of green water. It would need to be completely redone—new liner and probably a new pump, and who knew what else.

An image flashed through my mind. Floating facedown,

unable to breathe. Someone grabbing the back of my shirt and pulling me, sputtering, from the warm water.

I squeezed my eyes shut, shook my head. No. I didn't want to think about that night. I'd fought so hard to forget the faces all staring down at me. Music blaring from somewhere, and voices all questioning. "Is she all right? Didn't even know anyone was in there ... should we call the paramedics? Is she drunk?"

Inhaling sharply, I tromped out of the room, tripping over grabby vines and brambles.

I hadn't thought about that night in months. The past week or so, all of these memories suddenly replayed in my mind.

"After a few months of sobriety, your memory will start to resurface," Corky had warned me. "You'll remember things ... and then you'll wish you hadn't."

Someone had pulled me out of the water that night, administered CPR. Saved my life. A man.

I'd never even had a chance to thank him. Couldn't think who it was.

What a disgusting mess I'd been.

Trembling, I moved back into the foyer and looked up at the overhead chandelier. Angela said it was original to the house. Imported from France in 1918. It was impressive—nearly filled the whole ceiling—its crystal teardrops dangling like real tears clustered around lights intended to look like candles.

Then it moved.

No. That wasn't possible.

But yes, it had. The crystals clanked together as though someone had given the chandelier a push.

I froze. Stared. Waited.

Finally, it stopped and stilled.

Looking around, I considered whether there had been a slight earthquake. It wasn't unheard of in Virginia. Or even moths could have brushed against the crystals.

I started to move toward the kitchen when a sound echoed out of the upstairs. A door shutting?

I stood at the bottom of the stairs, grasping the dust-covered banister and staring into the darkened second story. "Hello?"

Was one of the workers already here? I hadn't thought anyone was here but me.

But then … footsteps. I was sure of it. Someone else was upstairs.

My throat constricted. Should I go up there? Check it out? This was my house now, and I was responsible for taking care of things. But my legs felt as though they might give out. What if a squatter had been staying in the abandoned house? What if they were violent?

Angela had told me that Waterloo housed an eclectic population—druids or something like that. I hadn't known what she was talking about, nor had I cared, but now I wondered.

Maybe I should call the police.

A car door shutting sounded from outside. Relieved, I rushed to the front door and pushed it open.

The construction crew had arrived. Burly men carrying tools.

I'd let them figure out if someone was milling around upstairs.

Grab your copy…
vinci-books.com/themeadow

About the Author

London Clarke is the award-winning author of eight novels, including the Legacy of Darkness series, the Dunmoor series, *Wildfell*, and *The Neighbor*. Her books have repeatedly been #1 Amazon category bestsellers in ghost thrillers and vampire suspense.

Clarke lives in South Carolina with her husband and two Italian greyhounds.

Acknowledgments

If you're reading this, you might need a minute. And maybe a deep breath. I know I do.

First, to my fearless beta readers—the ones who willingly climbed aboard the tour bus, stood in the wings or under blinding stage lights, and who sat with Brynn in those quiet, breaking-point hotel room moments—thank you.

Ruth Buchanan, Deborah Harris, Bonnie Burskey, Doreen Fernandes, Arianna Siegel, and Teresa Cook—you are the reason this book is stronger, sharper, and braver than its earliest drafts. You told me when Brynn needed to speak up or when Sullivan needed to unravel a little more. You pushed for deeper tension, clearer stakes, and more emotional honesty, especially in the moments that would've been easier to leave ambiguous.

You sometimes answered my "Is this too much?" questions with, "No. Make it worse," or "Add more." The book is better for it.

To the incredible beta readers who joined through Hidden Gems—thank you for stepping into this world with such thoughtful insight. Letting new readers see an early draft is always vulnerable work, and your feedback helped refine pacing, clarify motivations, and strengthen the emotional arc in ways that matter deeply.

To my readers—thank you for loving complicated characters. Thank you for embracing stories where devotion isn't easy, stability isn't guaranteed, and love sometimes has to fight through noise, ego, fear, and the past. Thank you for indulging my love of rock music and musicians and for trusting me to take you into uncomfortable (but sometimes really fun) places—backstage corridors, long highway stretches, Woodstock, and Y2K. You are the reason these characters get to live beyond the page.

To Vinci Books—thank you for believing in this series and helping bring Sullivan and Brynn's journey to readers. Publishing is never a solo act, and I'm grateful to be part of a team that understands the vulnerability and the power of stories like this one.

Thanks to S.H. Editorial Services for the edits and proofreading!

And finally—to anyone who has ever loved someone brilliant but broken, who has wrestled with the difference between passion and peace, or who has learned that devotion without stability can cost more than it gives—this one was for you.

www.ingramcontent.com/pod-product-compliance
Lightning Source LLC
Chambersburg PA
CBHW012026110726
47995CB00006B/1150